Garfield

BY JIM DAVIS ®

VOLUME 8

ROSS RICHIE CEO & Founder • MATT GAGNON Editor-in-Chief • FILIP SABLIK President of Publishing & Marketing • STEPHEN CHRISTY President of Development • LANCE KREITER VP of Licensing & Merchandising • PHIL BARBARO VP of Finance • BRYCE CARLSON Managing Editor • MEL CAYLO Marketing Manager • SCOTT NEWMAN Production Design Manager • IRENE BRADISH Operations Manager CHRISTINE DINH Brand Communications Manager • Sierra Hahn Senior Editor • DAFNA PLEBAN Editor • SHANNON WATTERS Editor • ERIC HARBURN Editor • WHITNEY LEOPARD Associate Editor JASMINE AMIRI Associate Editor • CHRIS ROSA Associate Editor • ALEX GALER Assistant Editor • CAMERON CHITTOCK Assistant Editor • MARY GUMPORT Assistant Editor • KELSEY DIETERICH Production Designer JILLIAN CRAB Production Designer • MICHELLE ANKLEY Production Design Assistant • AARON FERRARA Operations Coordinator • ELIZABETH LOUGHRIDGE Accounting Coordinator JOSÉ MEZA Sales Assistant • JAMES ARRIOLA Mailroom Assistant • STEPHANIE HOCUTT Marketing Assistant • SAM KUSEK Direct Market Representative • HILLARY LEVI Executive Assistant

kaboom!

GARFIELD Volume Eight, May 2016. Published by KaBOOM!, a division of Boom Entertainment, Inc. Garfield is © 2016 PAWS, INCORPORATED. ALL RIGHTS RESERVED. "GARFIELD" and the GARFIELD characters are registered and unregistered trademarks of Paws, Inc. Originally published in single issue form as GARFIELD No. 29-32. Copyright © 2014 PAWS, INCORPORATED. ALL RIGHTS RESERVED. KaBOOM!™ and the KaBOOM! logo are trademarks of Boom Entertainment, Inc., registered in various countries and categories. All characters, events, and institutions depicted herein are fictional. Any similarity between any of the names, characters, persons, events, and/or institutions in this publication to actual names, characters, and persons, whether living or dead, events, and/or institutions is unintended and purely coincidental. KaBOOM! does not read or accept unsolicited submissions of ideas, stories, or artwork.

A catalog record of this book is available from OCLC and from the KaBOOM! website, www.kaboom-studios.com, on the Librarians Page.

BOOM! Studios, 5670 Wilshire Boulevard, Suite 450, Los Angeles, CA 90036-5679. Printed in China. First Printing.
ISBN: 978-1-60886-801-8, eISBN: 978-1-61398-472-7

CHAPTER ONE

"MILKMAN AND THE MAKE-BELIEVERS"
WRITTEN BY
MARK EVANIER

ART BY
ANDY HIRSCH

COLORS BY
LISA MOORE

"SPACE ODDITY"
WRITTEN BY
SCOTT NICKEL

ART BY
MARIS WICKS

CHAPTER TWO

"UP IS DOWN"
WRITTEN BY
MARK EVANIER

ART BY
ANDY HIRSCH

COLORS BY
LISA MOORE

"ALL IN A DAY'S COSPLAY"
WRITTEN BY
SCOTT NICKEL

ART BY
GENEVIEVE FT

CHAPTER THREE

"THANKS 4 GIVING"
WRITTEN BY
MARK EVANIER

ART BY
ANDY HIRSCH

COLORS BY
LISA MOORE

"LITTLE RED RIDING CAT"
WRITTEN BY
SCOTT NICKEL

ART BY
NNEKA MEYERS

CHAPTER FOUR

"ELF ESTEEM"
WRITTEN BY
MARK EVANIER

ART BY
ANDY HIRSCH

COLORS BY
LISA MOORE

"NERMAL AND THE THREE BEARS"
WRITTEN BY
SCOTT NICKEL

ART BY
LISSY MARLIN

LETTERS BY
STEVE WANDS

COVER BY
ANDY HIRSCH

DESIGNER
GRACE PARK

ASSISTANT EDITOR
CHRIS ROSA

EDITOR
SHANNON WATTERS

GARFIELD CREATED BY
JIM DAVIS
SPECIAL THANKS TO SCOTT NICKEL, DAVID REDDICK, AND THE ENTIRE PAWS, INC. TEAM.

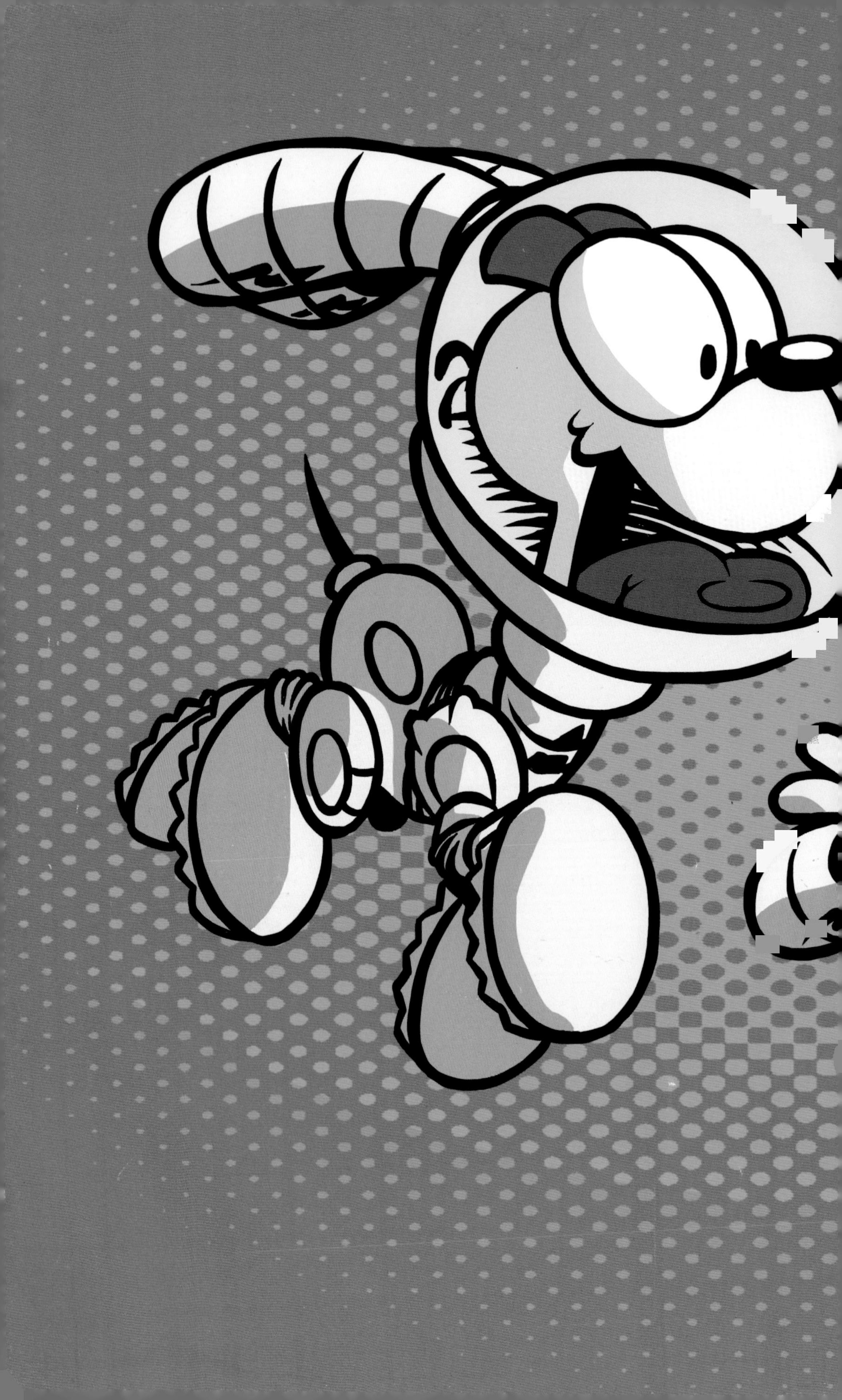

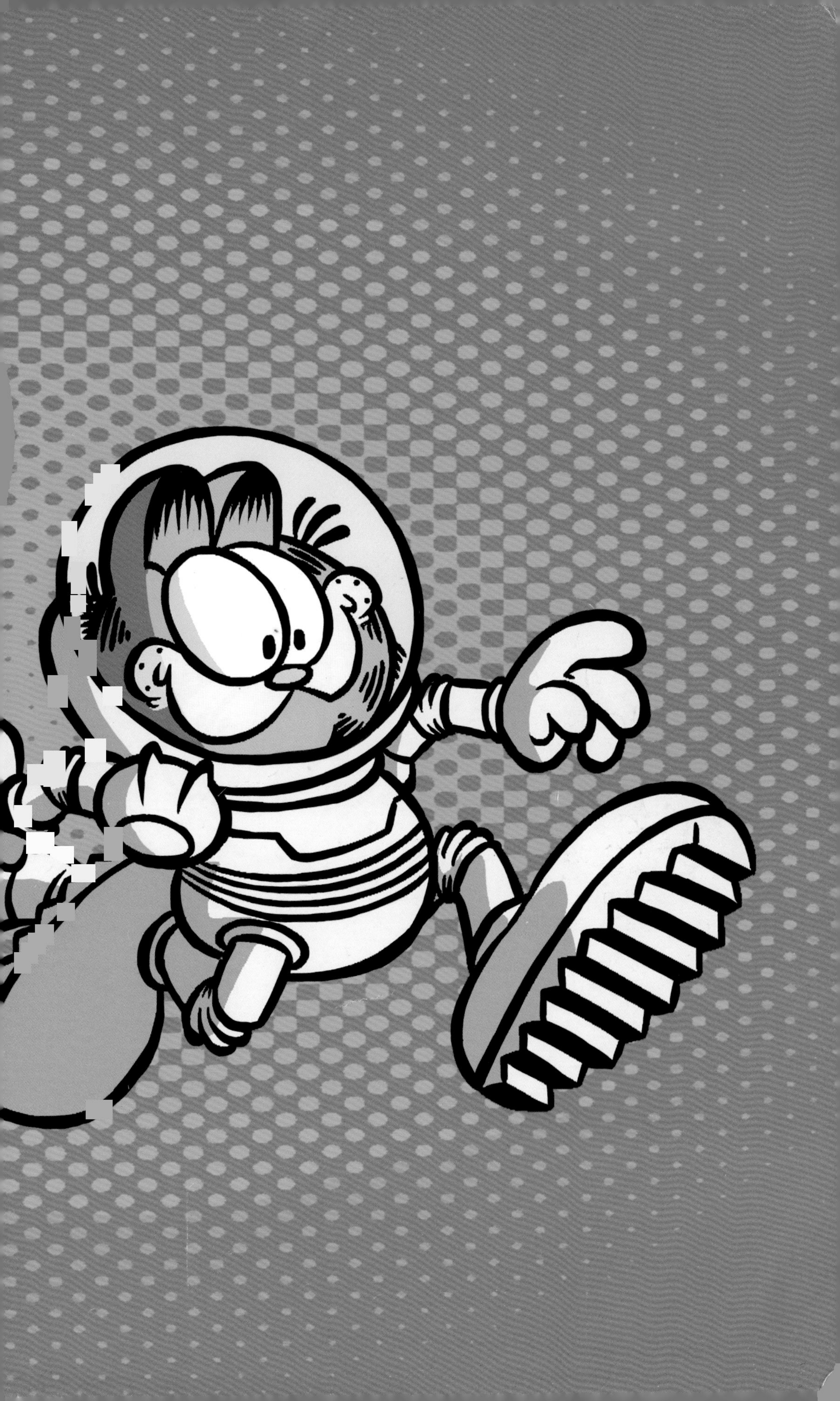

CHAPTER 1

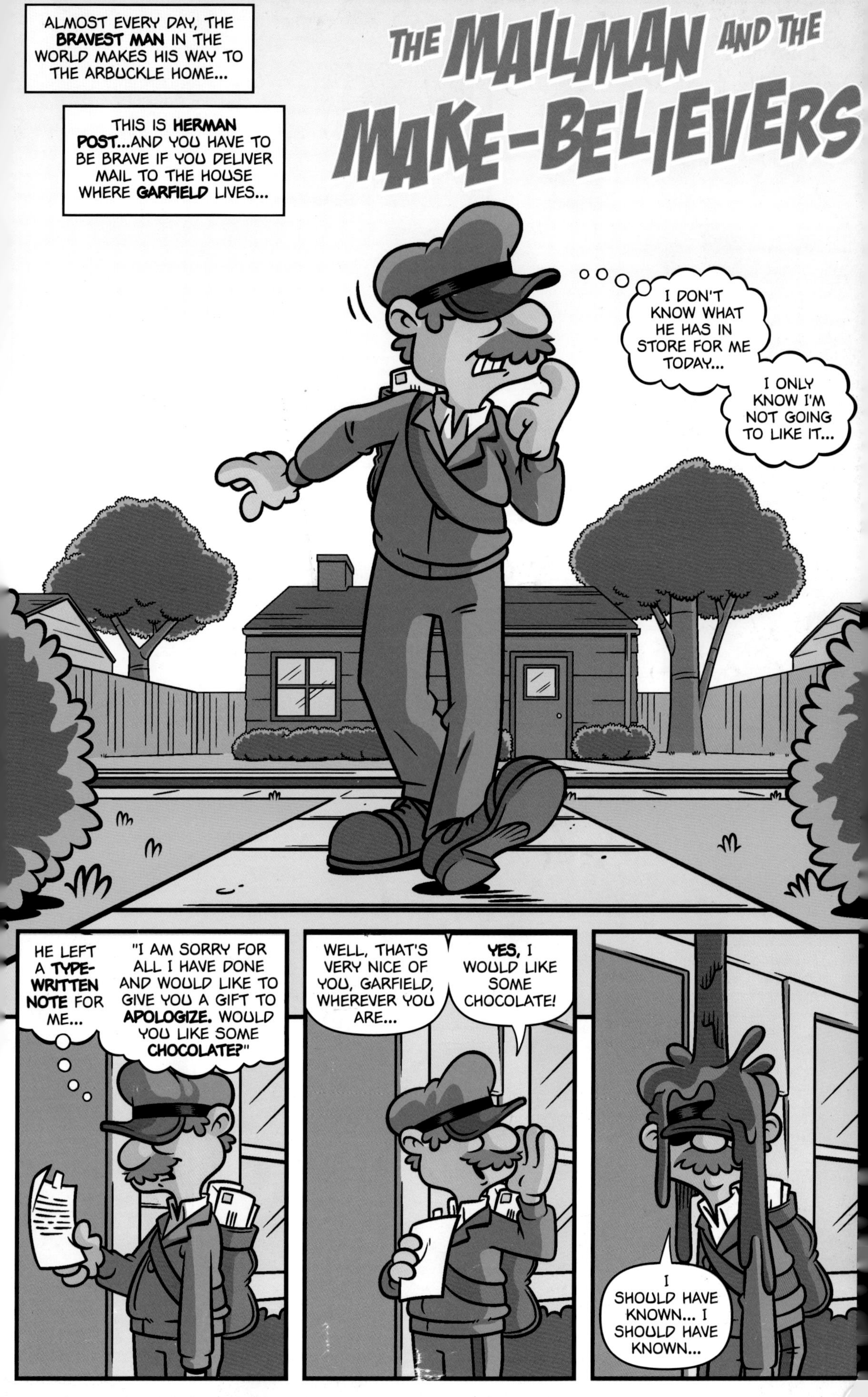

ALMOST EVERY DAY, THE BRAVEST MAN IN THE WORLD MAKES HIS WAY TO THE ARBUCKLE HOME...
THE MAILMAN AND THE MAKE-BELIEVERS
THIS IS HERMAN POST...AND YOU HAVE TO BE BRAVE IF YOU DELIVER MAIL TO THE HOUSE WHERE GARFIELD LIVES...
I DON'T KNOW WHAT HE HAS IN STORE FOR ME TODAY...
I ONLY KNOW I'M NOT GOING TO LIKE IT...
HE LEFT A TYPE-WRITTEN NOTE FOR ME...
"I AM SORRY FOR ALL I HAVE DONE AND WOULD LIKE TO GIVE YOU A GIFT TO APOLOGIZE. WOULD YOU LIKE SOME CHOCOLATE?"
WELL, THAT'S VERY NICE OF YOU, GARFIELD, WHEREVER YOU ARE...
YES, I WOULD LIKE SOME CHOCOLATE!
I SHOULD HAVE KNOWN... I SHOULD HAVE KNOWN...

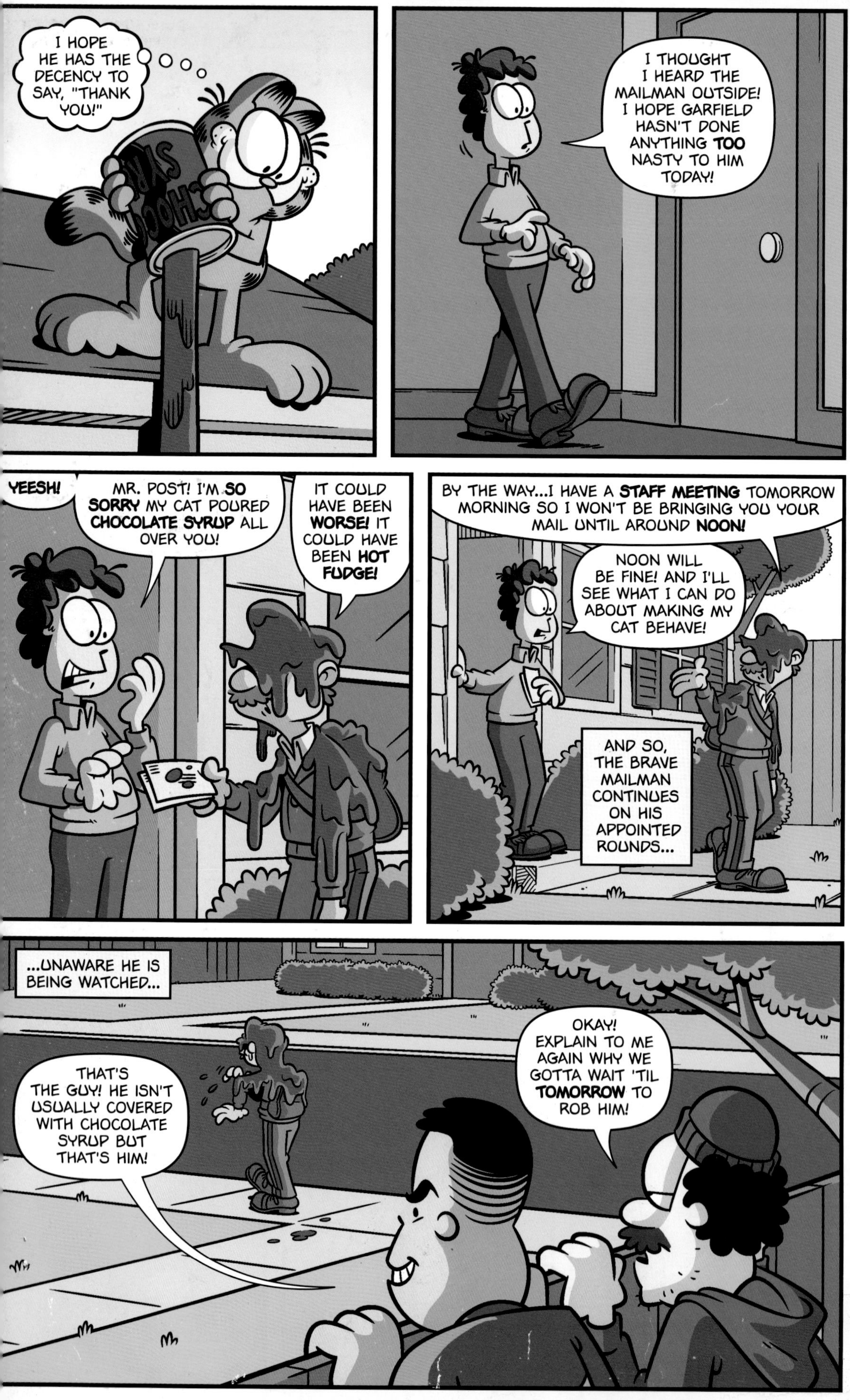

I HOPE HE HAS THE DECENCY TO SAY, "THANK YOU!"
SYRUP
I THOUGHT I HEARD THE MAILMAN OUTSIDE! I HOPE GARFIELD HASN'T DONE ANYTHING **TOO** NASTY TO HIM TODAY!
YEESH!
MR. POST! I'M **SO SORRY** MY CAT POURED **CHOCOLATE SYRUP** ALL OVER YOU!
IT COULD HAVE BEEN **WORSE!** IT COULD HAVE BEEN **HOT FUDGE!**
BY THE WAY...I HAVE A **STAFF MEETING** TOMORROW MORNING SO I WON'T BE BRINGING YOU YOUR MAIL UNTIL AROUND **NOON!**
NOON WILL BE FINE! AND I'LL SEE WHAT I CAN DO ABOUT MAKING MY CAT BEHAVE!
AND SO, THE BRAVE MAILMAN CONTINUES ON HIS APPOINTED ROUNDS...
...UNAWARE HE IS BEING WATCHED...
THAT'S THE GUY! HE ISN'T USUALLY COVERED WITH CHOCOLATE SYRUP BUT THAT'S HIM!
OKAY! EXPLAIN TO ME AGAIN WHY WE GOTTA WAIT 'TIL **TOMORROW** TO ROB HIM!

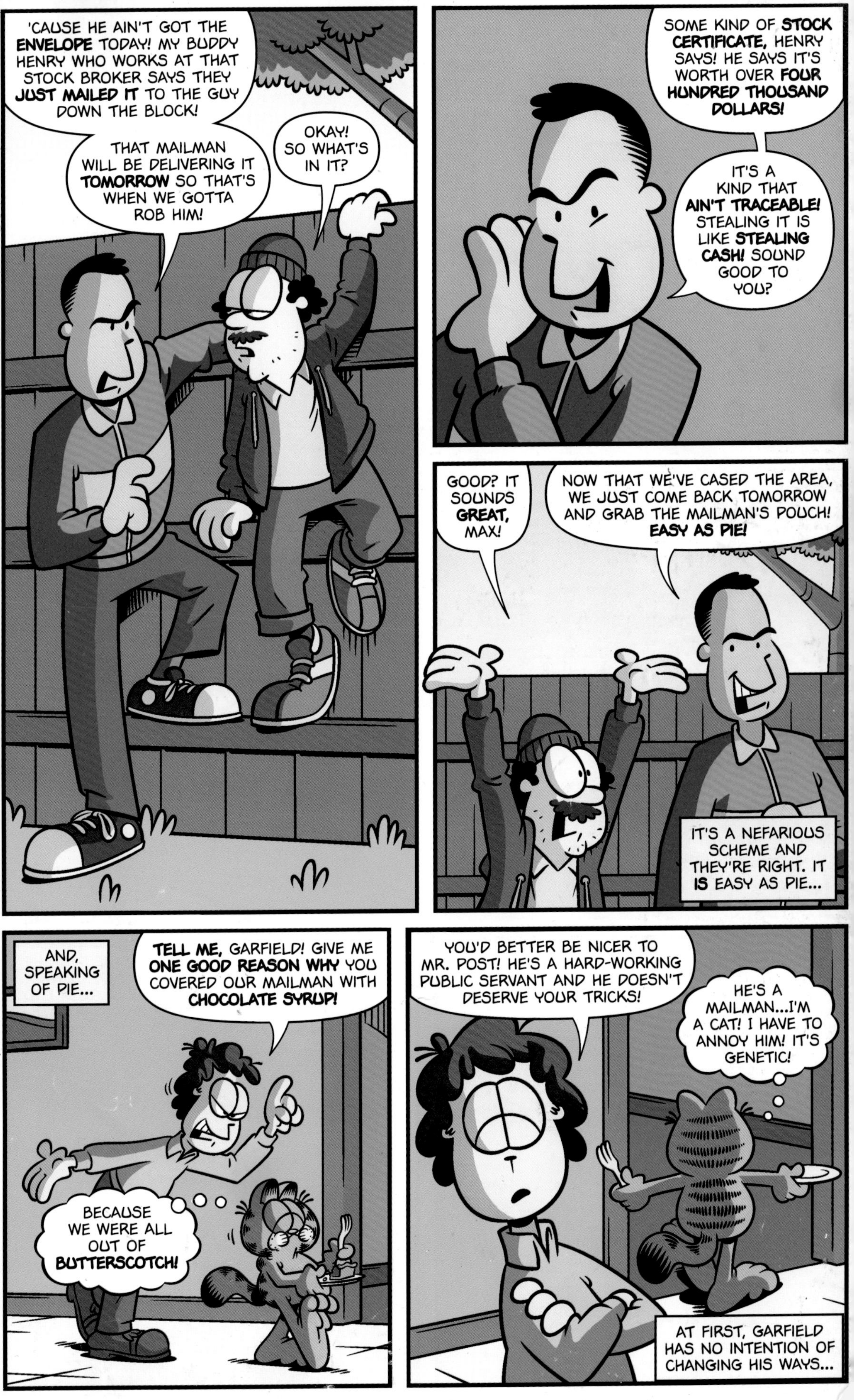
'CAUSE HE AIN'T GOT THE ENVELOPE TODAY! MY BUDDY HENRY WHO WORKS AT THAT STOCK BROKER SAYS THEY JUST MAILED IT TO THE GUY DOWN THE BLOCK!
THAT MAILMAN WILL BE DELIVERING IT TOMORROW SO THAT'S WHEN WE GOTTA ROB HIM!
OKAY! SO WHAT'S IN IT?
SOME KIND OF STOCK CERTIFICATE, HENRY SAYS! HE SAYS IT'S WORTH OVER FOUR HUNDRED THOUSAND DOLLARS!
IT'S A KIND THAT AIN'T TRACEABLE! STEALING IT IS LIKE STEALING CASH! SOUND GOOD TO YOU?
GOOD? IT SOUNDS GREAT, MAX!
NOW THAT WE'VE CASED THE AREA, WE JUST COME BACK TOMORROW AND GRAB THE MAILMAN'S POUCH! EASY AS PIE!
IT'S A NEFARIOUS SCHEME AND THEY'RE RIGHT. IT IS EASY AS PIE...
AND, SPEAKING OF PIE...
TELL ME, GARFIELD! GIVE ME ONE GOOD REASON WHY YOU COVERED OUR MAILMAN WITH CHOCOLATE SYRUP!
BECAUSE WE WERE ALL OUT OF BUTTERSCOTCH!
YOU'D BETTER BE NICER TO MR. POST! HE'S A HARD-WORKING PUBLIC SERVANT AND HE DOESN'T DESERVE YOUR TRICKS!
HE'S A MAILMAN...I'M A CAT! I HAVE TO ANNOY HIM! IT'S GENETIC!
AT FIRST, GARFIELD HAS NO INTENTION OF CHANGING HIS WAYS...

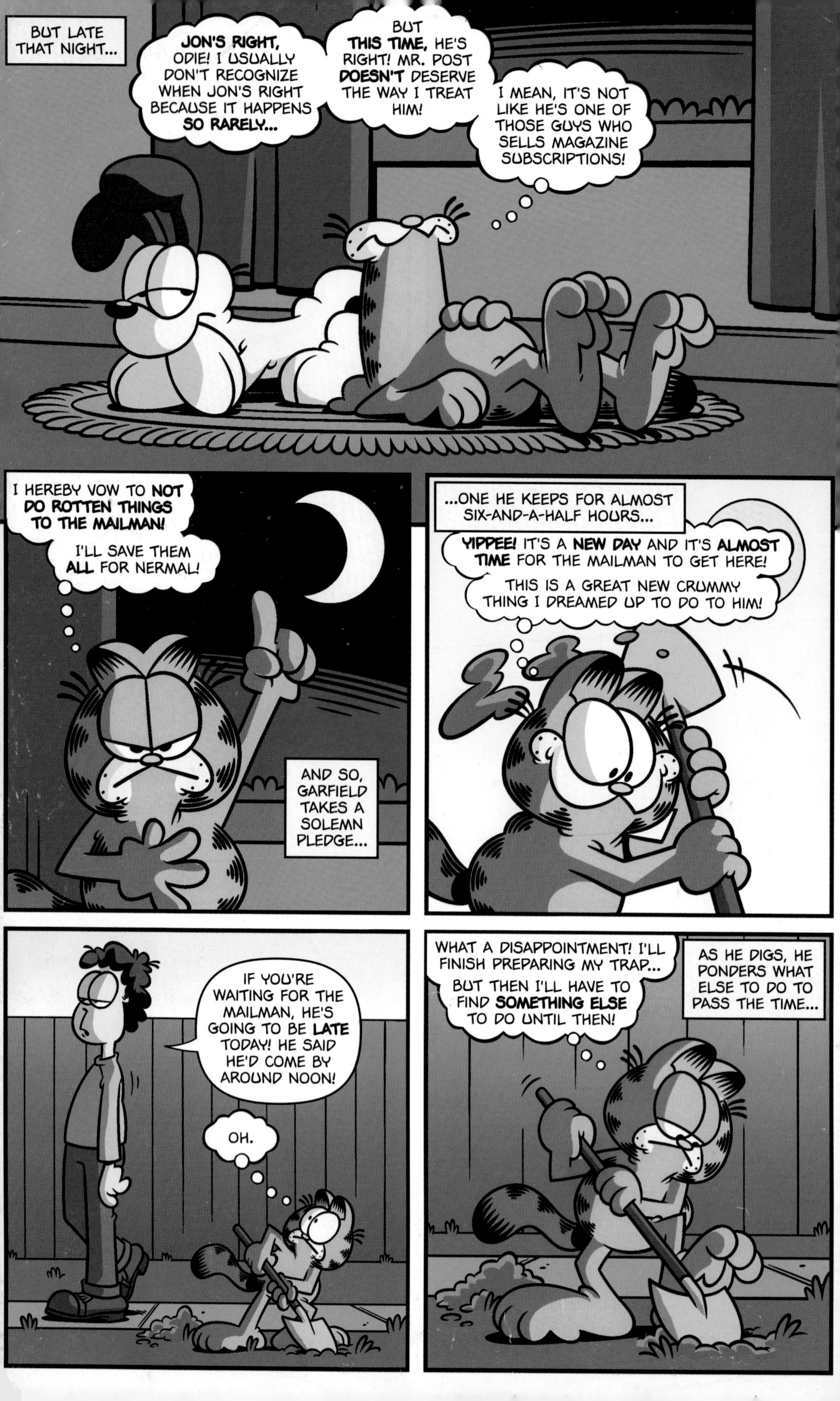
BUT LATE THAT NIGHT...
JON'S RIGHT, ODIE! I USUALLY DON'T RECOGNIZE WHEN JON'S RIGHT BECAUSE IT HAPPENS SO RARELY...
BUT THIS TIME, HE'S RIGHT! MR. POST DOESN'T DESERVE THE WAY I TREAT HIM!
I MEAN, IT'S NOT LIKE HE'S ONE OF THOSE GUYS WHO SELLS MAGAZINE SUBSCRIPTIONS!
I HEREBY VOW TO NOT DO ROTTEN THINGS TO THE MAILMAN!
I'LL SAVE THEM ALL FOR NERMAL!
AND SO, GARFIELD TAKES A SOLEMN PLEDGE...
...ONE HE KEEPS FOR ALMOST SIX-AND-A-HALF HOURS...
YIPPEE! IT'S A NEW DAY AND IT'S ALMOST TIME FOR THE MAILMAN TO GET HERE!
THIS IS A GREAT NEW CRUMMY THING I DREAMED UP TO DO TO HIM!
IF YOU'RE WAITING FOR THE MAILMAN, HE'S GOING TO BE LATE TODAY! HE SAID HE'D COME BY AROUND NOON!
OH.
WHAT A DISAPPOINTMENT! I'LL FINISH PREPARING MY TRAP...
BUT THEN I'LL HAVE TO FIND SOMETHING ELSE TO DO UNTIL THEN!
AS HE DIGS, HE PONDERS WHAT ELSE TO DO TO PASS THE TIME...

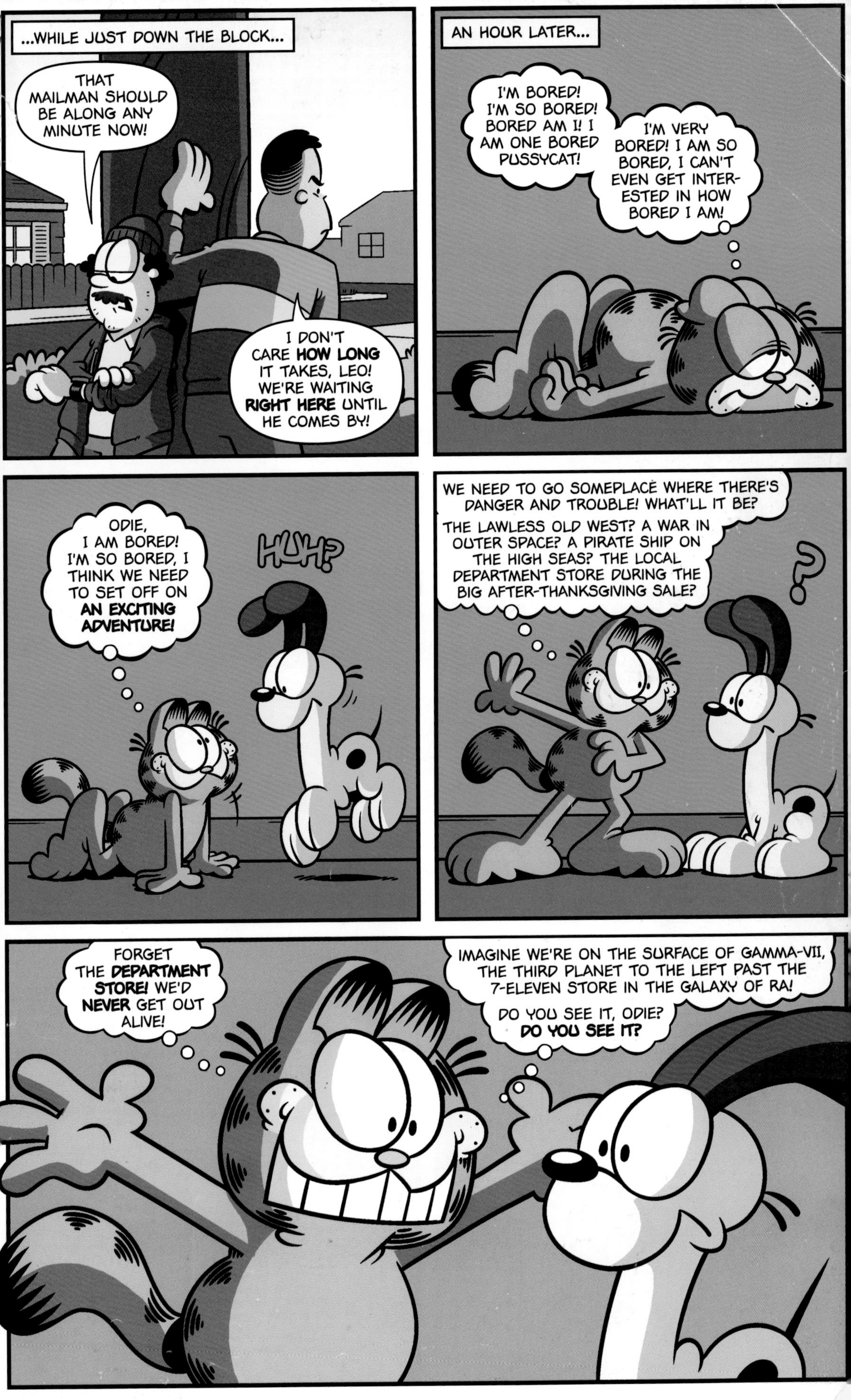
...WHILE JUST DOWN THE BLOCK...
THAT MAILMAN SHOULD BE ALONG ANY MINUTE NOW!
I DON'T CARE **HOW LONG** IT TAKES, LEO! WE'RE WAITING **RIGHT HERE** UNTIL HE COMES BY!
AN HOUR LATER...
I'M BORED! I'M SO BORED! BORED AM I! I AM ONE BORED PUSSYCAT!
I'M VERY BORED! I AM SO BORED, I CAN'T EVEN GET INTER-ESTED IN HOW BORED I AM!
ODIE, I AM BORED! I'M SO BORED, I THINK WE NEED TO SET OFF ON **AN EXCITING ADVENTURE!**
HUH?
WE NEED TO GO SOMEPLACE WHERE THERE'S DANGER AND TROUBLE! WHAT'LL IT BE?
THE LAWLESS OLD WEST? A WAR IN OUTER SPACE? A PIRATE SHIP ON THE HIGH SEAS? THE LOCAL DEPARTMENT STORE DURING THE BIG AFTER-THANKSGIVING SALE?
?
FORGET THE **DEPARTMENT STORE!** WE'D **NEVER** GET OUT ALIVE!
IMAGINE WE'RE ON THE SURFACE OF GAMMA-VII, THE THIRD PLANET TO THE LEFT PAST THE 7-ELEVEN STORE IN THE GALAXY OF RA!
DO YOU SEE IT, ODIE? **DO YOU SEE IT?**

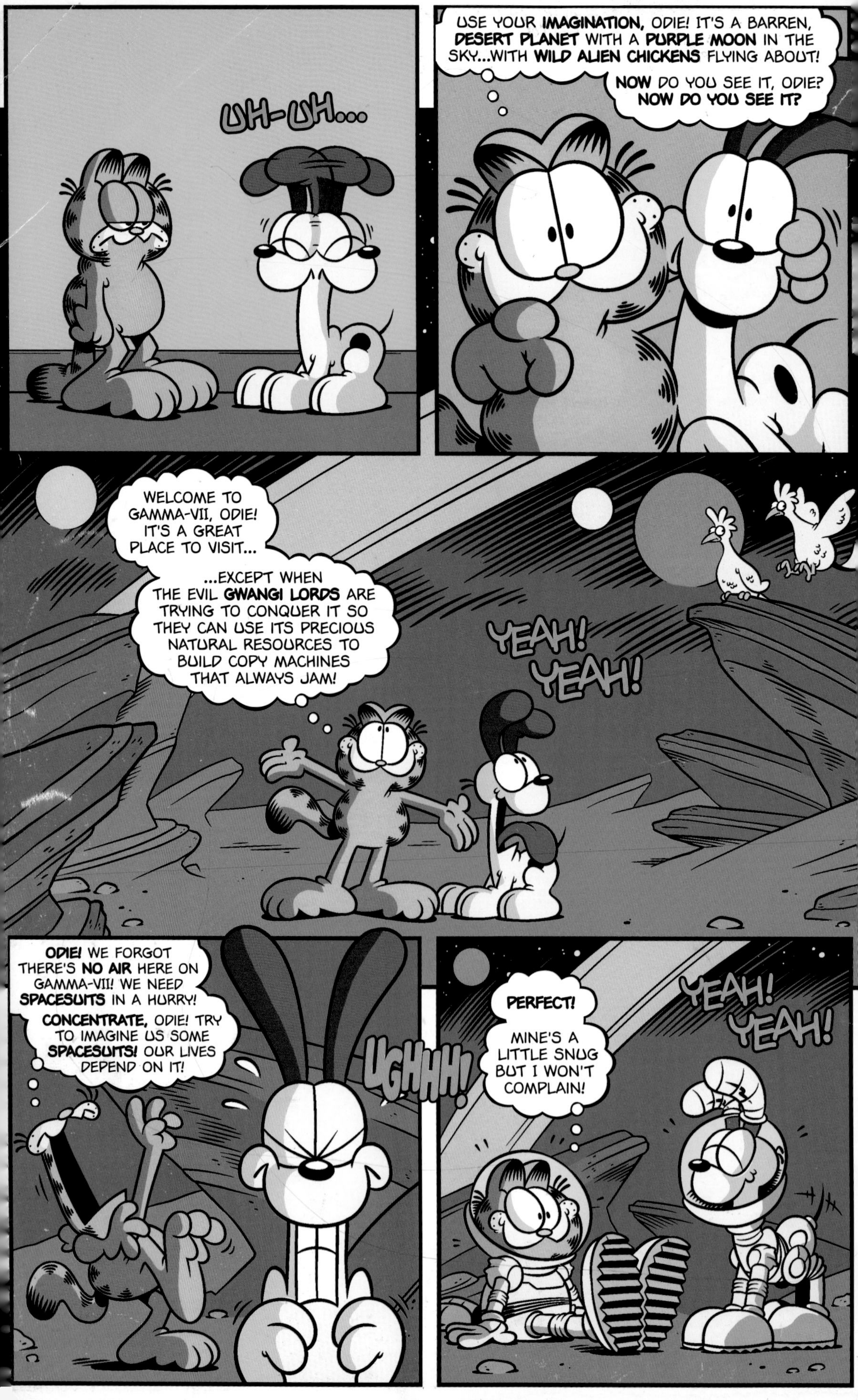
UH-UH...
USE YOUR IMAGINATION, ODIE! IT'S A BARREN, DESERT PLANET WITH A PURPLE MOON IN THE SKY...WITH WILD ALIEN CHICKENS FLYING ABOUT!
NOW DO YOU SEE IT, ODIE? NOW DO YOU SEE IT?
WELCOME TO GAMMA-VII, ODIE! IT'S A GREAT PLACE TO VISIT...
...EXCEPT WHEN THE EVIL GWANGI LORDS ARE TRYING TO CONQUER IT SO THEY CAN USE ITS PRECIOUS NATURAL RESOURCES TO BUILD COPY MACHINES THAT ALWAYS JAM!
YEAH! YEAH!
ODIE! WE FORGOT THERE'S NO AIR HERE ON GAMMA-VII! WE NEED SPACESUITS IN A HURRY!
CONCENTRATE, ODIE! TRY TO IMAGINE US SOME SPACESUITS! OUR LIVES DEPEND ON IT!
UGHHH!
PERFECT!
MINE'S A LITTLE SNUG BUT I WON'T COMPLAIN!
YEAH! YEAH!

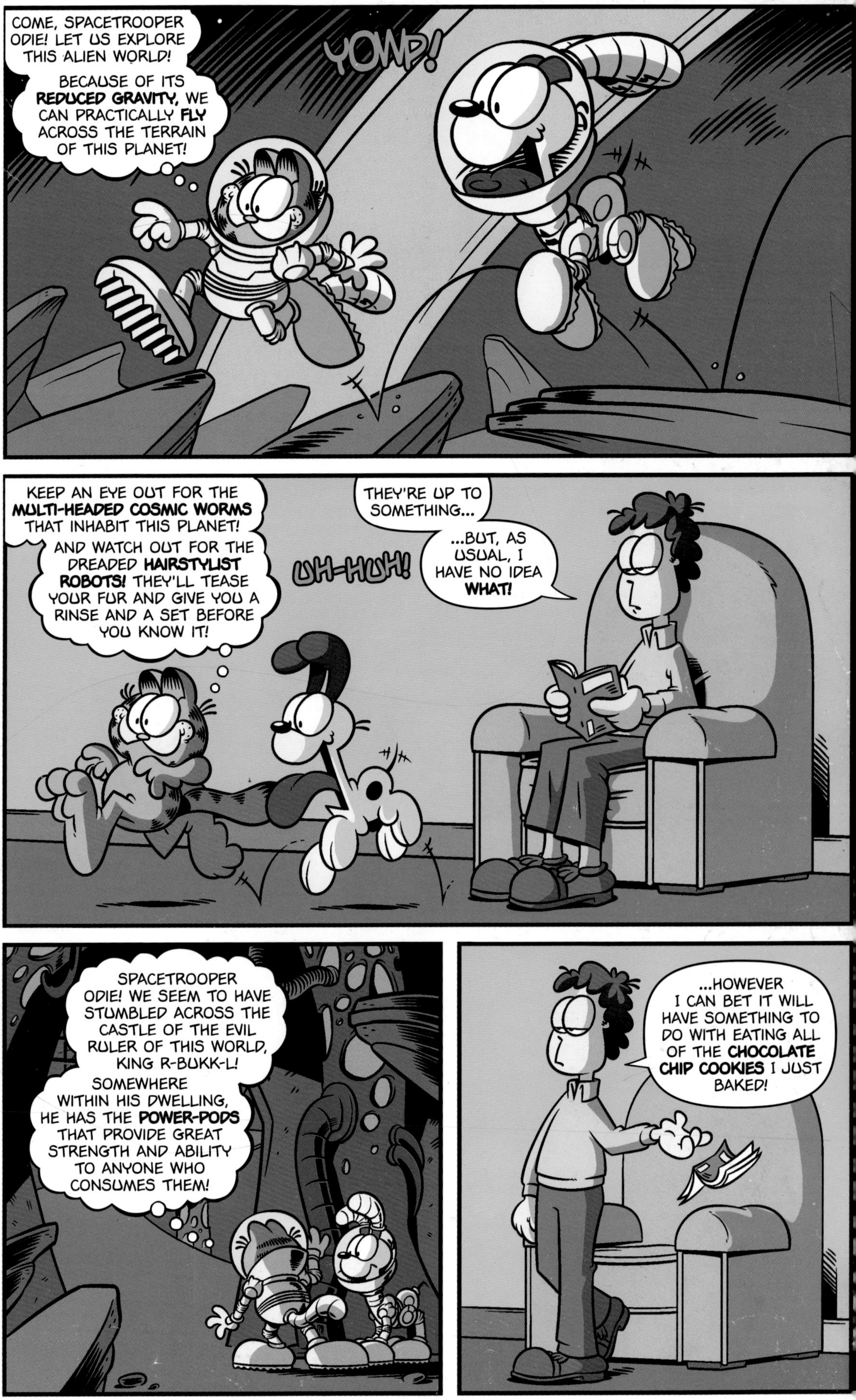
COME, SPACETROOPER ODIE! LET US EXPLORE THIS ALIEN WORLD!
BECAUSE OF ITS REDUCED GRAVITY, WE CAN PRACTICALLY FLY ACROSS THE TERRAIN OF THIS PLANET!
YOMP!
KEEP AN EYE OUT FOR THE MULTI-HEADED COSMIC WORMS THAT INHABIT THIS PLANET!
AND WATCH OUT FOR THE DREADED HAIRSTYLIST ROBOTS! THEY'LL TEASE YOUR FUR AND GIVE YOU A RINSE AND A SET BEFORE YOU KNOW IT!
UH-HUH!
THEY'RE UP TO SOMETHING...
...BUT, AS USUAL, I HAVE NO IDEA WHAT!
SPACETROOPER ODIE! WE SEEM TO HAVE STUMBLED ACROSS THE CASTLE OF THE EVIL RULER OF THIS WORLD, KING R-BUKK-L!
SOMEWHERE WITHIN HIS DWELLING, HE HAS THE POWER-PODS THAT PROVIDE GREAT STRENGTH AND ABILITY TO ANYONE WHO CONSUMES THEM!
...HOWEVER I CAN BET IT WILL HAVE SOMETHING TO DO WITH EATING ALL OF THE CHOCOLATE CHIP COOKIES I JUST BAKED!

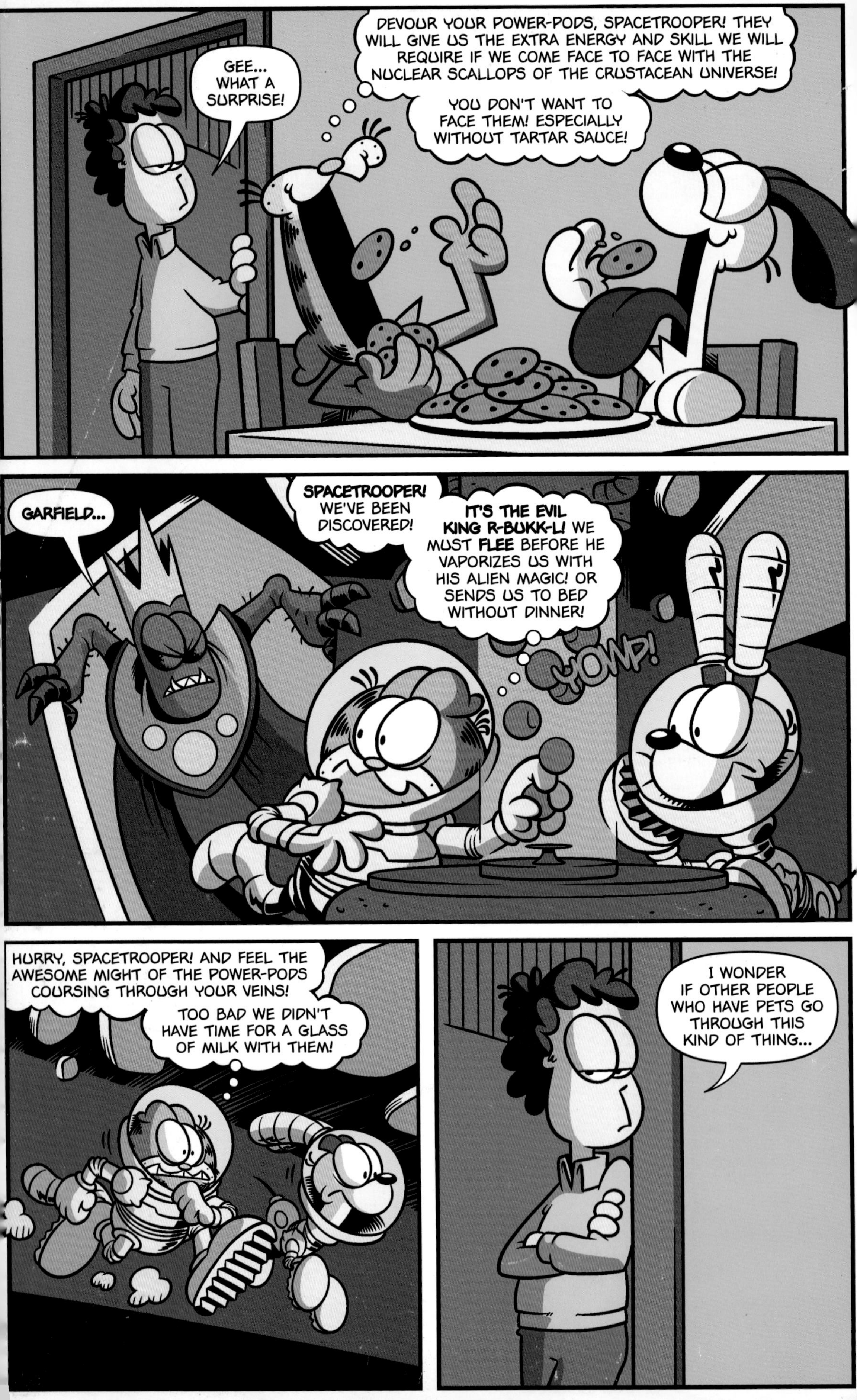
GEE... WHAT A SURPRISE!
DEVOUR YOUR POWER-PODS, SPACETROOPER! THEY WILL GIVE US THE EXTRA ENERGY AND SKILL WE WILL REQUIRE IF WE COME FACE TO FACE WITH THE NUCLEAR SCALLOPS OF THE CRUSTACEAN UNIVERSE!
YOU DON'T WANT TO FACE THEM! ESPECIALLY WITHOUT TARTAR SAUCE!
GARFIELD...
SPACETROOPER! WE'VE BEEN DISCOVERED!
IT'S THE EVIL KING R-BUKK-L! WE MUST FLEE BEFORE HE VAPORIZES US WITH HIS ALIEN MAGIC! OR SENDS US TO BED WITHOUT DINNER!
YOMP!
HURRY, SPACETROOPER! AND FEEL THE AWESOME MIGHT OF THE POWER-PODS COURSING THROUGH YOUR VEINS!
TOO BAD WE DIDN'T HAVE TIME FOR A GLASS OF MILK WITH THEM!
I WONDER IF OTHER PEOPLE WHO HAVE PETS GO THROUGH THIS KIND OF THING...

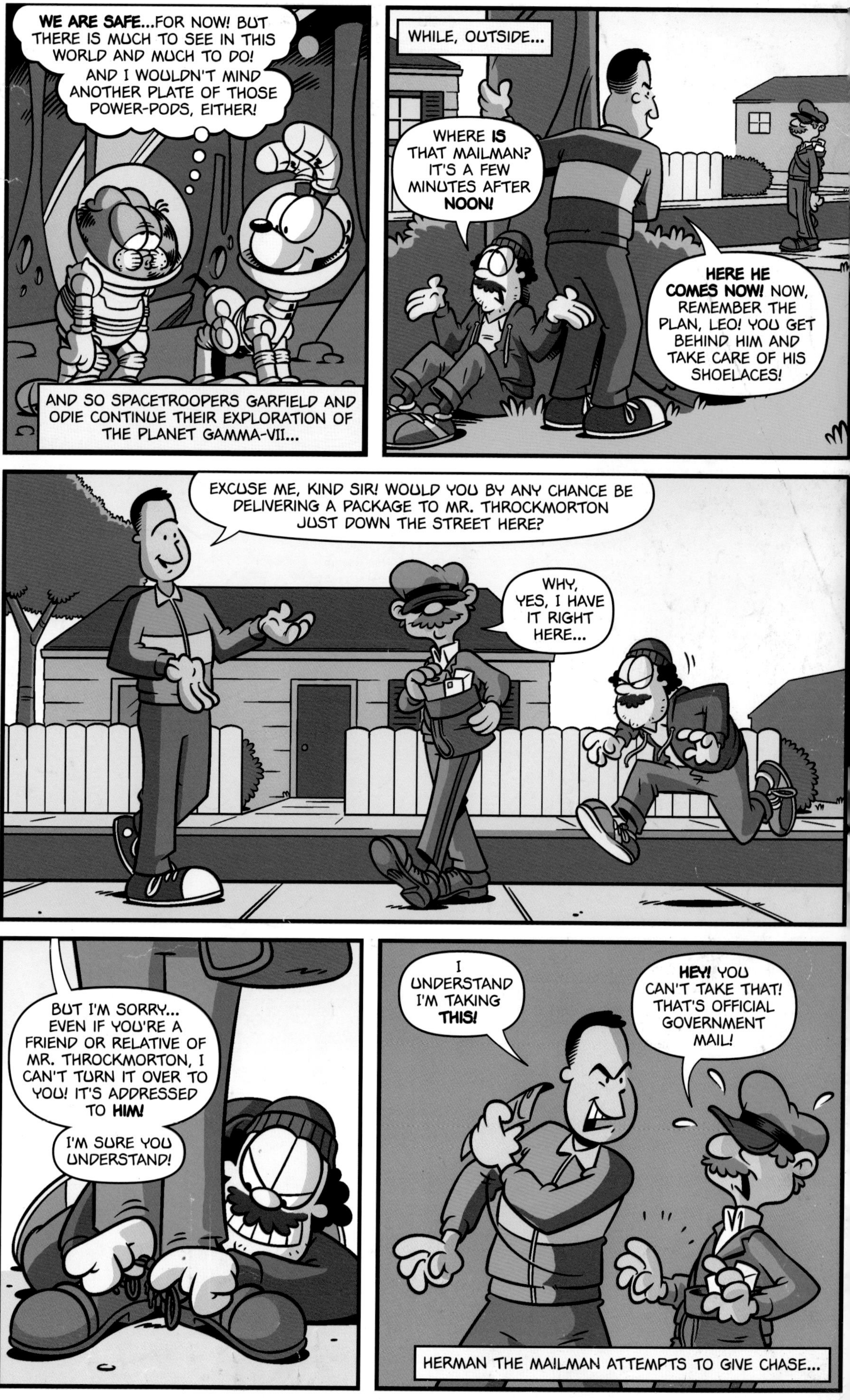
WE ARE SAFE...FOR NOW! BUT THERE IS MUCH TO SEE IN THIS WORLD AND MUCH TO DO!
AND I WOULDN'T MIND ANOTHER PLATE OF THOSE POWER-PODS, EITHER!
AND SO SPACETROOPERS GARFIELD AND ODIE CONTINUE THEIR EXPLORATION OF THE PLANET GAMMA-VII...
WHILE, OUTSIDE...
WHERE IS THAT MAILMAN? IT'S A FEW MINUTES AFTER NOON!
HERE HE COMES NOW! NOW, REMEMBER THE PLAN, LEO! YOU GET BEHIND HIM AND TAKE CARE OF HIS SHOELACES!
EXCUSE ME, KIND SIR! WOULD YOU BY ANY CHANCE BE DELIVERING A PACKAGE TO MR. THROCKMORTON JUST DOWN THE STREET HERE?
WHY, YES, I HAVE IT RIGHT HERE...
BUT I'M SORRY... EVEN IF YOU'RE A FRIEND OR RELATIVE OF MR. THROCKMORTON, I CAN'T TURN IT OVER TO YOU! IT'S ADDRESSED TO HIM!
I'M SURE YOU UNDERSTAND!
I UNDERSTAND I'M TAKING THIS!
HEY! YOU CAN'T TAKE THAT! THAT'S OFFICIAL GOVERNMENT MAIL!
HERMAN THE MAILMAN ATTEMPTS TO GIVE CHASE...

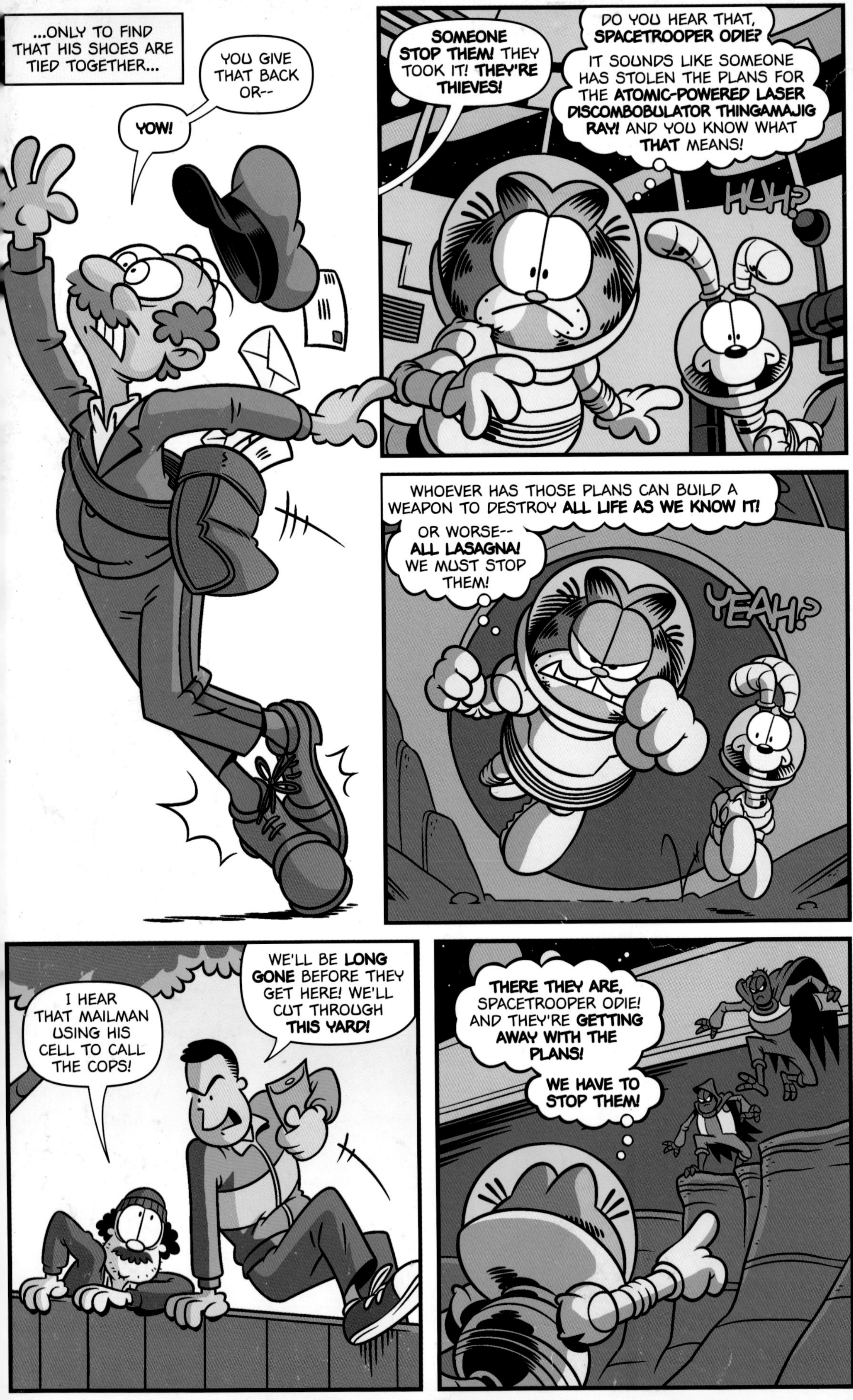

...ONLY TO FIND THAT HIS SHOES ARE TIED TOGETHER...
YOU GIVE THAT BACK OR--
YOW!
SOMEONE STOP THEM! THEY TOOK IT! THEY'RE THIEVES!
DO YOU HEAR THAT, SPACETROOPER ODIE?
IT SOUNDS LIKE SOMEONE HAS STOLEN THE PLANS FOR THE ATOMIC-POWERED LASER DISCOMBOBULATOR THINGAMAJIG RAY! AND YOU KNOW WHAT THAT MEANS!
HUH?
WHOEVER HAS THOSE PLANS CAN BUILD A WEAPON TO DESTROY ALL LIFE AS WE KNOW IT!
OR WORSE-- ALL LASAGNA! WE MUST STOP THEM!
YEAH!?
I HEAR THAT MAILMAN USING HIS CELL TO CALL THE COPS!
WE'LL BE LONG GONE BEFORE THEY GET HERE! WE'LL CUT THROUGH THIS YARD!
THERE THEY ARE, SPACETROOPER ODIE! AND THEY'RE GETTING AWAY WITH THE PLANS!
WE HAVE TO STOP THEM!

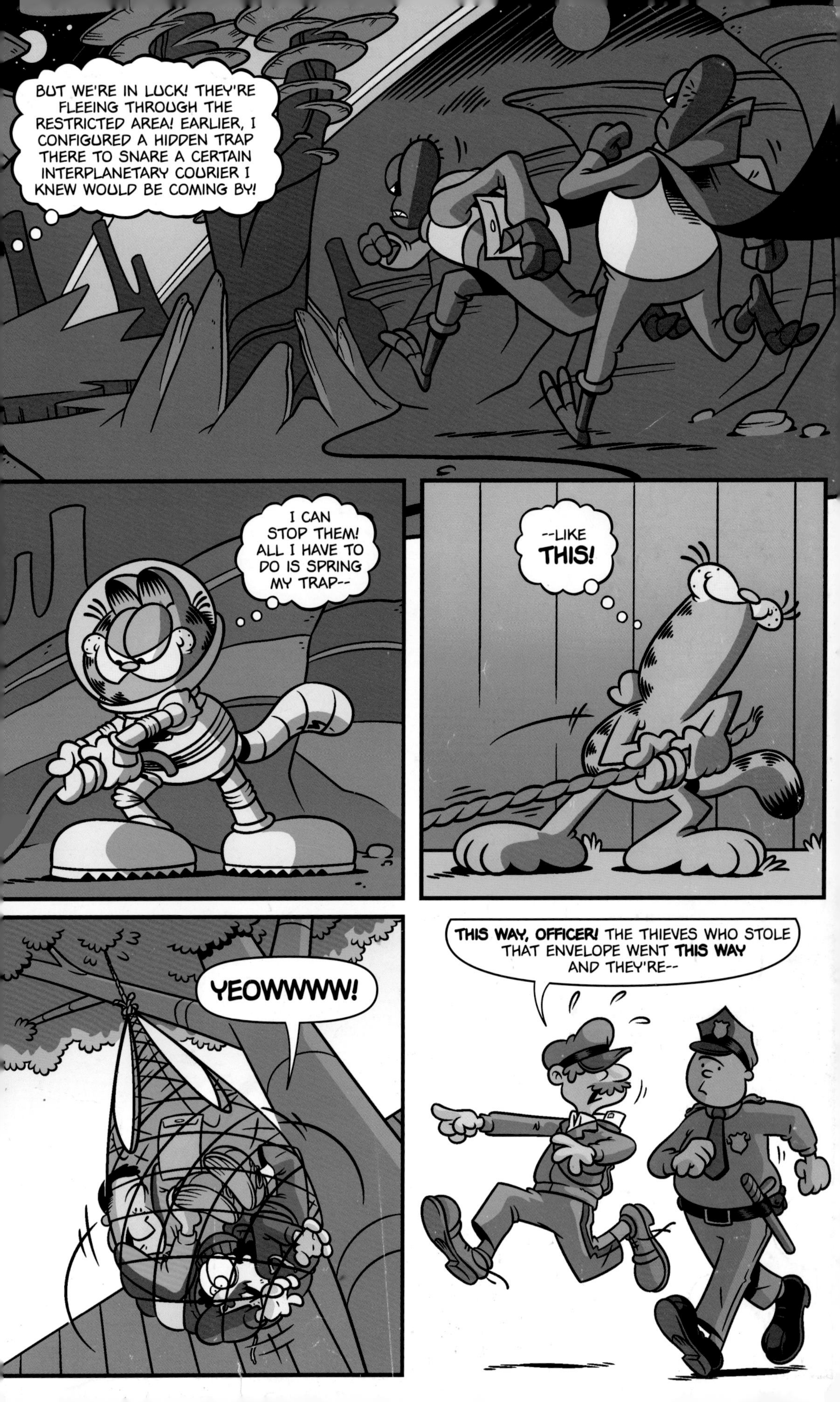
BUT WE'RE IN LUCK! THEY'RE FLEEING THROUGH THE RESTRICTED AREA! EARLIER, I CONFIGURED A HIDDEN TRAP THERE TO SNARE A CERTAIN INTERPLANETARY COURIER I KNEW WOULD BE COMING BY!
I CAN STOP THEM! ALL I HAVE TO DO IS SPRING MY TRAP--
--LIKE **THIS!**
YEOWWWW!
THIS WAY, OFFICER! THE THIEVES WHO STOLE THAT ENVELOPE WENT **THIS WAY** AND THEY'RE--

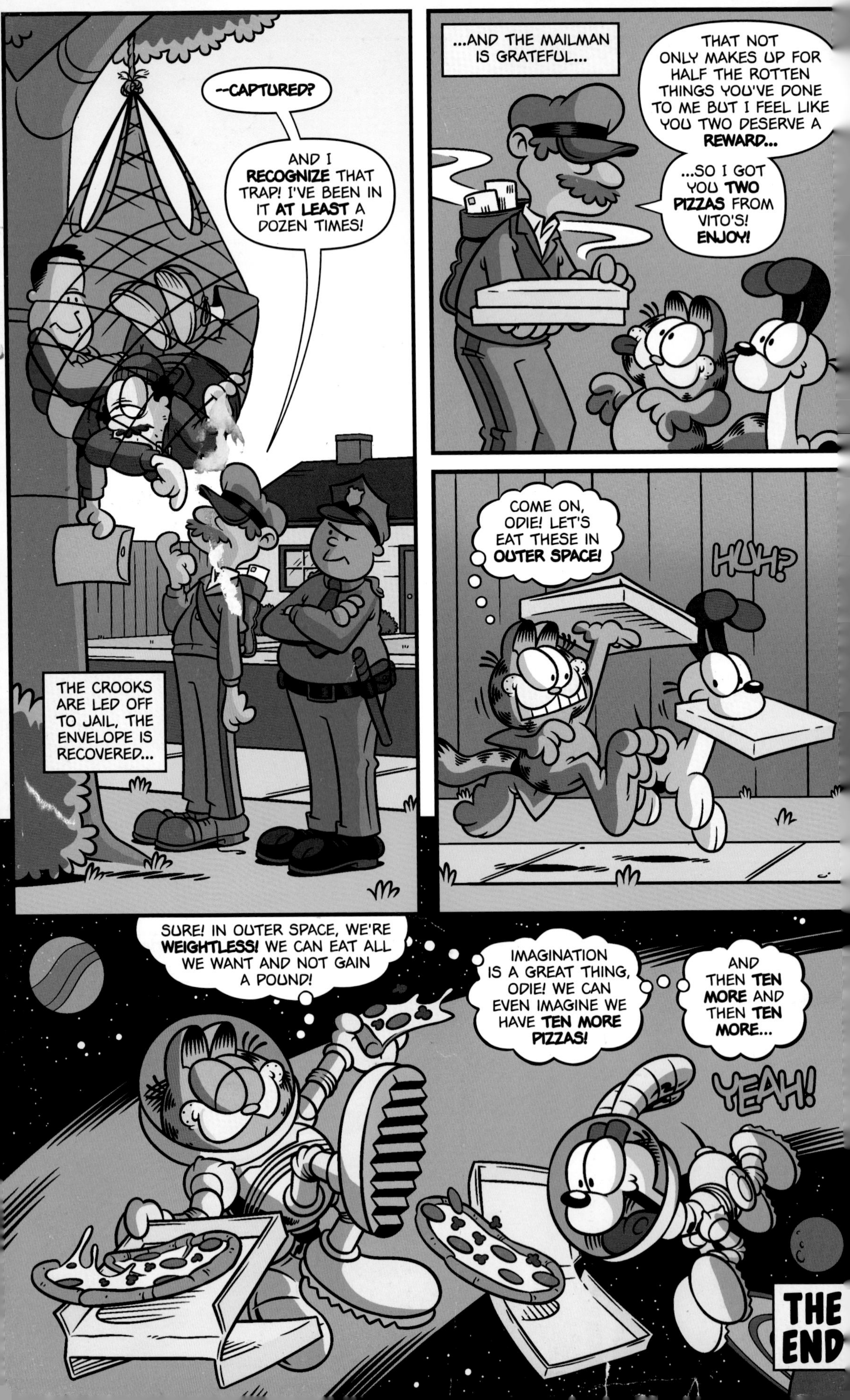
--CAPTURED?
AND I RECOGNIZE THAT TRAP! I'VE BEEN IN IT AT LEAST A DOZEN TIMES!
THE CROOKS ARE LED OFF TO JAIL, THE ENVELOPE IS RECOVERED...
...AND THE MAILMAN IS GRATEFUL...
THAT NOT ONLY MAKES UP FOR HALF THE ROTTEN THINGS YOU'VE DONE TO ME BUT I FEEL LIKE YOU TWO DESERVE A REWARD...
...SO I GOT YOU TWO PIZZAS FROM VITO'S! ENJOY!
COME ON, ODIE! LET'S EAT THESE IN OUTER SPACE!
HUH?
SURE! IN OUTER SPACE, WE'RE WEIGHTLESS! WE CAN EAT ALL WE WANT AND NOT GAIN A POUND!
IMAGINATION IS A GREAT THING, ODIE! WE CAN EVEN IMAGINE WE HAVE TEN MORE PIZZAS!
AND THEN TEN MORE AND THEN TEN MORE...
YEAH!
THE END

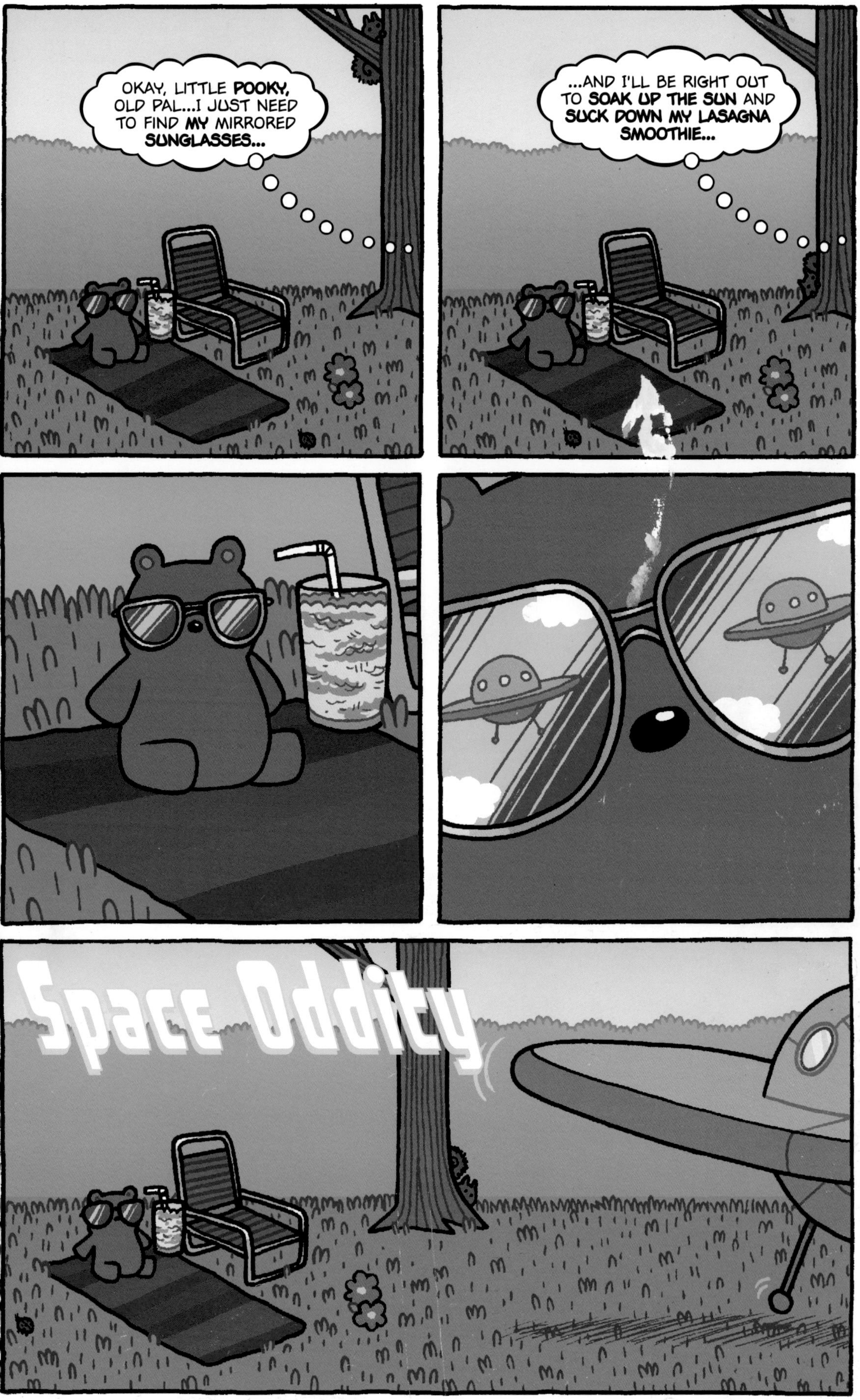
OKAY, LITTLE POOKY, OLD PAL...I JUST NEED TO FIND MY MIRRORED SUNGLASSES...
...AND I'LL BE RIGHT OUT TO SOAK UP THE SUN AND SUCK DOWN MY LASAGNA SMOOTHIE...
Space Oddity

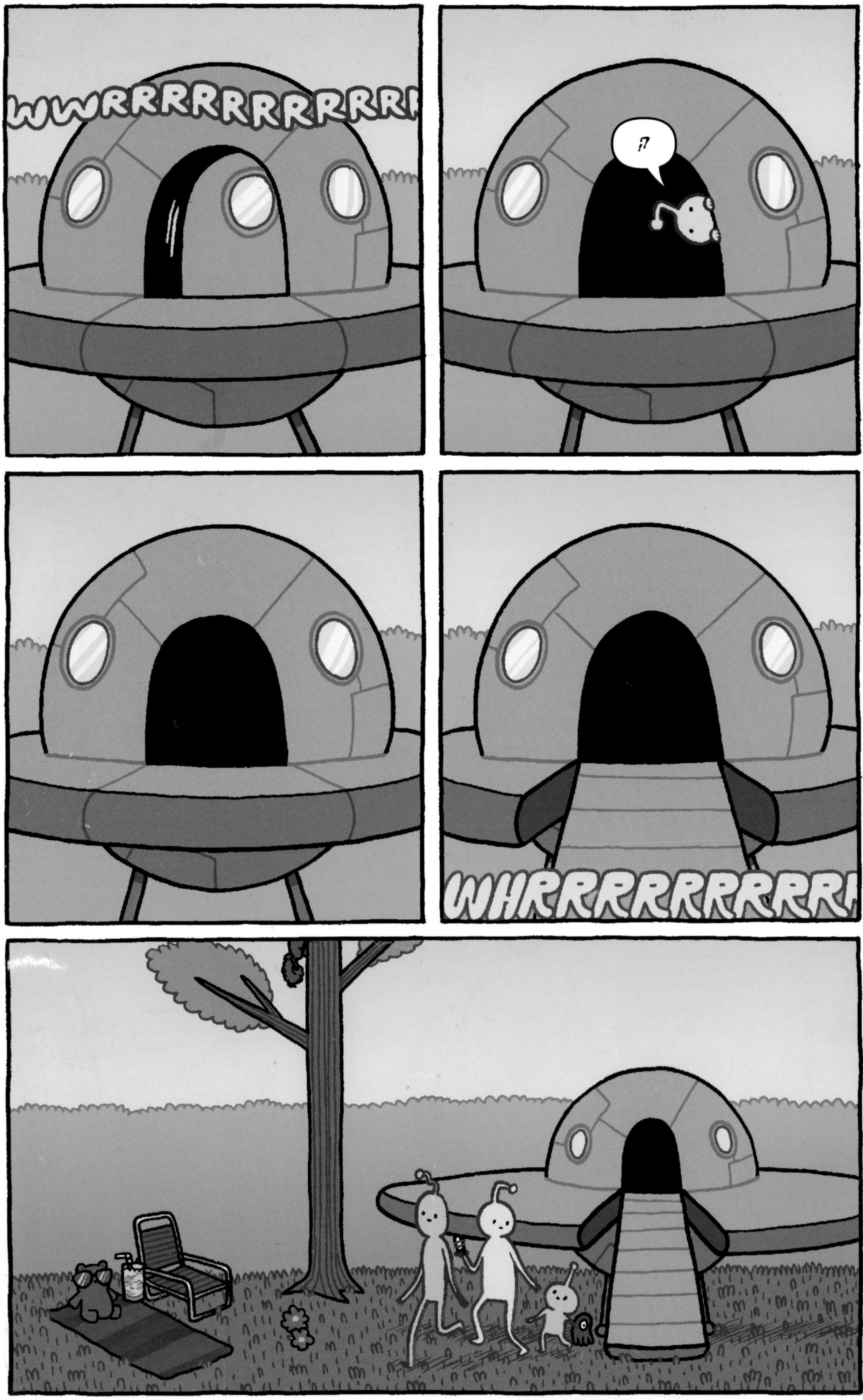
WWRRRRRRRRRR
WHRRRRRRRRRR

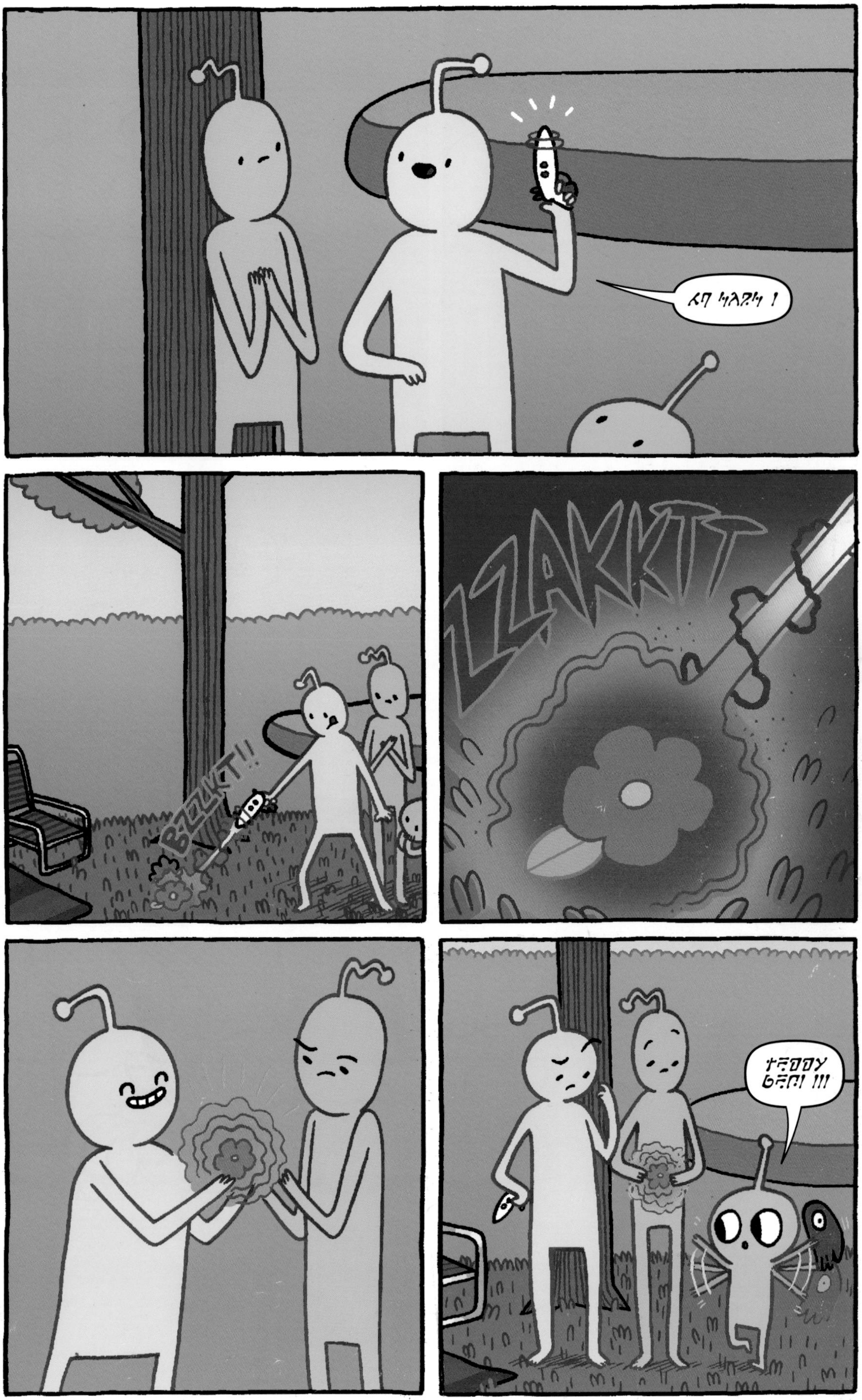
BZZKT!!
ZZAKKTT

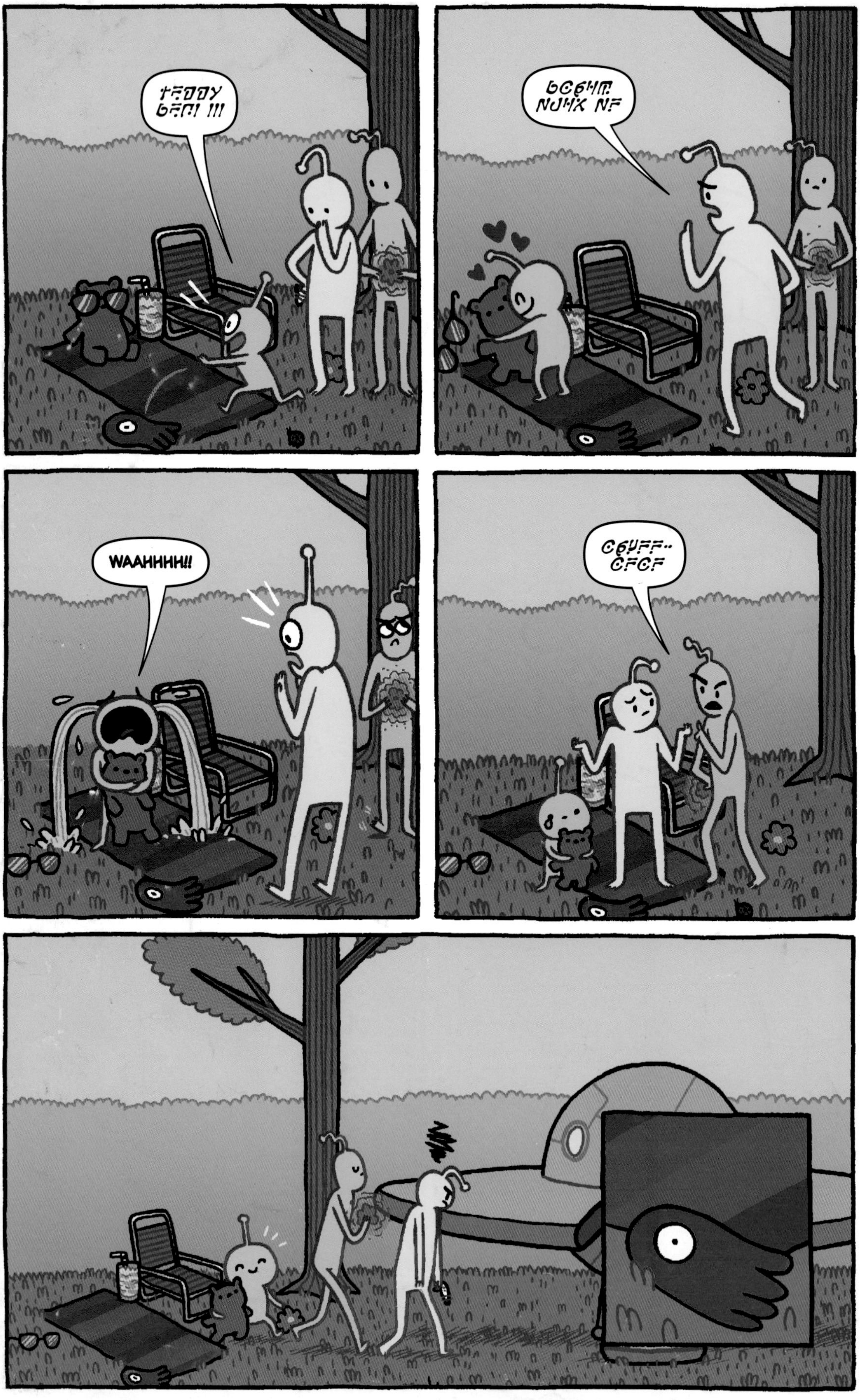
WAAHHHH!!

BUMP
BOOMP

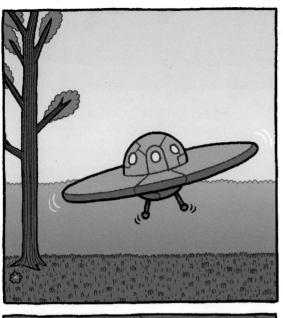

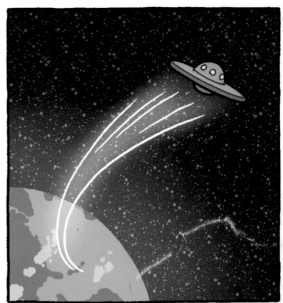

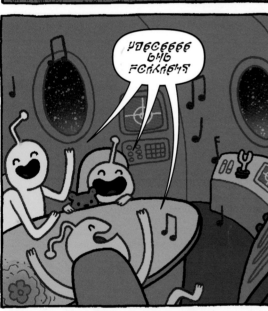

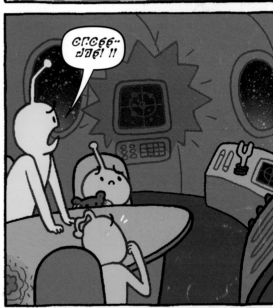

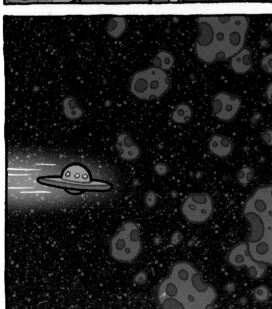

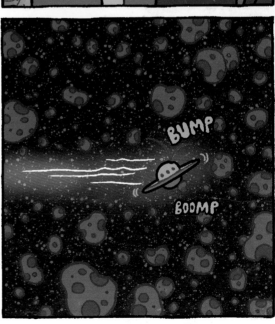

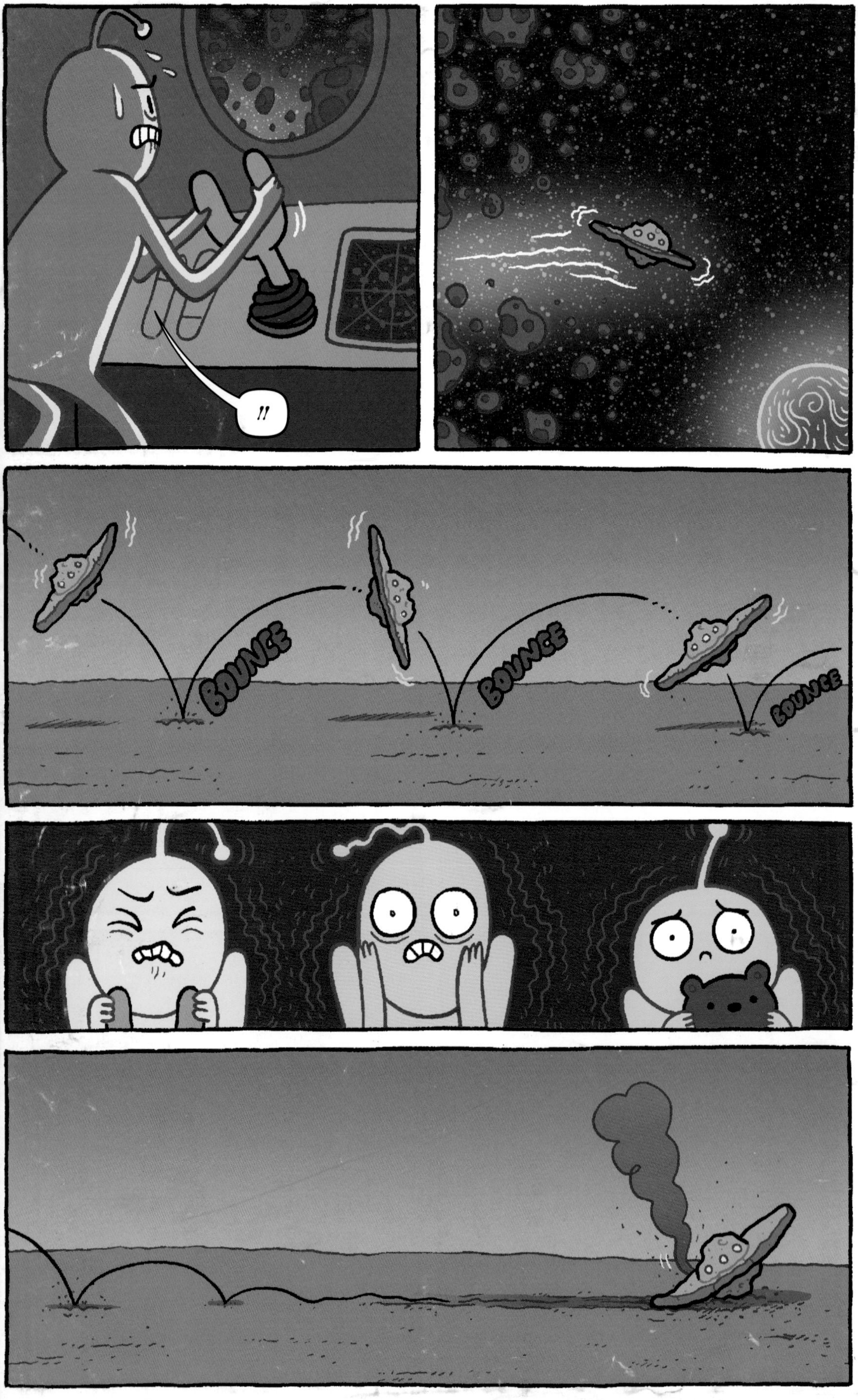
!!
BOUNCE
BOUNCE
BOUNCE

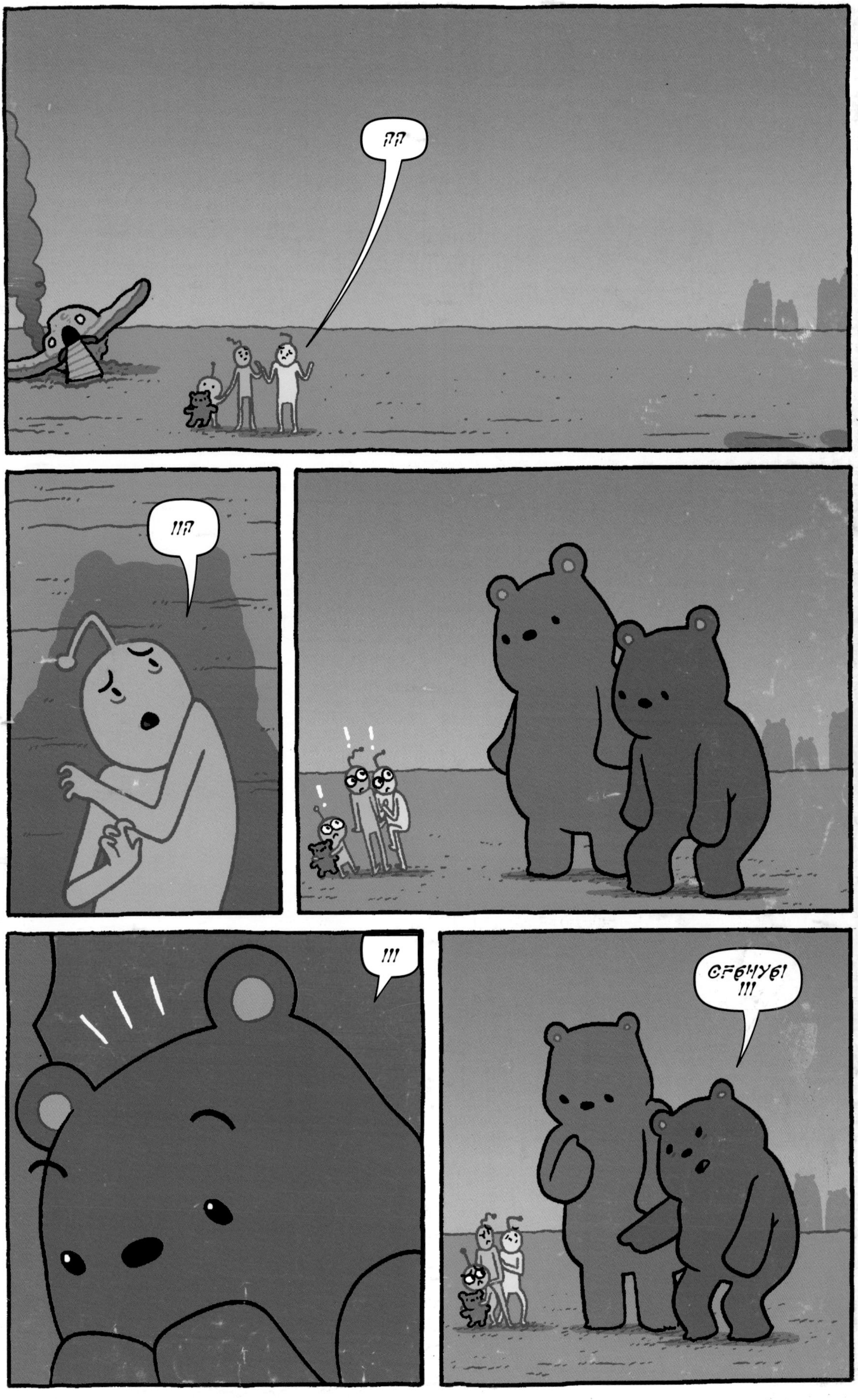
??
!!?
!!!
CF6HY6!
!!!

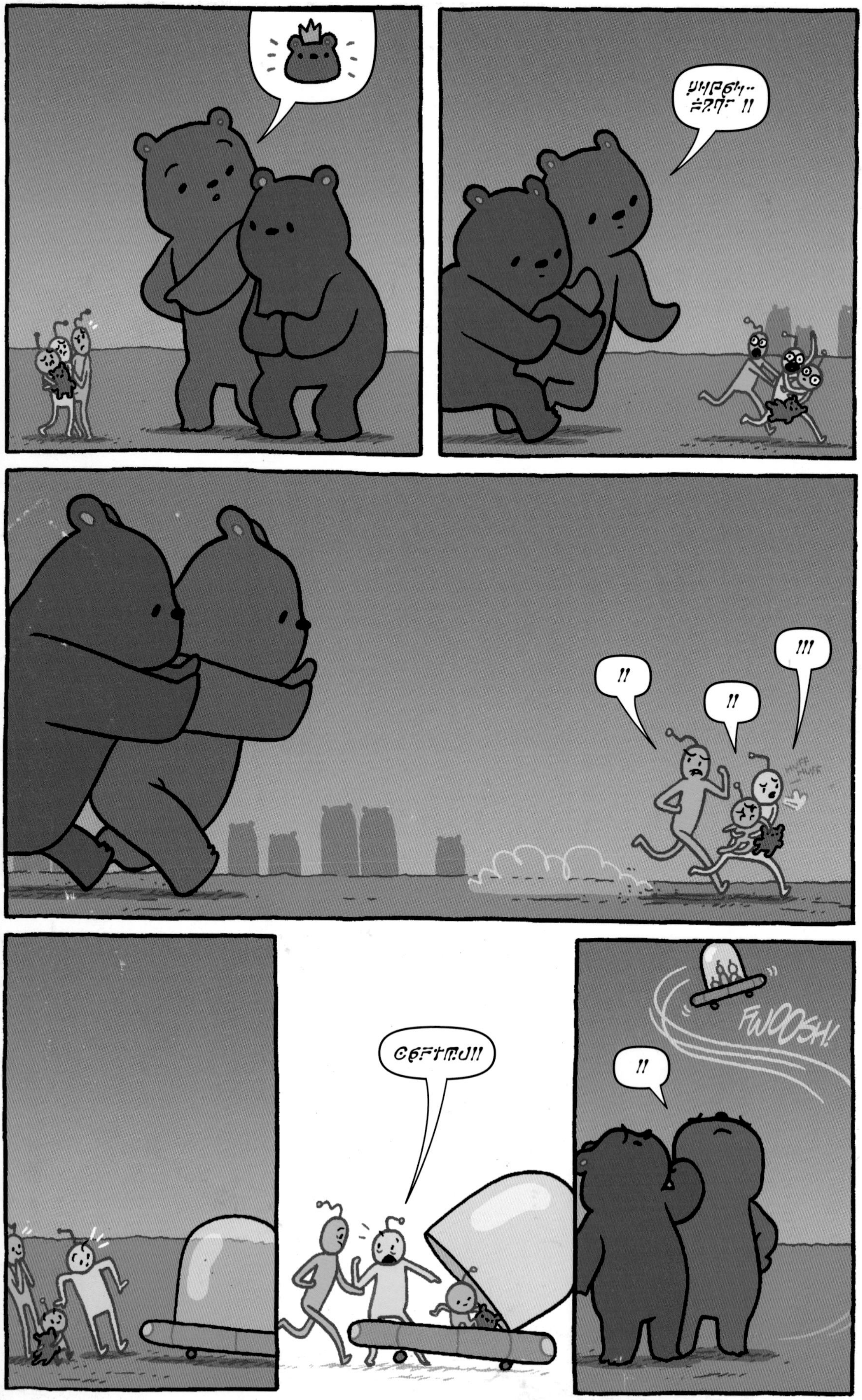
!!
!!
!!!
HUFF HUFF
!!
FWOOSH!

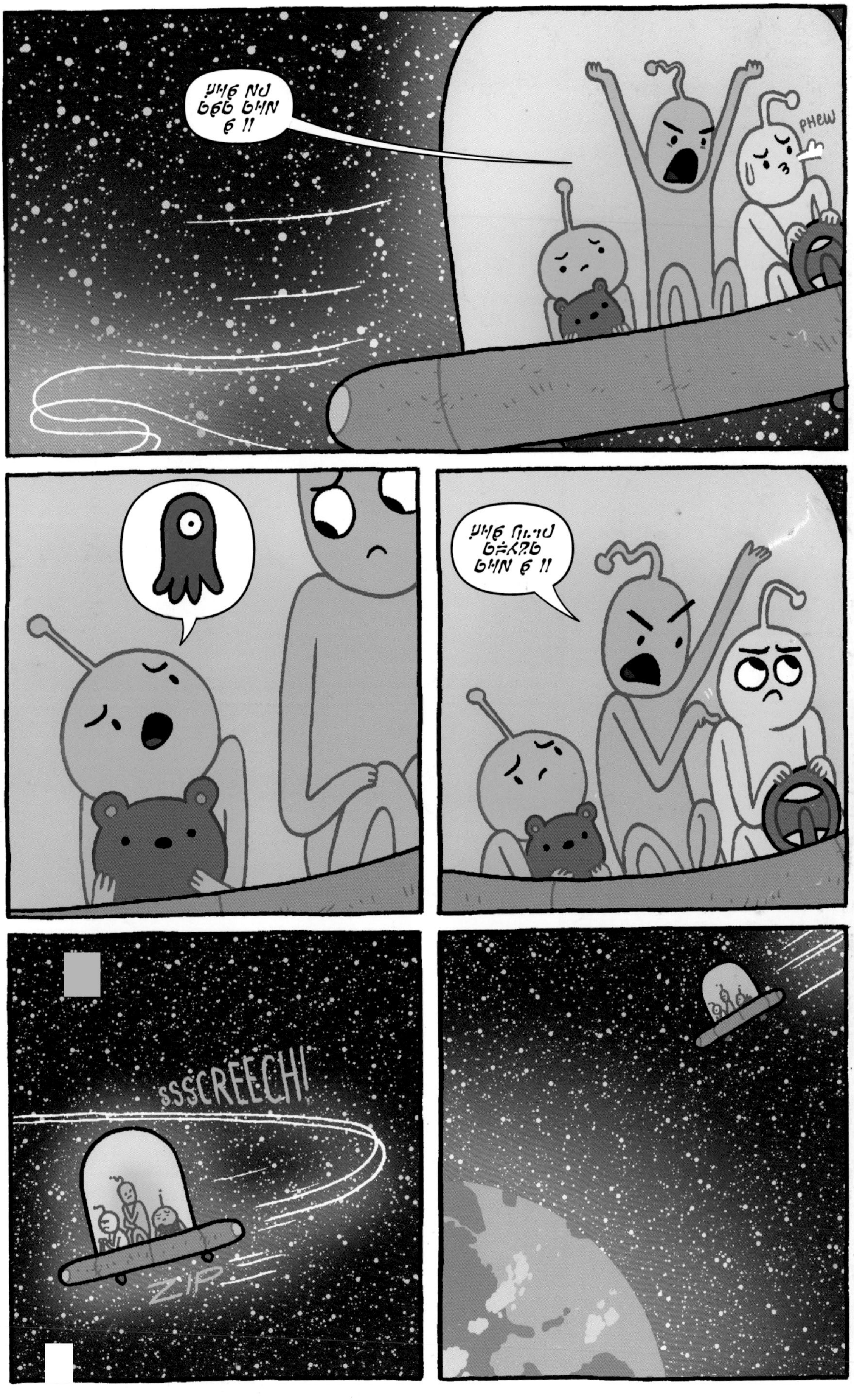
PHEW
SSSCREECH!
ZIP

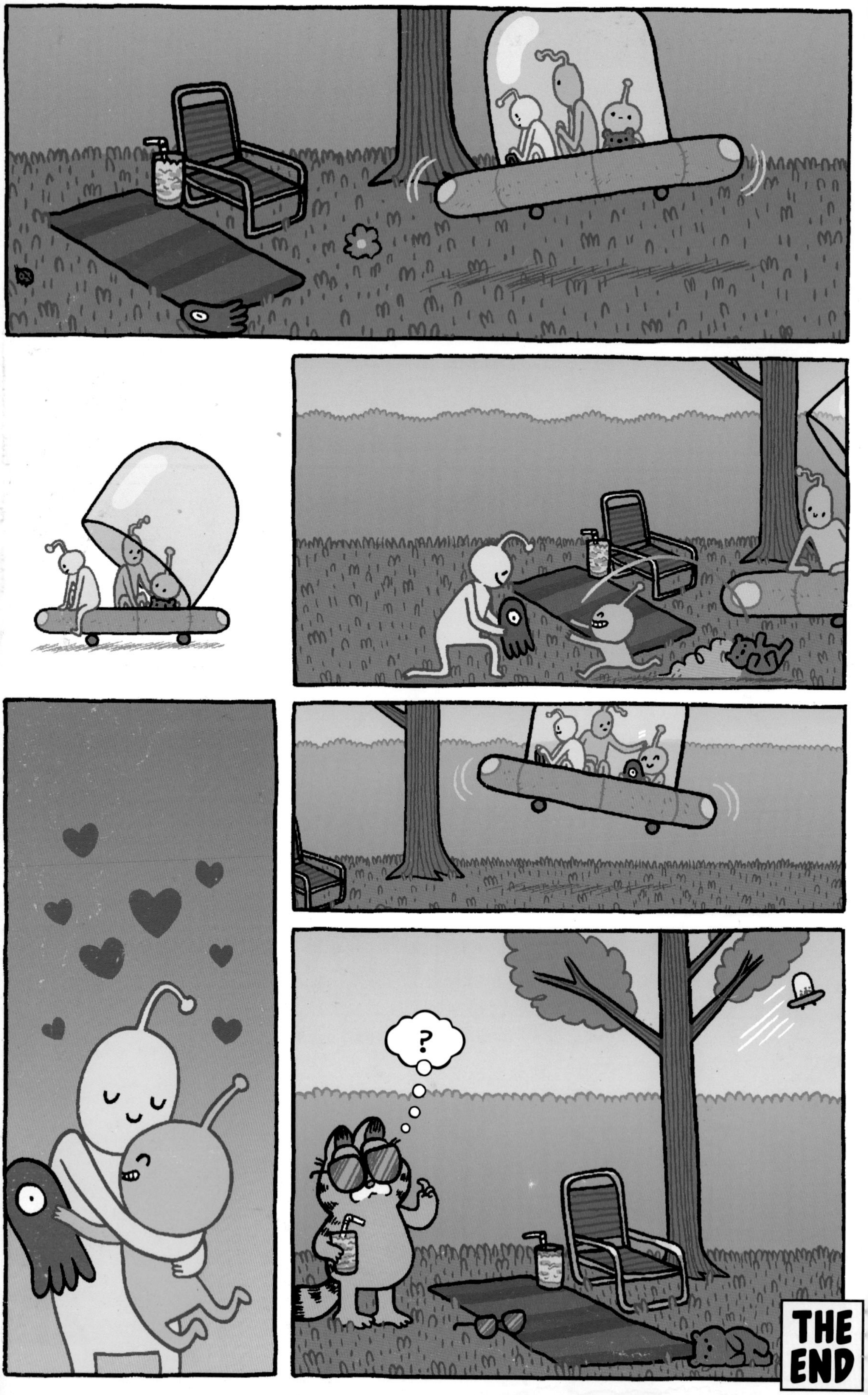
?
THE END

Garfield Sunday Classics

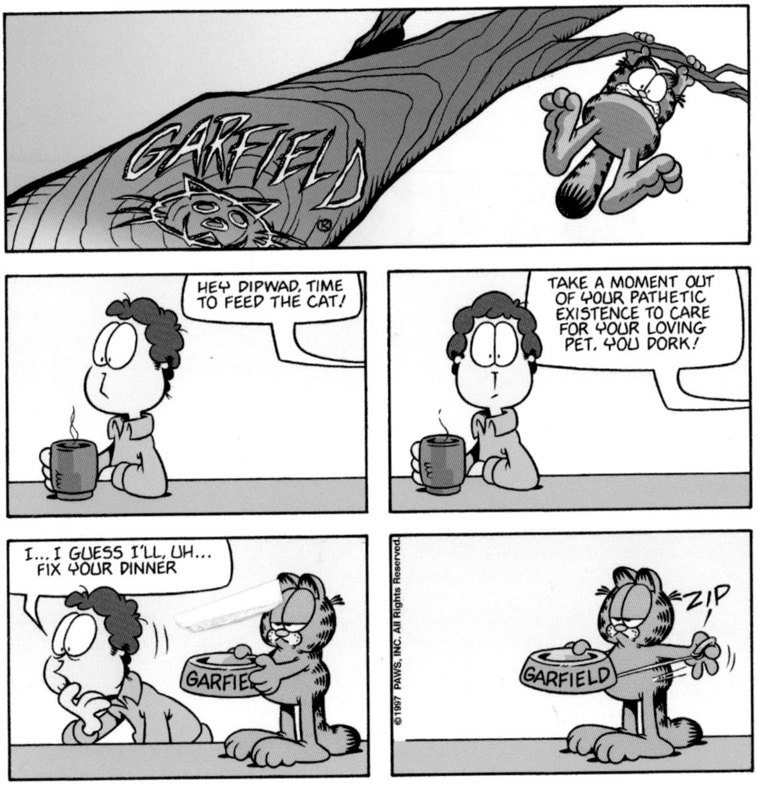

GARFIELD
HEY DIPWAD, TIME TO FEED THE CAT!
TAKE A MOMENT OUT OF YOUR PATHETIC EXISTENCE TO CARE FOR YOUR LOVING PET, YOU DORK!
GARFIE
I... I GUESS I'LL, UH... FIX YOUR DINNER
GARFIE
©1997 PAWS, INC. All Rights Reserved.
ZIP
GARFIELD
AND MAKE IT SNAPPY, GEEK BOY!
I LOVE THIS THING
GARFIELD
JIM DAVIS 5-4

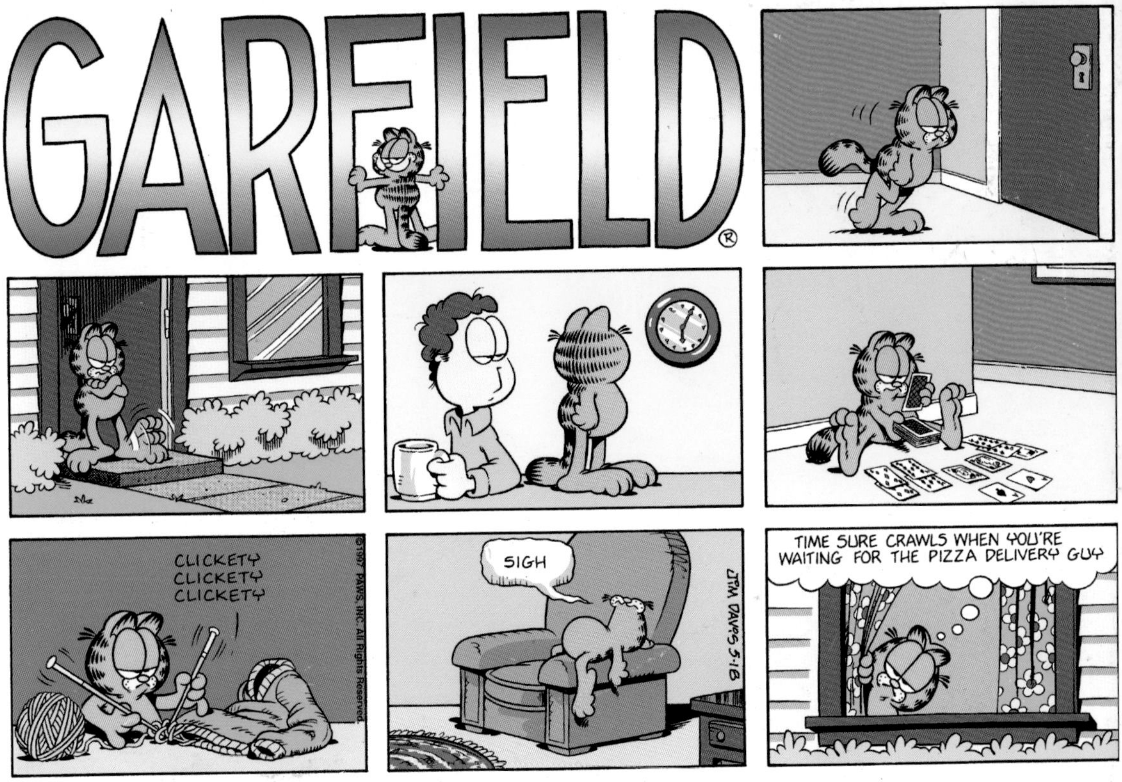

GARFIELD
CLICKETY CLICKETY CLICKETY
©1997 PAWS, INC. All Rights Reserved.
SIGH
JIM DAVIS 5-18
TIME SURE CRAWLS WHEN YOU'RE WAITING FOR THE PIZZA DELIVERY GUY

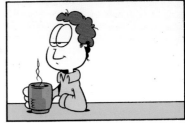

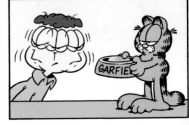

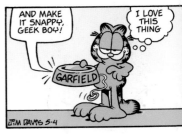

CHAPTER 2

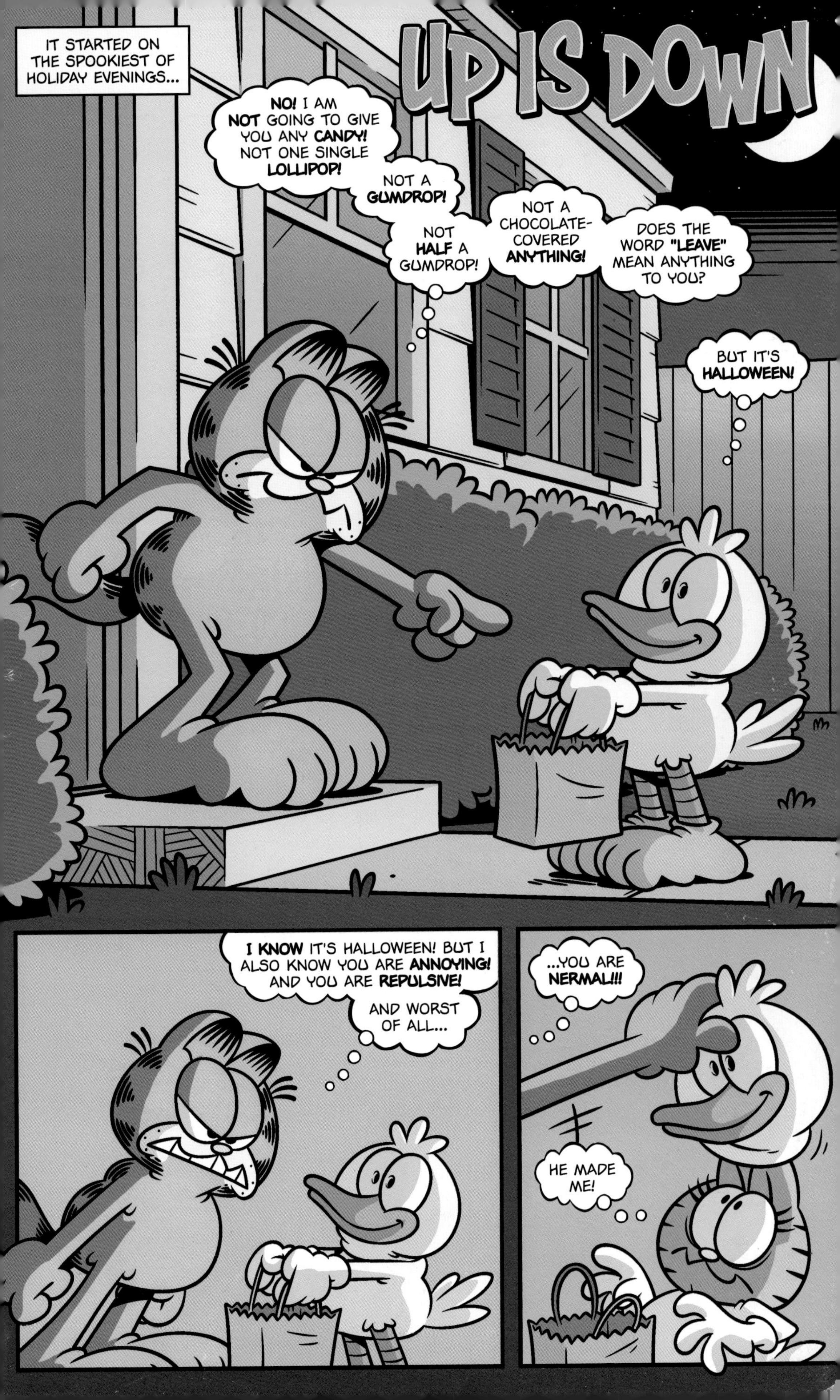
IT STARTED ON THE SPOOKIEST OF HOLIDAY EVENINGS...
UP IS DOWN
NO! I AM NOT GOING TO GIVE YOU ANY CANDY! NOT ONE SINGLE LOLLIPOP!
NOT A GUMDROP!
NOT HALF A GUMDROP!
NOT A CHOCOLATE-COVERED ANYTHING!
DOES THE WORD "LEAVE" MEAN ANYTHING TO YOU?
BUT IT'S HALLOWEEN!
I KNOW IT'S HALLOWEEN! BUT I ALSO KNOW YOU ARE ANNOYING! AND YOU ARE REPULSIVE!
AND WORST OF ALL...
...YOU ARE NERMAL!!!
HE MADE ME!

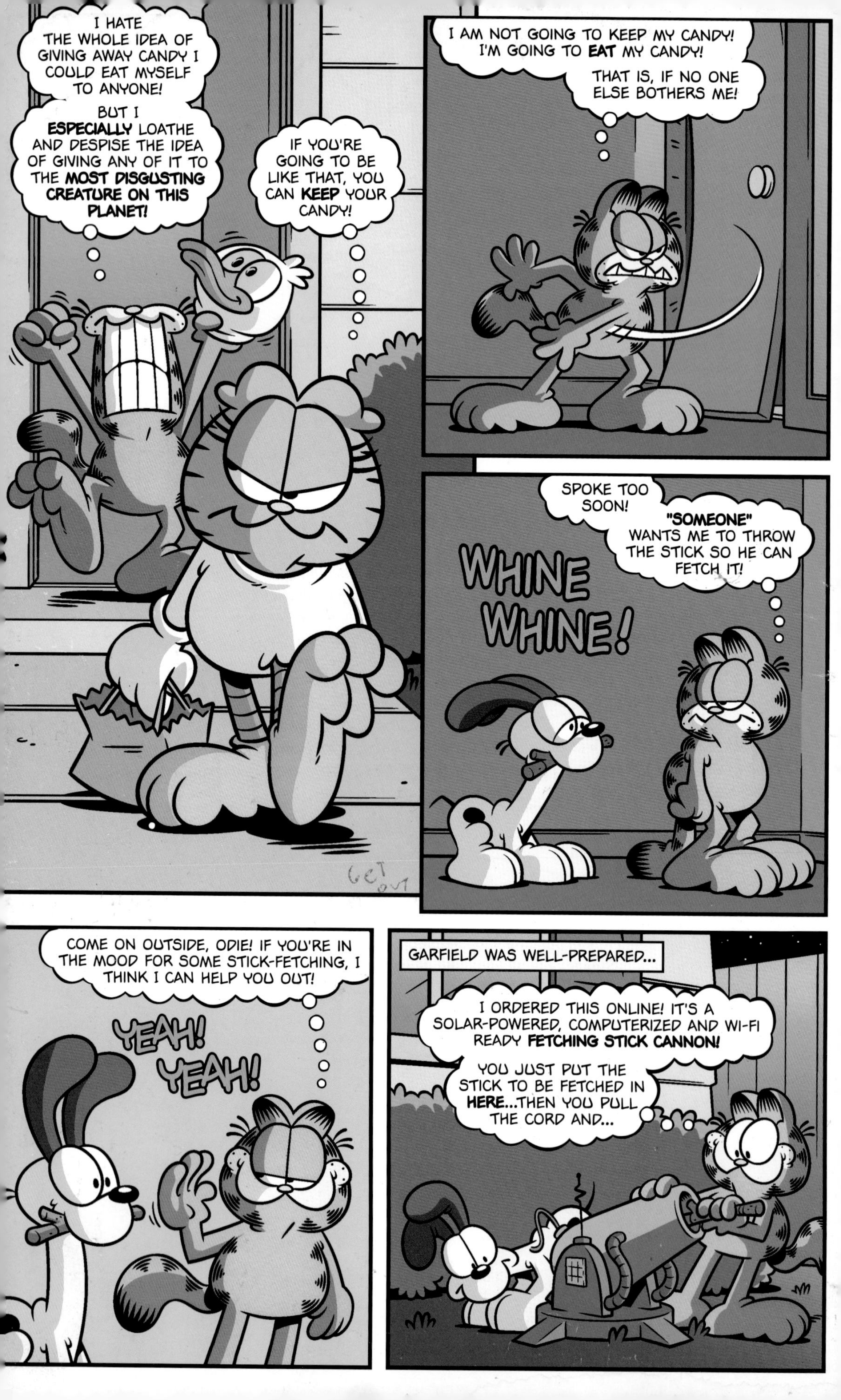

I HATE THE WHOLE IDEA OF GIVING AWAY CANDY I COULD EAT MYSELF TO ANYONE!
BUT I ESPECIALLY LOATHE AND DESPISE THE IDEA OF GIVING ANY OF IT TO THE MOST DISGUSTING CREATURE ON THIS PLANET!
IF YOU'RE GOING TO BE LIKE THAT, YOU CAN KEEP YOUR CANDY!
I AM NOT GOING TO KEEP MY CANDY! I'M GOING TO EAT MY CANDY!
THAT IS, IF NO ONE ELSE BOTHERS ME!
SPOKE TOO SOON!
"SOMEONE" WANTS ME TO THROW THE STICK SO HE CAN FETCH IT!
WHINE WHINE!
COME ON OUTSIDE, ODIE! IF YOU'RE IN THE MOOD FOR SOME STICK-FETCHING, I THINK I CAN HELP YOU OUT!
YEAH! YEAH!
GARFIELD WAS WELL-PREPARED...
I ORDERED THIS ONLINE! IT'S A SOLAR-POWERED, COMPUTERIZED AND WI-FI READY FETCHING STICK CANNON!
YOU JUST PUT THE STICK TO BE FETCHED IN HERE...THEN YOU PULL THE CORD AND...

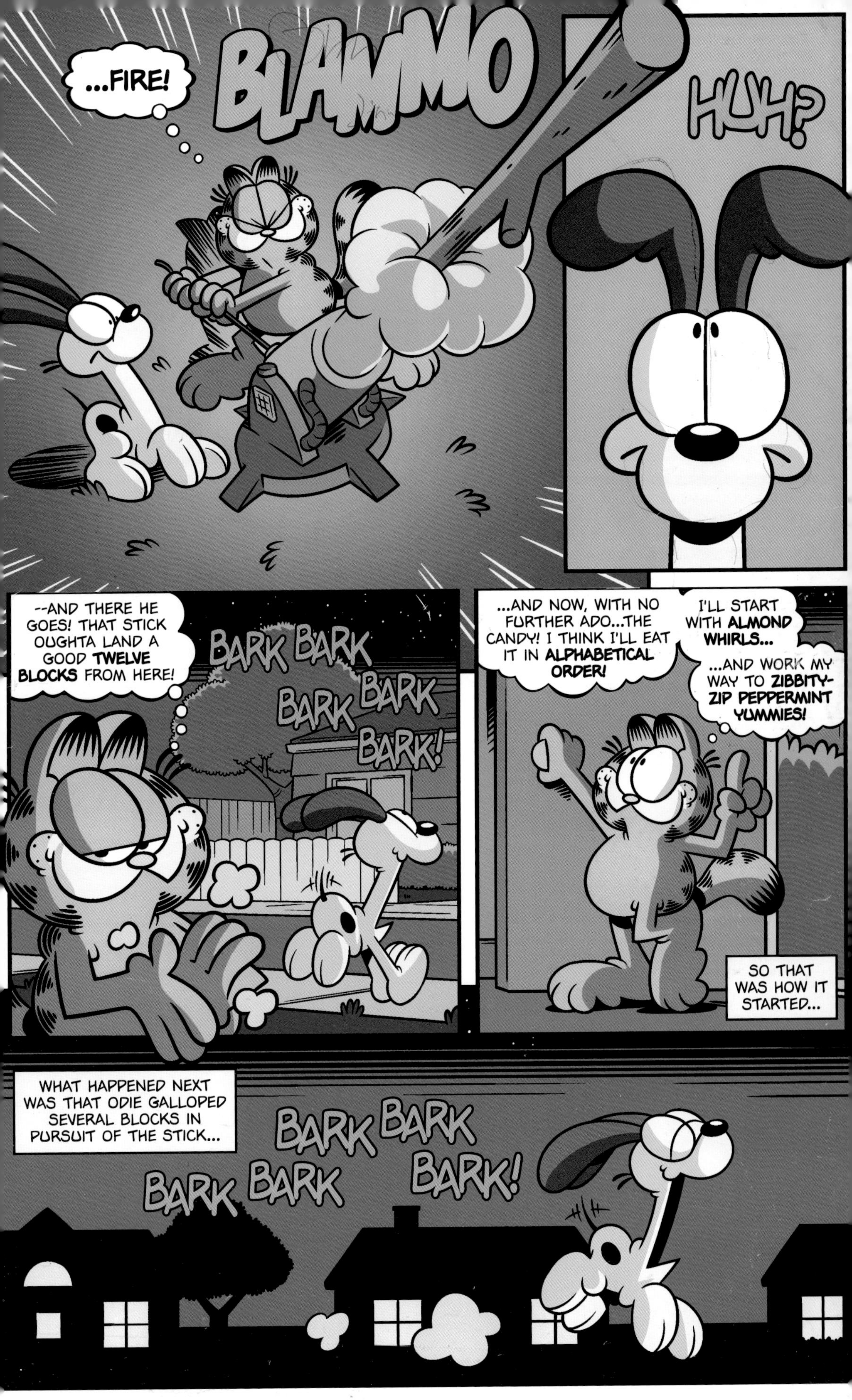

...FIRE!
BLAMMO
HUH?
--AND THERE HE GOES! THAT STICK OUGHTA LAND A GOOD TWELVE BLOCKS FROM HERE!
BARK BARK
BARK BARK
BARK!
...AND NOW, WITH NO FURTHER ADO...THE CANDY! I THINK I'LL EAT IT IN ALPHABETICAL ORDER!
I'LL START WITH ALMOND WHIRLS...
...AND WORK MY WAY TO ZIBBITY-ZIP PEPPERMINT YUMMIES!
SO THAT WAS HOW IT STARTED...
WHAT HAPPENED NEXT WAS THAT ODIE GALLOPED SEVERAL BLOCKS IN PURSUIT OF THE STICK...
BARK BARK
BARK BARK
BARK!

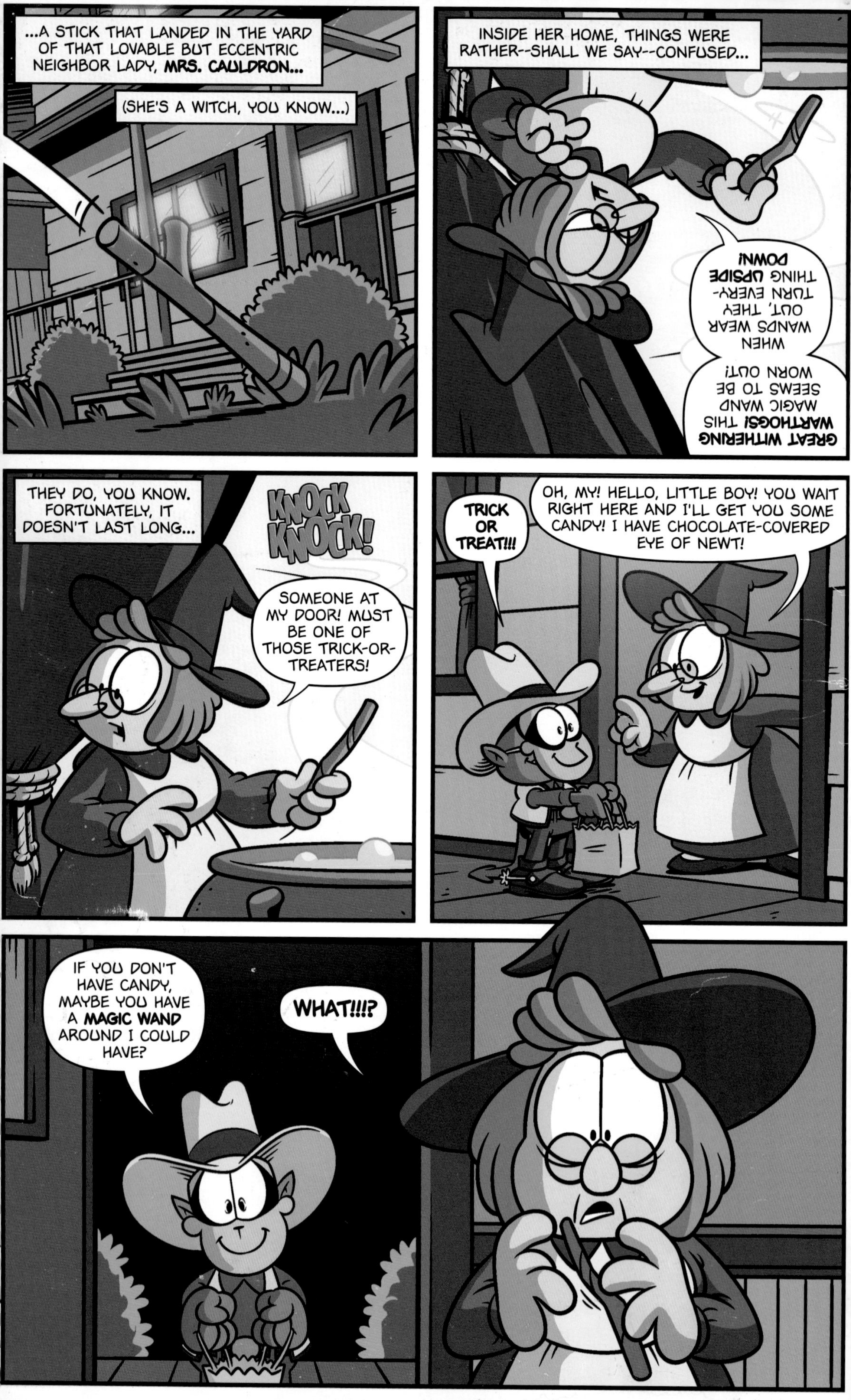
...A STICK THAT LANDED IN THE YARD OF THAT LOVABLE BUT ECCENTRIC NEIGHBOR LADY, **MRS. CAULDRON...**
(SHE'S A WITCH, YOU KNOW...)
INSIDE HER HOME, THINGS WERE RATHER--SHALL WE SAY--CONFUSED...
GREAT WITHERING WARTHOGS! THIS MAGIC WAND SEEMS TO BE WORN OUT!
WHEN WANDS WEAR OUT, THEY TURN EVERY-THING **UPSIDE DOWN!**
THEY DO, YOU KNOW. FORTUNATELY, IT DOESN'T LAST LONG...
KNOCK KNOCK!
SOMEONE AT MY DOOR! MUST BE ONE OF THOSE TRICK-OR-TREATERS!
TRICK OR TREAT!!!
OH, MY! HELLO, LITTLE BOY! YOU WAIT RIGHT HERE AND I'LL GET YOU SOME CANDY! I HAVE CHOCOLATE-COVERED EYE OF NEWT!
IF YOU DON'T HAVE CANDY, MAYBE YOU HAVE A **MAGIC WAND** AROUND I COULD HAVE?
WHAT!!!?

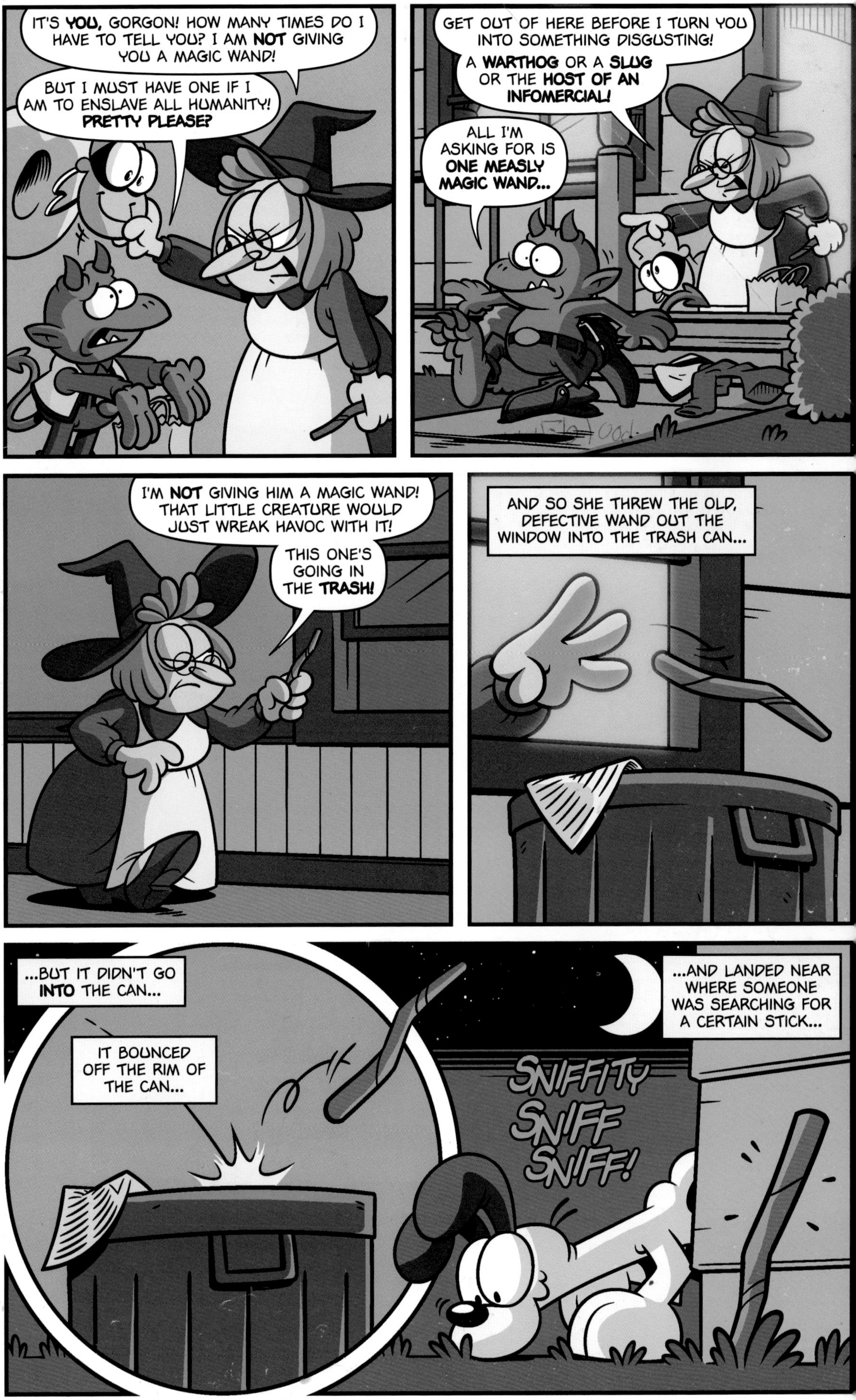

IT'S **YOU,** GORGON! HOW MANY TIMES DO I HAVE TO TELL YOU? I AM **NOT** GIVING YOU A MAGIC WAND!
BUT I MUST HAVE ONE IF I AM TO ENSLAVE ALL HUMANITY! **PRETTY PLEASE?**
GET OUT OF HERE BEFORE I TURN YOU INTO SOMETHING DISGUSTING!
A **WARTHOG** OR A **SLUG** OR THE **HOST OF AN INFOMERCIAL!**
ALL I'M ASKING FOR IS **ONE MEASLY MAGIC WAND...**
I'M **NOT** GIVING HIM A MAGIC WAND! THAT LITTLE CREATURE WOULD JUST WREAK HAVOC WITH IT!
THIS ONE'S GOING IN THE **TRASH!**
AND SO SHE THREW THE OLD, DEFECTIVE WAND OUT THE WINDOW INTO THE TRASH CAN...
...BUT IT DIDN'T GO **INTO** THE CAN...
IT BOUNCED OFF THE RIM OF THE CAN...
...AND LANDED NEAR WHERE SOMEONE WAS SEARCHING FOR A CERTAIN STICK...
SNIFFITY SNIFF SNIFF!

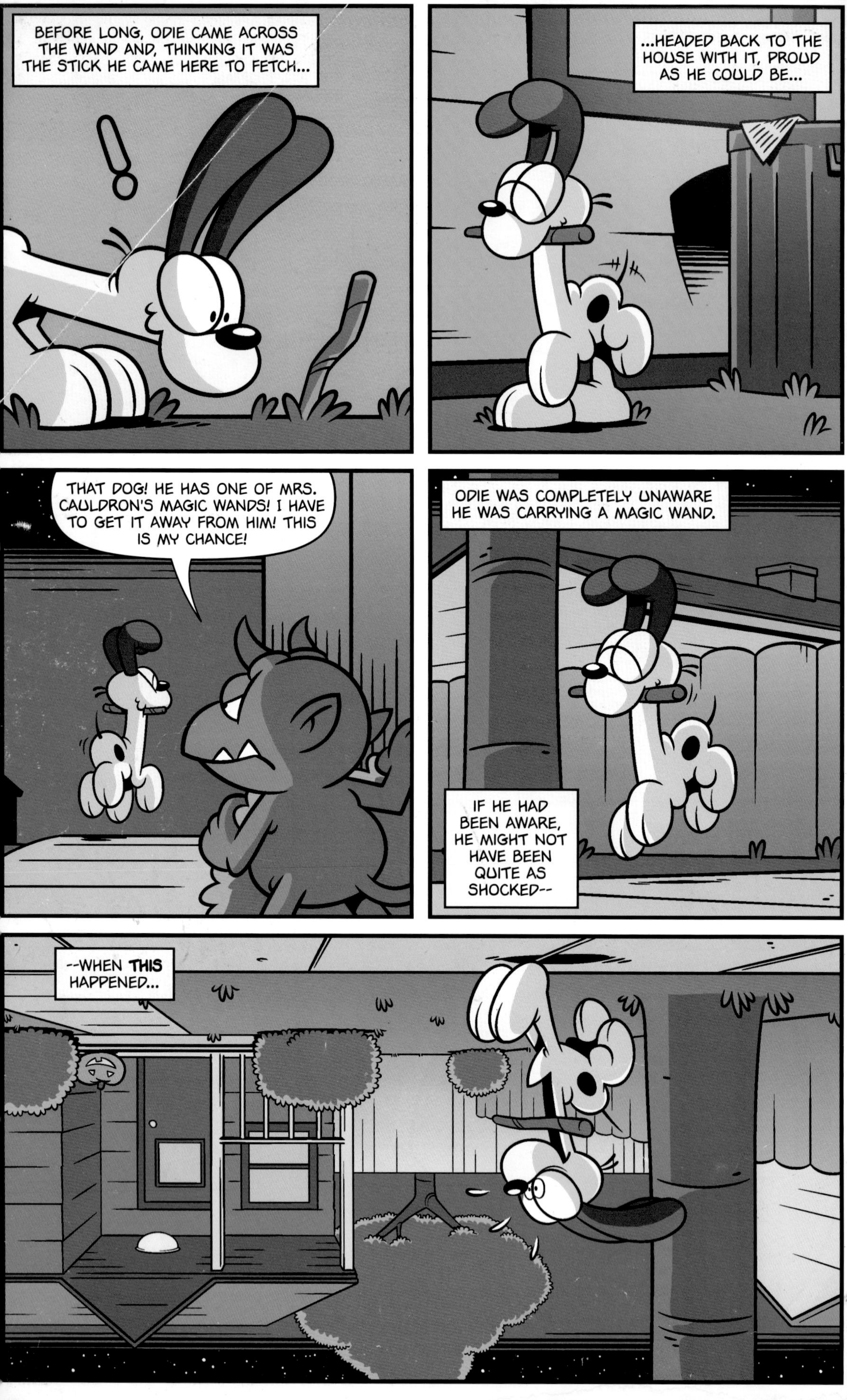
BEFORE LONG, ODIE CAME ACROSS THE WAND AND, THINKING IT WAS THE STICK HE CAME HERE TO FETCH...
...HEADED BACK TO THE HOUSE WITH IT, PROUD AS HE COULD BE...
THAT DOG! HE HAS ONE OF MRS. CAULDRON'S MAGIC WANDS! I HAVE TO GET IT AWAY FROM HIM! THIS IS MY CHANCE!
ODIE WAS COMPLETELY UNAWARE HE WAS CARRYING A MAGIC WAND.
IF HE HAD BEEN AWARE, HE MIGHT NOT HAVE BEEN QUITE AS SHOCKED--
--WHEN **THIS** HAPPENED...

HE WAS PRETTY FRIGHTENED--

--WHO WOULDN'T BE?--

--BUT BEFORE HE COULD FIGURE OUT WHAT WAS HAPPENING...

THERE WAS NOTHING TO FIGURE OUT...

HUH?

SO ODIE MADE A MAD DASH TO GET HOME WHERE HE FIGURED HE MIGHT BE SAFE...

WHEN HE GOT THERE, HE RAN AROUND TO THE BACK...

...AND ENTERED THROUGH THE DOGGY-DOOR...

...WHICH WAS MOMENTARILY NOT WHERE IT SHOULD BE.

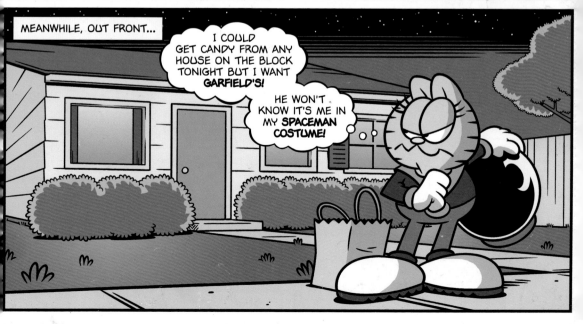

MEANWHILE, OUT FRONT...

I COULD GET CANDY FROM ANY HOUSE ON THE BLOCK TONIGHT BUT I WANT GARFIELD'S!

HE WON'T KNOW IT'S ME IN MY SPACEMAN COSTUME!

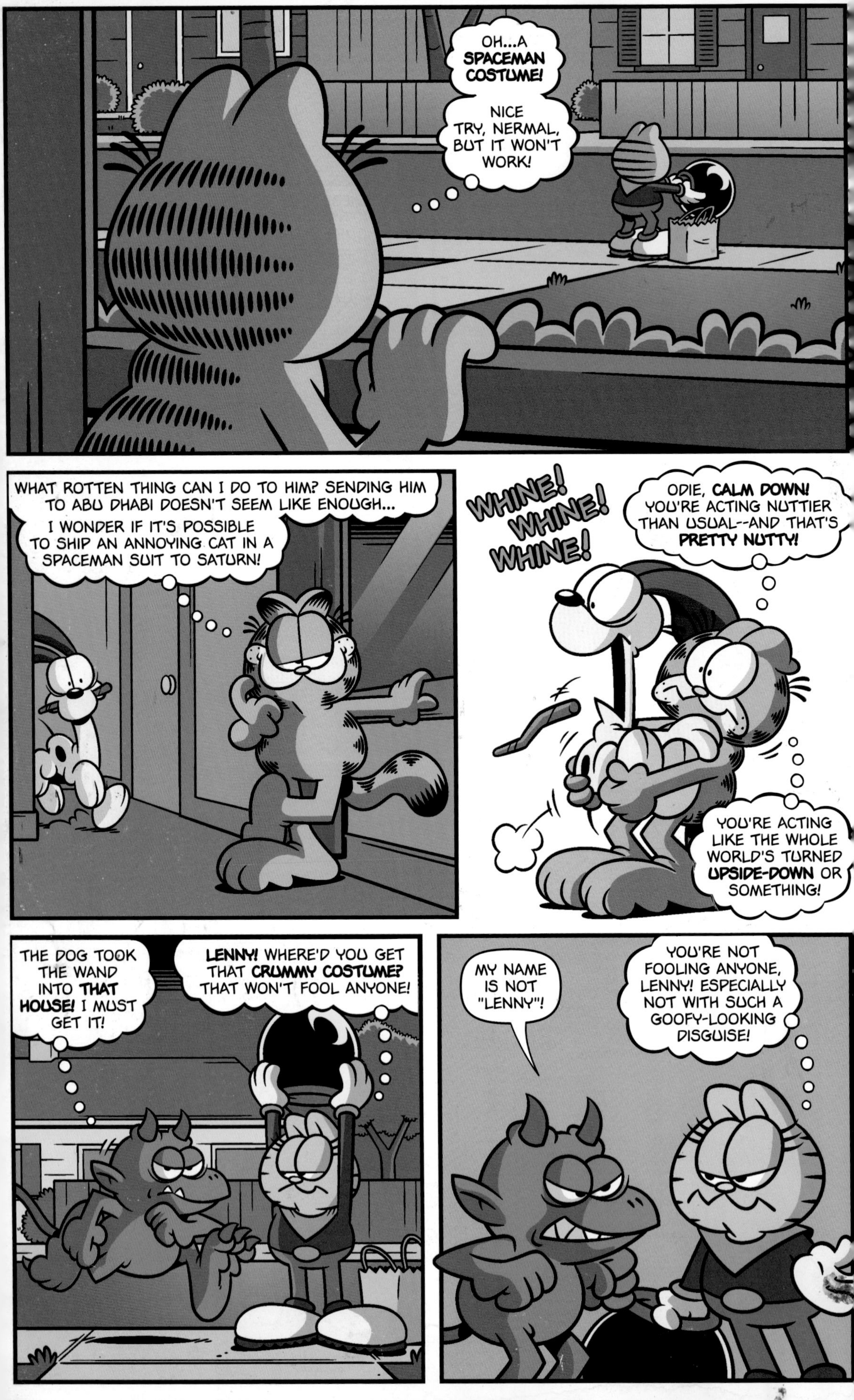
OH...A SPACEMAN COSTUME!
NICE TRY, NERMAL, BUT IT WON'T WORK!
WHAT ROTTEN THING CAN I DO TO HIM? SENDING HIM TO ABU DHABI DOESN'T SEEM LIKE ENOUGH...
I WONDER IF IT'S POSSIBLE TO SHIP AN ANNOYING CAT IN A SPACEMAN SUIT TO SATURN!
WHINE! WHINE! WHINE!
ODIE, CALM DOWN! YOU'RE ACTING NUTTIER THAN USUAL--AND THAT'S PRETTY NUTTY!
YOU'RE ACTING LIKE THE WHOLE WORLD'S TURNED UPSIDE-DOWN OR SOMETHING!
THE DOG TOOK THE WAND INTO THAT HOUSE! I MUST GET IT!
LENNY! WHERE'D YOU GET THAT CRUMMY COSTUME? THAT WON'T FOOL ANYONE!
MY NAME IS NOT "LENNY"!
YOU'RE NOT FOOLING ANYONE, LENNY! ESPECIALLY NOT WITH SUCH A GOOFY-LOOKING DISGUISE!

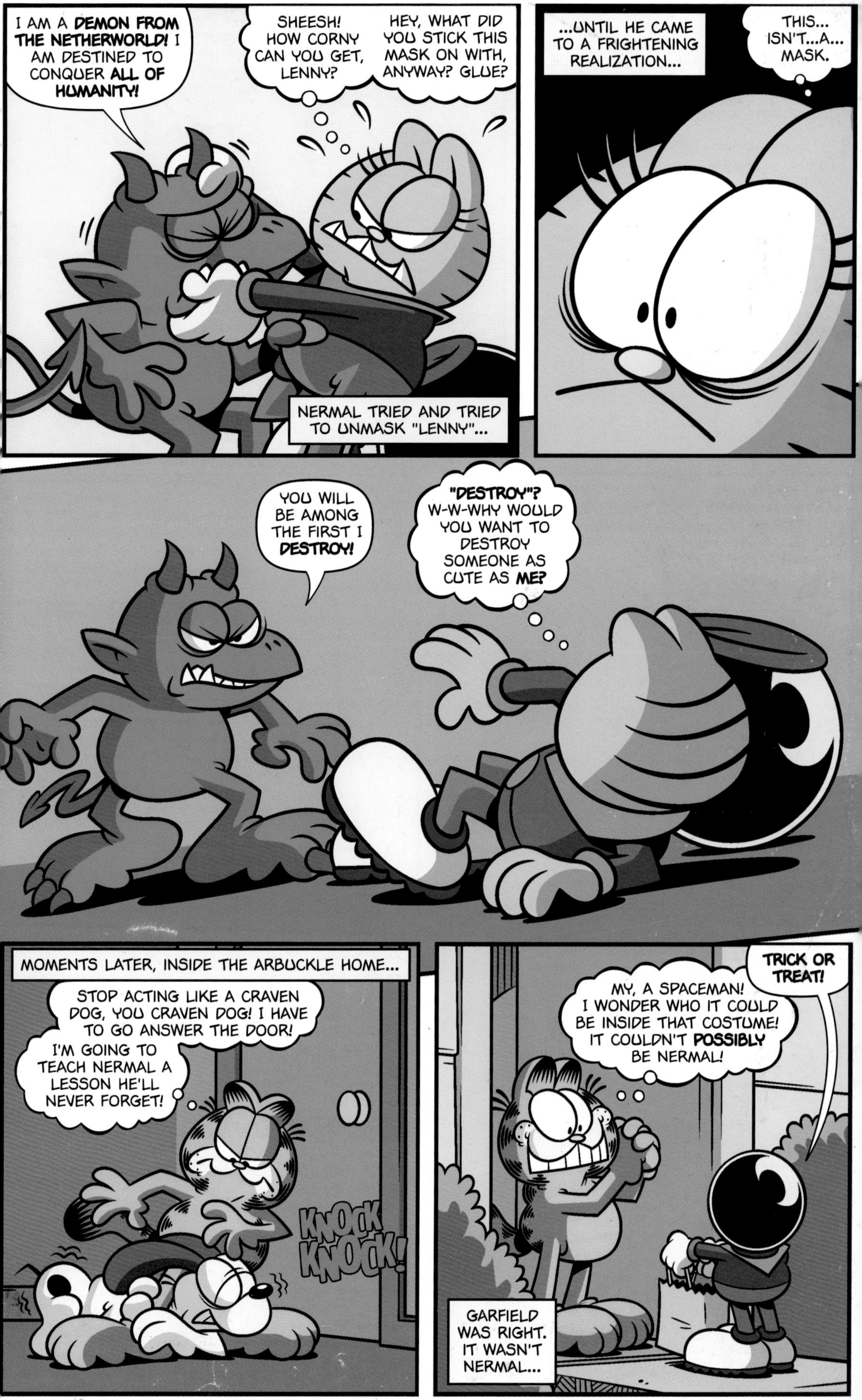
I AM A **DEMON FROM THE NETHERWORLD!** I AM DESTINED TO CONQUER **ALL OF HUMANITY!**
SHEESH! HOW CORNY CAN YOU GET, LENNY?
HEY, WHAT DID YOU STICK THIS MASK ON WITH, ANYWAY? GLUE?
NERMAL TRIED AND TRIED TO UNMASK "LENNY"...
...UNTIL HE CAME TO A FRIGHTENING REALIZATION...
THIS... ISN'T...A... MASK.
YOU WILL BE AMONG THE FIRST I **DESTROY!**
"DESTROY"? W-W-WHY WOULD YOU WANT TO DESTROY SOMEONE AS CUTE AS **ME?**
MOMENTS LATER, INSIDE THE ARBUCKLE HOME...
STOP ACTING LIKE A CRAVEN DOG, YOU CRAVEN DOG! I HAVE TO GO ANSWER THE DOOR!
I'M GOING TO TEACH NERMAL A LESSON HE'LL NEVER FORGET!
KNOCK KNOCK!
TRICK OR TREAT!
MY, A SPACEMAN! I WONDER WHO IT COULD BE INSIDE THAT COSTUME! IT COULDN'T **POSSIBLY** BE NERMAL!
GARFIELD WAS RIGHT. IT WASN'T NERMAL...

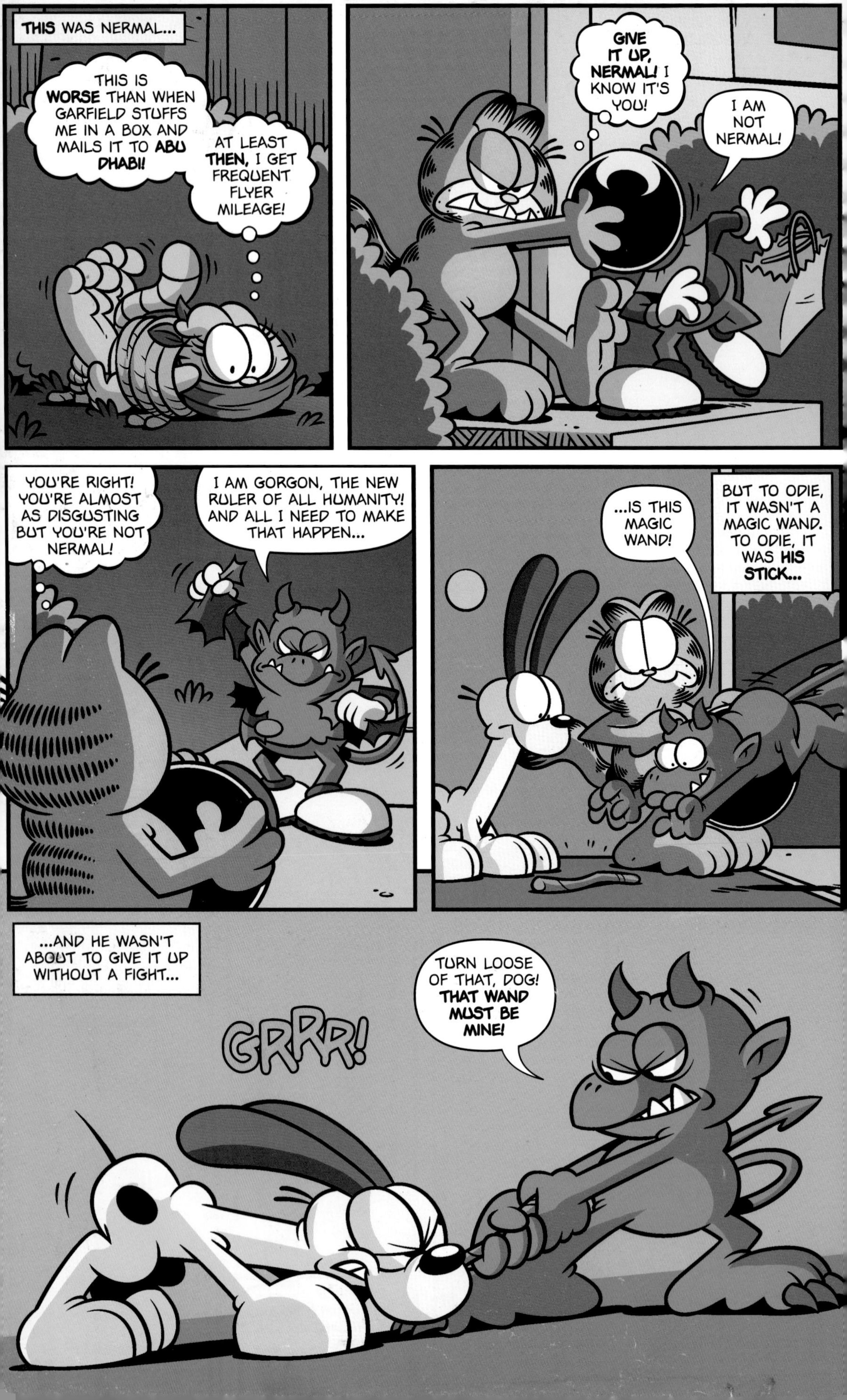
THIS WAS NERMAL...
THIS IS WORSE THAN WHEN GARFIELD STUFFS ME IN A BOX AND MAILS IT TO ABU DHABI!
AT LEAST THEN, I GET FREQUENT FLYER MILEAGE!
GIVE IT UP, NERMAL! I KNOW IT'S YOU!
I AM NOT NERMAL!
YOU'RE RIGHT! YOU'RE ALMOST AS DISGUSTING BUT YOU'RE NOT NERMAL!
I AM GORGON, THE NEW RULER OF ALL HUMANITY! AND ALL I NEED TO MAKE THAT HAPPEN...
...IS THIS MAGIC WAND!
BUT TO ODIE, IT WASN'T A MAGIC WAND. TO ODIE, IT WAS HIS STICK...
...AND HE WASN'T ABOUT TO GIVE IT UP WITHOUT A FIGHT...
GRRR!
TURN LOOSE OF THAT, DOG! THAT WAND MUST BE MINE!

I HAD A HUNCH SOMETHING LIKE THIS WAS GOING ON!
MRS. CAULDRON! YOU WON'T STOP ME BECAUSE NOW, **I HAVE THE WAND!**
THAT'S THE OLD, MODEL 3.0 MAGIC WAND! IT'S NO MATCH FOR THE NEW 4.0 MODEL!
NO! **NO!**
WOW! WHERE'D YOU SEND HIM?
SOMEWHERE WHERE HE WON'T BE BACK UNTIL **NEXT HALLOWEEN!**
THAT SEEMED TO BE THE END OF THE STORY...
BUT IT WASN'T...
YOU'LL HAVE TO FORGIVE THE MESS, LIZ! I'VE BEEN TOO BUSY TO TIDY UP AND THE WHOLE HOUSE HAS BEEN TURNED UPSIDE-DOWN!
IT CAN'T BE **THAT BAD!**
...BECAUSE THERE WAS STILL THE MATTER OF THAT OLD, BROKEN-DOWN MAGIC WAND...
ODIE! PUT THAT WAND DOWN! YOU DON'T KNOW WHAT YOU'RE DEALING WITH HERE!

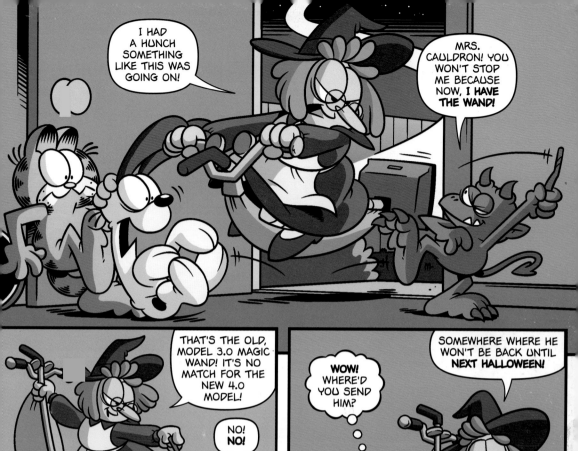

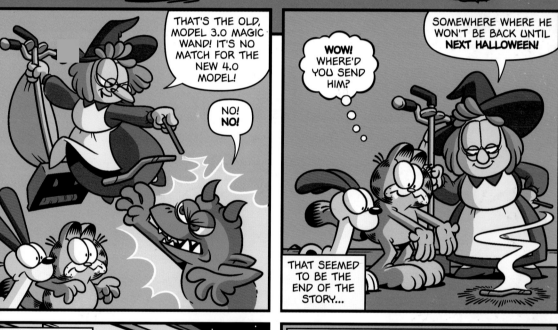

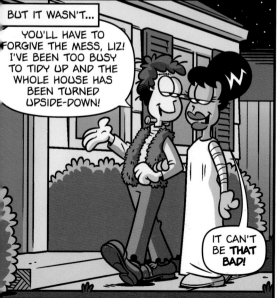

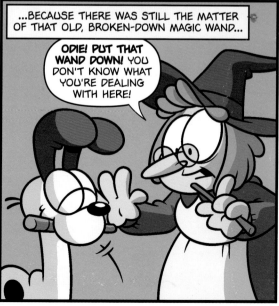

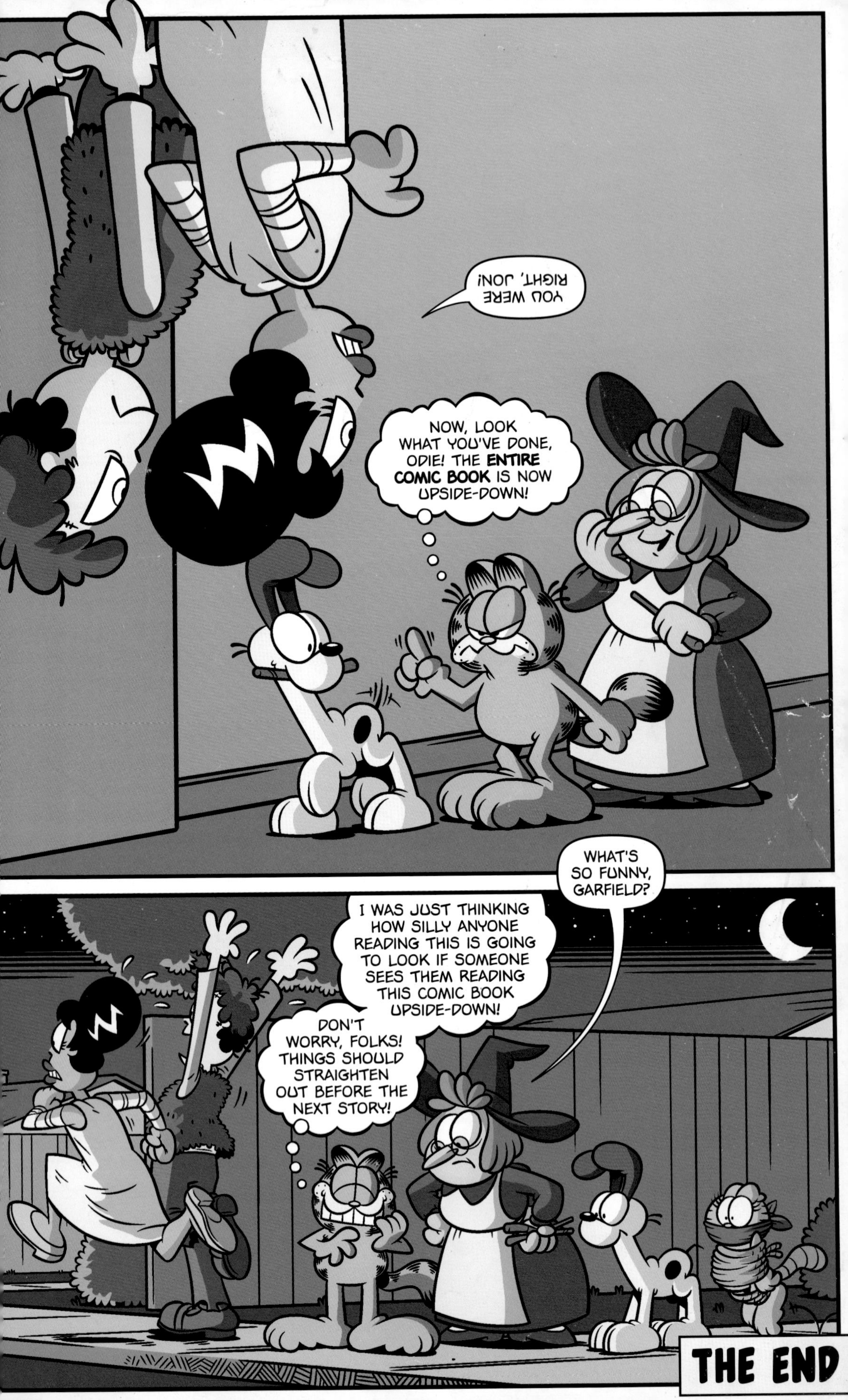
YOU WERE RIGHT, JON!
NOW, LOOK WHAT YOU'VE DONE, ODIE! THE **ENTIRE COMIC BOOK** IS NOW UPSIDE-DOWN!
WHAT'S SO FUNNY, GARFIELD?
I WAS JUST THINKING HOW SILLY ANYONE READING THIS IS GOING TO LOOK IF SOMEONE SEES THEM READING THIS COMIC BOOK UPSIDE-DOWN!
DON'T WORRY, FOLKS! THINGS SHOULD STRAIGHTEN OUT BEFORE THE NEXT STORY!
THE END

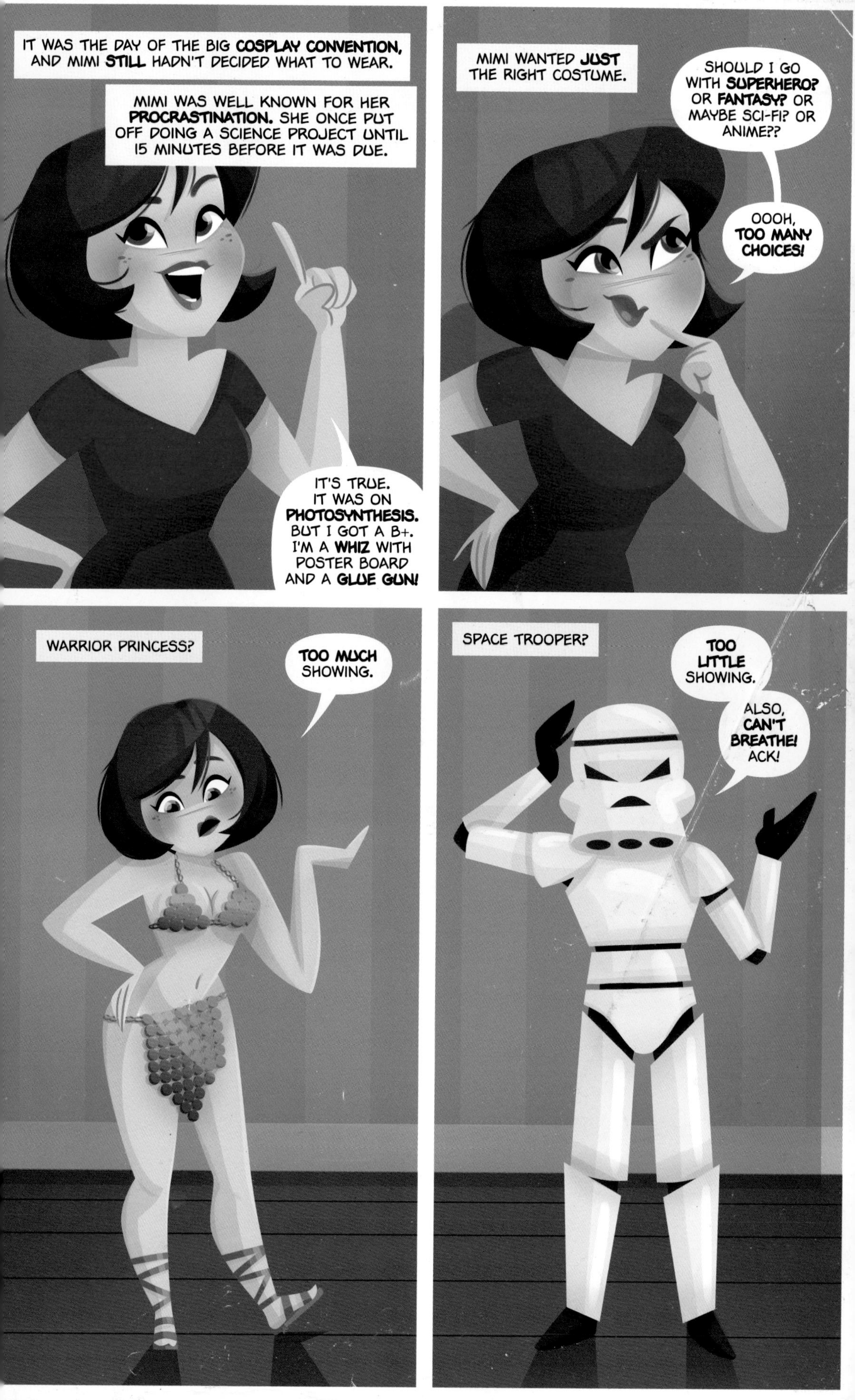
IT WAS THE DAY OF THE BIG **COSPLAY CONVENTION,** AND MIMI **STILL** HADN'T DECIDED WHAT TO WEAR.
MIMI WAS WELL KNOWN FOR HER **PROCRASTINATION.** SHE ONCE PUT OFF DOING A SCIENCE PROJECT UNTIL 15 MINUTES BEFORE IT WAS DUE.
IT'S TRUE. IT WAS ON **PHOTOSYNTHESIS.** BUT I GOT A B+. I'M A **WHIZ** WITH POSTER BOARD AND A **GLUE GUN!**
MIMI WANTED **JUST** THE RIGHT COSTUME.
SHOULD I GO WITH **SUPERHERO?** OR **FANTASY?** OR MAYBE SCI-FI? OR ANIME??
OOOH, **TOO MANY CHOICES!**
WARRIOR PRINCESS?
TOO MUCH SHOWING.
SPACE TROOPER?
TOO LITTLE SHOWING.
ALSO, **CAN'T BREATHE!** ACK!

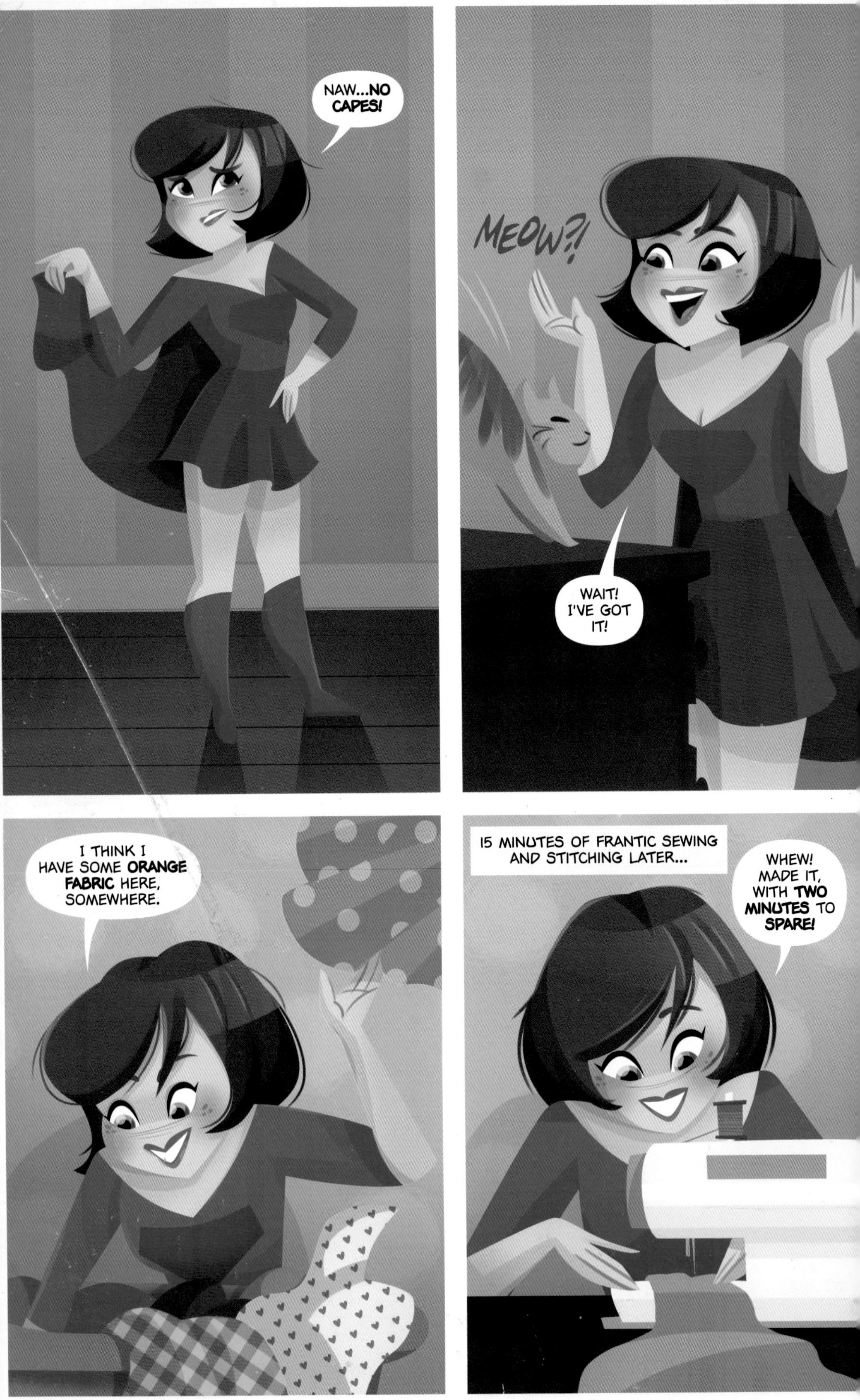
NAW...NO CAPES!
MEOW?!
WAIT! I'VE GOT IT!
I THINK I HAVE SOME ORANGE FABRIC HERE, SOMEWHERE.
15 MINUTES OF FRANTIC SEWING AND STITCHING LATER...
WHEW! MADE IT, WITH TWO MINUTES TO SPARE!

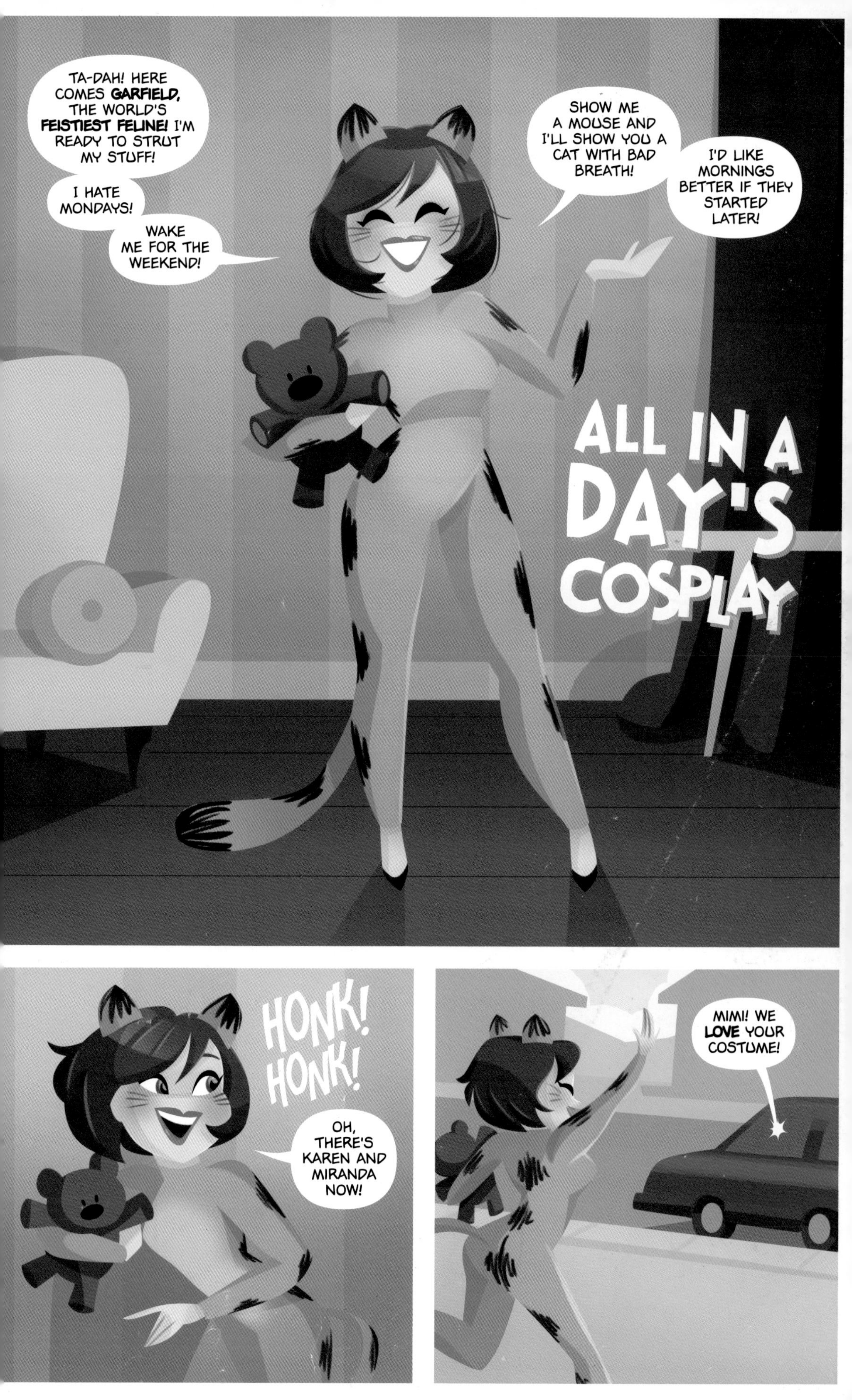
TA-DAH! HERE COMES GARFIELD, THE WORLD'S FEISTIEST FELINE! I'M READY TO STRUT MY STUFF!
I HATE MONDAYS!
WAKE ME FOR THE WEEKEND!
SHOW ME A MOUSE AND I'LL SHOW YOU A CAT WITH BAD BREATH!
I'D LIKE MORNINGS BETTER IF THEY STARTED LATER!
ALL IN A DAY'S COSPLAY
HONK! HONK!
OH, THERE'S KAREN AND MIRANDA NOW!
MIMI! WE LOVE YOUR COSTUME!

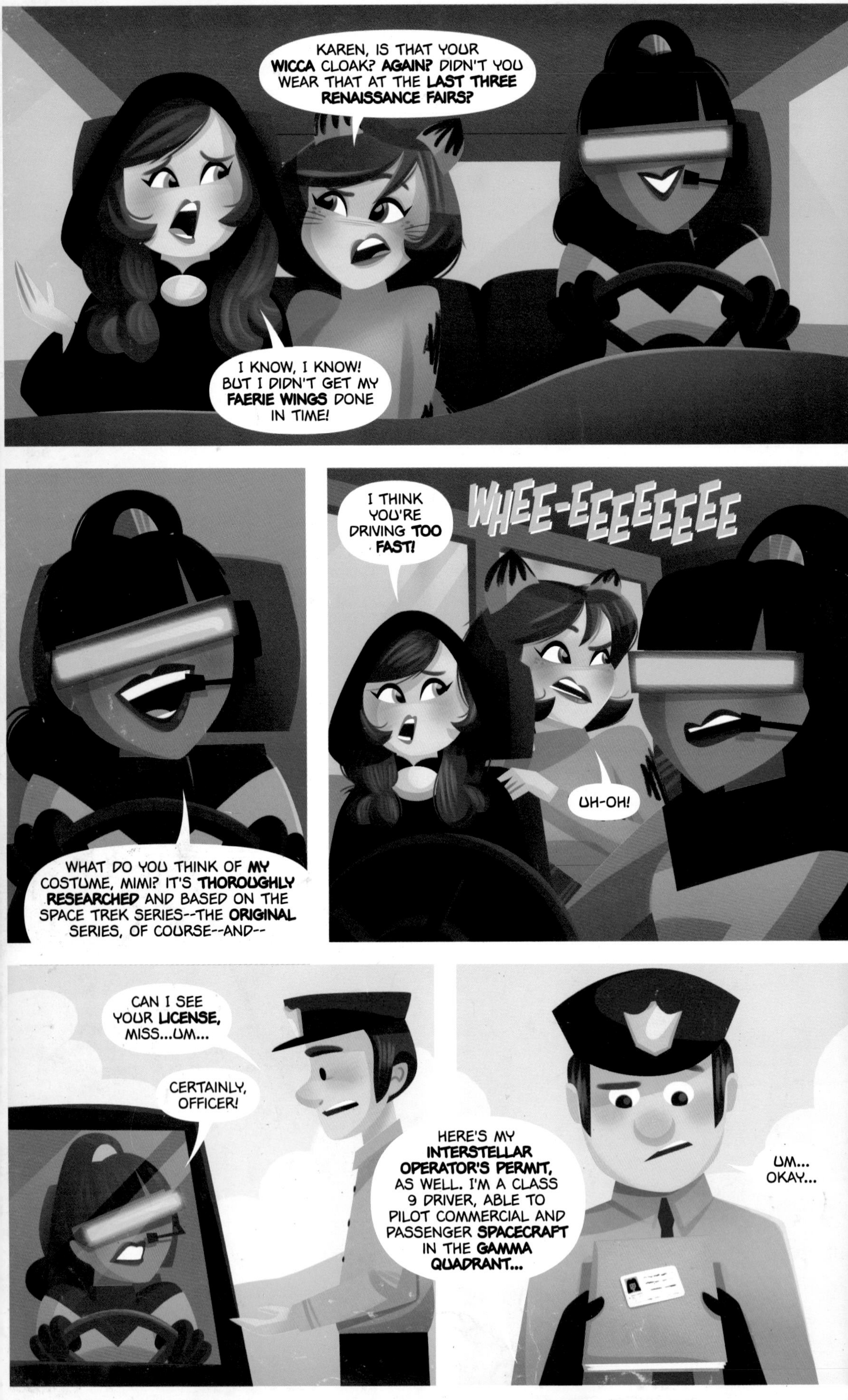
KAREN, IS THAT YOUR WICCA CLOAK? AGAIN? DIDN'T YOU WEAR THAT AT THE LAST THREE RENAISSANCE FAIRS?
I KNOW, I KNOW! BUT I DIDN'T GET MY FAERIE WINGS DONE IN TIME!
WHAT DO YOU THINK OF MY COSTUME, MIMI? IT'S THOROUGHLY RESEARCHED AND BASED ON THE SPACE TREK SERIES--THE ORIGINAL SERIES, OF COURSE--AND--
I THINK YOU'RE DRIVING TOO FAST!
WHEE-EEEEEEEE
UH-OH!
CAN I SEE YOUR LICENSE, MISS...UM...
CERTAINLY, OFFICER!
HERE'S MY INTERSTELLAR OPERATOR'S PERMIT, AS WELL. I'M A CLASS 9 DRIVER, ABLE TO PILOT COMMERCIAL AND PASSENGER SPACECRAFT IN THE GAMMA QUADRANT...
UM... OKAY...

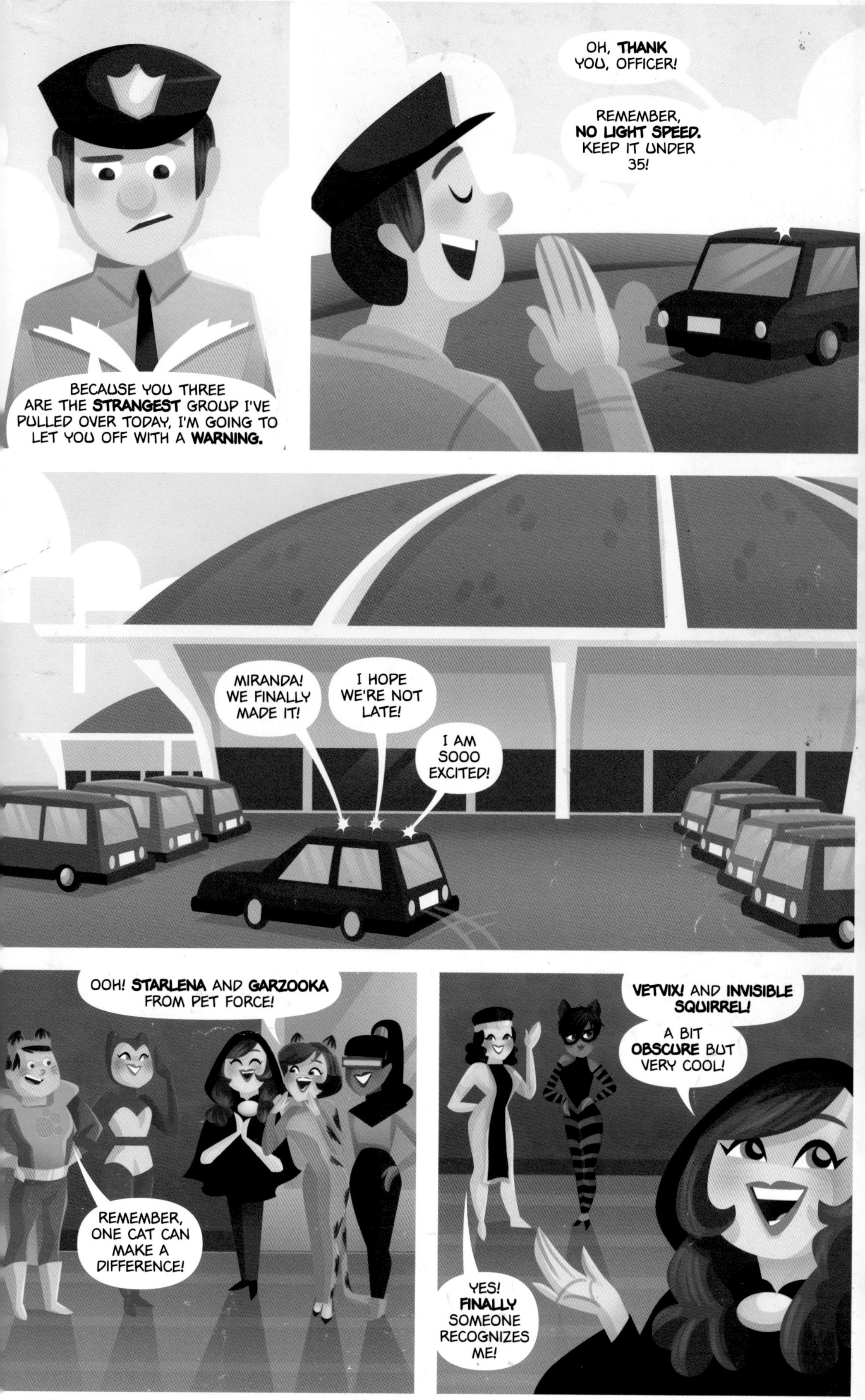
BECAUSE YOU THREE ARE THE **STRANGEST** GROUP I'VE PULLED OVER TODAY, I'M GOING TO LET YOU OFF WITH A **WARNING.**
OH, **THANK** YOU, OFFICER!
REMEMBER, **NO LIGHT SPEED.** KEEP IT UNDER 35!
MIRANDA! WE FINALLY MADE IT!
I HOPE WE'RE NOT LATE!
I AM SOOO EXCITED!
OOH! **STARLENA** AND **GARZOOKA** FROM PET FORCE!
REMEMBER, ONE CAT CAN MAKE A DIFFERENCE!
VETVIX! AND **INVISIBLE SQUIRREL!**
A BIT **OBSCURE** BUT VERY COOL!
YES! **FINALLY** SOMEONE RECOGNIZES ME!

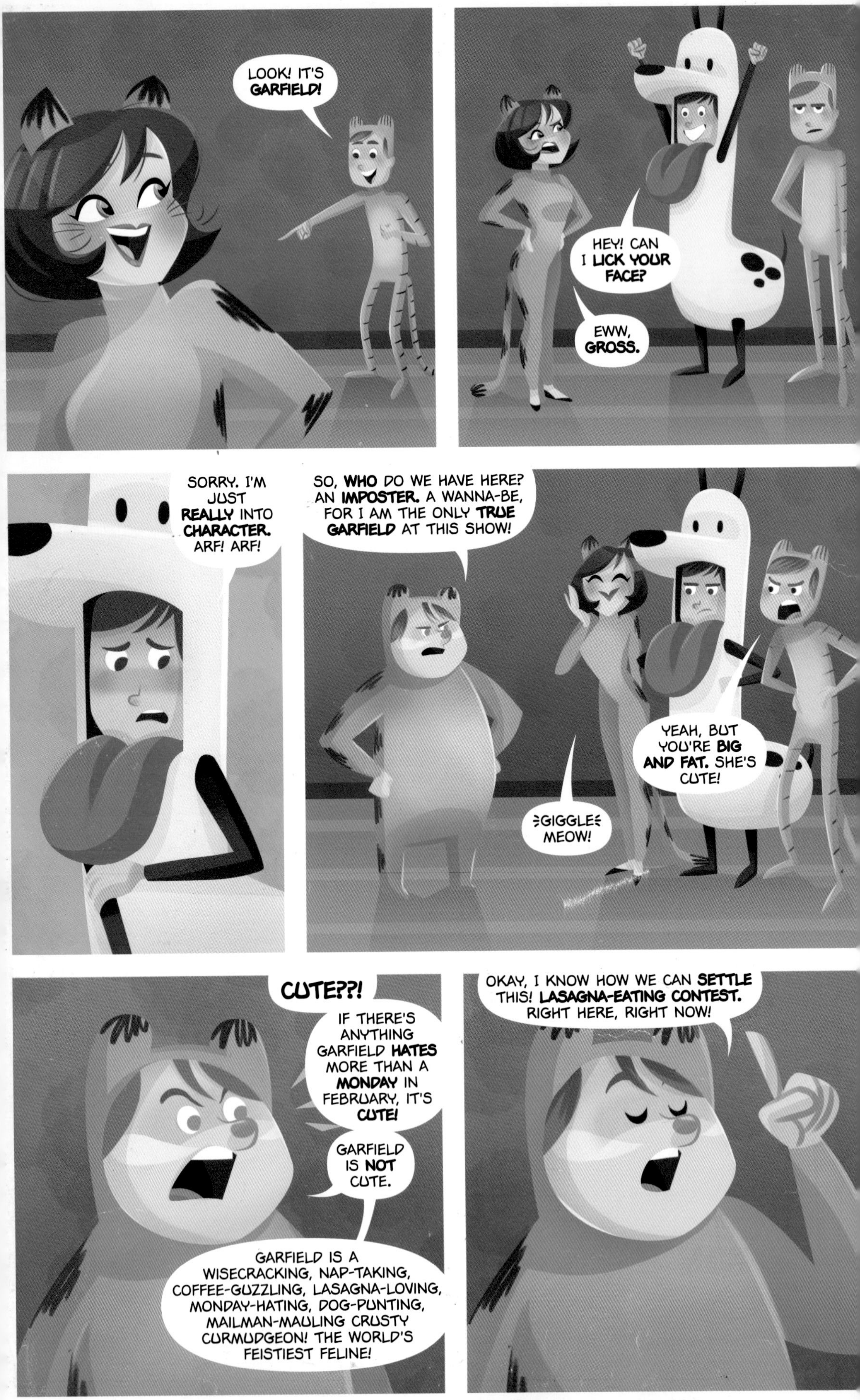
LOOK! IT'S GARFIELD!
HEY! CAN I LICK YOUR FACE?
EWW, GROSS.
SORRY. I'M JUST REALLY INTO CHARACTER. ARF! ARF!
SO, WHO DO WE HAVE HERE? AN IMPOSTER. A WANNA-BE, FOR I AM THE ONLY TRUE GARFIELD AT THIS SHOW!
GIGGLE MEOW!
YEAH, BUT YOU'RE BIG AND FAT. SHE'S CUTE!
CUTE??!
IF THERE'S ANYTHING GARFIELD HATES MORE THAN A MONDAY IN FEBRUARY, IT'S CUTE!
GARFIELD IS NOT CUTE.
GARFIELD IS A WISECRACKING, NAP-TAKING, COFFEE-GUZZLING, LASAGNA-LOVING, MONDAY-HATING, DOG-PUNTING, MAILMAN-MAULING CRUSTY CURMUDGEON! THE WORLD'S FEISTIEST FELINE!
OKAY, I KNOW HOW WE CAN SETTLE THIS! LASAGNA-EATING CONTEST. RIGHT HERE, RIGHT NOW!

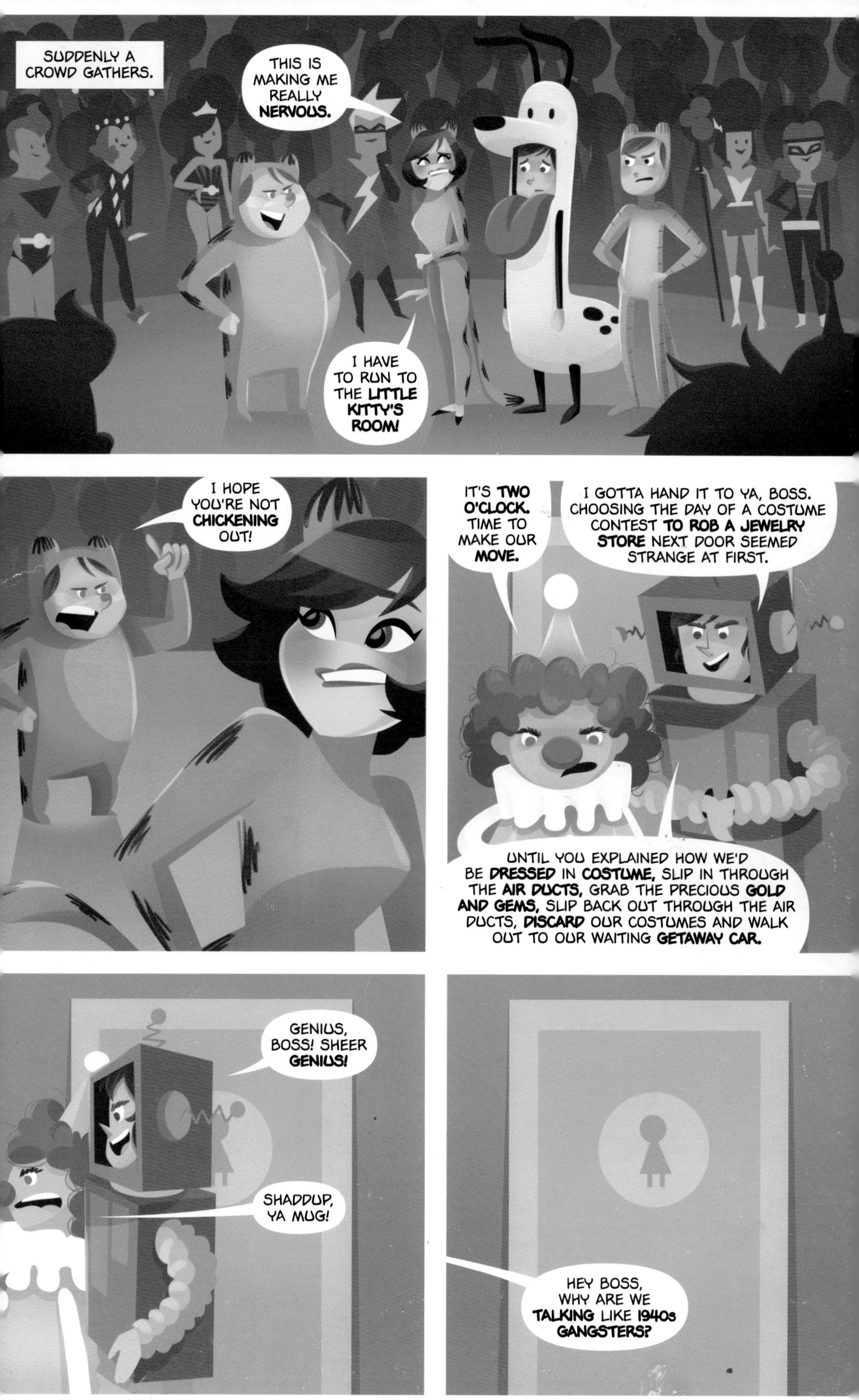
SUDDENLY A CROWD GATHERS.
THIS IS MAKING ME REALLY NERVOUS.
I HAVE TO RUN TO THE LITTLE KITTY'S ROOM!
I HOPE YOU'RE NOT CHICKENING OUT!
IT'S TWO O'CLOCK. TIME TO MAKE OUR MOVE.
I GOTTA HAND IT TO YA, BOSS. CHOOSING THE DAY OF A COSTUME CONTEST TO ROB A JEWELRY STORE NEXT DOOR SEEMED STRANGE AT FIRST.
UNTIL YOU EXPLAINED HOW WE'D BE DRESSED IN COSTUME, SLIP IN THROUGH THE AIR DUCTS, GRAB THE PRECIOUS GOLD AND GEMS, SLIP BACK OUT THROUGH THE AIR DUCTS, DISCARD OUR COSTUMES AND WALK OUT TO OUR WAITING GETAWAY CAR.
GENIUS, BOSS! SHEER GENIUS!
SHADDUP, YA MUG!
HEY BOSS, WHY ARE WE TALKING LIKE 1940s GANGSTERS?

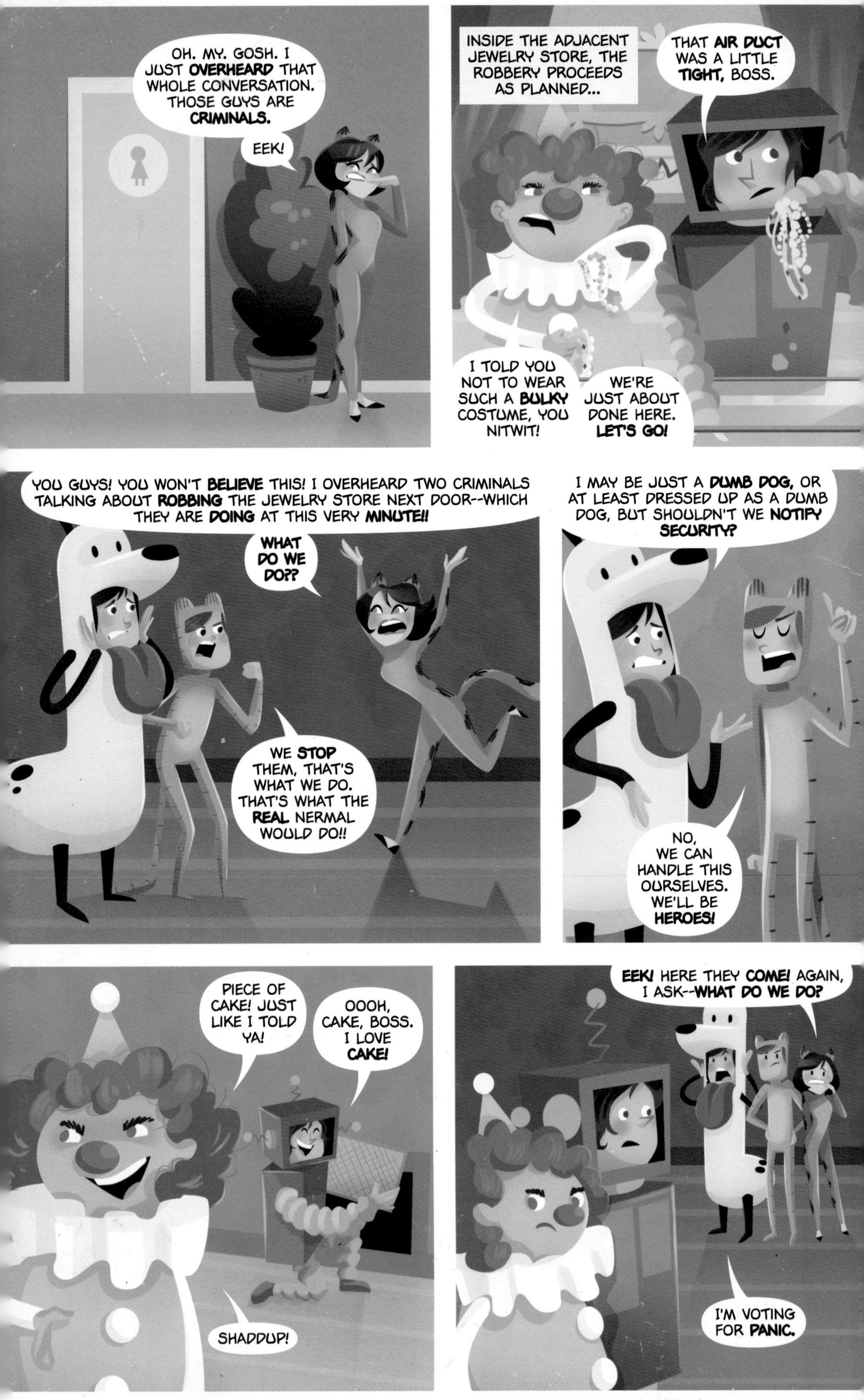

OH. MY. GOSH. I JUST **OVERHEARD** THAT WHOLE CONVERSATION. THOSE GUYS ARE **CRIMINALS.**
EEK!
INSIDE THE ADJACENT JEWELRY STORE, THE ROBBERY PROCEEDS AS PLANNED...
THAT **AIR DUCT** WAS A LITTLE **TIGHT**, BOSS.
I TOLD YOU NOT TO WEAR SUCH A **BULKY** COSTUME, YOU NITWIT!
WE'RE JUST ABOUT DONE HERE. **LET'S GO!**
YOU GUYS! YOU WON'T **BELIEVE** THIS! I OVERHEARD TWO CRIMINALS TALKING ABOUT **ROBBING** THE JEWELRY STORE NEXT DOOR--WHICH THEY ARE **DOING** AT THIS VERY **MINUTE!!**
WHAT DO WE DO??
WE **STOP** THEM, THAT'S WHAT WE DO. THAT'S WHAT THE **REAL** NERMAL WOULD DO!!
I MAY BE JUST A **DUMB DOG,** OR AT LEAST DRESSED UP AS A DUMB DOG, BUT SHOULDN'T WE **NOTIFY SECURITY?**
NO, WE CAN HANDLE THIS OURSELVES. WE'LL BE **HEROES!**
PIECE OF CAKE! JUST LIKE I TOLD YA!
OOOH, CAKE, BOSS. I LOVE **CAKE!**
SHADDUP!
EEK! HERE THEY COME! AGAIN, I ASK--**WHAT DO WE DO?**
I'M VOTING FOR **PANIC.**

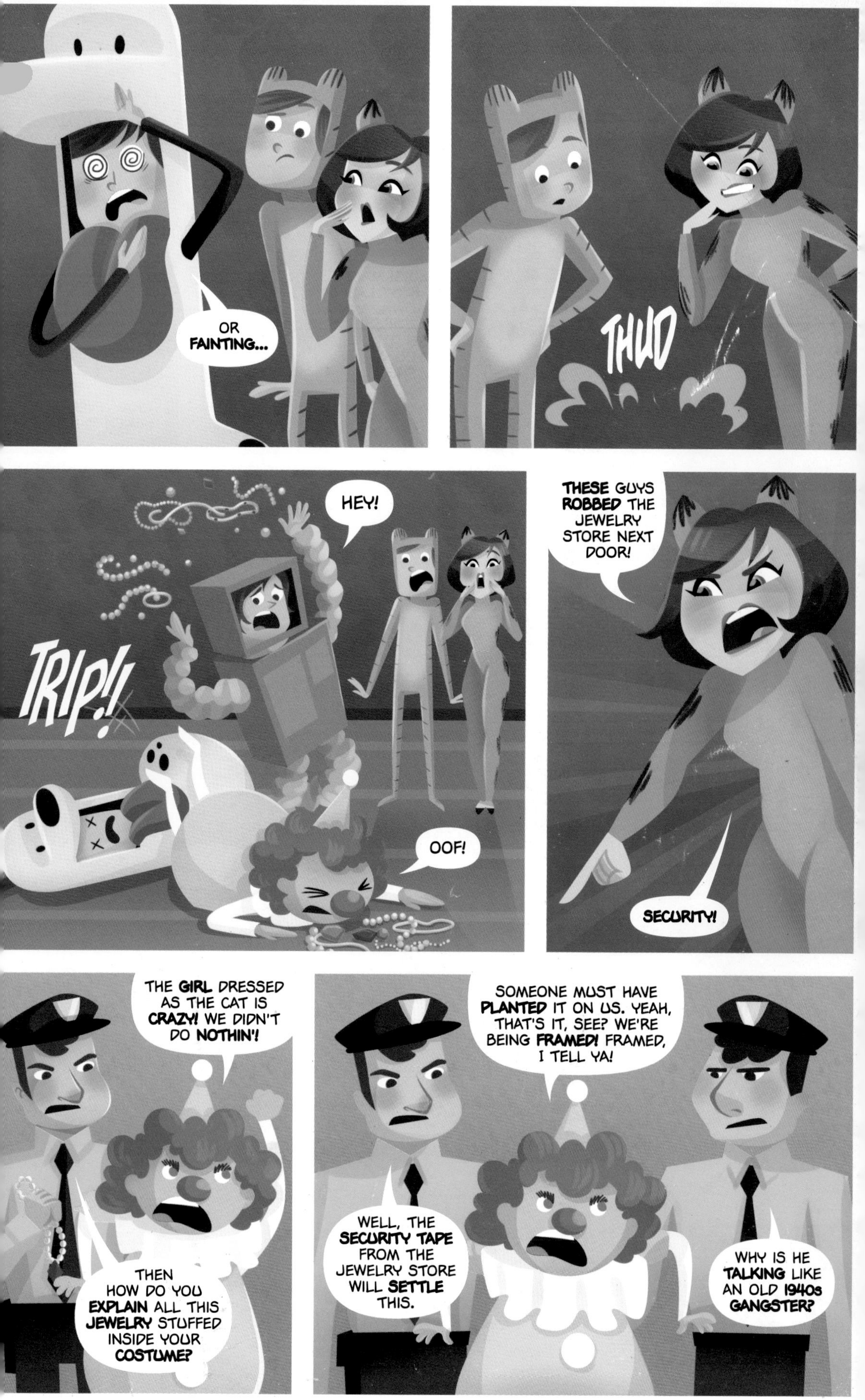
OR
FAINTING...
THUD
HEY!
TRIP!!
OOF!
THESE GUYS ROBBED THE JEWELRY STORE NEXT DOOR!
SECURITY!
THE GIRL DRESSED AS THE CAT IS CRAZY! WE DIDN'T DO NOTHIN'!
THEN HOW DO YOU EXPLAIN ALL THIS JEWELRY STUFFED INSIDE YOUR COSTUME?
SOMEONE MUST HAVE PLANTED IT ON US. YEAH, THAT'S IT, SEE? WE'RE BEING FRAMED! FRAMED, I TELL YA!
WELL, THE SECURITY TAPE FROM THE JEWELRY STORE WILL SETTLE THIS.
WHY IS HE TALKING LIKE AN OLD 1940s GANGSTER?

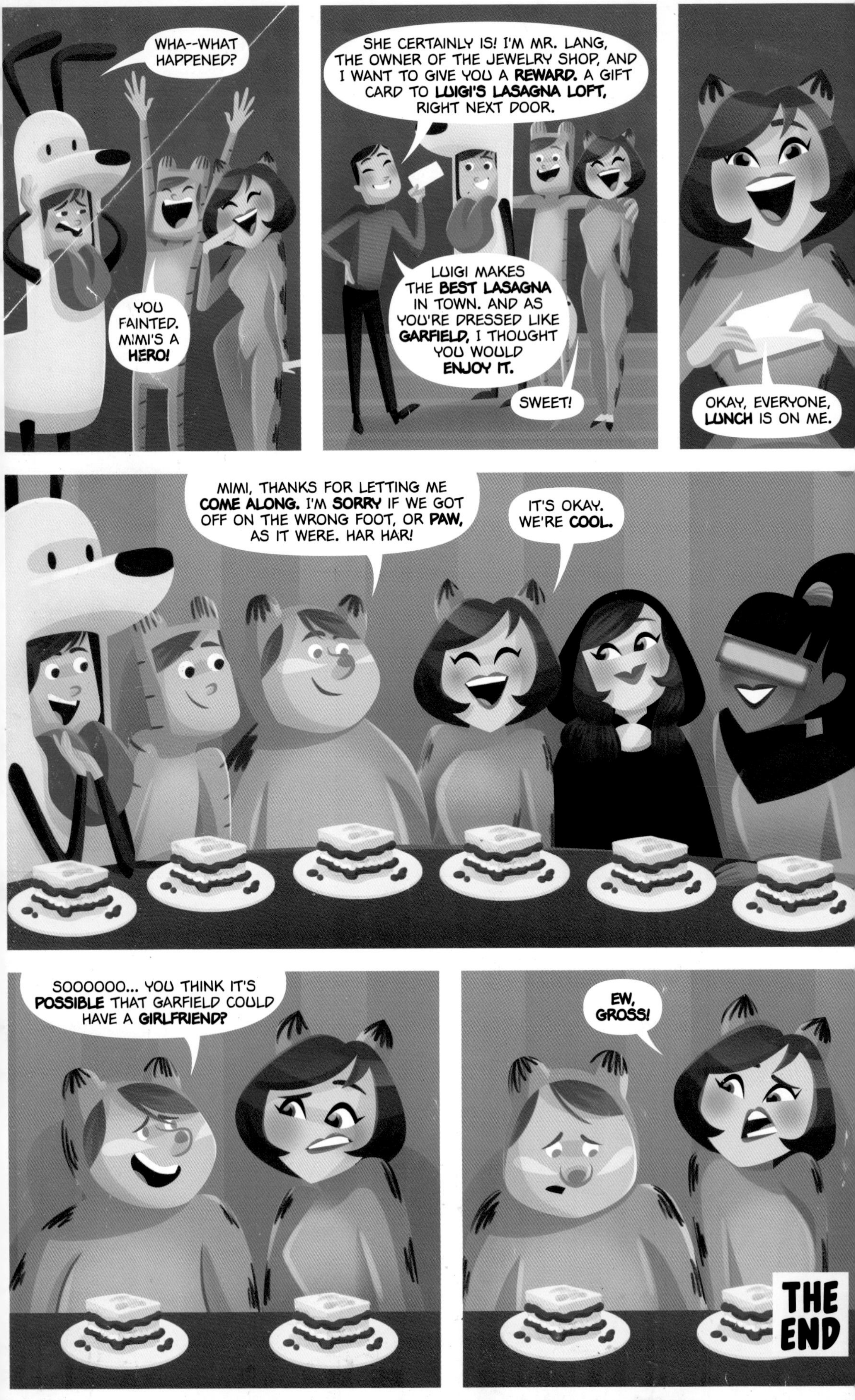
WHA--WHAT HAPPENED?
YOU FAINTED. MIMI'S A HERO!
SHE CERTAINLY IS! I'M MR. LANG, THE OWNER OF THE JEWELRY SHOP, AND I WANT TO GIVE YOU A REWARD. A GIFT CARD TO LUIGI'S LASAGNA LOFT, RIGHT NEXT DOOR.
LUIGI MAKES THE BEST LASAGNA IN TOWN. AND AS YOU'RE DRESSED LIKE GARFIELD, I THOUGHT YOU WOULD ENJOY IT.
SWEET!
OKAY, EVERYONE, LUNCH IS ON ME.
MIMI, THANKS FOR LETTING ME COME ALONG. I'M SORRY IF WE GOT OFF ON THE WRONG FOOT, OR PAW, AS IT WERE. HAR HAR!
IT'S OKAY. WE'RE COOL.
SOOOOOO... YOU THINK IT'S POSSIBLE THAT GARFIELD COULD HAVE A GIRLFRIEND?
EW, GROSS!
THE END

CREEPY COMICS

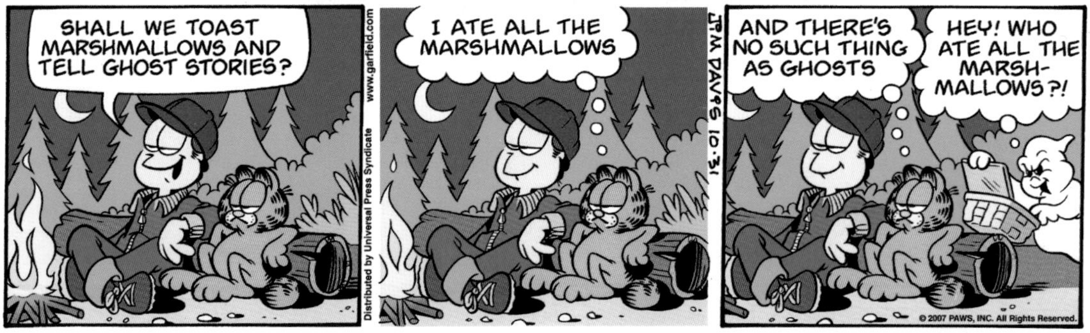
SHALL WE TOAST MARSHMALLOWS AND TELL GHOST STORIES?
www.garfield.com
Distributed by Universal Press Syndicate
I ATE ALL THE MARSHMALLOWS
JPM DAVPS 10-31
AND THERE'S NO SUCH THING AS GHOSTS
HEY! WHO ATE ALL THE MARSH-MALLOWS?!
© 2007 PAWS, INC. All Rights Reserved.

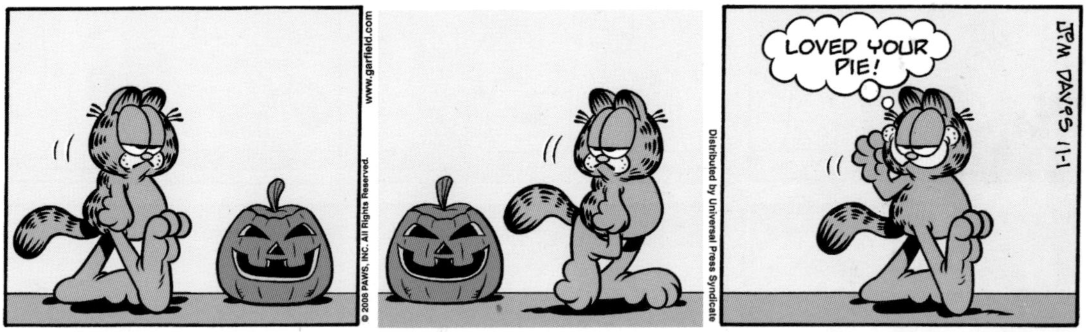
www.garfield.com
© 2008 PAWS, INC. All Rights Reserved.
Distributed by Universal Press Syndicate
LOVED YOUR PIE!
JPM DAVPS 11-1

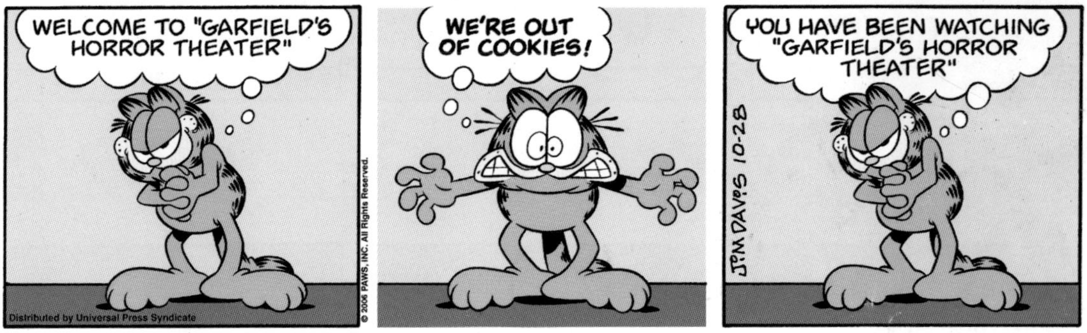
WELCOME TO "GARFIELD'S HORROR THEATER"
Distributed by Universal Press Syndicate
© 2006 PAWS, INC. All Rights Reserved.
WE'RE OUT OF COOKIES!
YOU HAVE BEEN WATCHING "GARFIELD'S HORROR THEATER"
JPM DAVPS 10-28

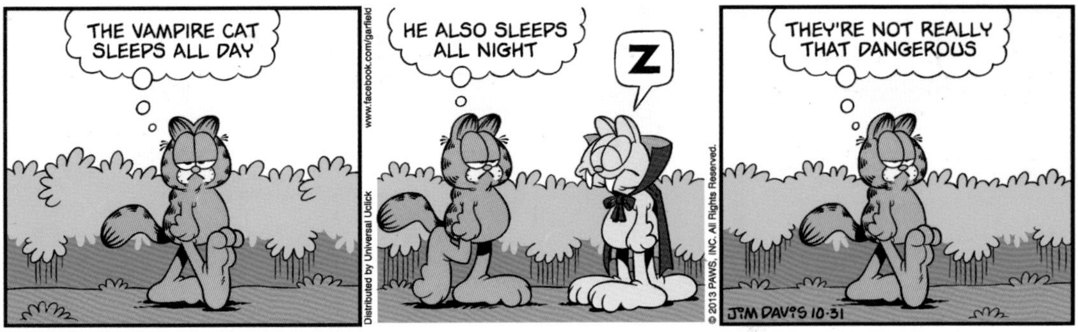
THE VAMPIRE CAT SLEEPS ALL DAY
www.facebook.com/garfield
Distributed by Universal Uclick
HE ALSO SLEEPS ALL NIGHT
Z
© 2013 PAWS, INC. All Rights Reserved.
THEY'RE NOT REALLY THAT DANGEROUS
JPM DAVPS 10-31

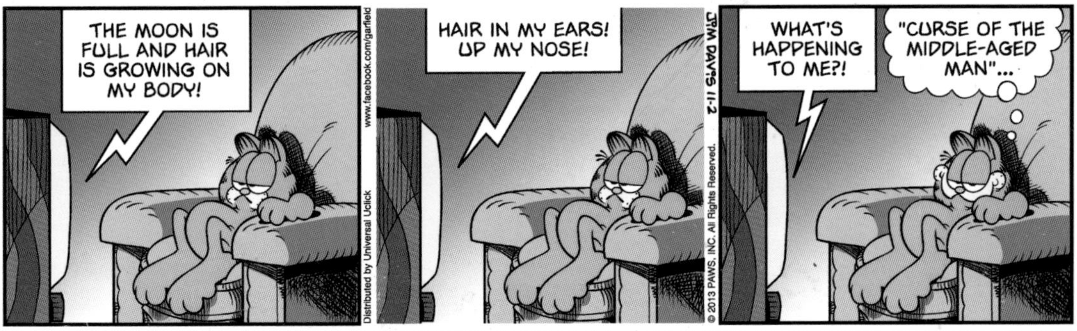
THE MOON IS FULL AND HAIR IS GROWING ON MY BODY!
www.facebook.com/garfield
Distributed by Universal Uclick
HAIR IN MY EARS! UP MY NOSE!
JPM DAVPS 11-2
© 2013 PAWS, INC. All Rights Reserved.
WHAT'S HAPPENING TO ME?!
"CURSE OF THE MIDDLE-AGED MAN"...

Garfield Sunday Classics

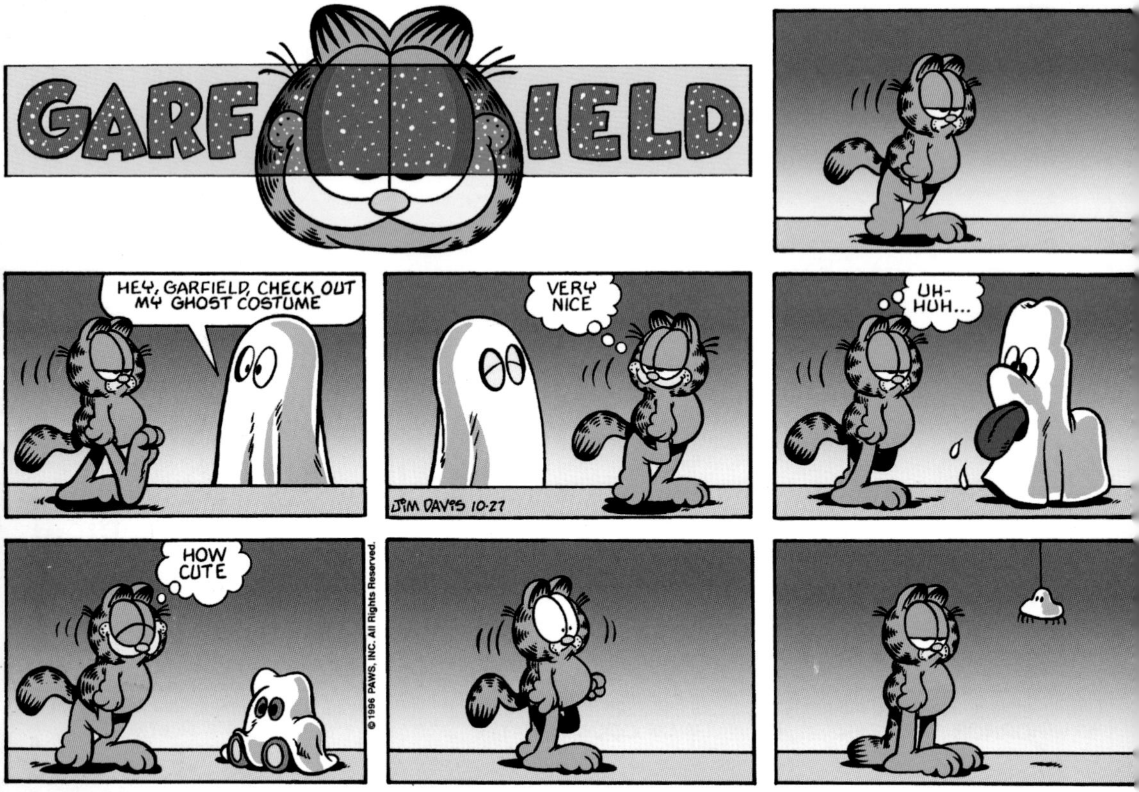
GARFIELD
HEY, GARFIELD, CHECK OUT MY GHOST COSTUME
VERY NICE
JIM DAVIS 10-27
UH-HUH...
HOW CUTE
© 1996 PAWS, INC. All Rights Reserved.

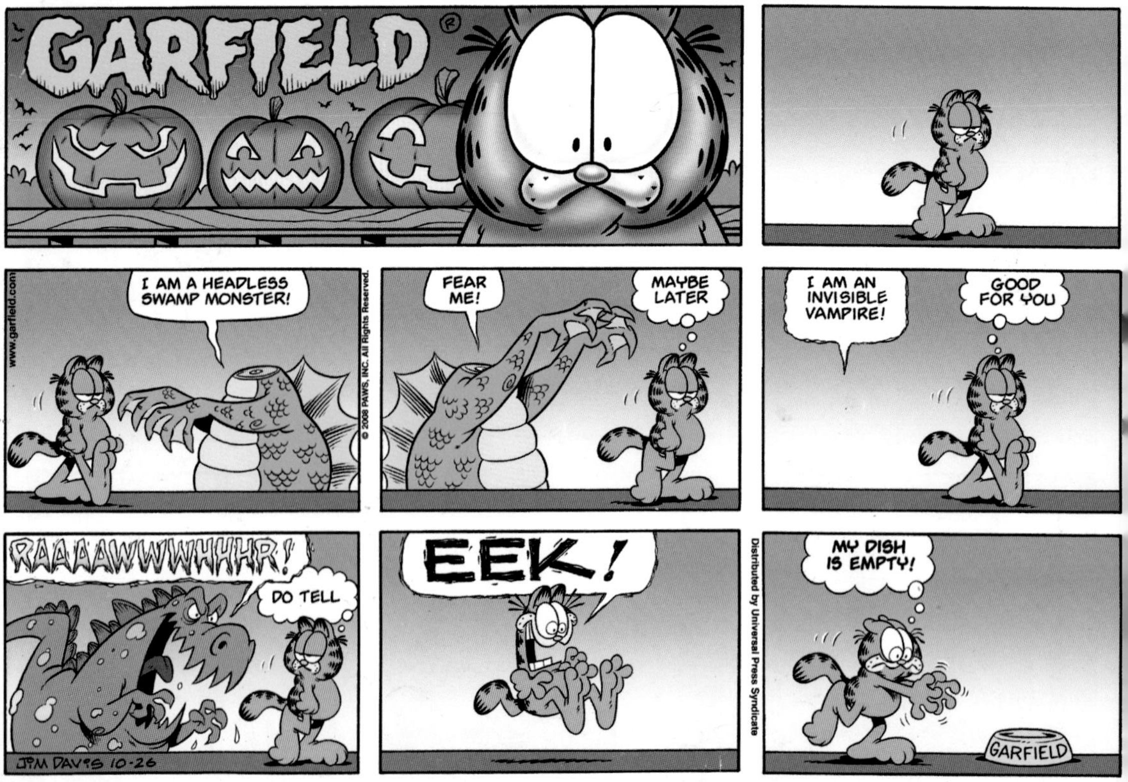
GARFIELD®
www.garfield.com
I AM A HEADLESS SWAMP MONSTER!
© 2008 PAWS, INC. All Rights Reserved.
FEAR ME!
MAYBE LATER
I AM AN INVISIBLE VAMPIRE!
GOOD FOR YOU
RAAAAWWWHHHR!
DO TELL
JIM DAVIS 10-26
EEK!
Distributed by Universal Press Syndicate
MY DISH IS EMPTY!
GARFIELD

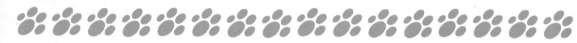

CHAPTER 3

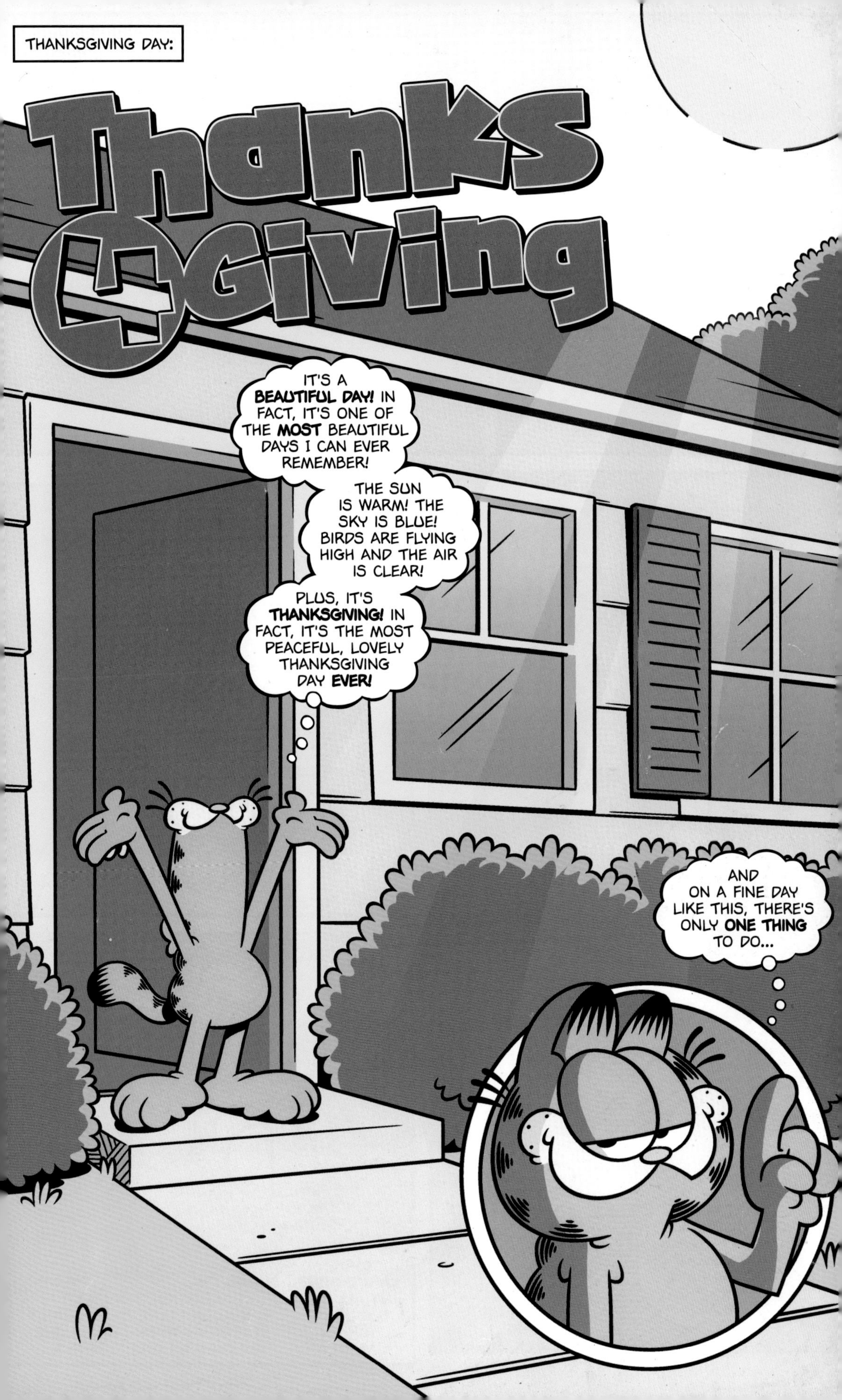
THANKSGIVING DAY:
Thanks Giving
IT'S A BEAUTIFUL DAY! IN FACT, IT'S ONE OF THE MOST BEAUTIFUL DAYS I CAN EVER REMEMBER!
THE SUN IS WARM! THE SKY IS BLUE! BIRDS ARE FLYING HIGH AND THE AIR IS CLEAR!
PLUS, IT'S THANKSGIVING! IN FACT, IT'S THE MOST PEACEFUL, LOVELY THANKSGIVING DAY EVER!
AND ON A FINE DAY LIKE THIS, THERE'S ONLY ONE THING TO DO...

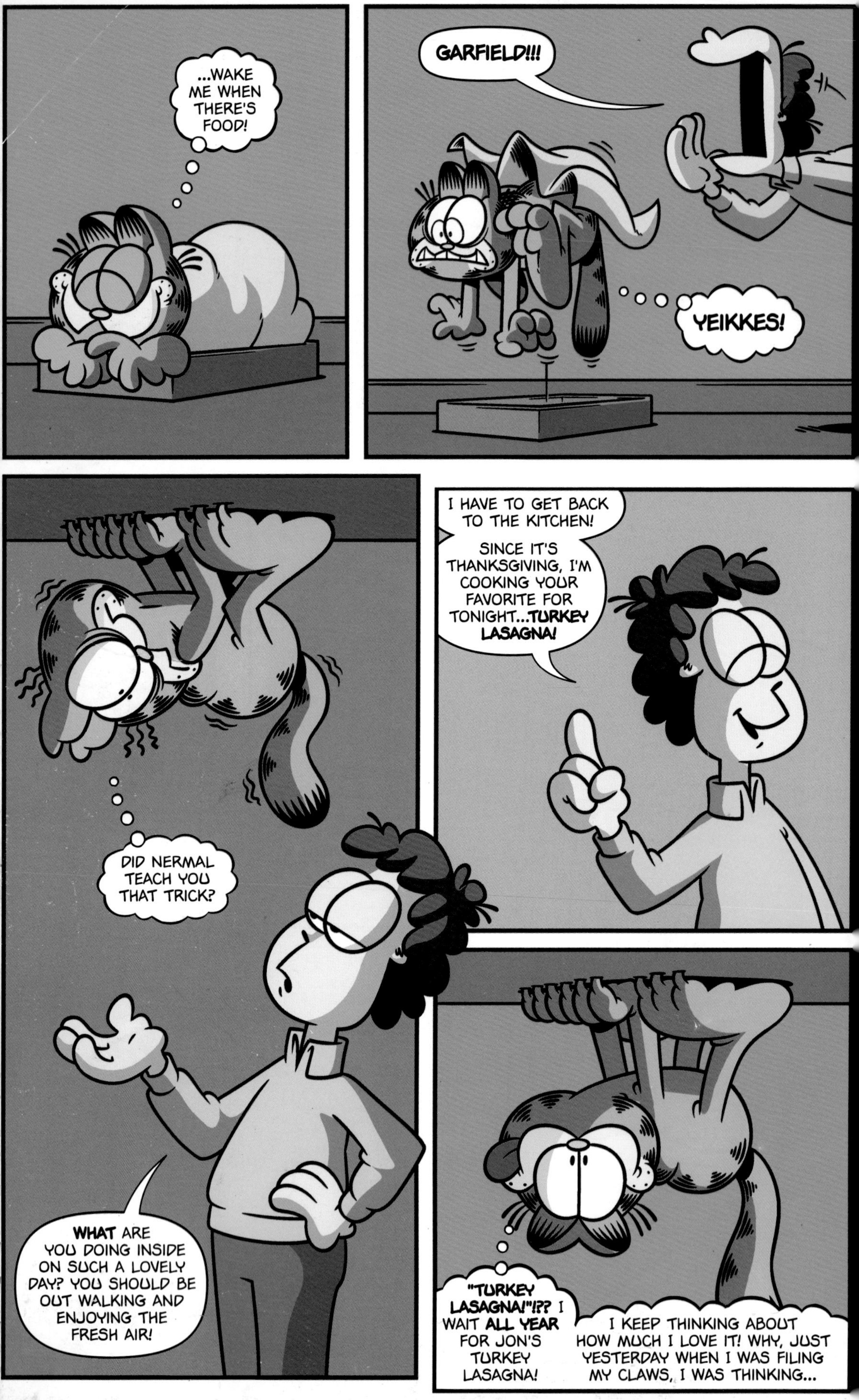
...WAKE ME WHEN THERE'S FOOD!
GARFIELD!!!
YEIKKES!
DID NERMAL TEACH YOU THAT TRICK?
WHAT ARE YOU DOING INSIDE ON SUCH A LOVELY DAY? YOU SHOULD BE OUT WALKING AND ENJOYING THE FRESH AIR!
I HAVE TO GET BACK TO THE KITCHEN!
SINCE IT'S THANKSGIVING, I'M COOKING YOUR FAVORITE FOR TONIGHT...TURKEY LASAGNA!
"TURKEY LASAGNA!"!?? I WAIT ALL YEAR FOR JON'S TURKEY LASAGNA!
I KEEP THINKING ABOUT HOW MUCH I LOVE IT! WHY, JUST YESTERDAY WHEN I WAS FILING MY CLAWS, I WAS THINKING...

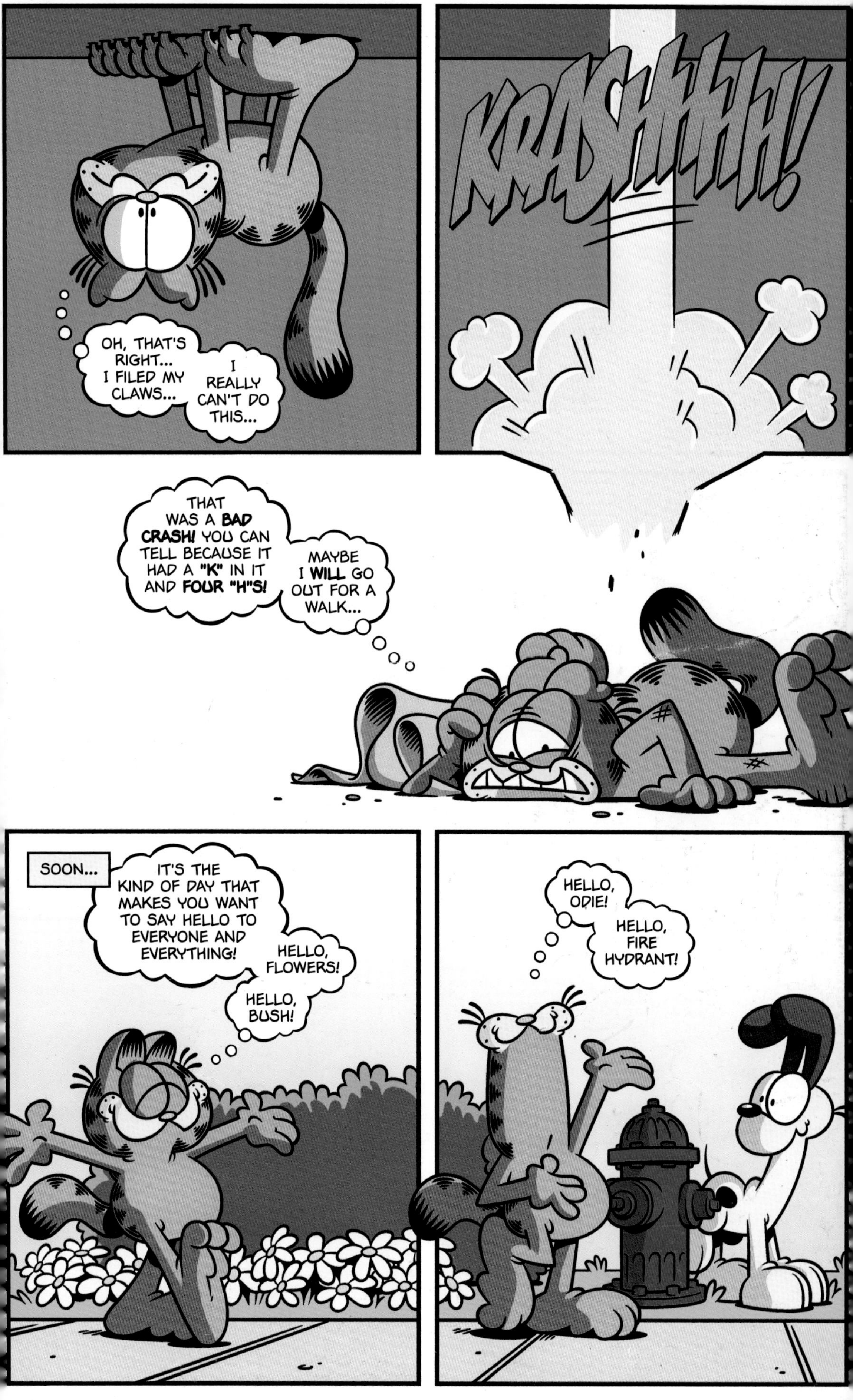

OH, THAT'S RIGHT... I FILED MY CLAWS...
I REALLY CAN'T DO THIS...
KRASHHHH!
THAT WAS A BAD CRASH! YOU CAN TELL BECAUSE IT HAD A "K" IN IT AND FOUR "H"S!
MAYBE I WILL GO OUT FOR A WALK...
SOON...
IT'S THE KIND OF DAY THAT MAKES YOU WANT TO SAY HELLO TO EVERYONE AND EVERYTHING!
HELLO, FLOWERS!
HELLO, BUSH!
HELLO, ODIE!
HELLO, FIRE HYDRANT!

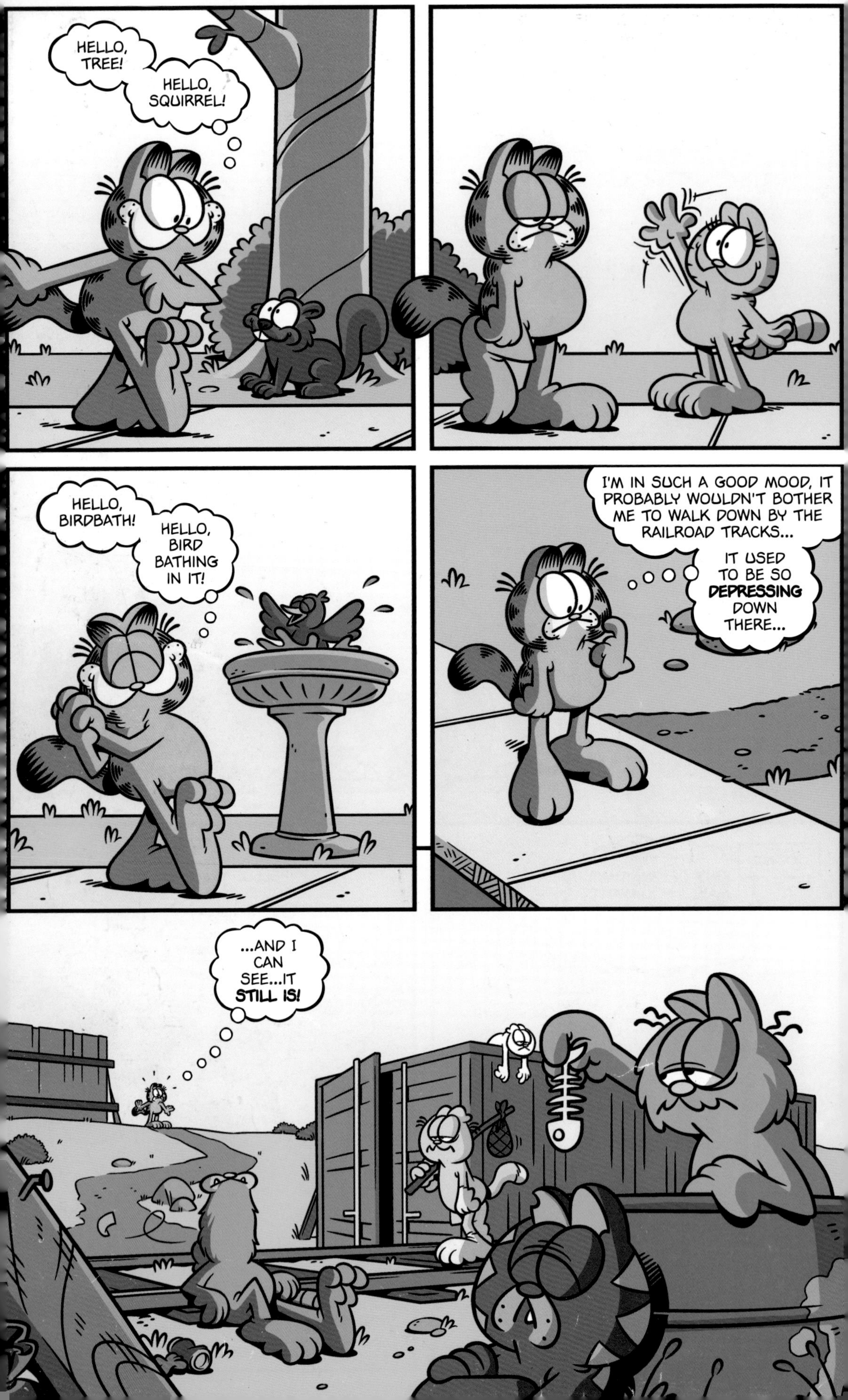
HELLO, TREE!
HELLO, SQUIRREL!
HELLO, BIRDBATH!
HELLO, BIRD BATHING IN IT!
I'M IN SUCH A GOOD MOOD, IT PROBABLY WOULDN'T BOTHER ME TO WALK DOWN BY THE RAILROAD TRACKS...
IT USED TO BE SO **DEPRESSING** DOWN THERE...
...AND I CAN SEE...IT **STILL IS!**

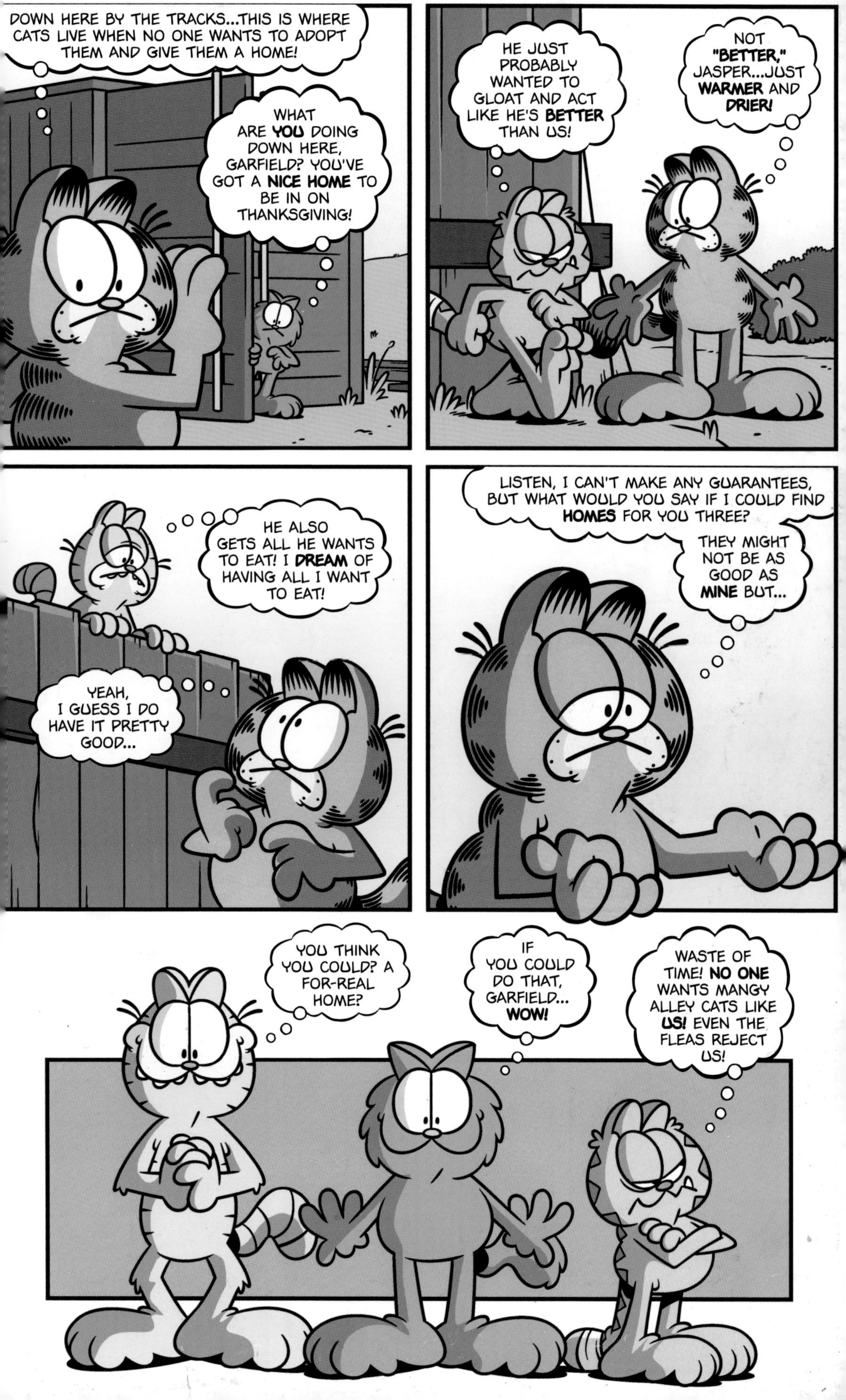

DOWN HERE BY THE TRACKS...THIS IS WHERE CATS LIVE WHEN NO ONE WANTS TO ADOPT THEM AND GIVE THEM A HOME!
WHAT ARE YOU DOING DOWN HERE, GARFIELD? YOU'VE GOT A NICE HOME TO BE IN ON THANKSGIVING!
HE JUST PROBABLY WANTED TO GLOAT AND ACT LIKE HE'S BETTER THAN US!
NOT "BETTER," JASPER...JUST WARMER AND DRIER!
HE ALSO GETS ALL HE WANTS TO EAT! I DREAM OF HAVING ALL I WANT TO EAT!
YEAH, I GUESS I DO HAVE IT PRETTY GOOD...
LISTEN, I CAN'T MAKE ANY GUARANTEES, BUT WHAT WOULD YOU SAY IF I COULD FIND HOMES FOR YOU THREE?
THEY MIGHT NOT BE AS GOOD AS MINE BUT...
YOU THINK YOU COULD? A FOR-REAL HOME?
IF YOU COULD DO THAT, GARFIELD... WOW!
WASTE OF TIME! NO ONE WANTS MANGY ALLEY CATS LIKE US! EVEN THE FLEAS REJECT US!

HEY, IT'S WORTH A TRY, JASPER! COME WITH ME AND LET'S SEE WHAT WILL HAPPEN!

I **KNOW** WHAT WILL HAPPEN AND I AIN'T GETTIN' MY HOPES UP AGAIN!

HAVE IT YOUR WAY! I'LL BE BACK IN A WHILE...

...HOPEFULLY WITHOUT BENJY AND ALF HERE!

I'LL SEE **ALL THREE** OF YOU LATER!

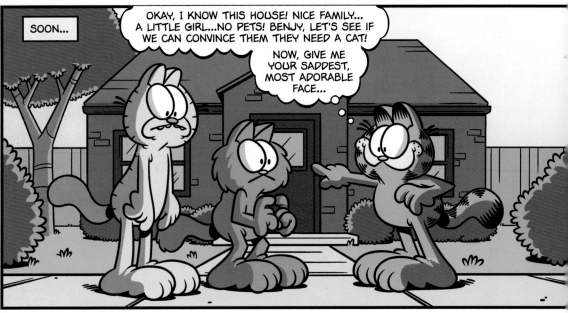

SOON...

OKAY, I KNOW THIS HOUSE! NICE FAMILY... A LITTLE GIRL...NO PETS! BENJY, LET'S SEE IF WE CAN CONVINCE THEM THEY NEED A CAT!

NOW, GIVE ME YOUR SADDEST, MOST ADORABLE FACE...

THAT'S NOT SAD ENOUGH! TRY TO LOOK **SADDER!**

BETTER! NOW, MAKE YOUR **EYES BIGGER** AND TURN UP THE CORNERS OF YOUR MOUTH INTO A **FAINT SMILE!**

PERFECT! LET'S GO RING THE DOORBELL!

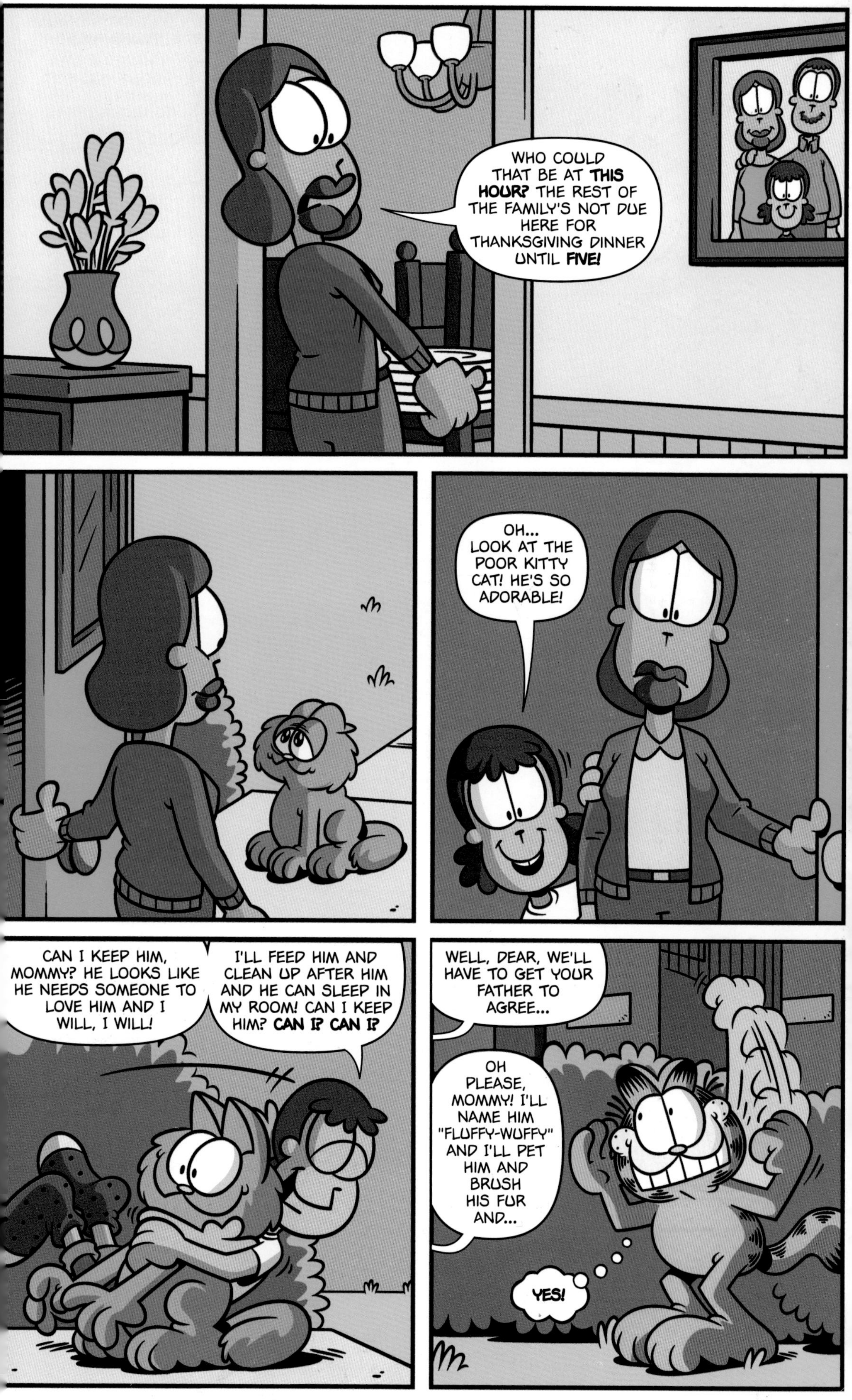
WHO COULD THAT BE AT **THIS HOUR?** THE REST OF THE FAMILY'S NOT DUE HERE FOR THANKSGIVING DINNER UNTIL **FIVE!**
OH... LOOK AT THE POOR KITTY CAT! HE'S SO ADORABLE!
CAN I KEEP HIM, MOMMY? HE LOOKS LIKE HE NEEDS SOMEONE TO LOVE HIM AND I WILL, I WILL!
I'LL FEED HIM AND CLEAN UP AFTER HIM AND HE CAN SLEEP IN MY ROOM! CAN I KEEP HIM? **CAN I? CAN I?**
WELL, DEAR, WE'LL HAVE TO GET YOUR FATHER TO AGREE...
OH PLEASE, MOMMY! I'LL NAME HIM "FLUFFY-WUFFY" AND I'LL PET HIM AND BRUSH HIS FUR AND...
YES!

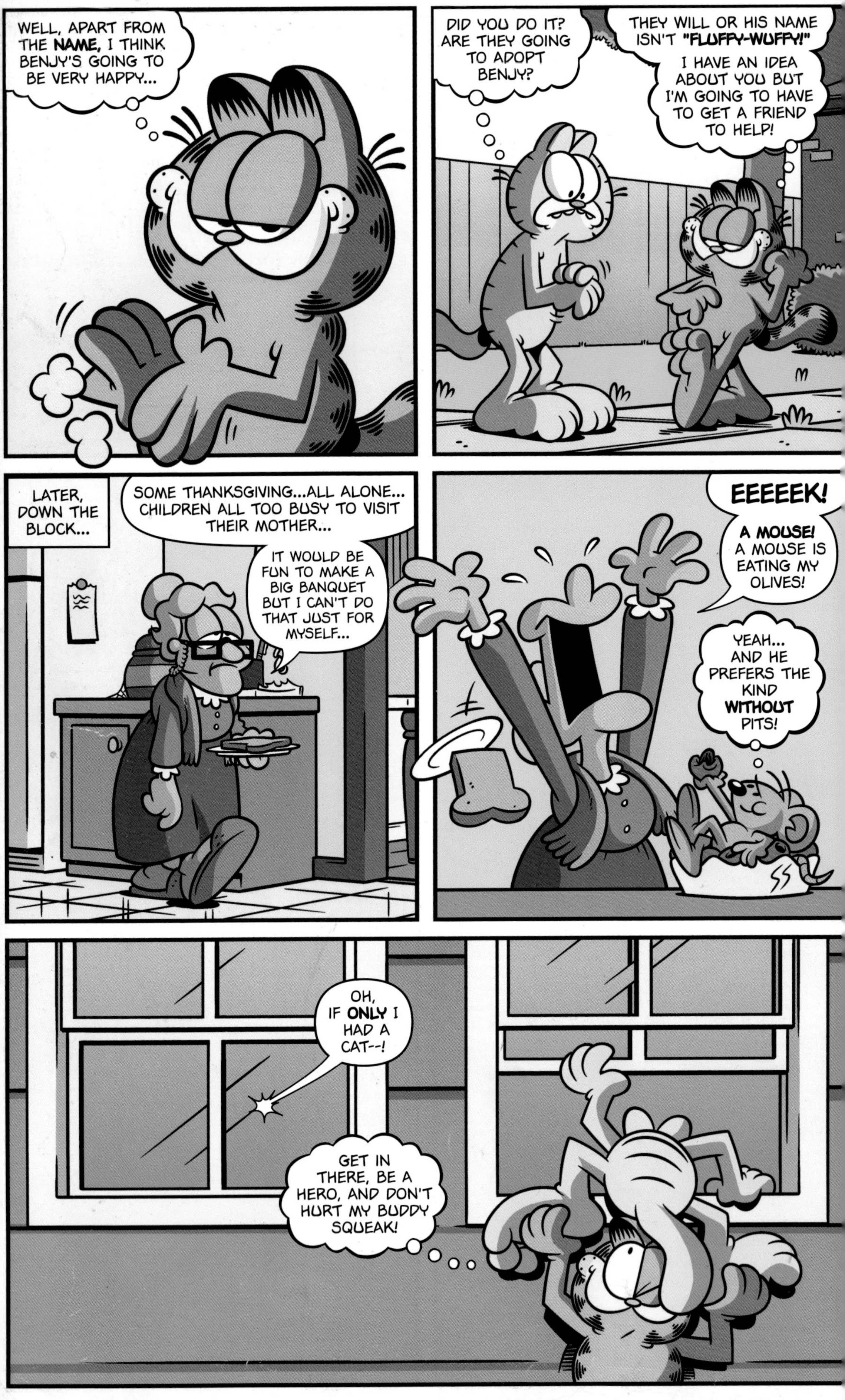
WELL, APART FROM THE NAME, I THINK BENJY'S GOING TO BE VERY HAPPY...
DID YOU DO IT? ARE THEY GOING TO ADOPT BENJY?
THEY WILL OR HIS NAME ISN'T "FLUFFY-WUFFY!"
I HAVE AN IDEA ABOUT YOU BUT I'M GOING TO HAVE TO GET A FRIEND TO HELP!
LATER, DOWN THE BLOCK...
SOME THANKSGIVING...ALL ALONE... CHILDREN ALL TOO BUSY TO VISIT THEIR MOTHER...
IT WOULD BE FUN TO MAKE A BIG BANQUET BUT I CAN'T DO THAT JUST FOR MYSELF...
EEEEEK!
A MOUSE! A MOUSE IS EATING MY OLIVES!
YEAH... AND HE PREFERS THE KIND WITHOUT PITS!
OH, IF ONLY I HAD A CAT--!
GET IN THERE, BE A HERO, AND DON'T HURT MY BUDDY SQUEAK!

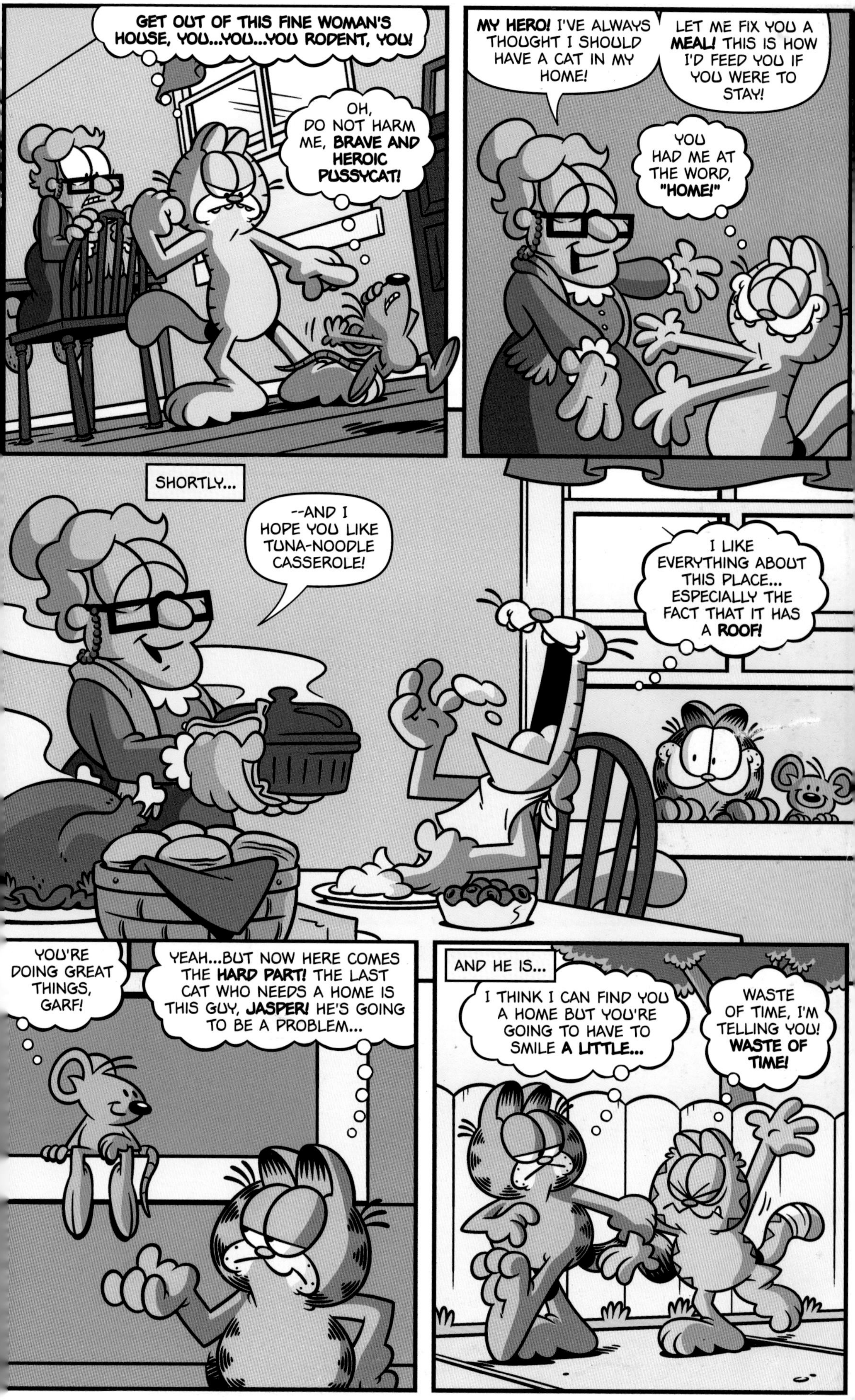
GET OUT OF THIS FINE WOMAN'S HOUSE, YOU...YOU...YOU RODENT, YOU!
OH, DO NOT HARM ME, BRAVE AND HEROIC PUSSYCAT!
MY HERO! I'VE ALWAYS THOUGHT I SHOULD HAVE A CAT IN MY HOME!
LET ME FIX YOU A MEAL! THIS IS HOW I'D FEED YOU IF YOU WERE TO STAY!
YOU HAD ME AT THE WORD, "HOME!"
SHORTLY...
--AND I HOPE YOU LIKE TUNA-NOODLE CASSEROLE!
I LIKE EVERYTHING ABOUT THIS PLACE... ESPECIALLY THE FACT THAT IT HAS A ROOF!
YOU'RE DOING GREAT THINGS, GARF!
YEAH...BUT NOW HERE COMES THE HARD PART! THE LAST CAT WHO NEEDS A HOME IS THIS GUY, JASPER! HE'S GOING TO BE A PROBLEM...
AND HE IS...
I THINK I CAN FIND YOU A HOME BUT YOU'RE GOING TO HAVE TO SMILE A LITTLE...
WASTE OF TIME, I'M TELLING YOU! WASTE OF TIME!

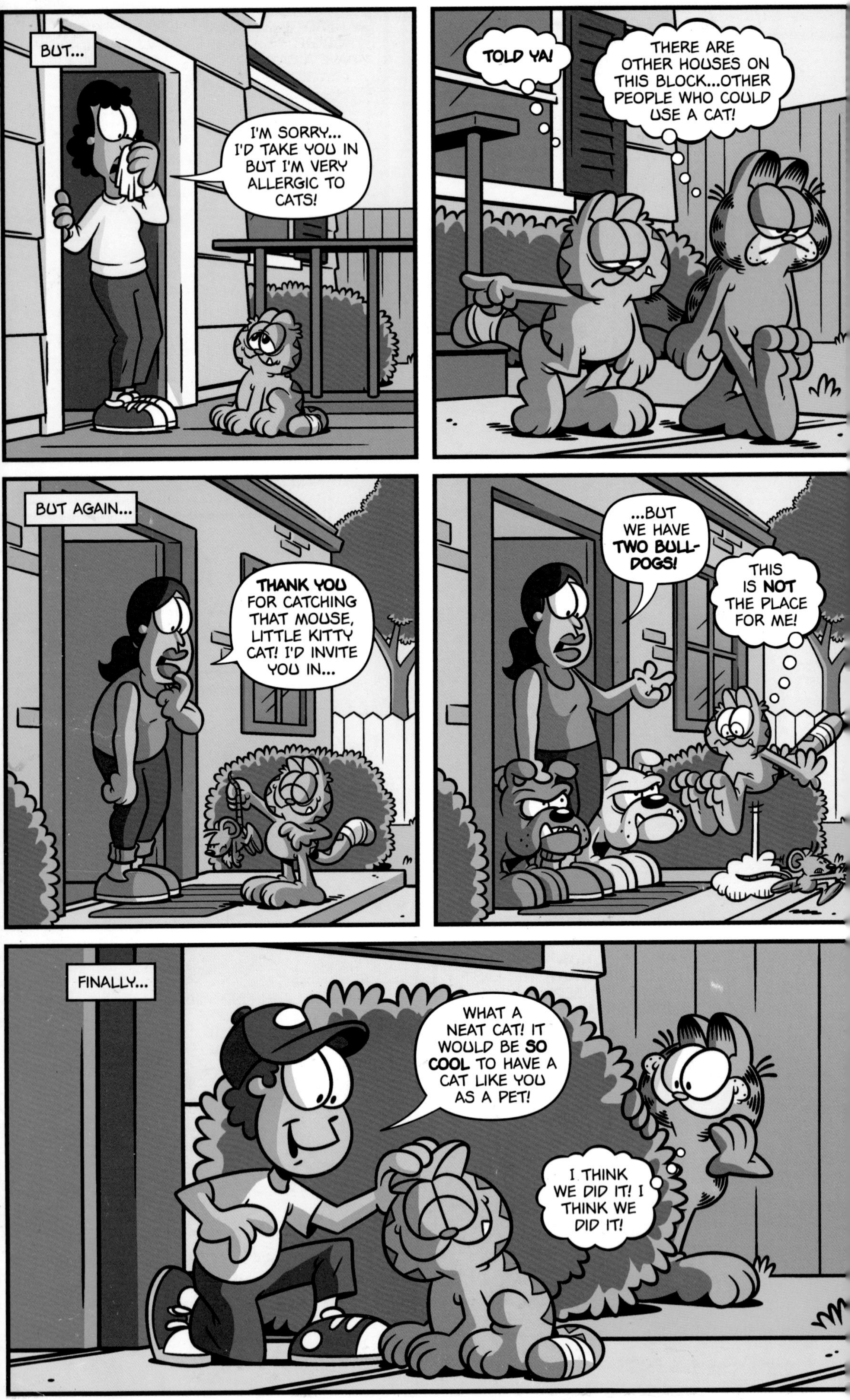
BUT...
I'M SORRY... I'D TAKE YOU IN BUT I'M VERY ALLERGIC TO CATS!
TOLD YA!
THERE ARE OTHER HOUSES ON THIS BLOCK...OTHER PEOPLE WHO COULD USE A CAT!
BUT AGAIN...
THANK YOU FOR CATCHING THAT MOUSE, LITTLE KITTY CAT! I'D INVITE YOU IN...
...BUT WE HAVE TWO BULL-DOGS!
THIS IS NOT THE PLACE FOR ME!
FINALLY...
WHAT A NEAT CAT! IT WOULD BE SO COOL TO HAVE A CAT LIKE YOU AS A PET!
I THINK WE DID IT! I THINK WE DID IT!

WE WILL NOT HAVE A CAT IN THIS HOUSE!

BUT, DAD...

WE'LL DISCUSS IT OVER DINNER BUT I DON'T THINK YOU CAN CHANGE MY MIND!

I GUESS WE DIDN'T DO IT. MAYBE OVER ON THE NEXT BLOCK...

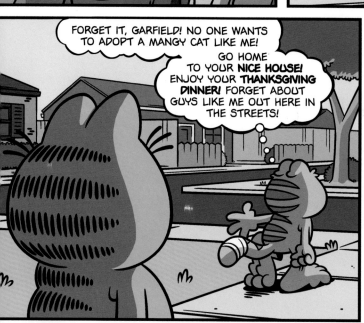

FORGET IT, GARFIELD! NO ONE WANTS TO ADOPT A MANGY CAT LIKE ME!

GO HOME TO YOUR NICE HOUSE! ENJOY YOUR THANKSGIVING DINNER! FORGET ABOUT GUYS LIKE ME OUT HERE IN THE STREETS!

I THOUGHT FOR SURE THAT LAST HOUSE WOULD TAKE HIM IN BUT...

WELL, MAYBE HE'S RIGHT...

AND SO...

HERE YOU GO, BOYS! GARFIELD'S FAVORITE THANKSGIVING TREAT--TURKEY LASAGNA! EAT IT UP!

YEAH! YEAH! YEAH!

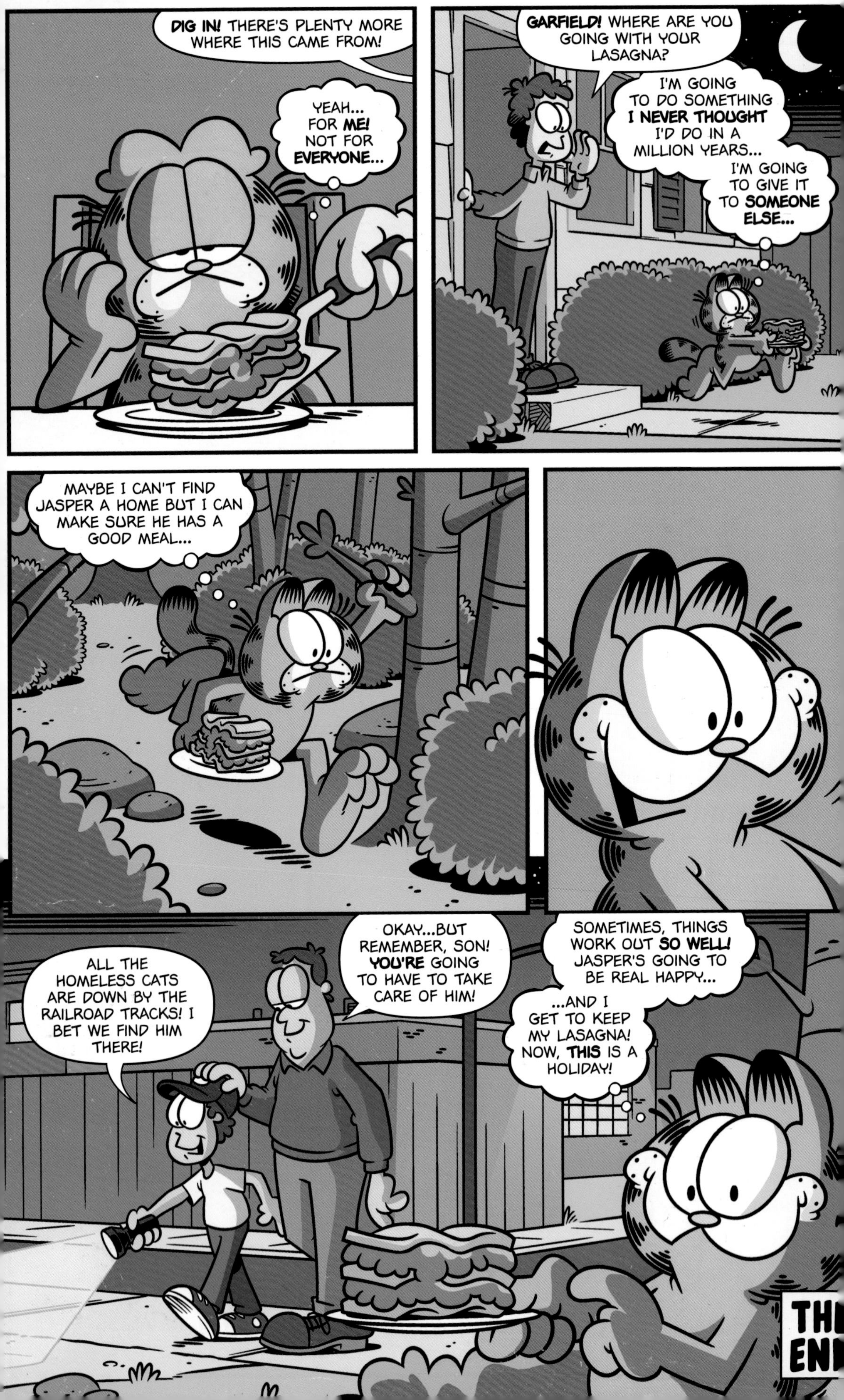
DIG IN! THERE'S PLENTY MORE WHERE THIS CAME FROM!
YEAH... FOR ME! NOT FOR EVERYONE...
GARFIELD! WHERE ARE YOU GOING WITH YOUR LASAGNA?
I'M GOING TO DO SOMETHING I NEVER THOUGHT I'D DO IN A MILLION YEARS...
I'M GOING TO GIVE IT TO SOMEONE ELSE...
MAYBE I CAN'T FIND JASPER A HOME BUT I CAN MAKE SURE HE HAS A GOOD MEAL...
ALL THE HOMELESS CATS ARE DOWN BY THE RAILROAD TRACKS! I BET WE FIND HIM THERE!
OKAY...BUT REMEMBER, SON! YOU'RE GOING TO HAVE TO TAKE CARE OF HIM!
SOMETIMES, THINGS WORK OUT SO WELL! JASPER'S GOING TO BE REAL HAPPY...
...AND I GET TO KEEP MY LASAGNA! NOW, THIS IS A HOLIDAY!

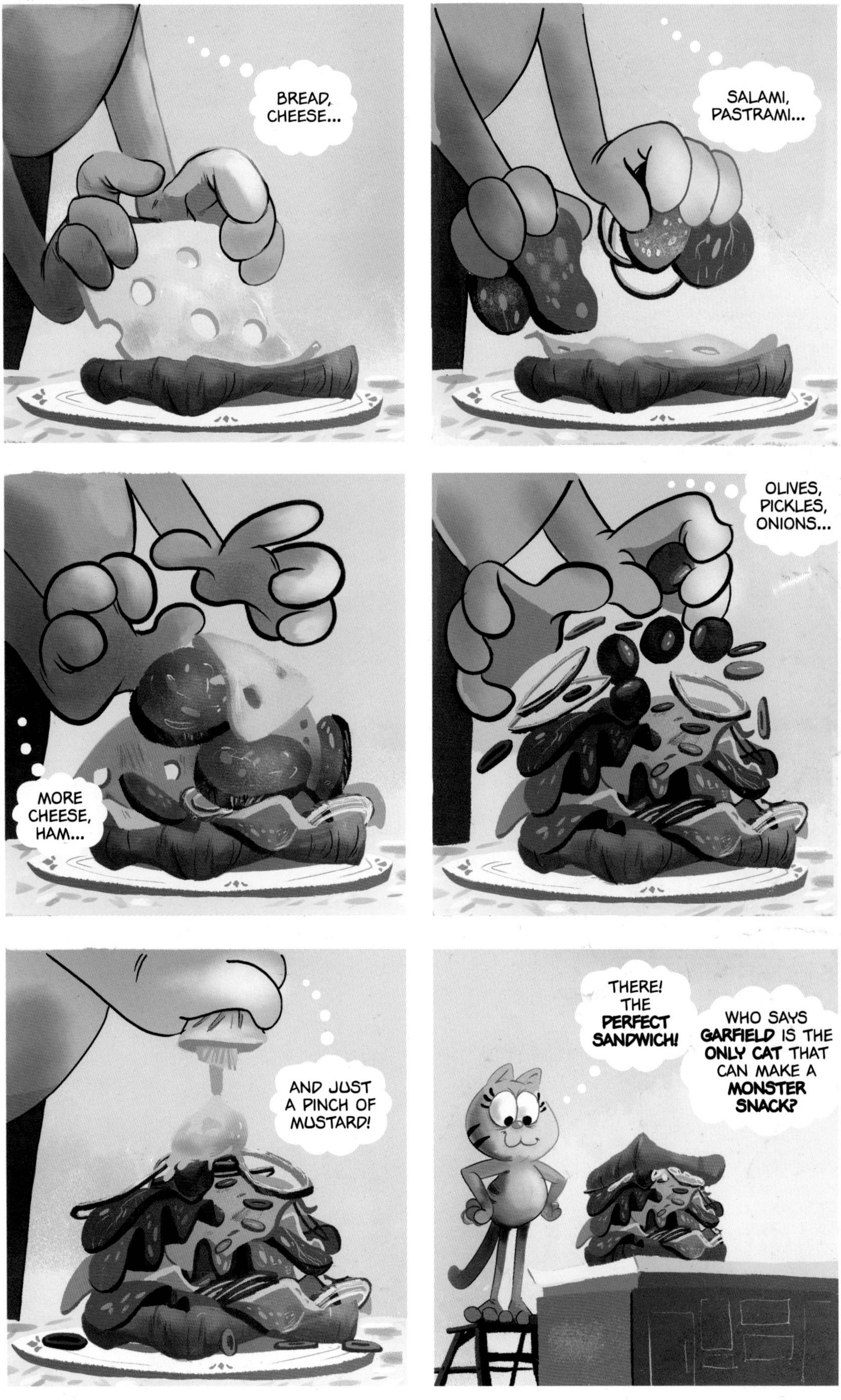
BREAD, CHEESE...
SALAMI, PASTRAMI...
MORE CHEESE, HAM...
OLIVES, PICKLES, ONIONS...
AND JUST A PINCH OF MUSTARD!
THERE! THE PERFECT SANDWICH!
WHO SAYS GARFIELD IS THE ONLY CAT THAT CAN MAKE A MONSTER SNACK?

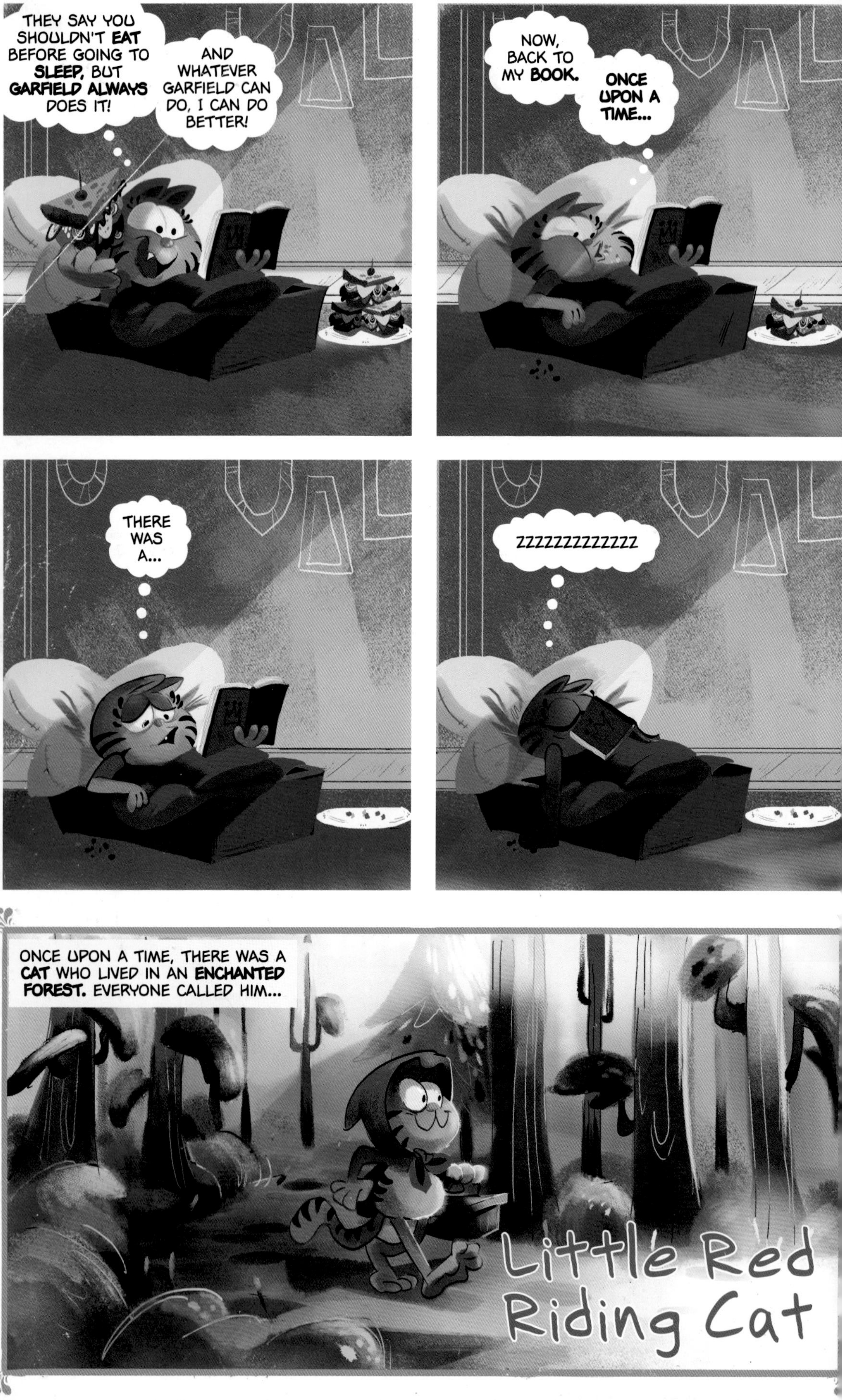

THEY SAY YOU SHOULDN'T EAT BEFORE GOING TO SLEEP, BUT GARFIELD ALWAYS DOES IT!
AND WHATEVER GARFIELD CAN DO, I CAN DO BETTER!
NOW, BACK TO MY BOOK.
ONCE UPON A TIME...
THERE WAS A...
ZZZZZZZZZZZZZZ
ONCE UPON A TIME, THERE WAS A CAT WHO LIVED IN AN ENCHANTED FOREST. EVERYONE CALLED HIM...
Little Red Riding Cat

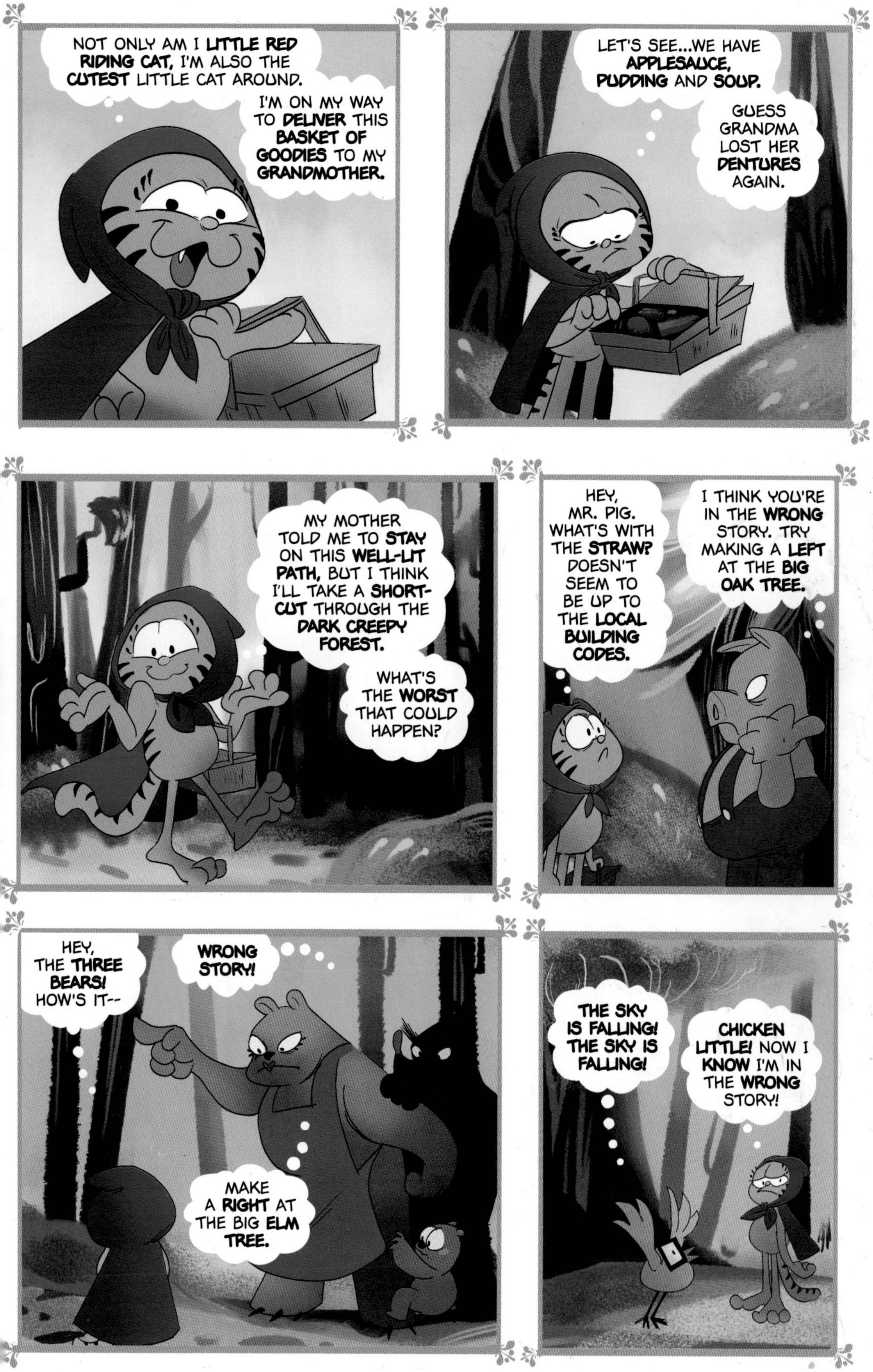
NOT ONLY AM I LITTLE RED RIDING CAT, I'M ALSO THE CUTEST LITTLE CAT AROUND.
I'M ON MY WAY TO DELIVER THIS BASKET OF GOODIES TO MY GRANDMOTHER.
LET'S SEE...WE HAVE APPLESAUCE, PUDDING AND SOUP.
GUESS GRANDMA LOST HER DENTURES AGAIN.
MY MOTHER TOLD ME TO STAY ON THIS WELL-LIT PATH, BUT I THINK I'LL TAKE A SHORT-CUT THROUGH THE DARK CREEPY FOREST.
WHAT'S THE WORST THAT COULD HAPPEN?
HEY, MR. PIG. WHAT'S WITH THE STRAW? DOESN'T SEEM TO BE UP TO THE LOCAL BUILDING CODES.
I THINK YOU'RE IN THE WRONG STORY. TRY MAKING A LEFT AT THE BIG OAK TREE.
HEY, THE THREE BEARS! HOW'S IT--
WRONG STORY!
MAKE A RIGHT AT THE BIG ELM TREE.
THE SKY IS FALLING! THE SKY IS FALLING!
CHICKEN LITTLE! NOW I KNOW I'M IN THE WRONG STORY!

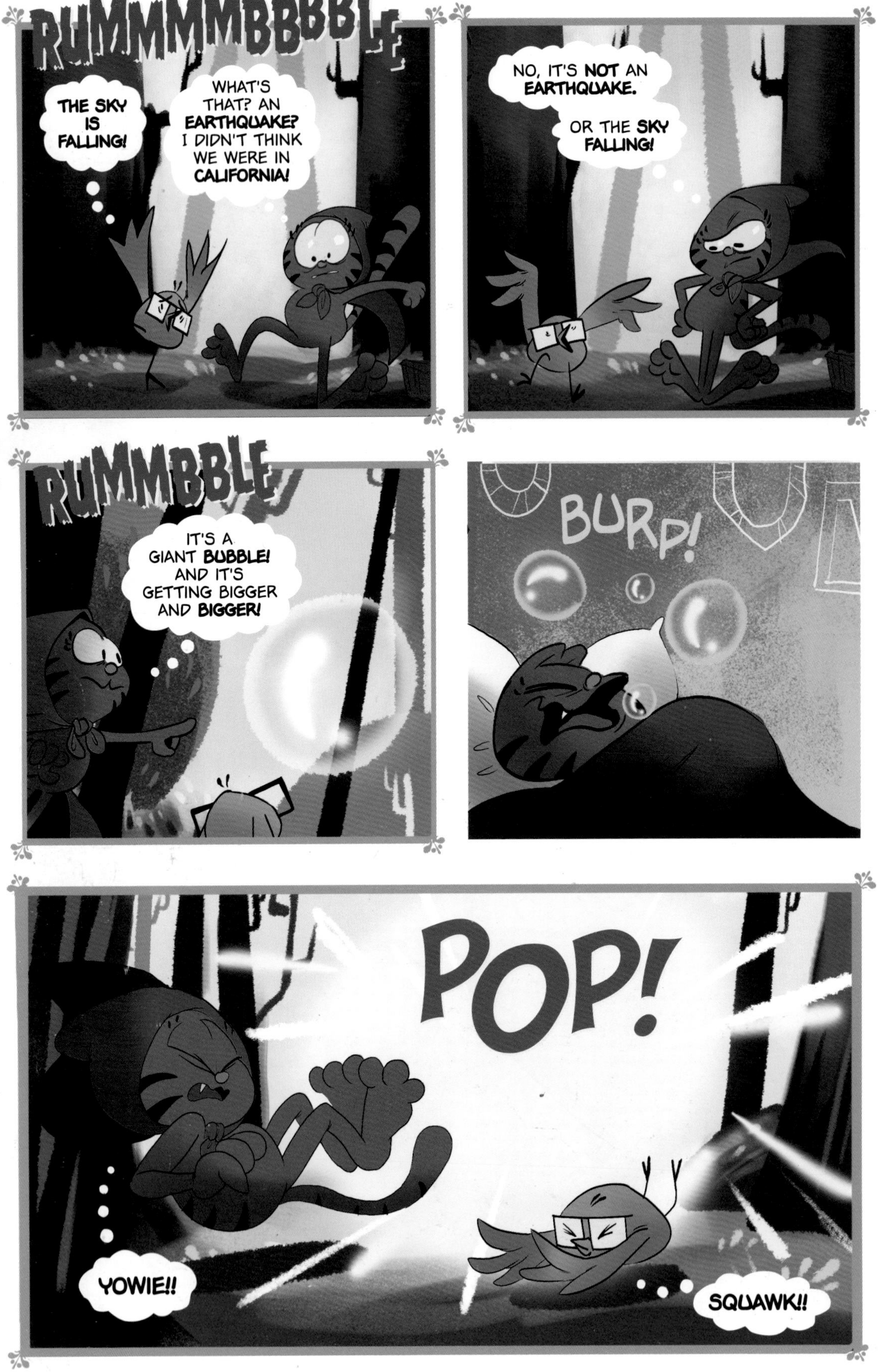
RUMMMMMBBBBBLE
THE SKY IS FALLING!
WHAT'S THAT? AN EARTHQUAKE? I DIDN'T THINK WE WERE IN CALIFORNIA!
NO, IT'S NOT AN EARTHQUAKE.
OR THE SKY FALLING!
RUMMBBLE
IT'S A GIANT BUBBLE! AND IT'S GETTING BIGGER AND BIGGER!
BURP!
POP!
YOWIE!!
SQUAWK!!

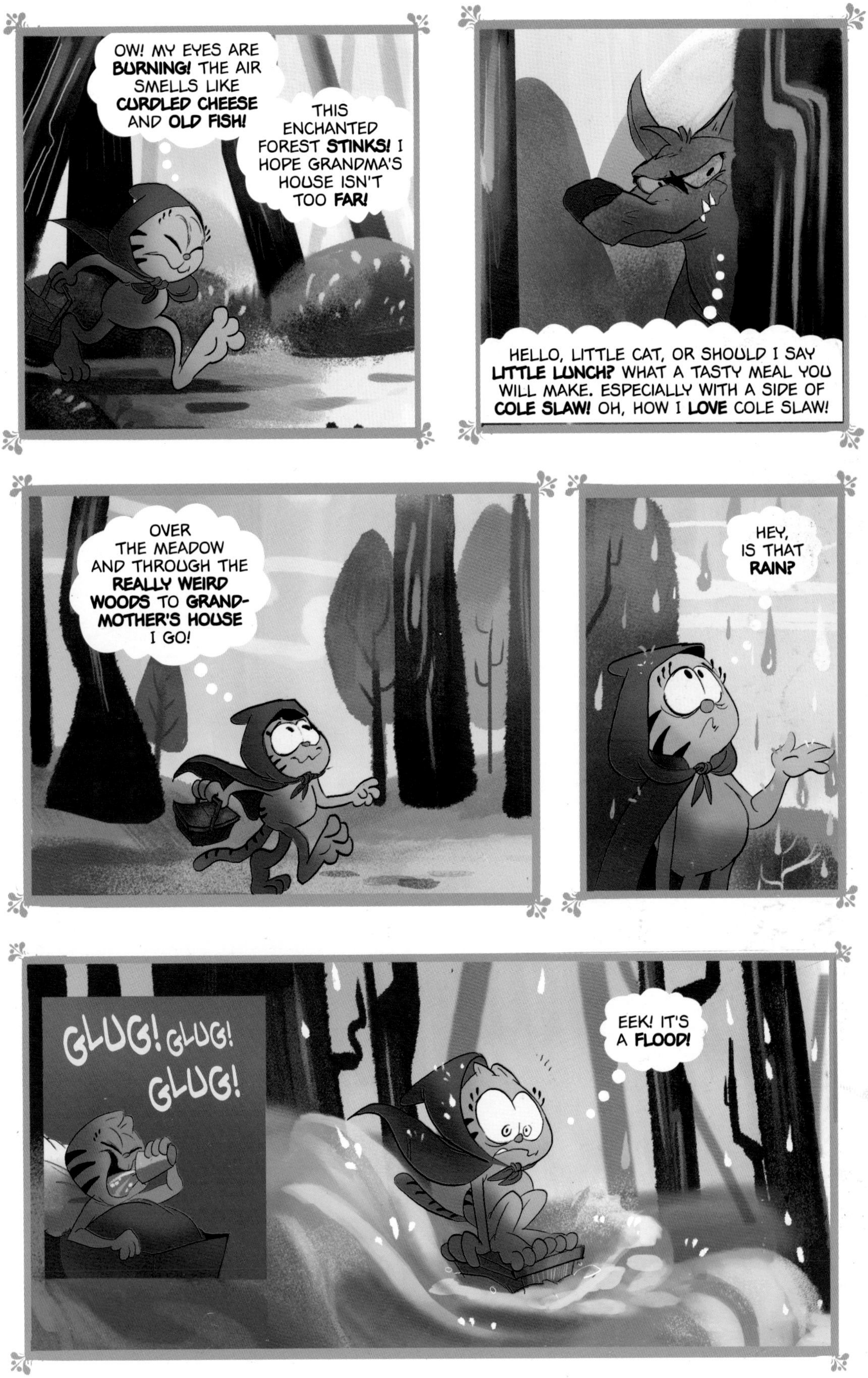

OW! MY EYES ARE **BURNING!** THE AIR SMELLS LIKE **CURDLED CHEESE** AND **OLD FISH!**
THIS ENCHANTED FOREST **STINKS!** I HOPE GRANDMA'S HOUSE ISN'T TOO **FAR!**
HELLO, LITTLE CAT, OR SHOULD I SAY **LITTLE LUNCH?** WHAT A TASTY MEAL YOU WILL MAKE. ESPECIALLY WITH A SIDE OF **COLE SLAW!** OH, HOW I **LOVE** COLE SLAW!
OVER THE MEADOW AND THROUGH THE **REALLY WEIRD WOODS** TO **GRAND-MOTHER'S HOUSE** I GO!
HEY, IS THAT **RAIN?**
GLUG! GLUG! GLUG!
EEK! IT'S A **FLOOD!**

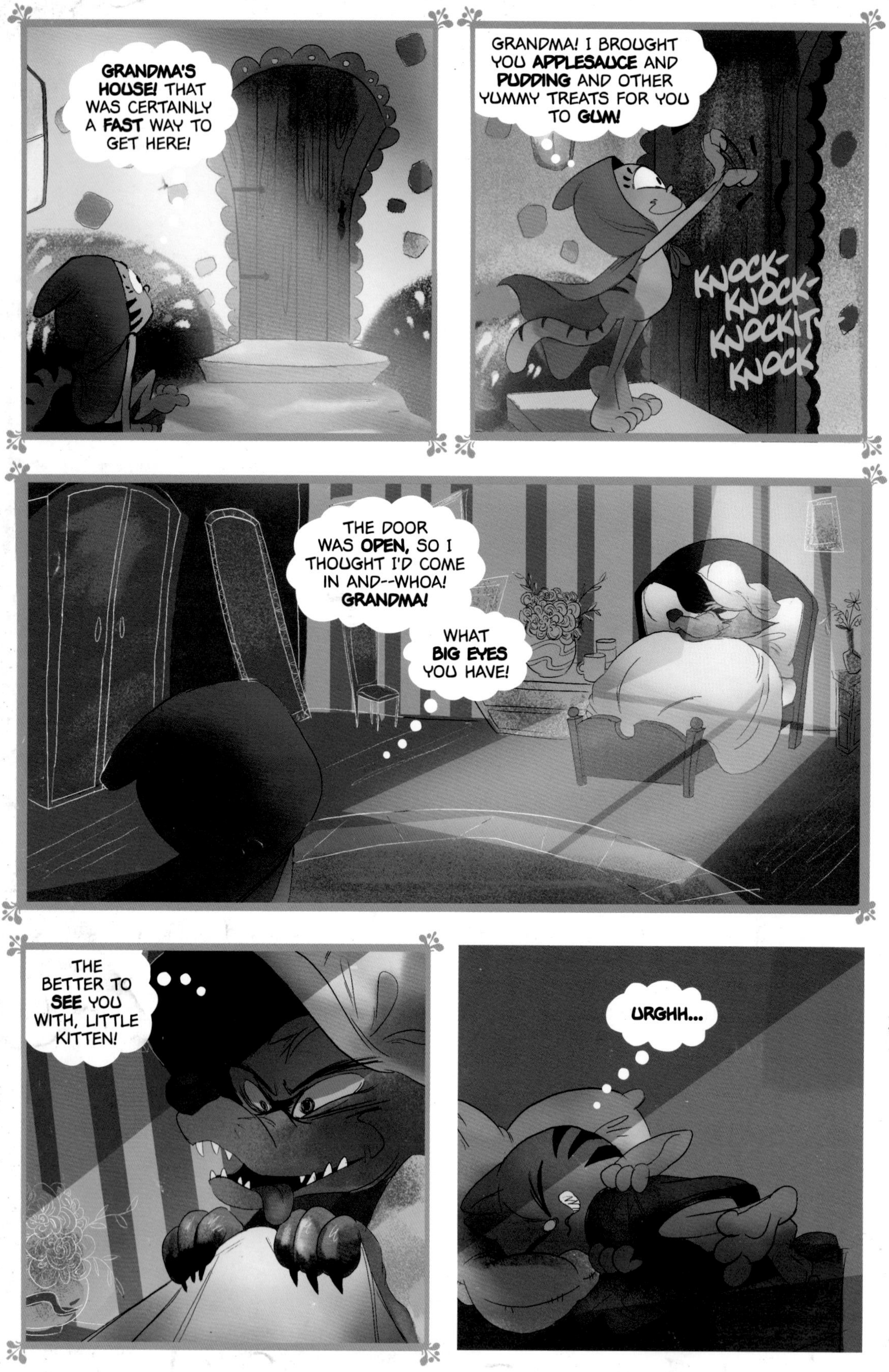

GRANDMA'S HOUSE! THAT WAS CERTAINLY A FAST WAY TO GET HERE!
GRANDMA! I BROUGHT YOU APPLESAUCE AND PUDDING AND OTHER YUMMY TREATS FOR YOU TO GUM!
KNOCK-KNOCK-KNOCKITY-KNOCK
THE DOOR WAS OPEN, SO I THOUGHT I'D COME IN AND--WHOA! GRANDMA!
WHAT BIG EYES YOU HAVE!
THE BETTER TO SEE YOU WITH, LITTLE KITTEN!
URGHH...

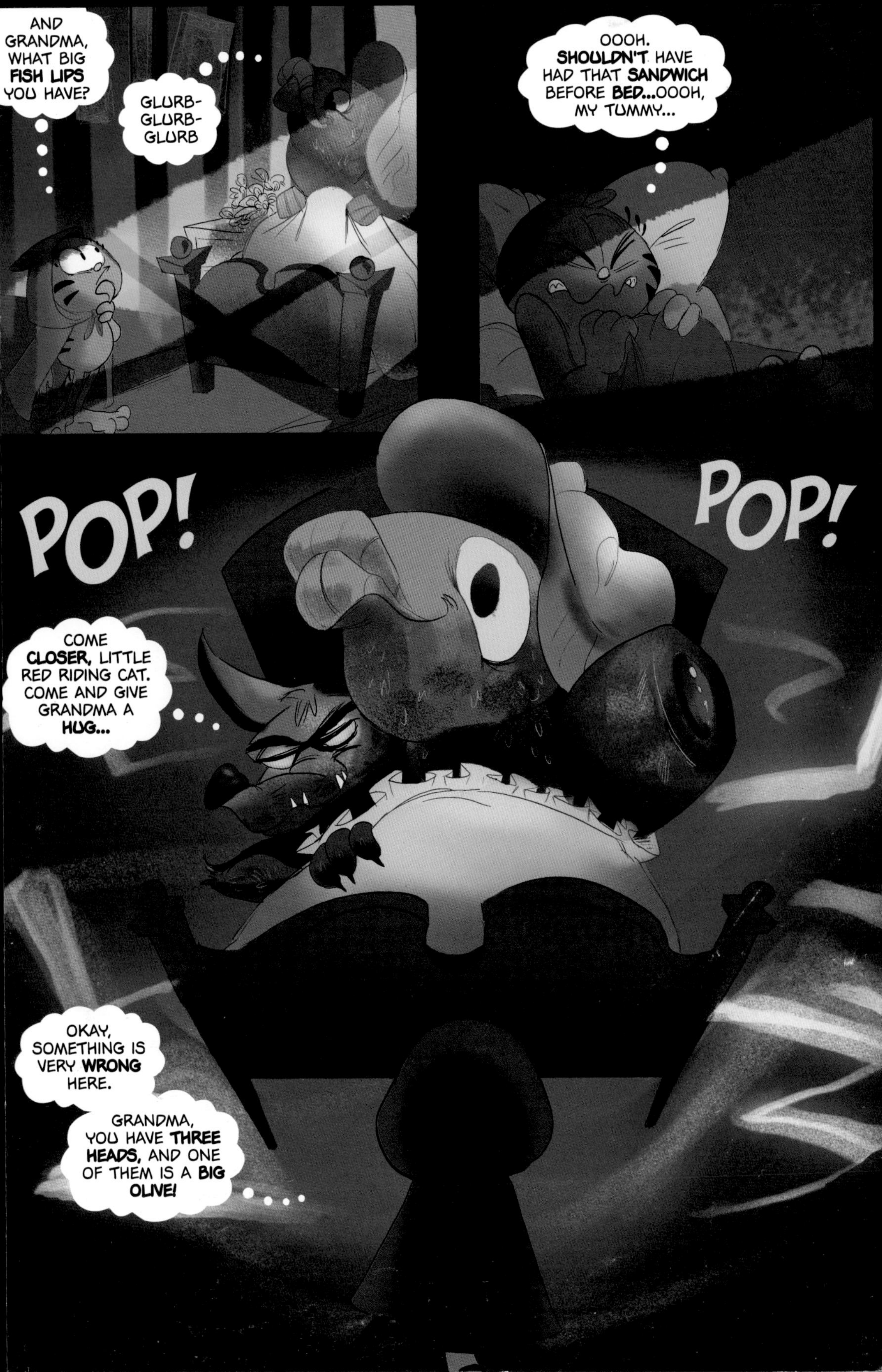
AND GRANDMA, WHAT BIG FISH LIPS YOU HAVE?
GLURB-GLURB-GLURB
OOOH. SHOULDN'T HAVE HAD THAT SANDWICH BEFORE BED...OOOH, MY TUMMY...
POP!
POP!
COME CLOSER, LITTLE RED RIDING CAT. COME AND GIVE GRANDMA A HUG...
OKAY, SOMETHING IS VERY WRONG HERE.
GRANDMA, YOU HAVE THREE HEADS, AND ONE OF THEM IS A BIG OLIVE!

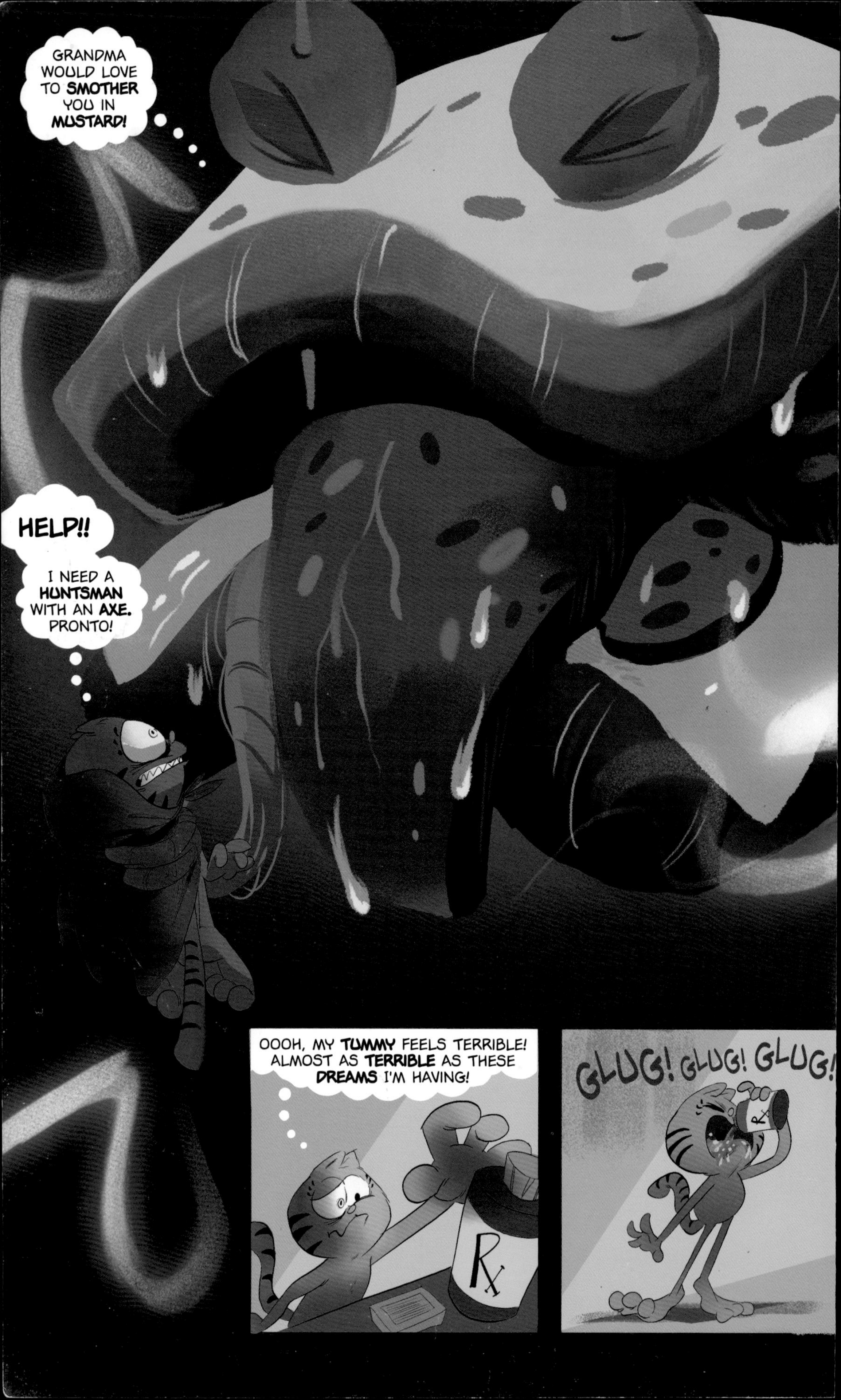
GRANDMA WOULD LOVE TO SMOTHER YOU IN MUSTARD!
HELP!!
I NEED A HUNTSMAN WITH AN AXE. PRONTO!
OOOH, MY TUMMY FEELS TERRIBLE! ALMOST AS TERRIBLE AS THESE DREAMS I'M HAVING!
GLUG! GLUG! GLUG!

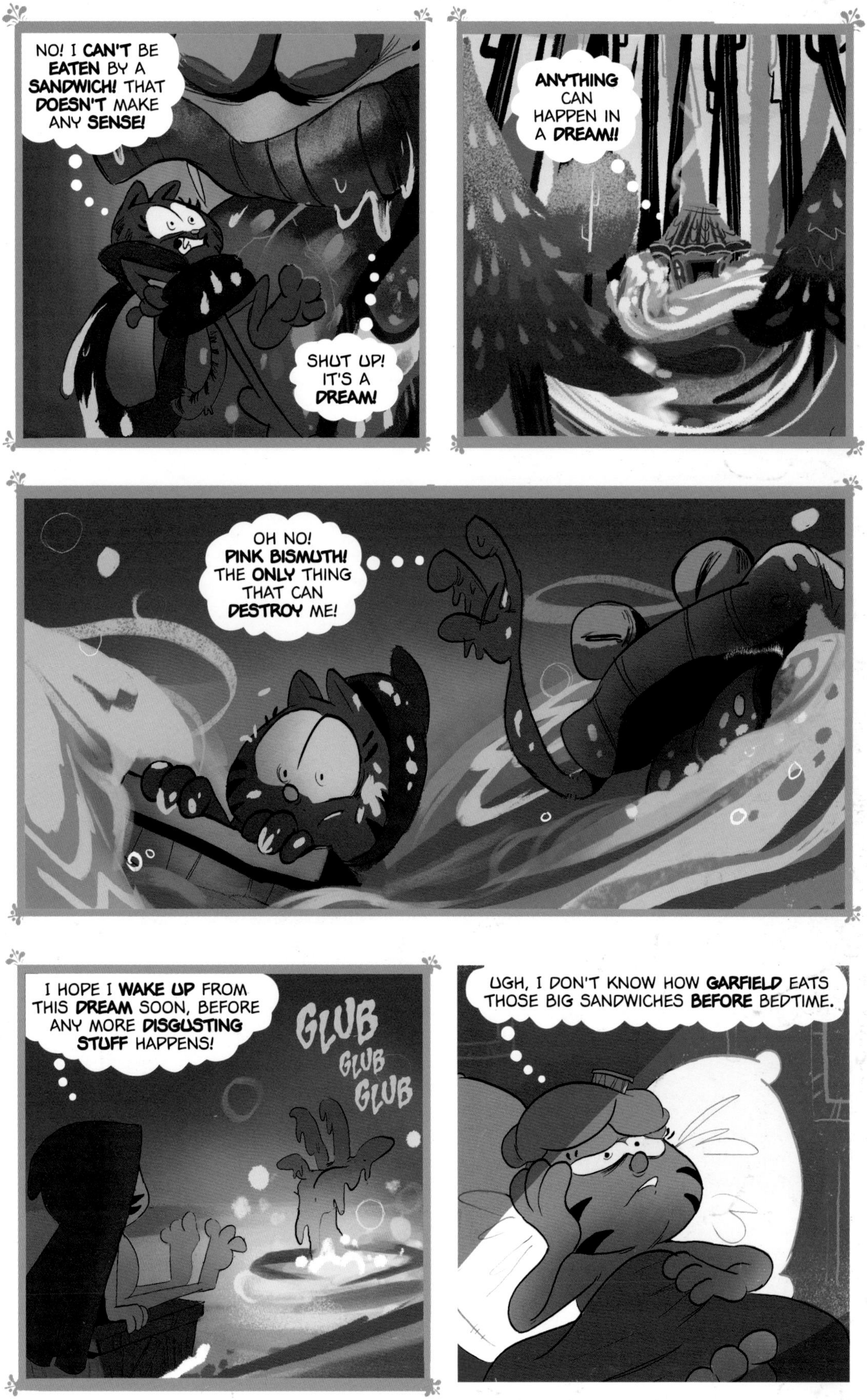
NO! I CAN'T BE EATEN BY A SANDWICH! THAT DOESN'T MAKE ANY SENSE!
SHUT UP! IT'S A DREAM!
ANYTHING CAN HAPPEN IN A DREAM!!
OH NO! PINK BISMUTH! THE ONLY THING THAT CAN DESTROY ME!
I HOPE I WAKE UP FROM THIS DREAM SOON, BEFORE ANY MORE DISGUSTING STUFF HAPPENS!
GLUB
GLUB
GLUB
UGH, I DON'T KNOW HOW GARFIELD EATS THOSE BIG SANDWICHES BEFORE BEDTIME.

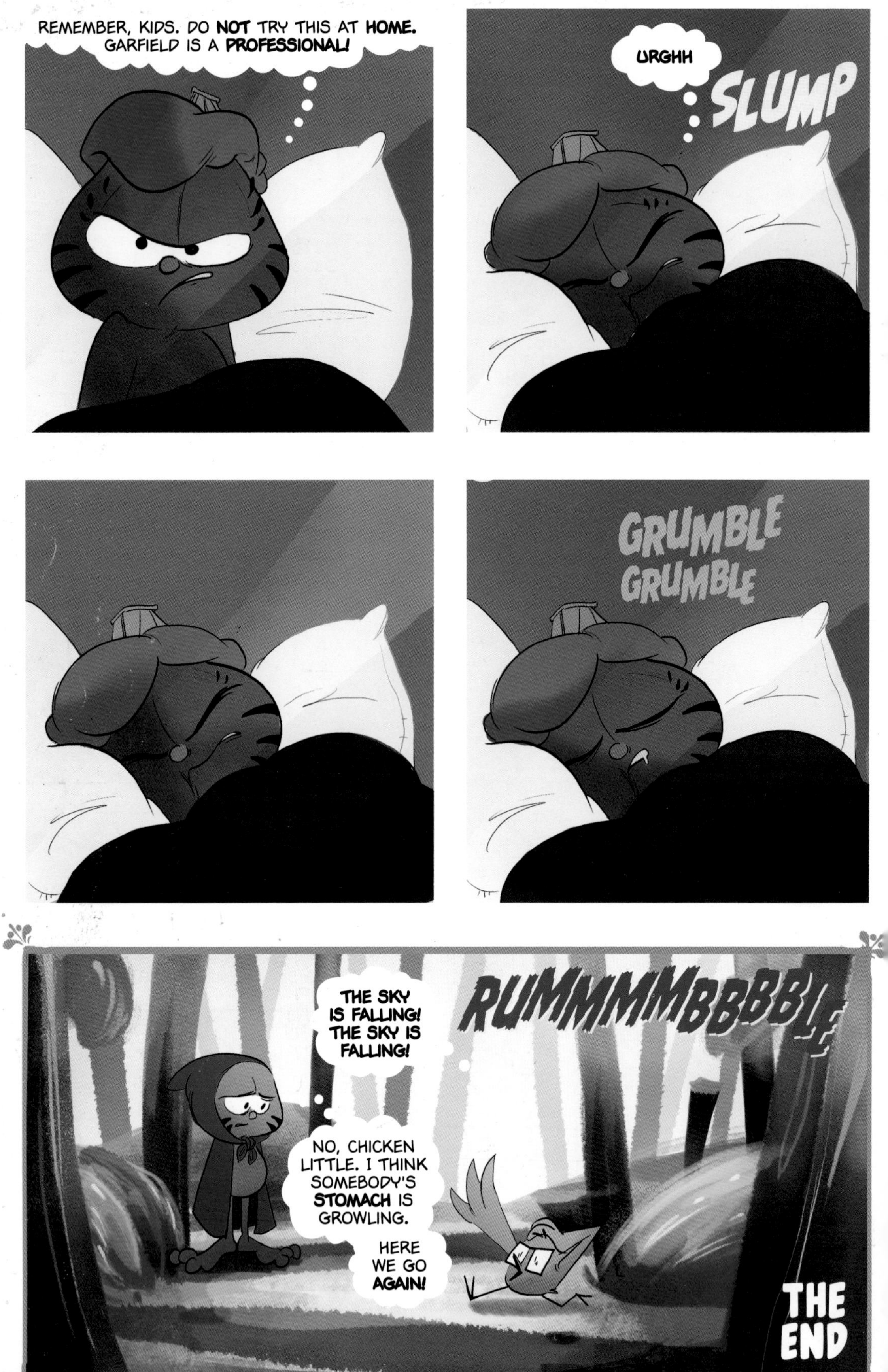
REMEMBER, KIDS. DO NOT TRY THIS AT HOME. GARFIELD IS A PROFESSIONAL!
URGHH
SLUMP
GRUMBLE GRUMBLE
THE SKY IS FALLING! THE SKY IS FALLING!
RUMMMMMBBBBLE
NO, CHICKEN LITTLE. I THINK SOMEBODY'S STOMACH IS GROWLING.
HERE WE GO AGAIN!
THE END

Garfield Sunday Classics

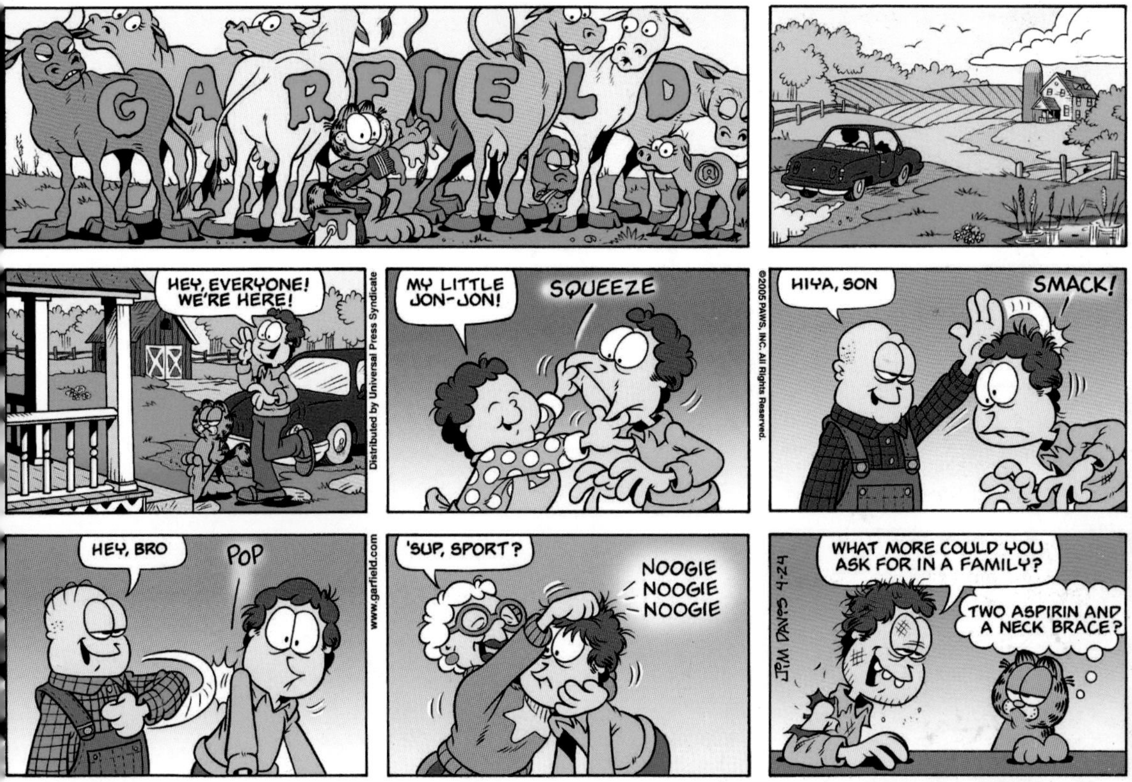

HEY, EVERYONE! WE'RE HERE!
Distributed by Universal Press Syndicate
MY LITTLE JON-JON!
SQUEEZE
©2005 PAWS, INC. All Rights Reserved.
HIYA, SON
SMACK!
HEY, BRO
POP
www.garfield.com
'SUP, SPORT?
NOOGIE NOOGIE NOOGIE
WHAT MORE COULD YOU ASK FOR IN A FAMILY?
TWO ASPIRIN AND A NECK BRACE?
JPM DAVPS 4-24

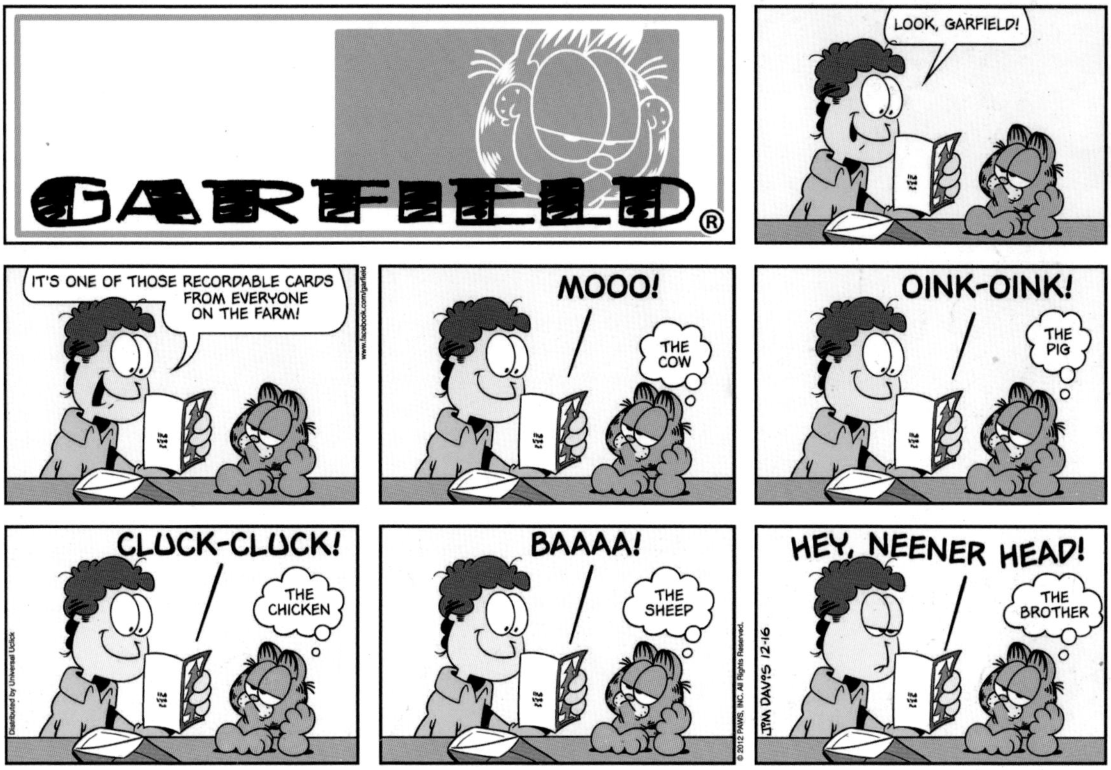

GARFIELD®
LOOK, GARFIELD!
IT'S ONE OF THOSE RECORDABLE CARDS FROM EVERYONE ON THE FARM!
www.facebook.com/garfield
MOOO!
THE COW
OINK-OINK!
THE PIG
CLUCK-CLUCK!
THE CHICKEN
Distributed by Universal Uclick
BAAAA!
THE SHEEP
© 2012 PAWS, INC. All Rights Reserved.
JPM DAVPS 12-16
HEY, NEENER HEAD!
THE BROTHER

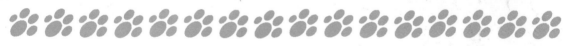

CHAPTER 4

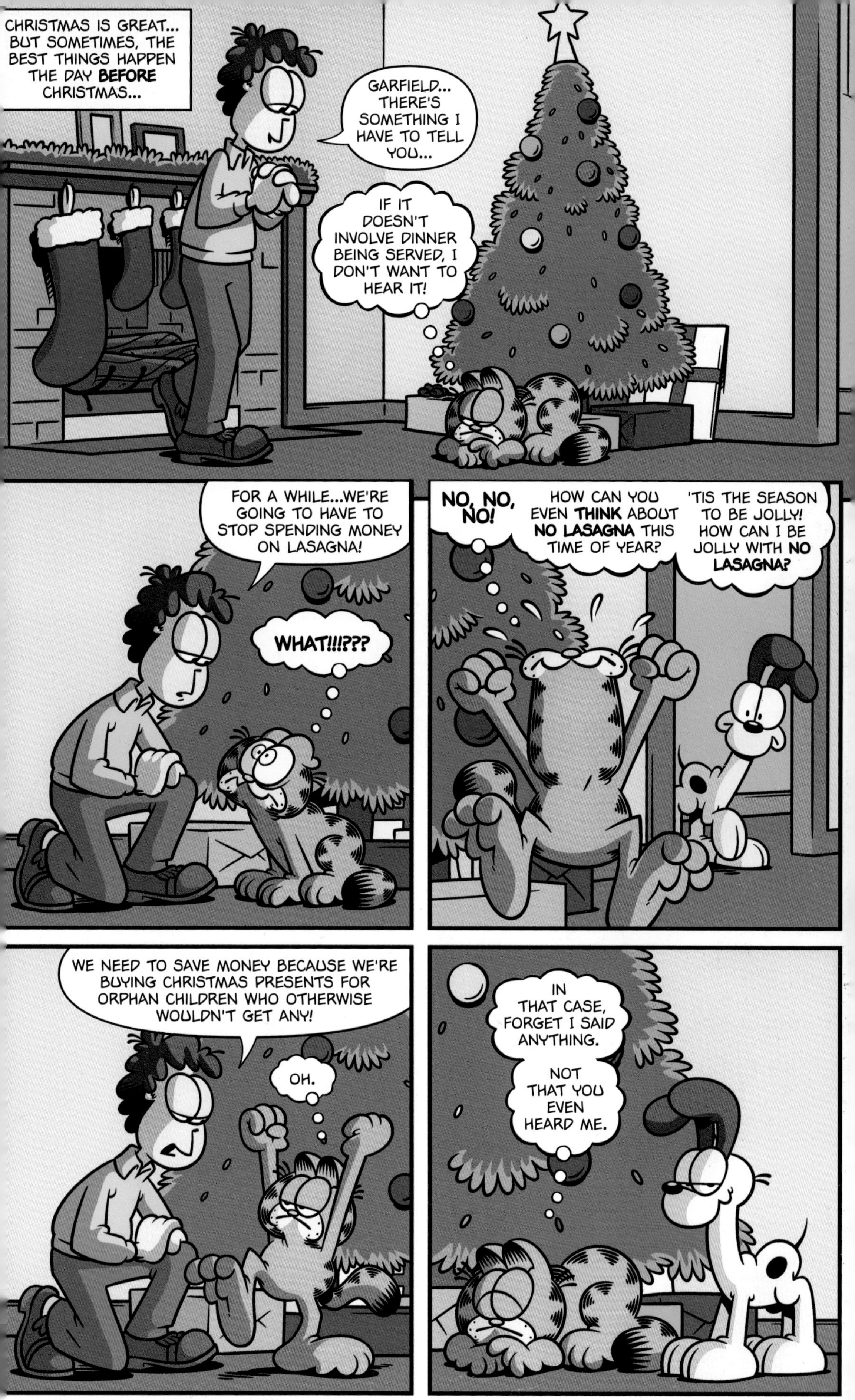

CHRISTMAS IS GREAT... BUT SOMETIMES, THE BEST THINGS HAPPEN THE DAY **BEFORE** CHRISTMAS...
GARFIELD... THERE'S SOMETHING I HAVE TO TELL YOU...
IF IT DOESN'T INVOLVE DINNER BEING SERVED, I DON'T WANT TO HEAR IT!
FOR A WHILE...WE'RE GOING TO HAVE TO STOP SPENDING MONEY ON LASAGNA!
WHAT!!!???
NO, NO, NO!
HOW CAN YOU EVEN **THINK** ABOUT **NO LASAGNA** THIS TIME OF YEAR?
'TIS THE SEASON TO BE JOLLY! HOW CAN I BE JOLLY WITH **NO LASAGNA?**
WE NEED TO SAVE MONEY BECAUSE WE'RE BUYING CHRISTMAS PRESENTS FOR ORPHAN CHILDREN WHO OTHERWISE WOULDN'T GET ANY!
OH.
IN THAT CASE, FORGET I SAID ANYTHING.
NOT THAT YOU EVEN HEARD ME.

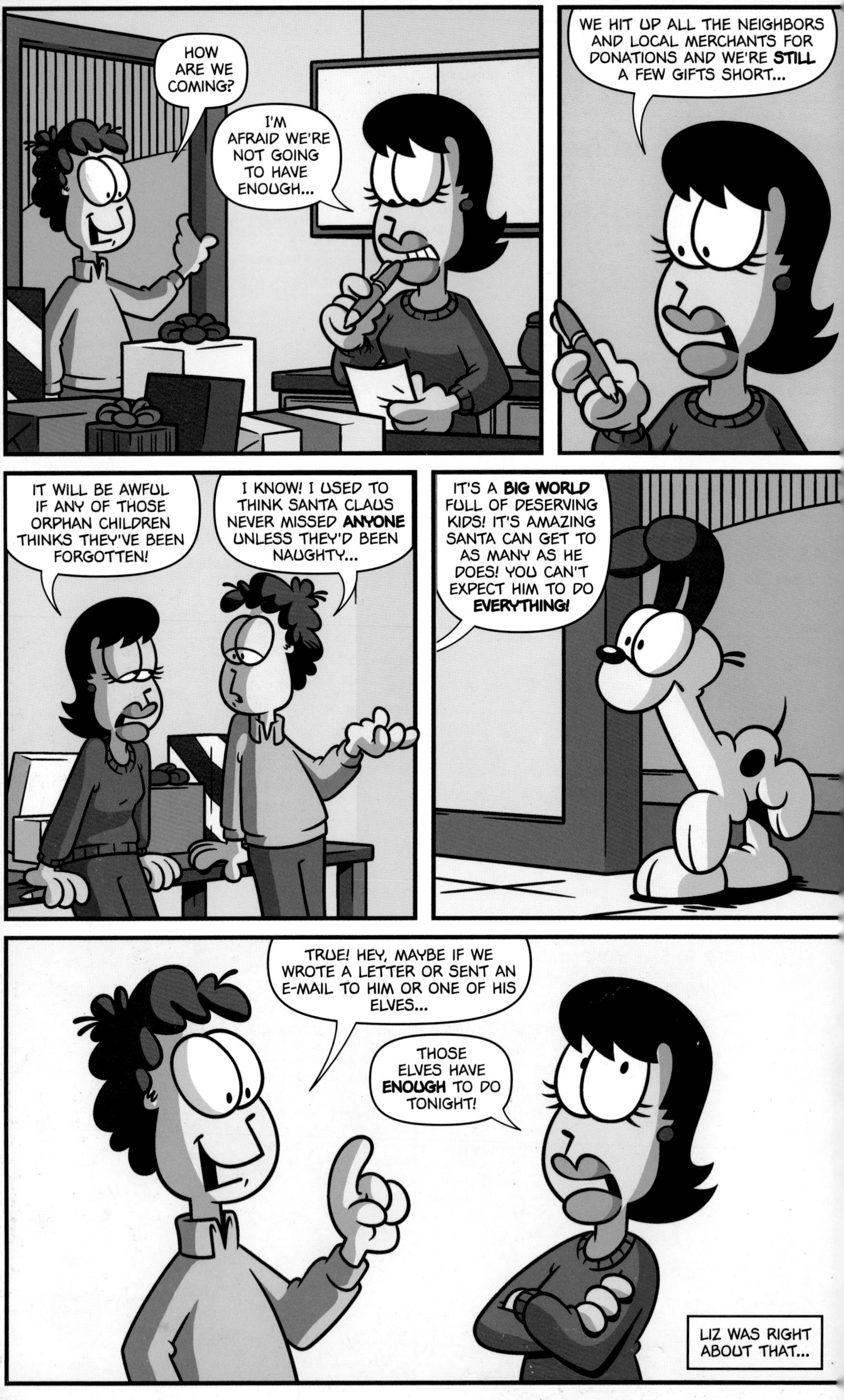
HOW ARE WE COMING?
I'M AFRAID WE'RE NOT GOING TO HAVE ENOUGH...
WE HIT UP ALL THE NEIGHBORS AND LOCAL MERCHANTS FOR DONATIONS AND WE'RE STILL A FEW GIFTS SHORT...
IT WILL BE AWFUL IF ANY OF THOSE ORPHAN CHILDREN THINKS THEY'VE BEEN FORGOTTEN!
I KNOW! I USED TO THINK SANTA CLAUS NEVER MISSED ANYONE UNLESS THEY'D BEEN NAUGHTY...
IT'S A BIG WORLD FULL OF DESERVING KIDS! IT'S AMAZING SANTA CAN GET TO AS MANY AS HE DOES! YOU CAN'T EXPECT HIM TO DO EVERYTHING!
TRUE! HEY, MAYBE IF WE WROTE A LETTER OR SENT AN E-MAIL TO HIM OR ONE OF HIS ELVES...
THOSE ELVES HAVE ENOUGH TO DO TONIGHT!
LIZ WAS RIGHT ABOUT THAT...

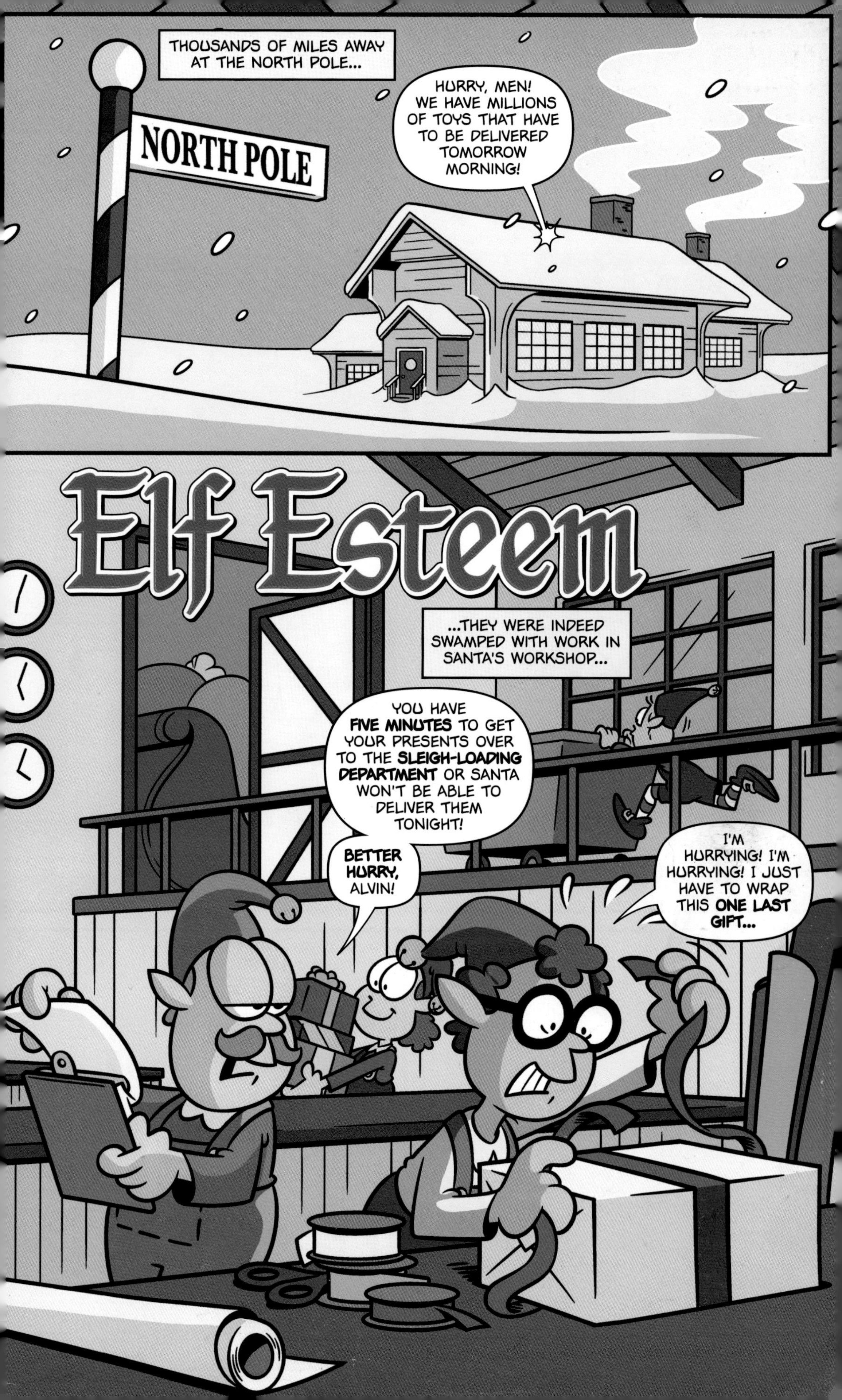
THOUSANDS OF MILES AWAY AT THE NORTH POLE...
NORTH POLE
HURRY, MEN! WE HAVE MILLIONS OF TOYS THAT HAVE TO BE DELIVERED TOMORROW MORNING!
Elf Esteem
...THEY WERE INDEED SWAMPED WITH WORK IN SANTA'S WORKSHOP...
YOU HAVE **FIVE MINUTES** TO GET YOUR PRESENTS OVER TO THE **SLEIGH-LOADING DEPARTMENT** OR SANTA WON'T BE ABLE TO DELIVER THEM TONIGHT!
BETTER HURRY, ALVIN!
I'M HURRYING! I'M HURRYING! I JUST HAVE TO WRAP THIS **ONE LAST GIFT...**

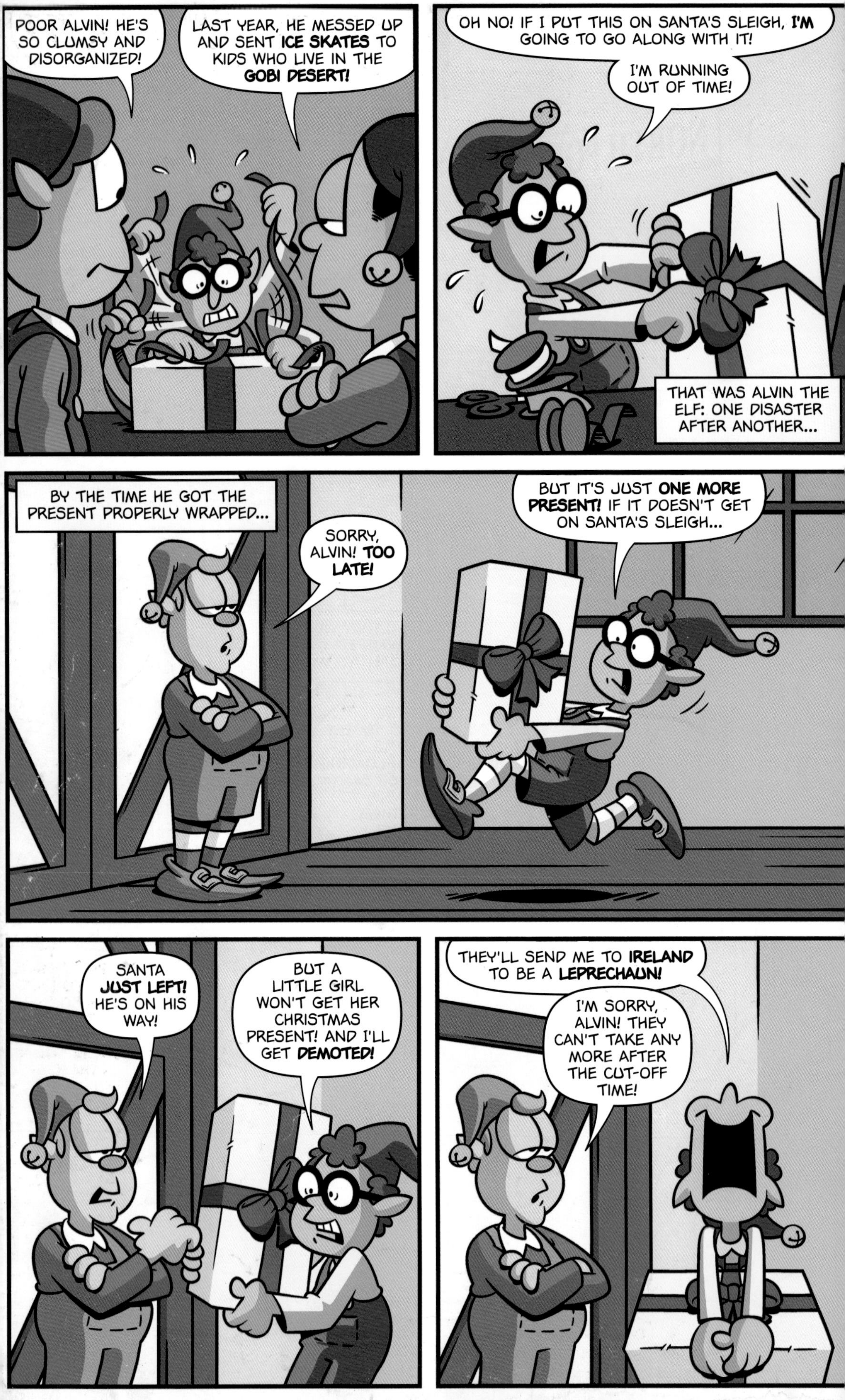
POOR ALVIN! HE'S SO CLUMSY AND DISORGANIZED!
LAST YEAR, HE MESSED UP AND SENT **ICE SKATES** TO KIDS WHO LIVE IN THE **GOBI DESERT!**
OH NO! IF I PUT THIS ON SANTA'S SLEIGH, **I'M** GOING TO GO ALONG WITH IT!
I'M RUNNING OUT OF TIME!
THAT WAS ALVIN THE ELF: ONE DISASTER AFTER ANOTHER...
BY THE TIME HE GOT THE PRESENT PROPERLY WRAPPED...
SORRY, ALVIN! **TOO LATE!**
BUT IT'S JUST **ONE MORE PRESENT!** IF IT DOESN'T GET ON SANTA'S SLEIGH...
SANTA **JUST LEFT!** HE'S ON HIS WAY!
BUT A LITTLE GIRL WON'T GET HER CHRISTMAS PRESENT! AND I'LL GET **DEMOTED!**
THEY'LL SEND ME TO **IRELAND** TO BE A **LEPRECHAUN!**
I'M SORRY, ALVIN! THEY CAN'T TAKE ANY MORE AFTER THE CUT-OFF TIME!

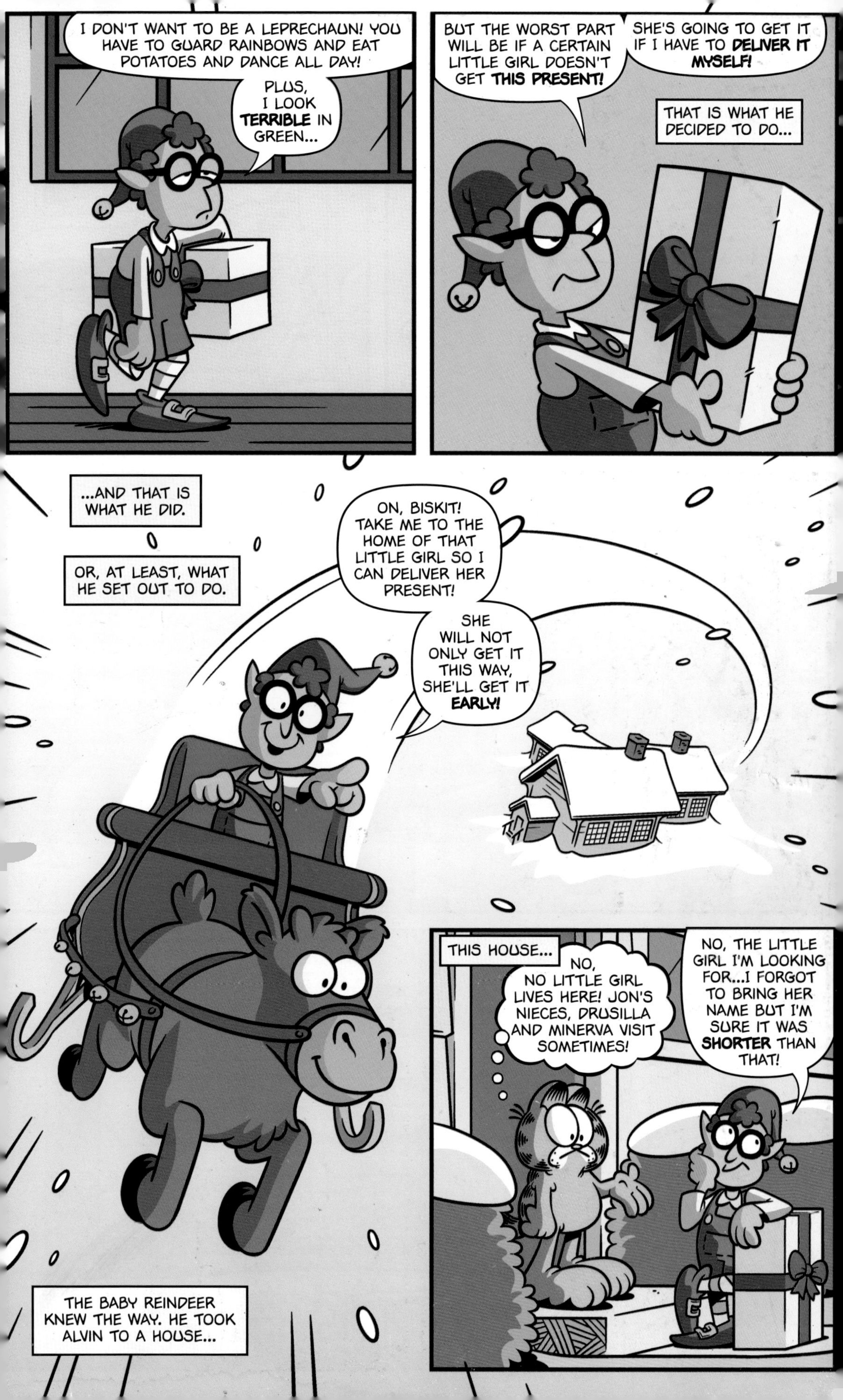
I DON'T WANT TO BE A LEPRECHAUN! YOU HAVE TO GUARD RAINBOWS AND EAT POTATOES AND DANCE ALL DAY!
PLUS, I LOOK **TERRIBLE** IN GREEN...
BUT THE WORST PART WILL BE IF A CERTAIN LITTLE GIRL DOESN'T GET **THIS PRESENT!**
SHE'S GOING TO GET IT IF I HAVE TO **DELIVER IT MYSELF!**
THAT IS WHAT HE DECIDED TO DO...
...AND THAT IS WHAT HE DID.
OR, AT LEAST, WHAT HE SET OUT TO DO.
ON, BISKIT! TAKE ME TO THE HOME OF THAT LITTLE GIRL SO I CAN DELIVER HER PRESENT!
SHE WILL NOT ONLY GET IT THIS WAY, SHE'LL GET IT **EARLY!**
THE BABY REINDEER KNEW THE WAY. HE TOOK ALVIN TO A HOUSE...
THIS HOUSE...
NO, NO LITTLE GIRL LIVES HERE! JON'S NIECES, DRUSILLA AND MINERVA VISIT SOMETIMES!
NO, THE LITTLE GIRL I'M LOOKING FOR...I FORGOT TO BRING HER NAME BUT I'M SURE IT WAS **SHORTER** THAN THAT!

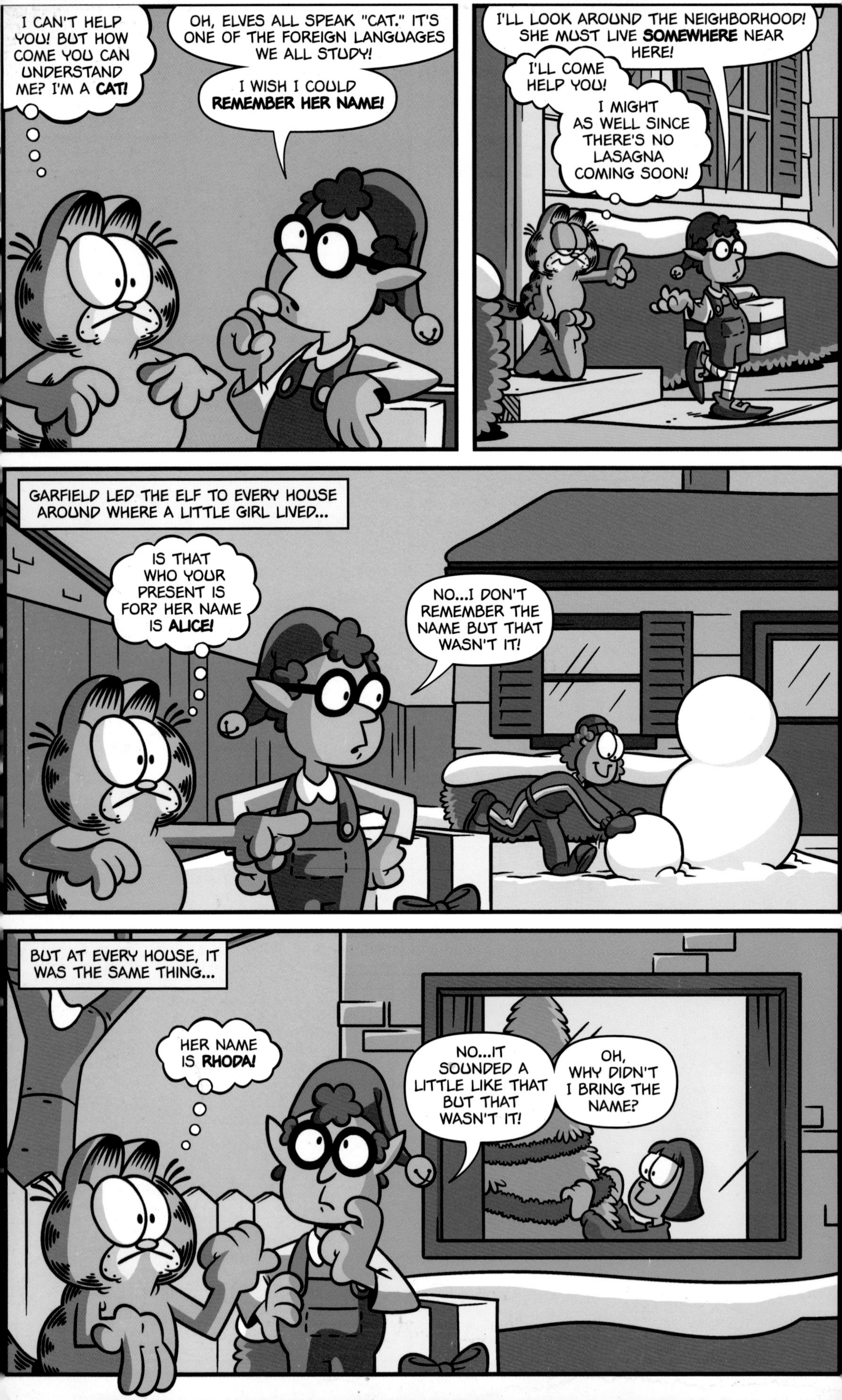
I CAN'T HELP YOU! BUT HOW COME YOU CAN UNDERSTAND ME? I'M A **CAT!**
OH, ELVES ALL SPEAK "CAT." IT'S ONE OF THE FOREIGN LANGUAGES WE ALL STUDY!
I WISH I COULD **REMEMBER HER NAME!**
I'LL LOOK AROUND THE NEIGHBORHOOD! SHE MUST LIVE **SOMEWHERE** NEAR HERE!
I'LL COME HELP YOU!
I MIGHT AS WELL SINCE THERE'S NO LASAGNA COMING SOON!
GARFIELD LED THE ELF TO EVERY HOUSE AROUND WHERE A LITTLE GIRL LIVED...
IS THAT WHO YOUR PRESENT IS FOR? HER NAME IS **ALICE!**
NO...I DON'T REMEMBER THE NAME BUT THAT WASN'T IT!
BUT AT EVERY HOUSE, IT WAS THE SAME THING...
HER NAME IS **RHODA!**
NO...IT SOUNDED A LITTLE LIKE THAT BUT THAT WASN'T IT!
OH, WHY DIDN'T I BRING THE NAME?

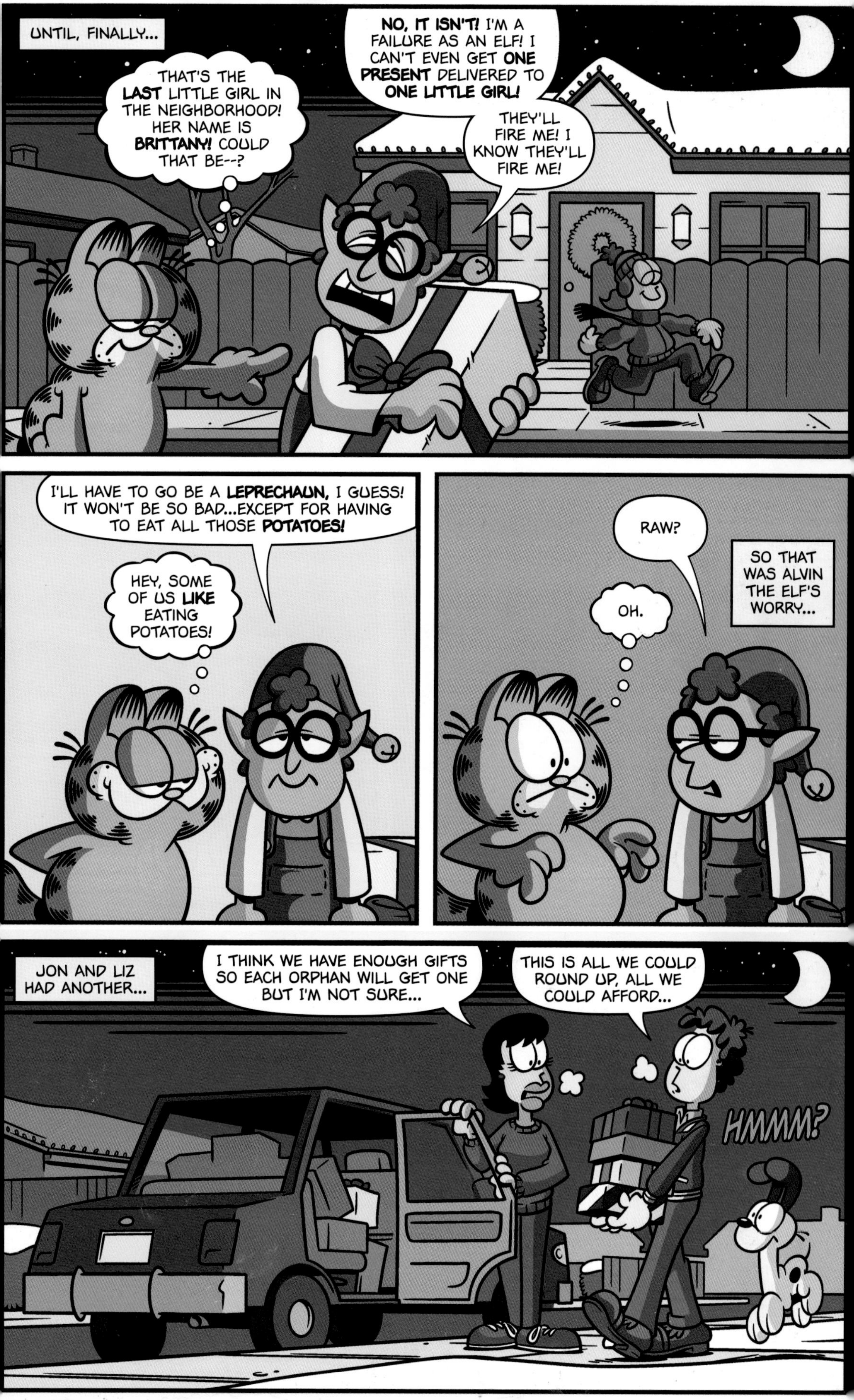

UNTIL, FINALLY...
THAT'S THE LAST LITTLE GIRL IN THE NEIGHBORHOOD! HER NAME IS BRITTANY! COULD THAT BE--?
NO, IT ISN'T! I'M A FAILURE AS AN ELF! I CAN'T EVEN GET ONE PRESENT DELIVERED TO ONE LITTLE GIRL!
THEY'LL FIRE ME! I KNOW THEY'LL FIRE ME!
I'LL HAVE TO GO BE A LEPRECHAUN, I GUESS! IT WON'T BE SO BAD...EXCEPT FOR HAVING TO EAT ALL THOSE POTATOES!
HEY, SOME OF US LIKE EATING POTATOES!
RAW?
SO THAT WAS ALVIN THE ELF'S WORRY...
OH.
JON AND LIZ HAD ANOTHER...
I THINK WE HAVE ENOUGH GIFTS SO EACH ORPHAN WILL GET ONE BUT I'M NOT SURE...
THIS IS ALL WE COULD ROUND UP, ALL WE COULD AFFORD...
HMMM?

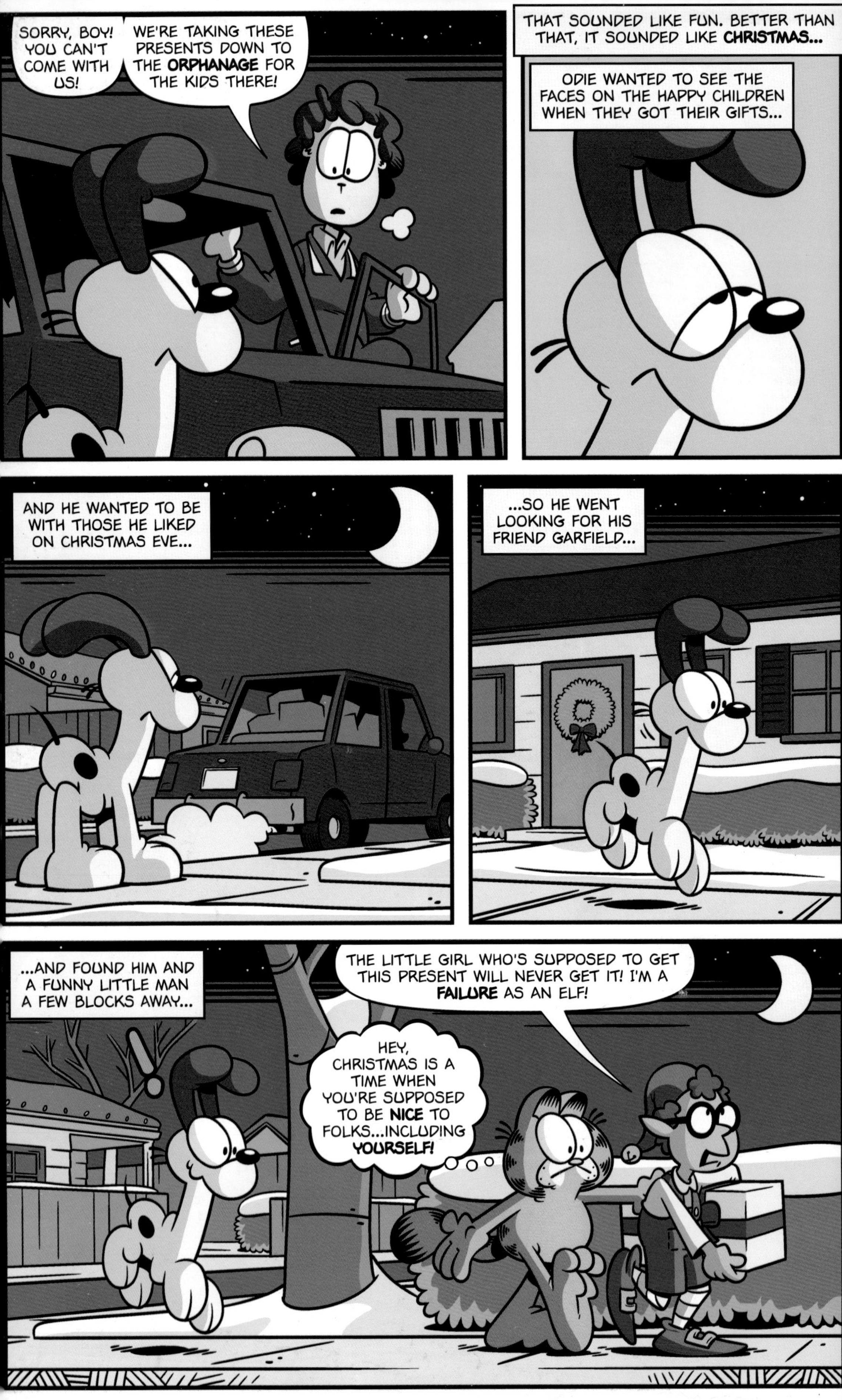
SORRY, BOY! YOU CAN'T COME WITH US!
WE'RE TAKING THESE PRESENTS DOWN TO THE **ORPHANAGE** FOR THE KIDS THERE!
THAT SOUNDED LIKE FUN. BETTER THAN THAT, IT SOUNDED LIKE **CHRISTMAS...**
ODIE WANTED TO SEE THE FACES ON THE HAPPY CHILDREN WHEN THEY GOT THEIR GIFTS...
AND HE WANTED TO BE WITH THOSE HE LIKED ON CHRISTMAS EVE...
...SO HE WENT LOOKING FOR HIS FRIEND GARFIELD...
...AND FOUND HIM AND A FUNNY LITTLE MAN A FEW BLOCKS AWAY...
THE LITTLE GIRL WHO'S SUPPOSED TO GET THIS PRESENT WILL NEVER GET IT! I'M A **FAILURE** AS AN ELF!
HEY, CHRISTMAS IS A TIME WHEN YOU'RE SUPPOSED TO BE **NICE** TO FOLKS...INCLUDING **YOURSELF!**

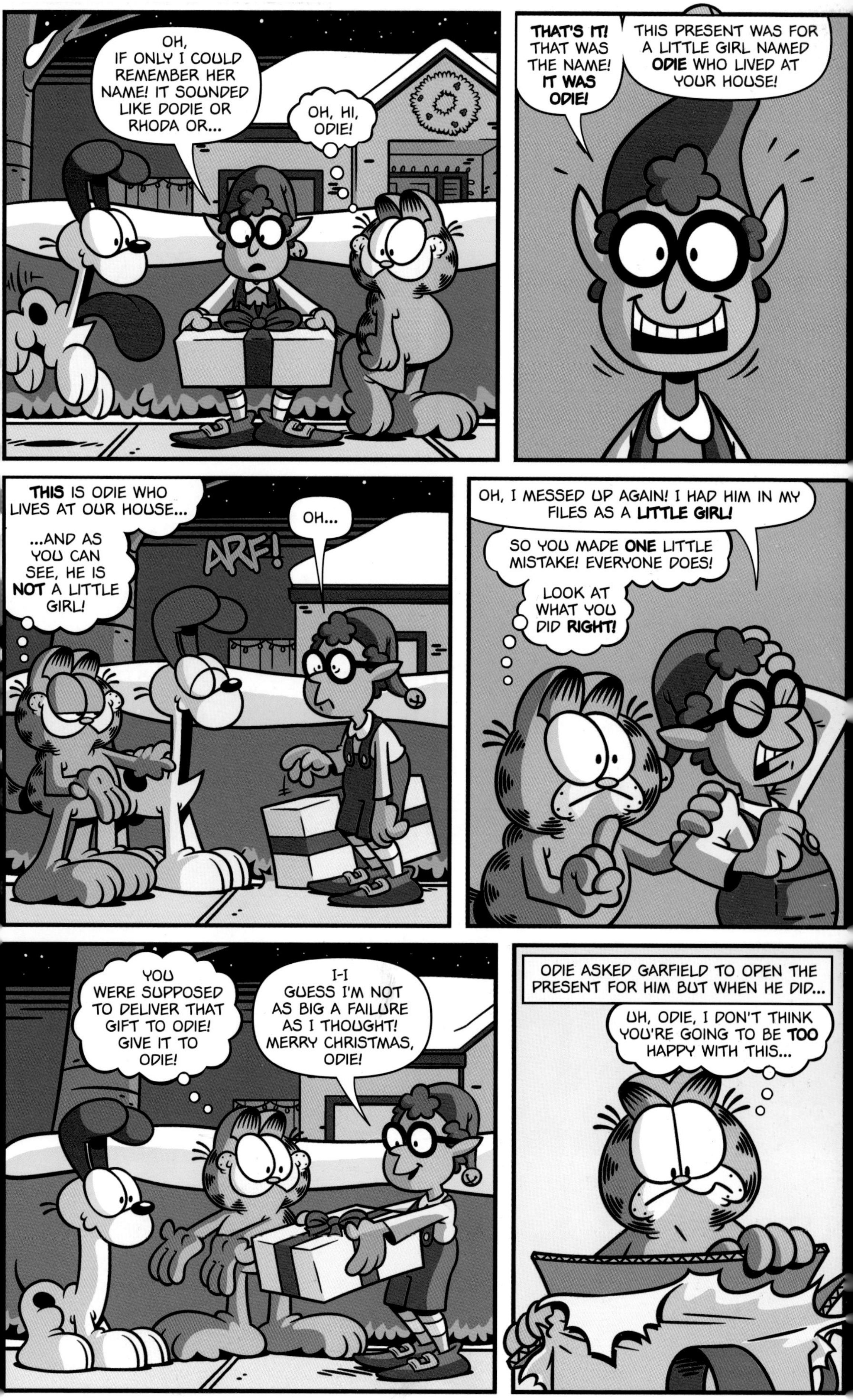

OH, IF ONLY I COULD REMEMBER HER NAME! IT SOUNDED LIKE DODIE OR RHODA OR...
OH, HI, ODIE!
THAT'S IT! THAT WAS THE NAME! IT WAS ODIE!
THIS PRESENT WAS FOR A LITTLE GIRL NAMED ODIE WHO LIVED AT YOUR HOUSE!
THIS IS ODIE WHO LIVES AT OUR HOUSE...
...AND AS YOU CAN SEE, HE IS NOT A LITTLE GIRL!
ARF!
OH...
OH, I MESSED UP AGAIN! I HAD HIM IN MY FILES AS A LITTLE GIRL!
SO YOU MADE ONE LITTLE MISTAKE! EVERYONE DOES!
LOOK AT WHAT YOU DID RIGHT!
YOU WERE SUPPOSED TO DELIVER THAT GIFT TO ODIE! GIVE IT TO ODIE!
I-I GUESS I'M NOT AS BIG A FAILURE AS I THOUGHT! MERRY CHRISTMAS, ODIE!
ODIE ASKED GARFIELD TO OPEN THE PRESENT FOR HIM BUT WHEN HE DID...
UH, ODIE, I DON'T THINK YOU'RE GOING TO BE TOO HAPPY WITH THIS...

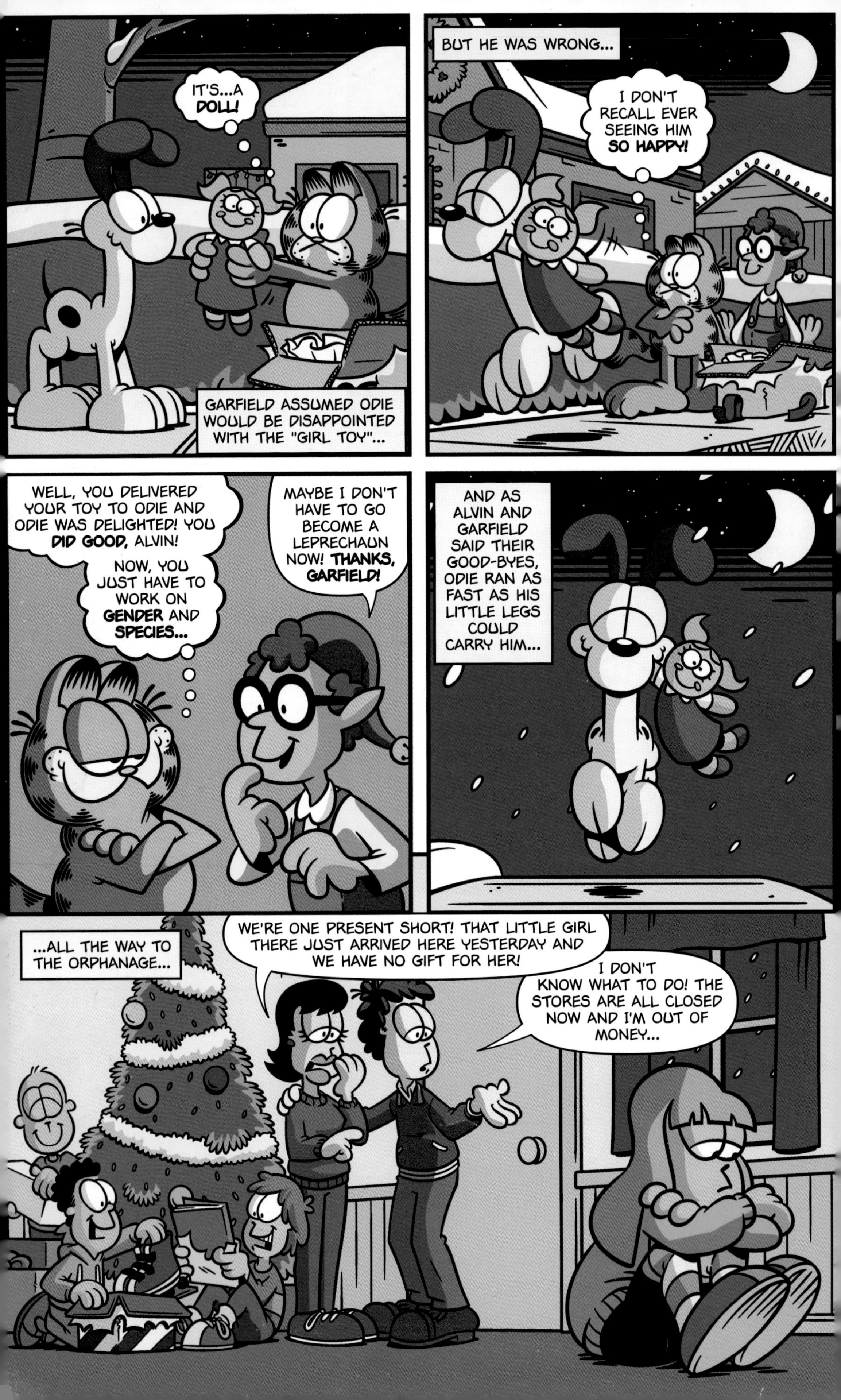
IT'S...A DOLL!
GARFIELD ASSUMED ODIE WOULD BE DISAPPOINTED WITH THE "GIRL TOY"...
BUT HE WAS WRONG...
I DON'T RECALL EVER SEEING HIM SO HAPPY!
WELL, YOU DELIVERED YOUR TOY TO ODIE AND ODIE WAS DELIGHTED! YOU DID GOOD, ALVIN!
NOW, YOU JUST HAVE TO WORK ON GENDER AND SPECIES...
MAYBE I DON'T HAVE TO GO BECOME A LEPRECHAUN NOW! THANKS, GARFIELD!
AND AS ALVIN AND GARFIELD SAID THEIR GOOD-BYES, ODIE RAN AS FAST AS HIS LITTLE LEGS COULD CARRY HIM...
...ALL THE WAY TO THE ORPHANAGE...
WE'RE ONE PRESENT SHORT! THAT LITTLE GIRL THERE JUST ARRIVED HERE YESTERDAY AND WE HAVE NO GIFT FOR HER!
I DON'T KNOW WHAT TO DO! THE STORES ARE ALL CLOSED NOW AND I'M OUT OF MONEY...

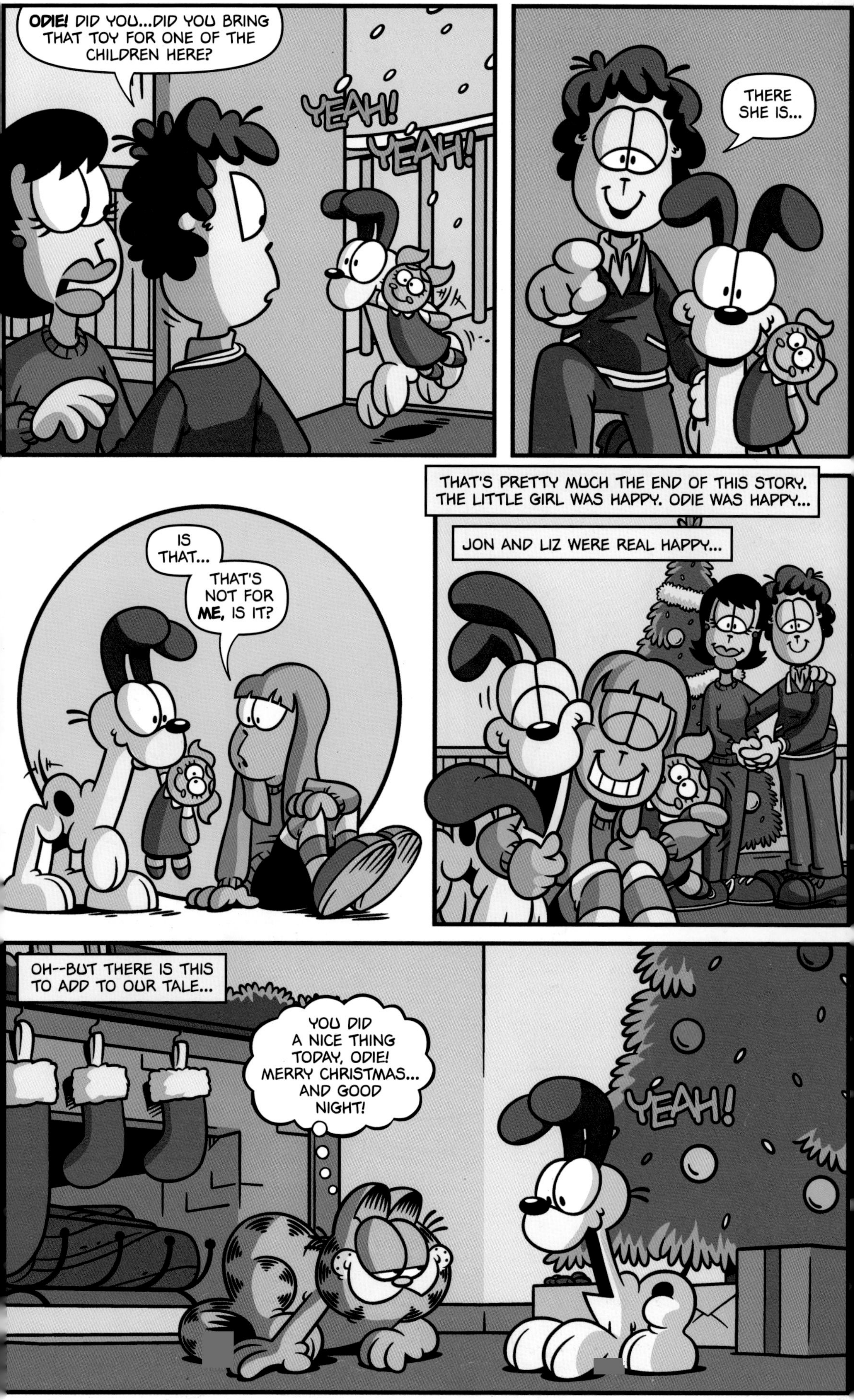

ODIE! DID YOU...DID YOU BRING THAT TOY FOR ONE OF THE CHILDREN HERE?
YEAH!
YEAH!
THERE SHE IS...
IS THAT...
THAT'S NOT FOR ME, IS IT?
THAT'S PRETTY MUCH THE END OF THIS STORY. THE LITTLE GIRL WAS HAPPY. ODIE WAS HAPPY...
JON AND LIZ WERE REAL HAPPY...
OH--BUT THERE IS THIS TO ADD TO OUR TALE...
YOU DID A NICE THING TODAY, ODIE! MERRY CHRISTMAS... AND GOOD NIGHT!
YEAH!

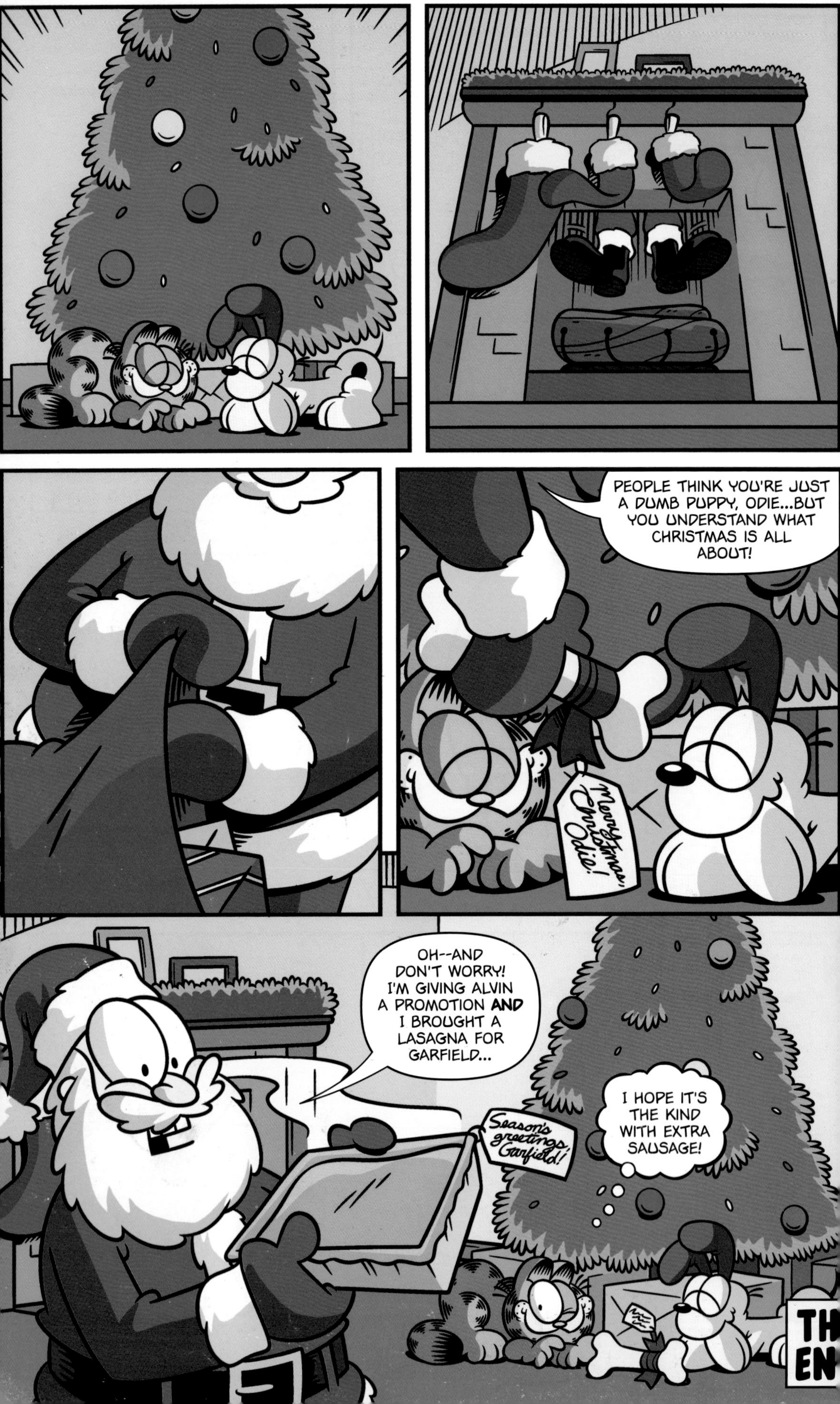
PEOPLE THINK YOU'RE JUST A DUMB PUPPY, ODIE...BUT YOU UNDERSTAND WHAT CHRISTMAS IS ALL ABOUT!
Merry Christmas, Odie!
OH--AND DON'T WORRY! I'M GIVING ALVIN A PROMOTION **AND** I BROUGHT A LASAGNA FOR GARFIELD...
Season's greetings, Garfield!
I HOPE IT'S THE KIND WITH EXTRA SAUSAGE!

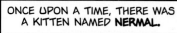

ONCE UPON A TIME, THERE WAS A KITTEN NAMED **NERMAL**.

HE WAS THE **CUTEST** KITTEN THAT **EVER LIVED**. IF YOU DON'T **BELIEVE US**, JUST **ASK** HIM.

IT'S TRUE. I **AM** THE WORLD'S CUTEST KITTEN.

I EVEN HAVE THIS **SIGNED DOCUMENT** FROM THE **INSTITUTE OF CUTENESS** TO PROVE IT.

ONE BEAUTIFUL DAY, NERMAL WAS WALKING IN THE **WOODS**.

THE WOODS? UM, I LIVE IN THE **SUBURBS**. HOW ABOUT I WALK THROUGH A **PARK** OR A **MINI-MALL**?

HE CAME UPON A SMALL COTTAGE. IT WAS THE **COTTAGE** OF THE THREE BEARS.

WHAT?

OKAY, NOW **WAIT** A MINUTE. **THREE BEARS?** SERIOUSLY?

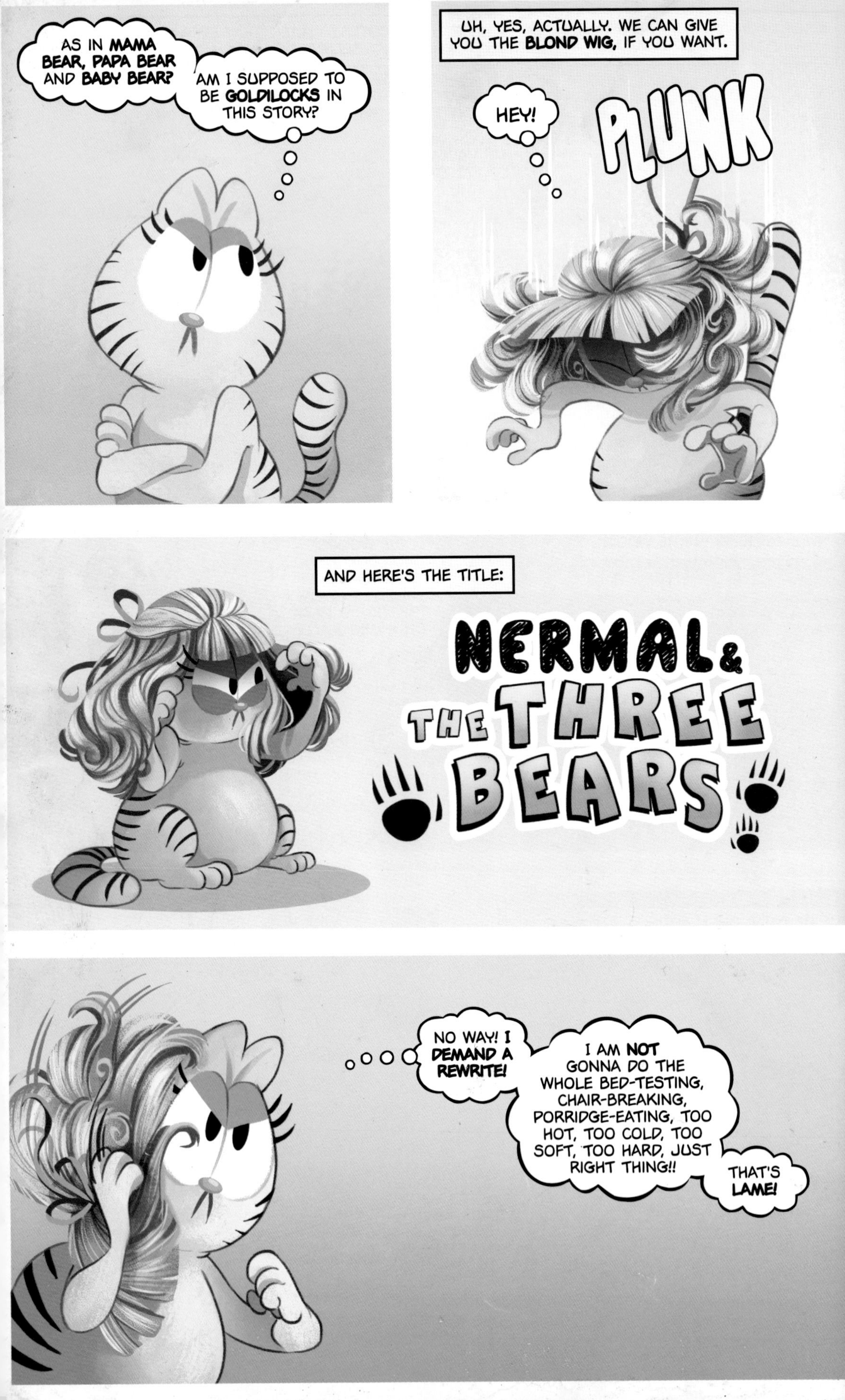

AS IN **MAMA** **BEAR, PAPA BEAR** AND **BABY BEAR?**
AM I SUPPOSED TO BE **GOLDILOCKS** IN THIS STORY?
UH, YES, ACTUALLY. WE CAN GIVE YOU THE **BLOND WIG**, IF YOU WANT.
HEY!
PLUNK
AND HERE'S THE TITLE:
NERMAL & THE THREE BEARS
NO WAY! **I DEMAND A REWRITE!**
I AM **NOT** GONNA DO THE WHOLE BED-TESTING, CHAIR-BREAKING, PORRIDGE-EATING, TOO HOT, TOO COLD, TOO SOFT, TOO HARD, JUST RIGHT THING!!
THAT'S **LAME!**

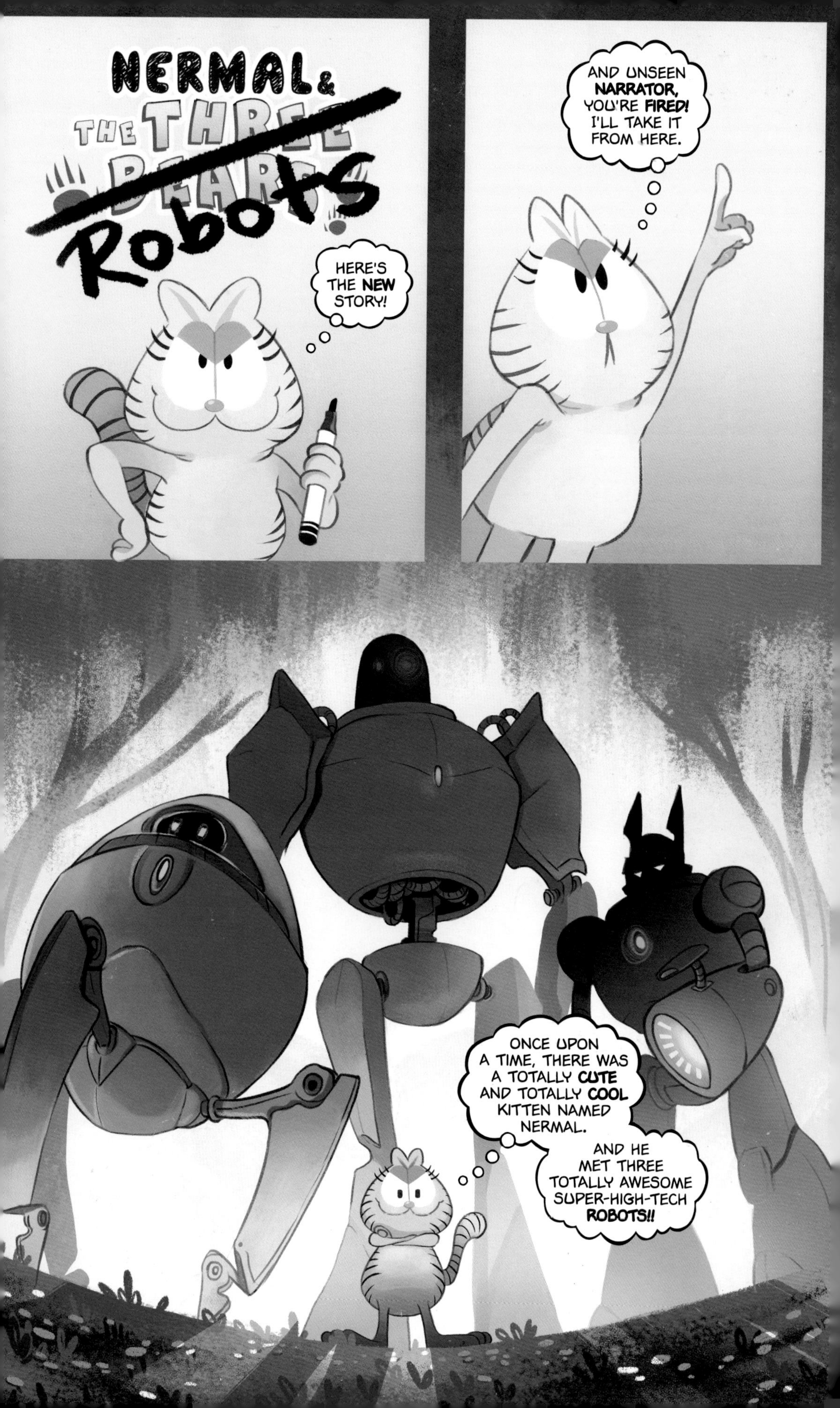

NERMAL &
THE THREE BEARS Robots
HERE'S THE NEW STORY!
AND UNSEEN NARRATOR, YOU'RE FIRED! I'LL TAKE IT FROM HERE.
ONCE UPON A TIME, THERE WAS A TOTALLY CUTE AND TOTALLY COOL KITTEN NAMED NERMAL.
AND HE MET THREE TOTALLY AWESOME SUPER-HIGH-TECH ROBOTS!!

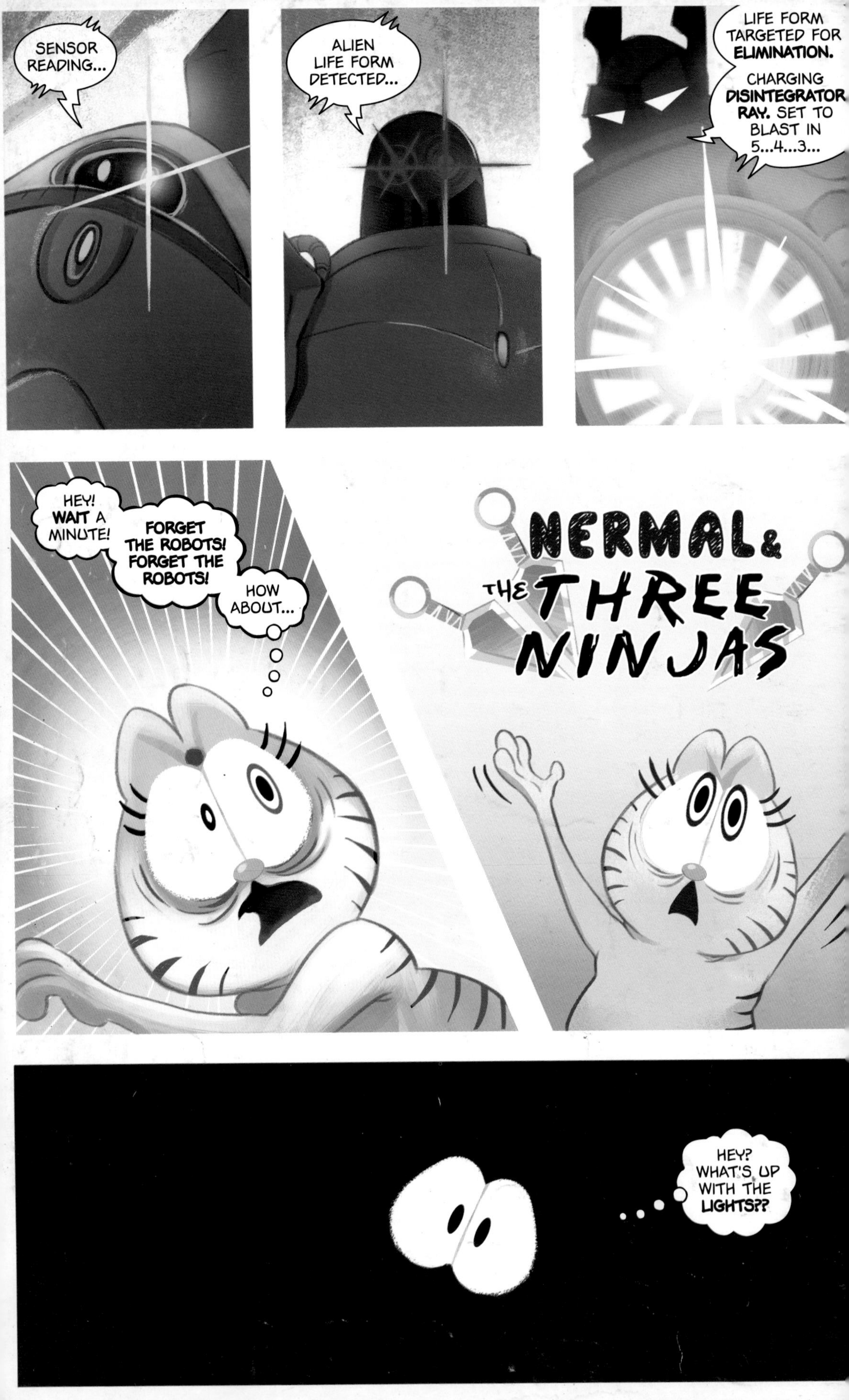
SENSOR READING...
ALIEN LIFE FORM DETECTED...
LIFE FORM TARGETED FOR **ELIMINATION.**
CHARGING **DISINTEGRATOR RAY.** SET TO BLAST IN 5...4...3...
HEY! **WAIT** A MINUTE!
FORGET THE ROBOTS! FORGET THE ROBOTS!
HOW ABOUT...
NERMAL & THE THREE NINJAS
HEY? WHAT'S UP WITH THE **LIGHTS??**

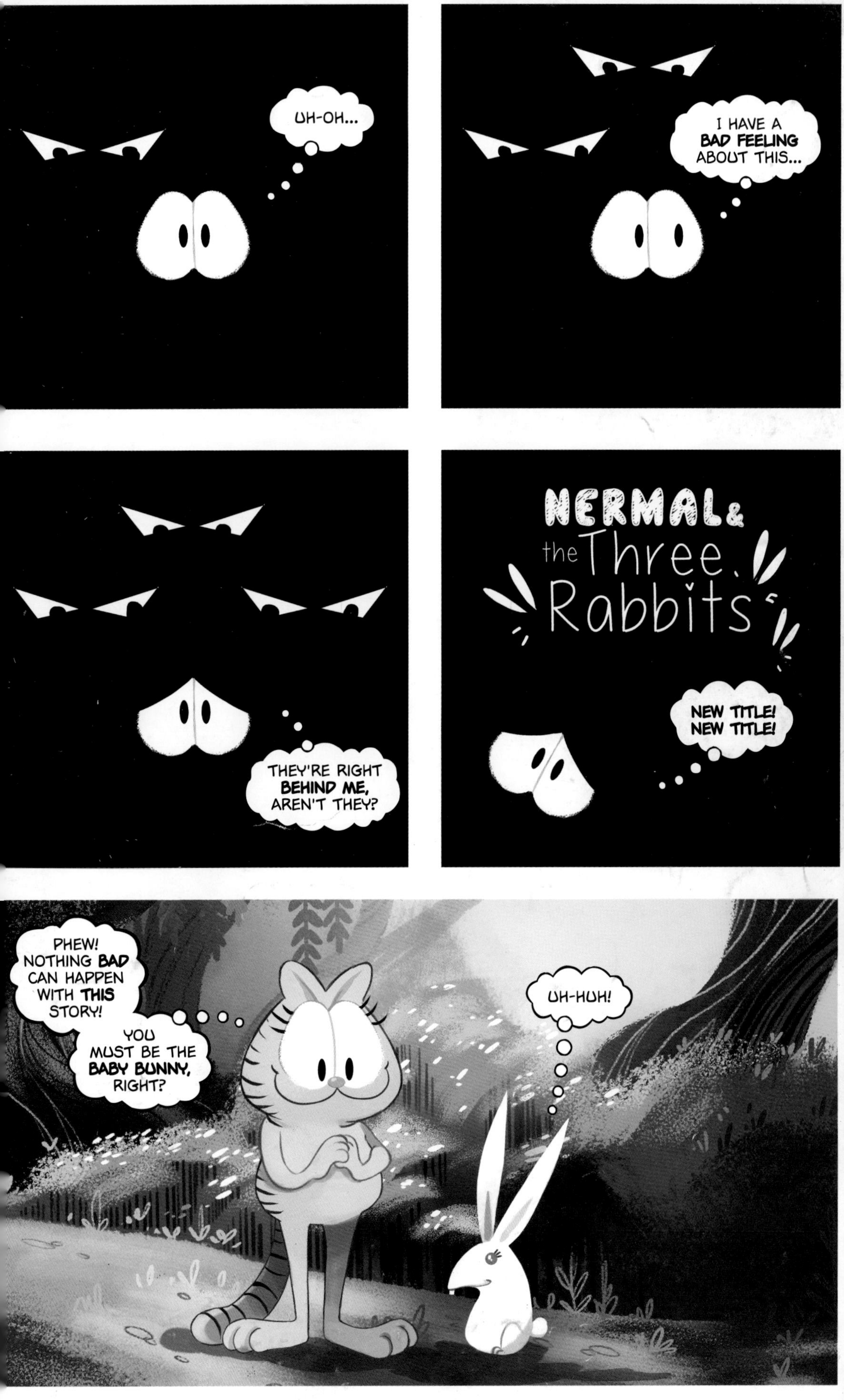
UH-OH...
I HAVE A BAD FEELING ABOUT THIS...
THEY'RE RIGHT BEHIND ME, AREN'T THEY?
NERMAL & the Three Rabbits
NEW TITLE! NEW TITLE!
PHEW! NOTHING BAD CAN HAPPEN WITH THIS STORY!
YOU MUST BE THE BABY BUNNY, RIGHT?
UH-HUH!

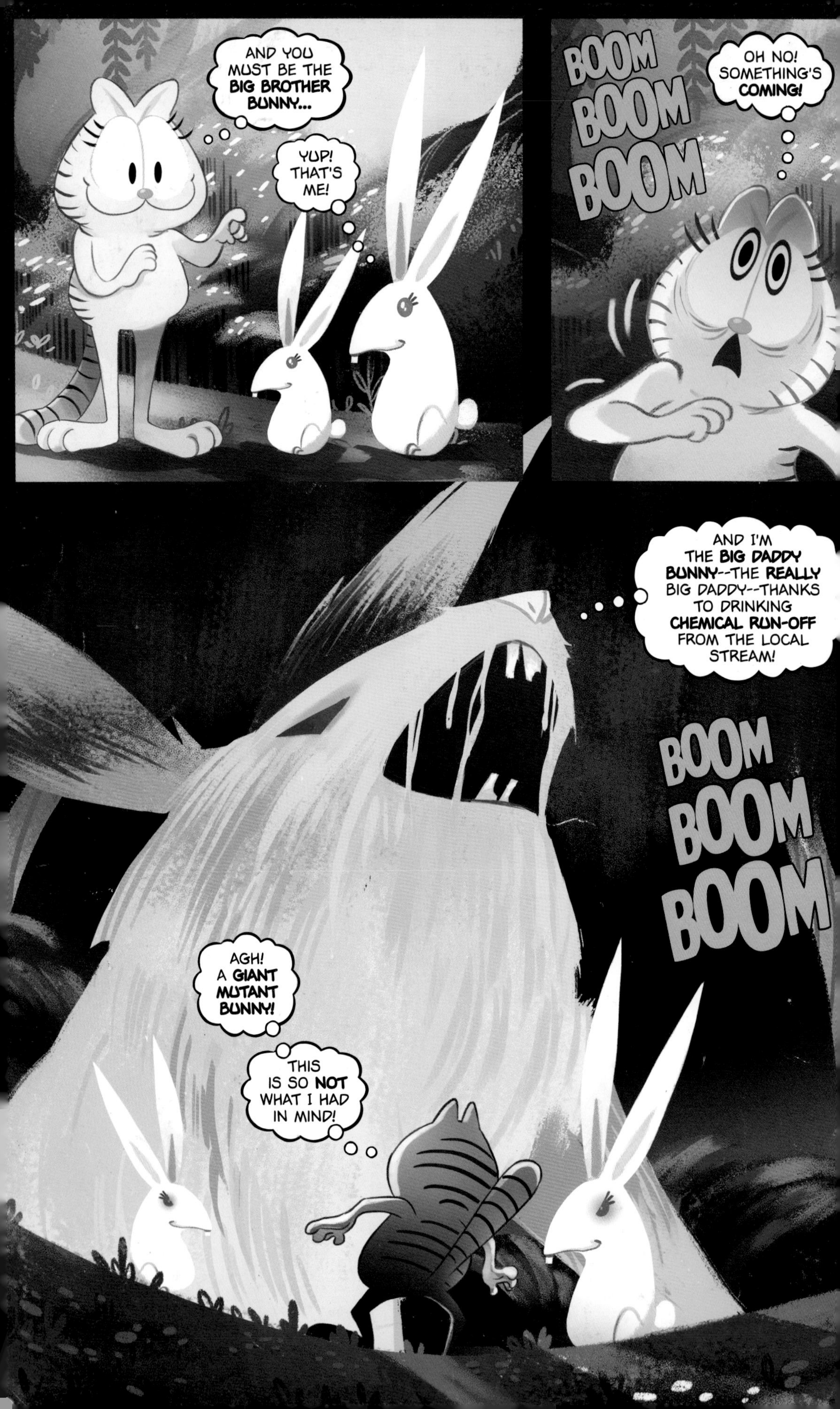
AND YOU MUST BE THE BIG BROTHER BUNNY...
YUP! THAT'S ME!
BOOM BOOM BOOM
OH NO! SOMETHING'S COMING!
AND I'M THE BIG DADDY BUNNY--THE REALLY BIG DADDY--THANKS TO DRINKING CHEMICAL RUN-OFF FROM THE LOCAL STREAM!
BOOM BOOM BOOM
AGH! A GIANT MUTANT BUNNY!
THIS IS SO NOT WHAT I HAD IN MIND!

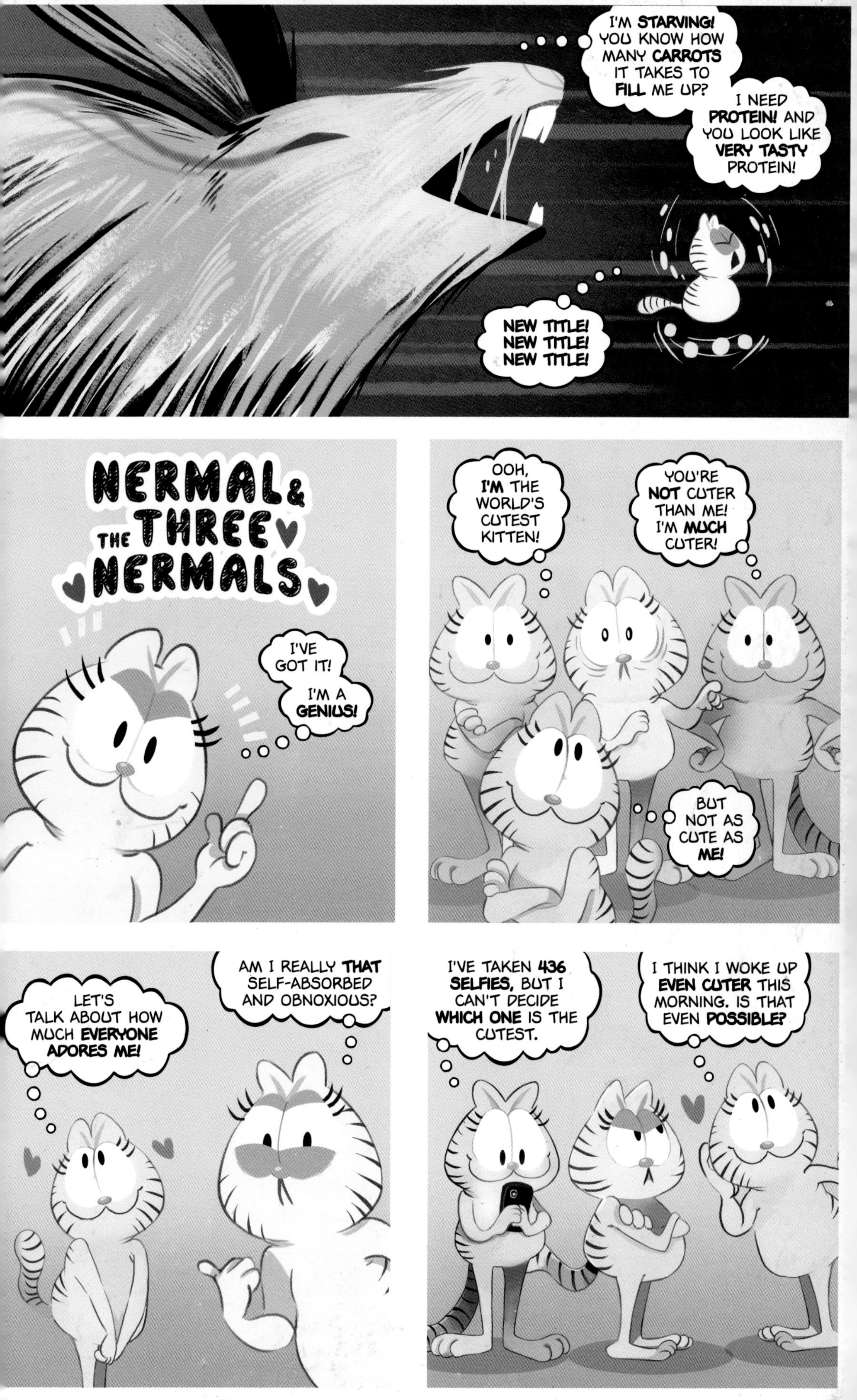

I'M STARVING! YOU KNOW HOW MANY CARROTS IT TAKES TO FILL ME UP?
I NEED PROTEIN! AND YOU LOOK LIKE VERY TASTY PROTEIN!
NEW TITLE! NEW TITLE! NEW TITLE!
NERMAL & THE THREE NERMALS
I'VE GOT IT!
I'M A GENIUS!
OOH, I'M THE WORLD'S CUTEST KITTEN!
YOU'RE NOT CUTER THAN ME! I'M MUCH CUTER!
BUT NOT AS CUTE AS ME!
LET'S TALK ABOUT HOW MUCH EVERYONE ADORES ME!
AM I REALLY THAT SELF-ABSORBED AND OBNOXIOUS?
I'VE TAKEN 436 SELFIES, BUT I CAN'T DECIDE WHICH ONE IS THE CUTEST.
I THINK I WOKE UP EVEN CUTER THIS MORNING. IS THAT EVEN POSSIBLE?

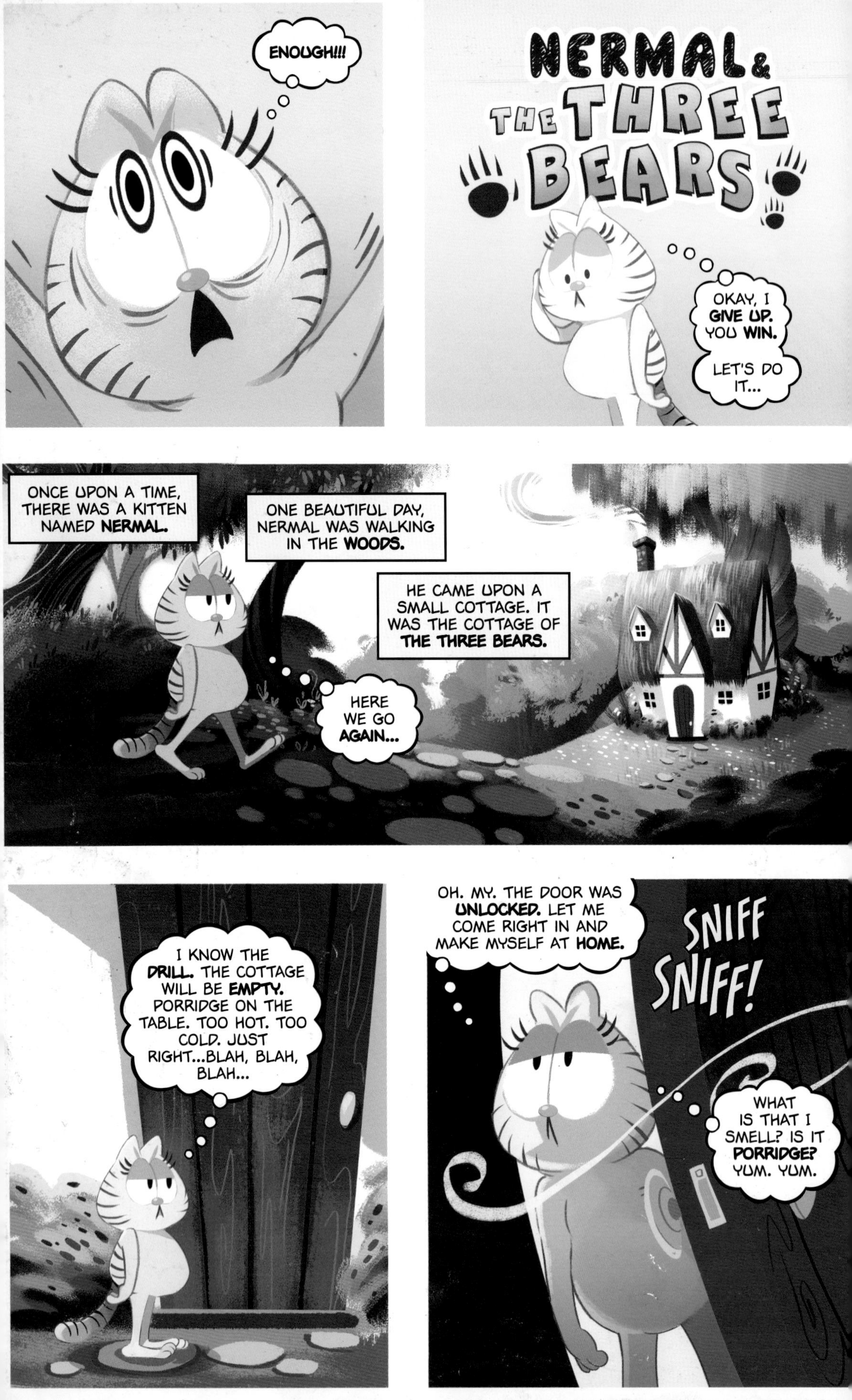
ENOUGH!!!
NERMAL & THE THREE BEARS
OKAY, I GIVE UP. YOU WIN.
LET'S DO IT...
ONCE UPON A TIME, THERE WAS A KITTEN NAMED NERMAL.
ONE BEAUTIFUL DAY, NERMAL WAS WALKING IN THE WOODS.
HE CAME UPON A SMALL COTTAGE. IT WAS THE COTTAGE OF THE THREE BEARS.
HERE WE GO AGAIN...
I KNOW THE DRILL. THE COTTAGE WILL BE EMPTY. PORRIDGE ON THE TABLE. TOO HOT. TOO COLD. JUST RIGHT...BLAH, BLAH, BLAH...
OH. MY. THE DOOR WAS UNLOCKED. LET ME COME RIGHT IN AND MAKE MYSELF AT HOME.
SNIFF SNIFF!
WHAT IS THAT I SMELL? IS IT PORRIDGE? YUM. YUM.

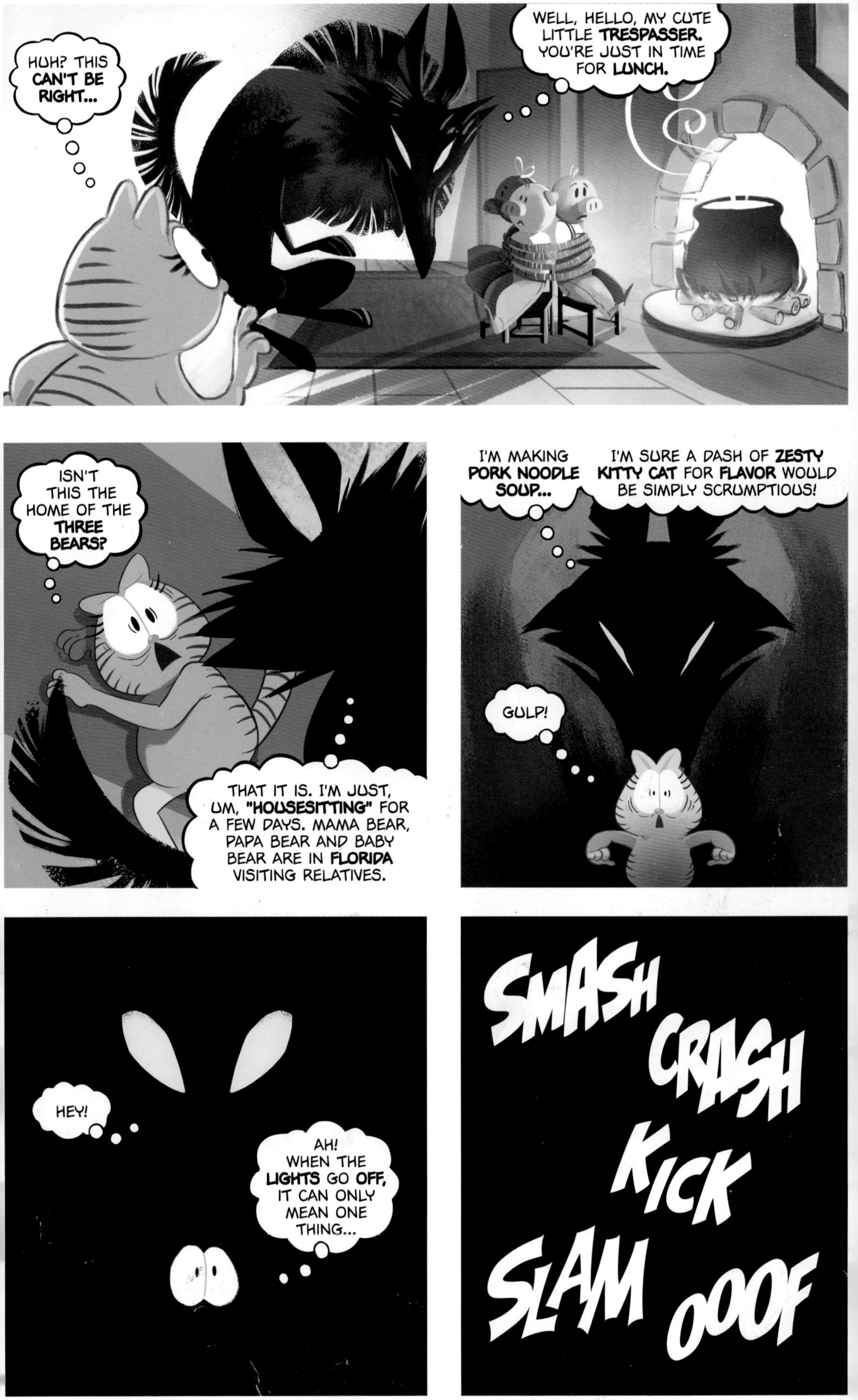
HUH? THIS CAN'T BE RIGHT...
WELL, HELLO, MY CUTE LITTLE TRESPASSER. YOU'RE JUST IN TIME FOR LUNCH.
ISN'T THIS THE HOME OF THE THREE BEARS?
THAT IT IS. I'M JUST, UM, "HOUSESITTING" FOR A FEW DAYS. MAMA BEAR, PAPA BEAR AND BABY BEAR ARE IN FLORIDA VISITING RELATIVES.
I'M MAKING PORK NOODLE SOUP...
I'M SURE A DASH OF ZESTY KITTY CAT FOR FLAVOR WOULD BE SIMPLY SCRUMPTIOUS!
GULP!
HEY!
AH! WHEN THE LIGHTS GO OFF, IT CAN ONLY MEAN ONE THING...
SMASH
CRASH
KICK
SLAM
OOOF

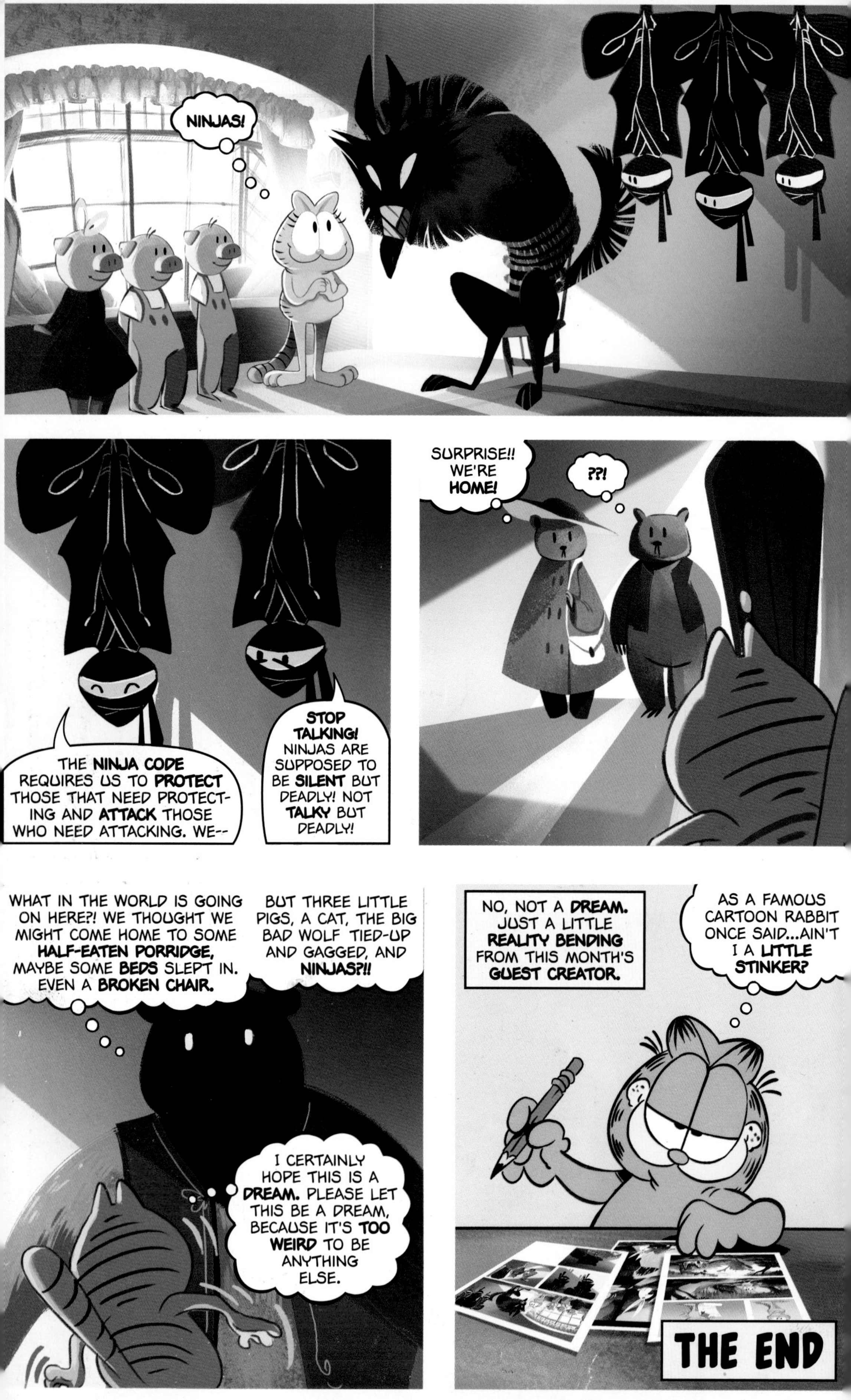
NINJAS!
THE NINJA CODE REQUIRES US TO PROTECT THOSE THAT NEED PROTECTING AND ATTACK THOSE WHO NEED ATTACKING. WE--
STOP TALKING! NINJAS ARE SUPPOSED TO BE SILENT BUT DEADLY! NOT TALKY BUT DEADLY!
SURPRISE!! WE'RE HOME!
??!
WHAT IN THE WORLD IS GOING ON HERE?! WE THOUGHT WE MIGHT COME HOME TO SOME HALF-EATEN PORRIDGE, MAYBE SOME BEDS SLEPT IN. EVEN A BROKEN CHAIR.
BUT THREE LITTLE PIGS, A CAT, THE BIG BAD WOLF TIED-UP AND GAGGED, AND NINJAS?!!
I CERTAINLY HOPE THIS IS A DREAM. PLEASE LET THIS BE A DREAM, BECAUSE IT'S TOO WEIRD TO BE ANYTHING ELSE.
NO, NOT A DREAM. JUST A LITTLE REALITY BENDING FROM THIS MONTH'S GUEST CREATOR.
AS A FAMOUS CARTOON RABBIT ONCE SAID...AIN'T I A LITTLE STINKER?
THE END

Christmas Cheer

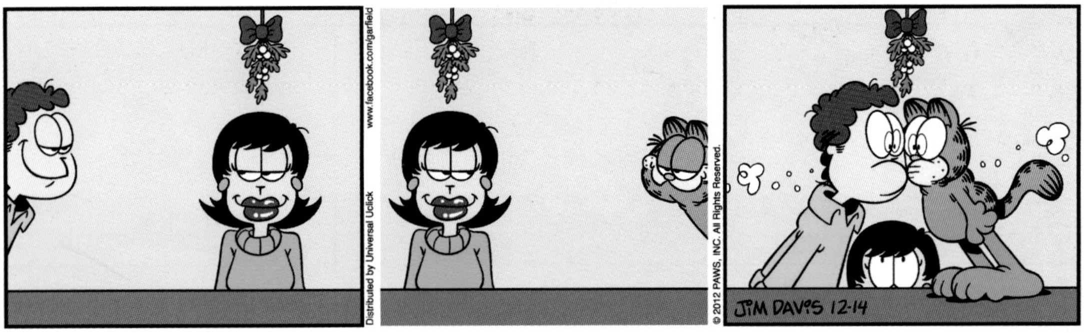

www.facebook.com/garfield
Distributed by Universal Uclick
© 2012 PAWS, INC. All Rights Reserved.
JIM DAVIS 12-14

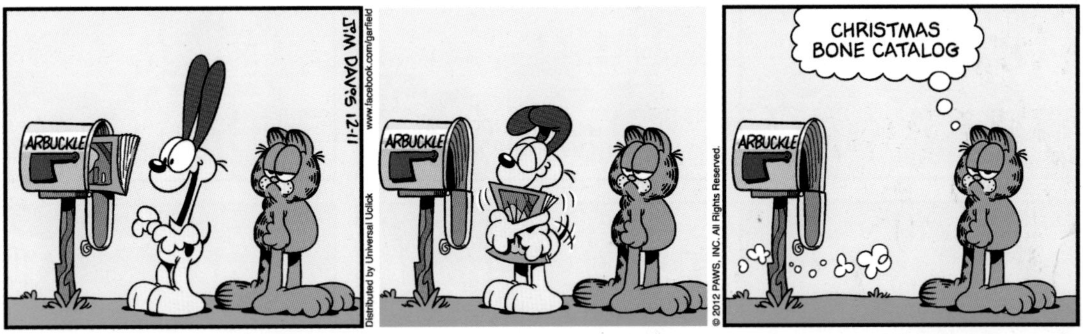

ARBUCKLE
JIM DAVIS 12-11
www.facebook.com/garfield
Distributed by Universal Uclick
© 2012 PAWS, INC. All Rights Reserved.
CHRISTMAS BONE CATALOG

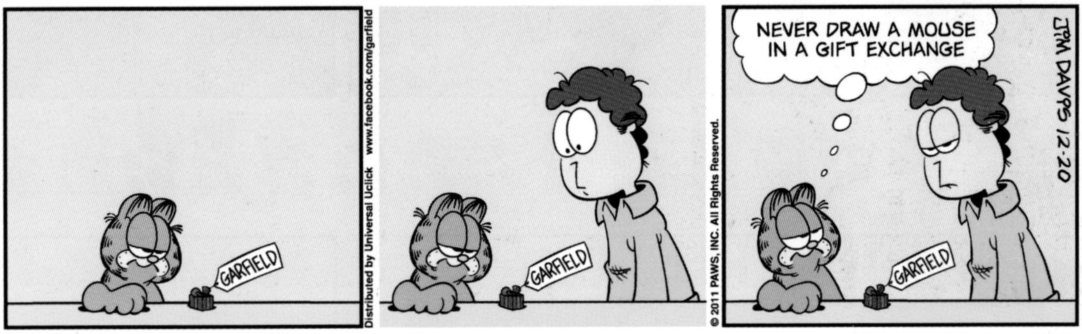

GARFIELD
www.facebook.com/garfield
Distributed by Universal Uclick
© 2011 PAWS, INC. All Rights Reserved.
NEVER DRAW A MOUSE IN A GIFT EXCHANGE
JIM DAVIS 12-20

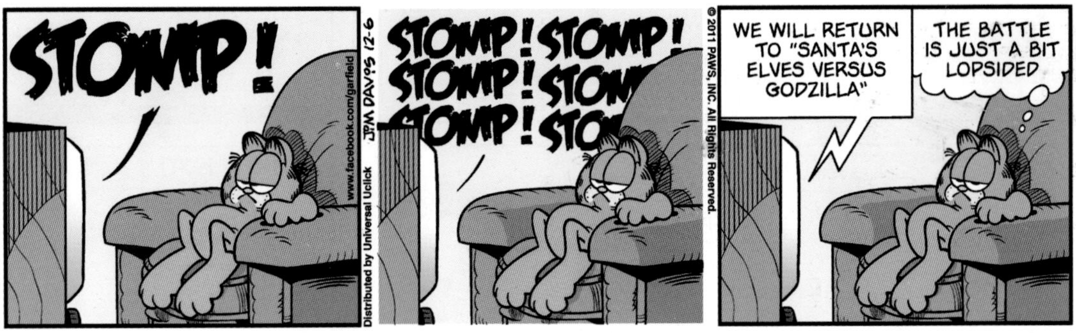

STOMP!
www.facebook.com/garfield
JIM DAVIS 12-6
Distributed by Universal Uclick
STOMP! STOMP!
STOMP! STOM
STOMP! STO
© 2011 PAWS, INC. All Rights Reserved.
WE WILL RETURN TO "SANTA'S ELVES VERSUS GODZILLA"
THE BATTLE IS JUST A BIT LOPSIDED

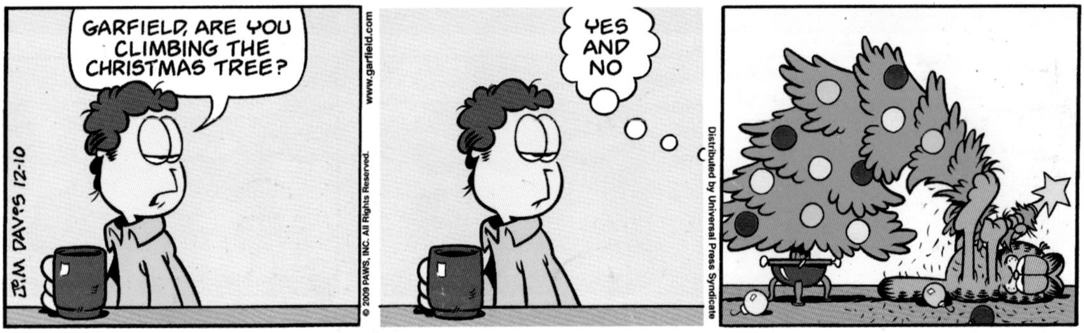

GARFIELD, ARE YOU CLIMBING THE CHRISTMAS TREE?
JIM DAVIS 12-10
www.garfield.com
© 2009 PAWS, INC. All Rights Reserved.
YES AND NO
Distributed by Universal Press Syndicate

Garfield Sunday Classics

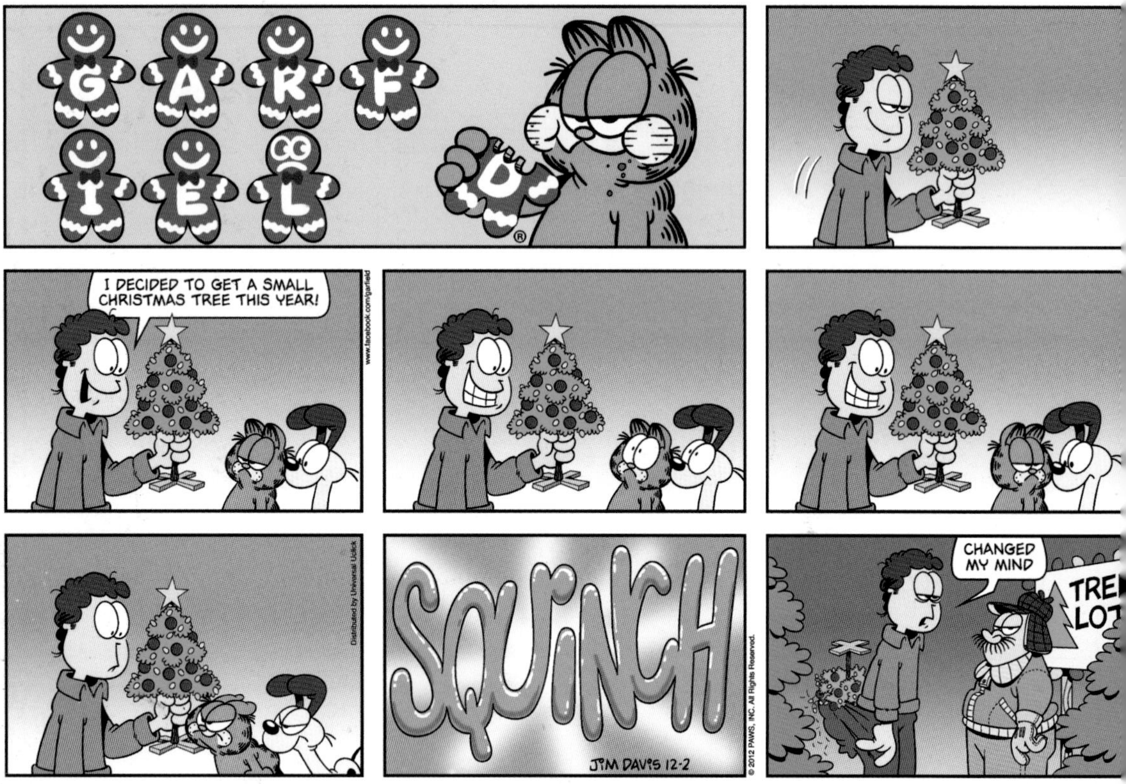

G A R F I E L D
I DECIDED TO GET A SMALL CHRISTMAS TREE THIS YEAR!
www.facebook.com/garfield
Distributed by Universal Uclick
SQUINCH
JIM DAVIS 12-2
© 2012 PAWS, INC. All Rights Reserved.
CHANGED MY MIND

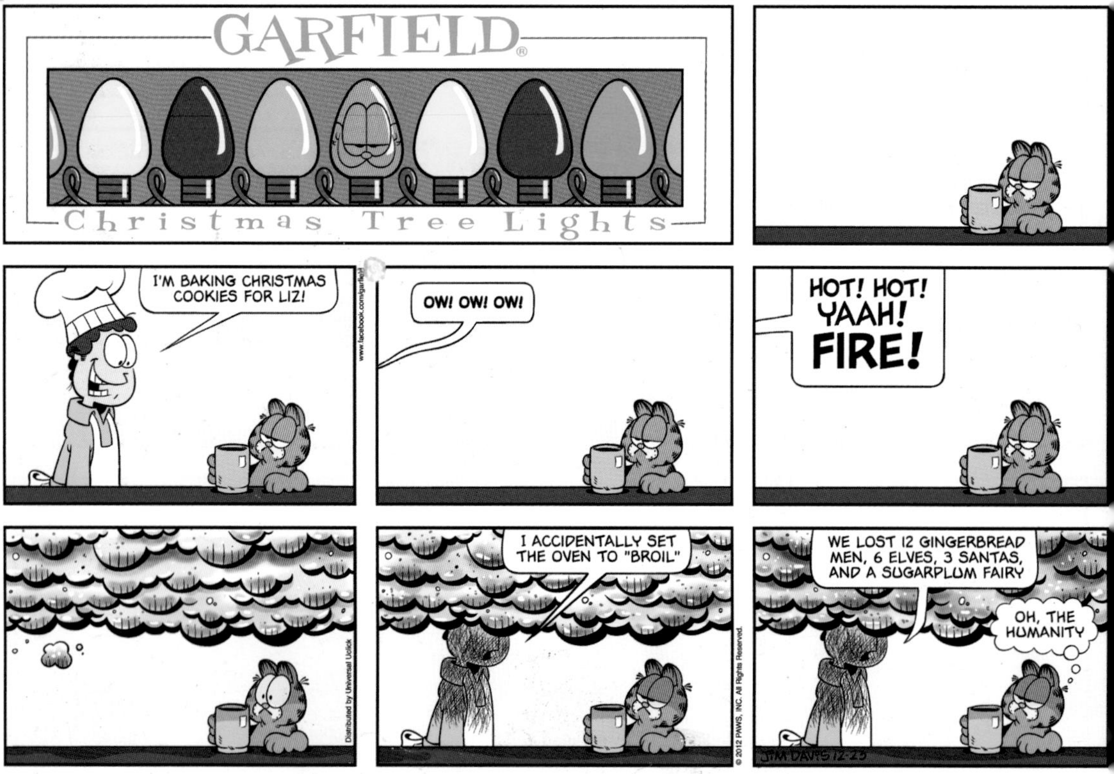

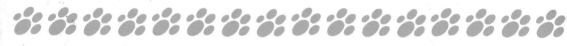

GARFIELD®
Christmas Tree Lights
I'M BAKING CHRISTMAS COOKIES FOR LIZ!
www.facebook.com/garfield
OW! OW! OW!
HOT! HOT! YAAH! FIRE!
Distributed by Universal Uclick
I ACCIDENTALLY SET THE OVEN TO "BROIL"
© 2012 PAWS, INC. All Rights Reserved.
WE LOST 12 GINGERBREAD MEN, 6 ELVES, 3 SANTAS, AND A SUGARPLUM FAIRY
OH, THE HUMANITY
JIM DAVIS 12-23

COVER GALLERY

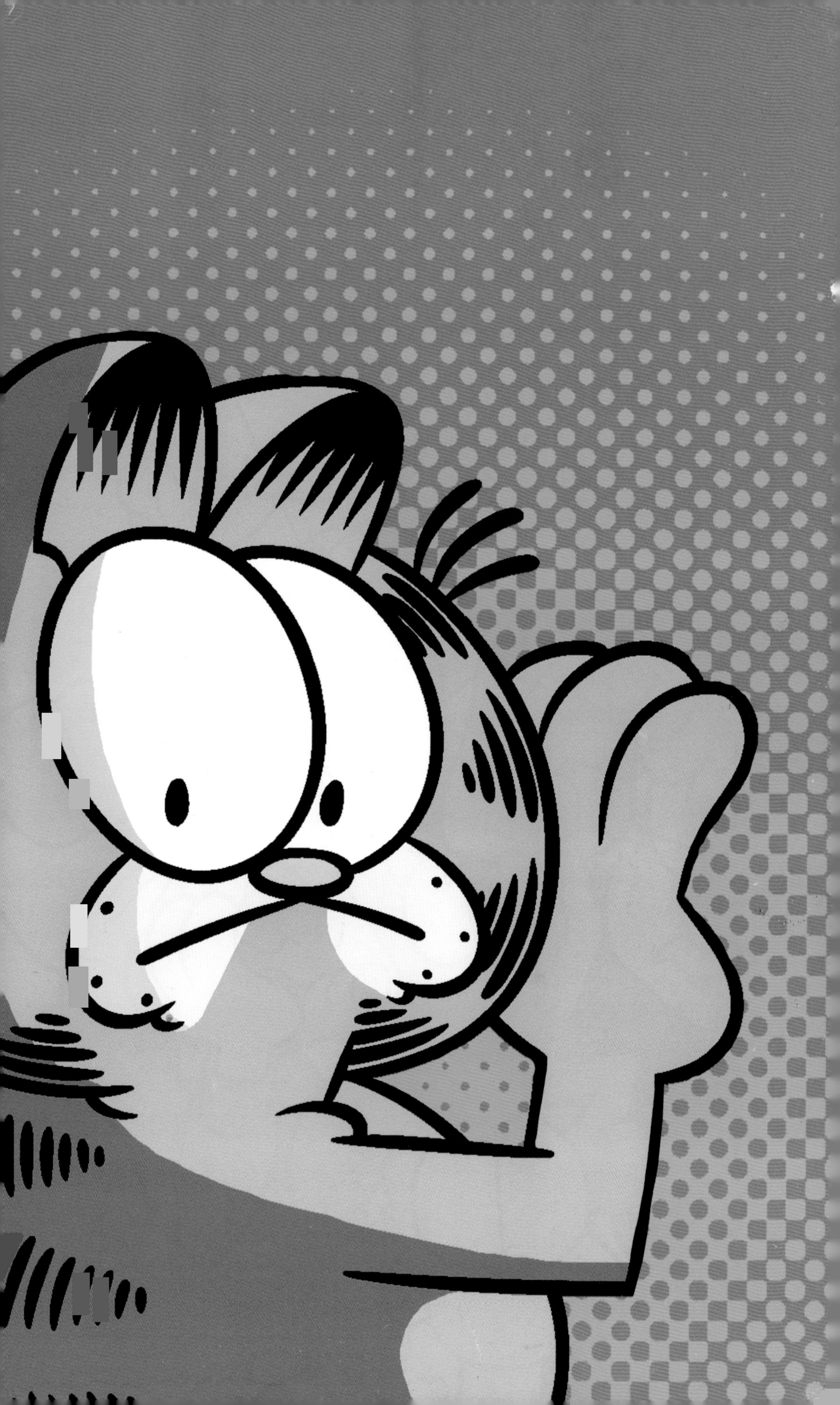

ISSUE 29 COVER BY
ANDY HIRSCH

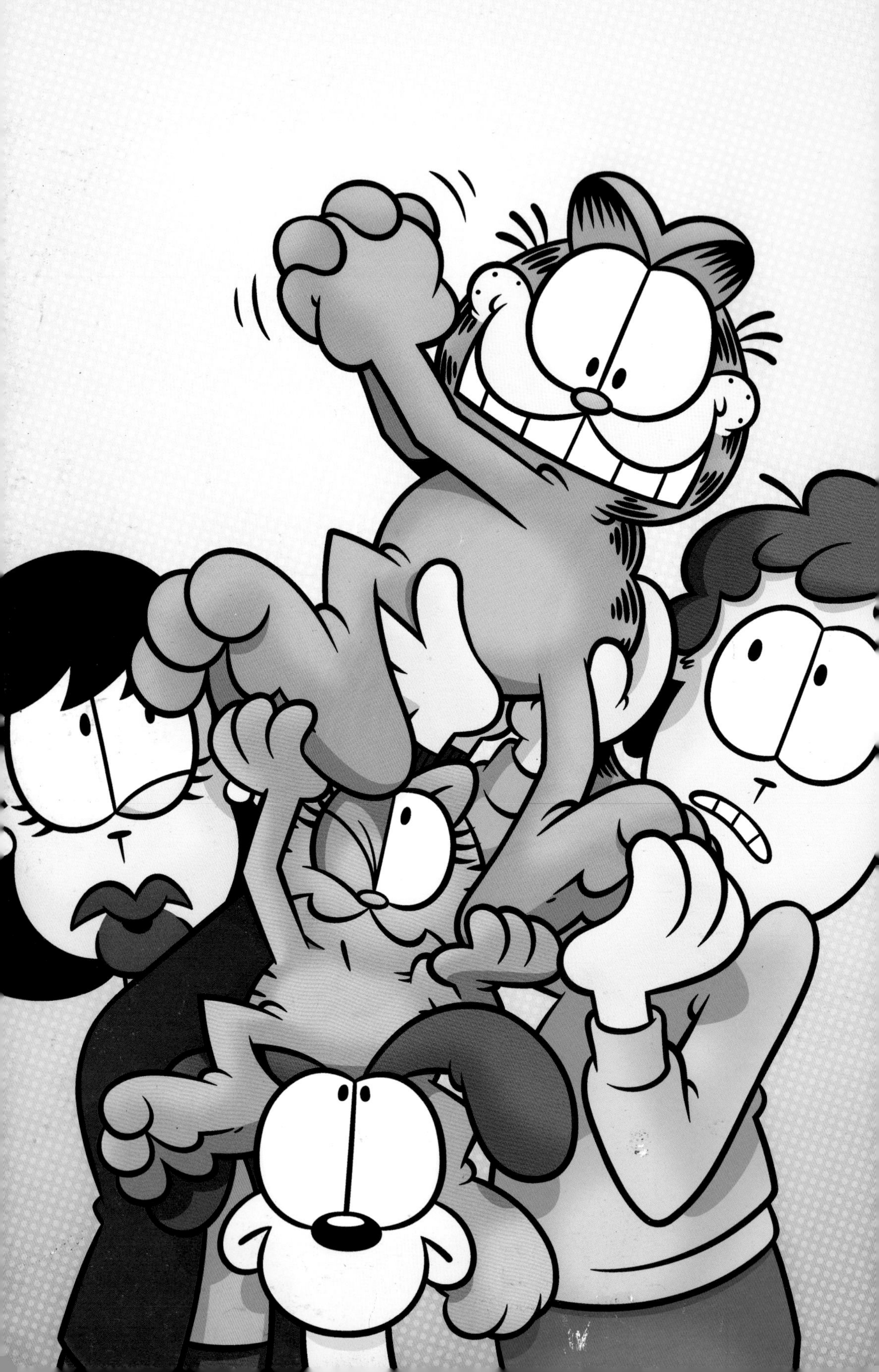

ISSUE 30 COVER BY
ANDY HIRSCH

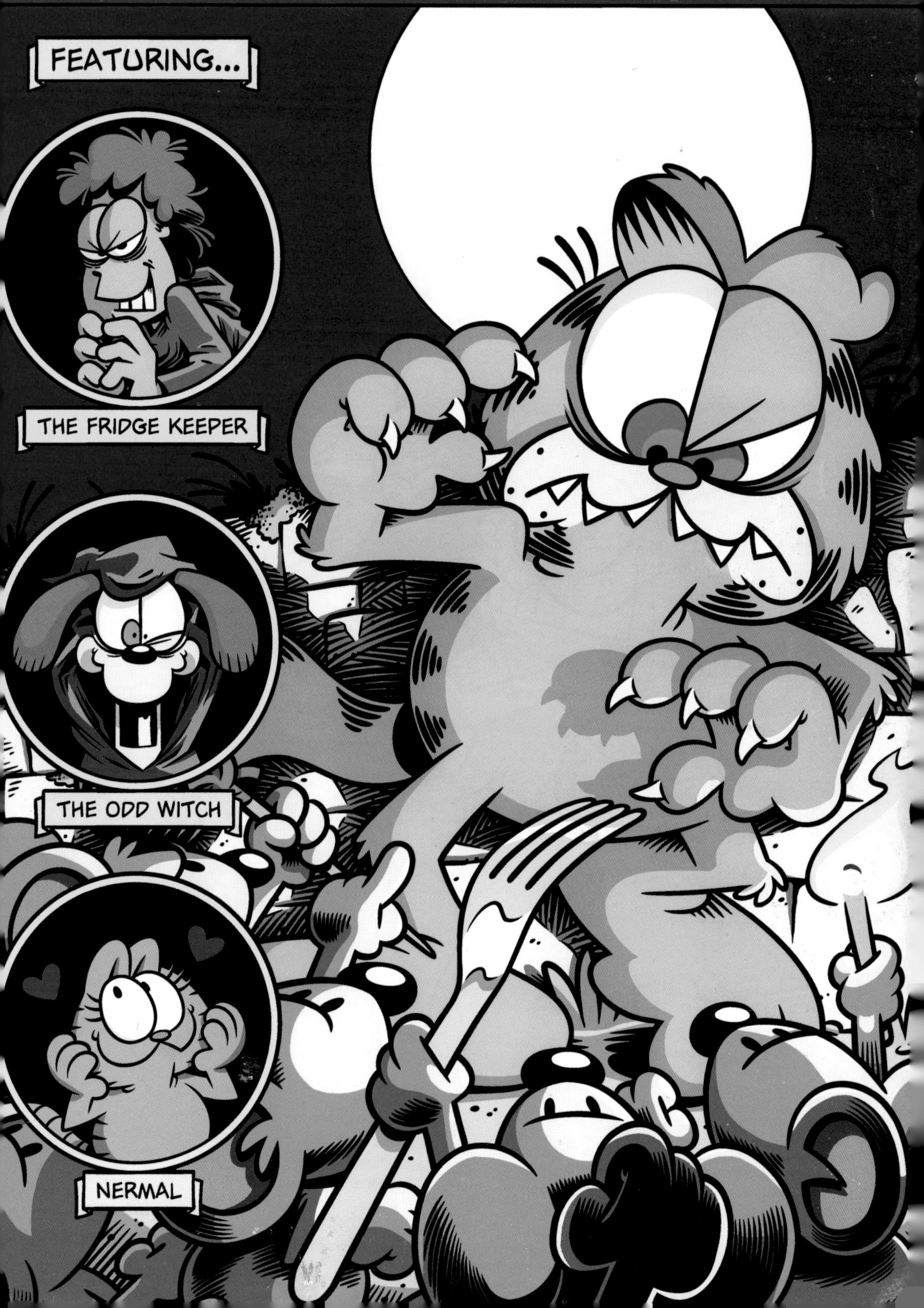
FEATURING...
THE FRIDGE KEEPER
THE ODD WITCH
NERMAL

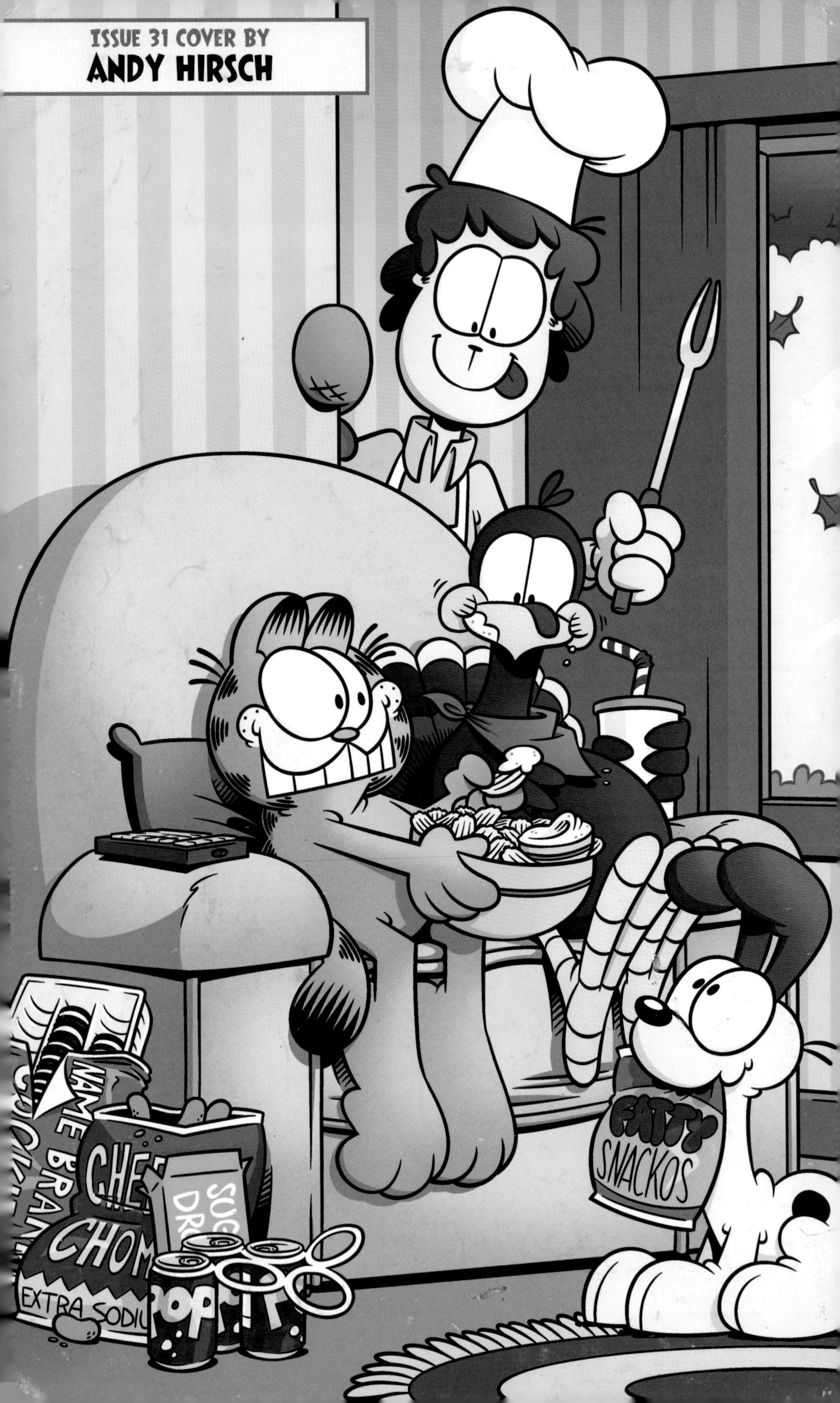
NAME
BRAN
CHE
CHOM
EXTRA SODIU
SUG
DR
POP
FATTY
SNACKOS

ISSUE 31 COVER BY
ANDY HIRSCH

ISSUE 32 COVER BY
ANDY HIRSCH

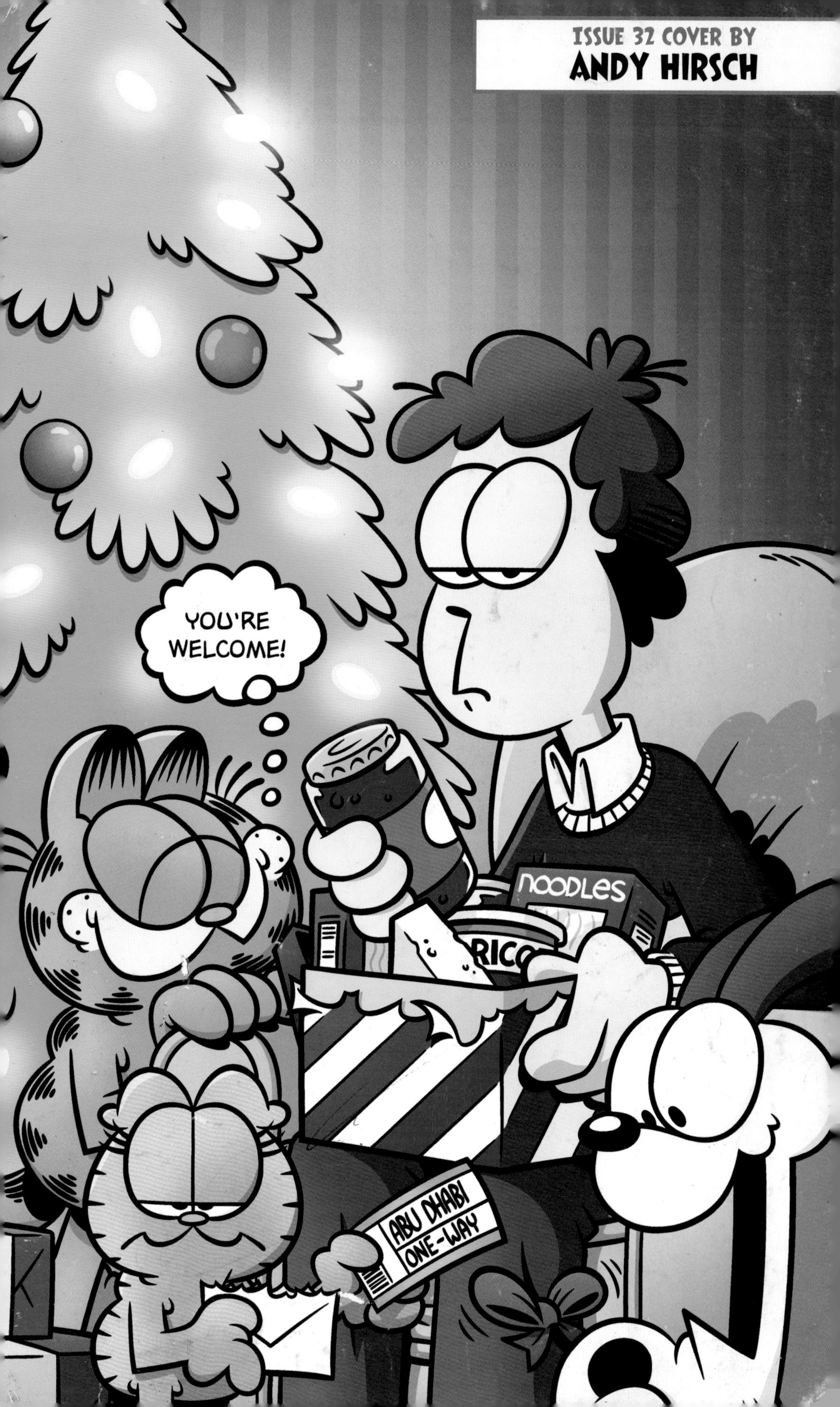
YOU'RE WELCOME!
NOODLES
RICO
ABU DHABI ONE-WAY